# Best Intentions

Sasha has every intention of being a better parent than his parents were.

Maryana has every intention of making this baby her very last – more so than the previous five times she said that.

Valeria and Galina have every intention of holding their family together.

Alexei has every intention of putting himself first.

Viktor has every intention of ending the nightmare.

Katerina has every intention of keeping the peace, just like Mother.

Dmitri has every intention of being taken seriously by Val.

David has every intention of making Father pay.

Sergei has every intention of staying out of the way.

Vlad's only intention is staying with Sarah.

Sarah's only intention is to get her diploma on schedule, even if it kills her.

Elizabyeta's only intention is to get her way.

Nikky wants a Dune Digger.

Tomas fully intends to absolve his guilt.

**Best Intentions. Everyone has them. Few ever go as planned.**

# Best
# Intentions

Susan Staneslow Olesen

This is an original work of fiction.
Names, characters, places and politics are
the work of the author's imagination. Any
similarity to persons living or dead is
entirely coincidental.

With grateful thanks to
Barbara Bloy, PhD,
the first doctor Sarah ever trusted

and

to my dad, Bob Staneslow,
who understands the zen
of grammar in too many languages

# The Kirushenko Family

(as of February 2263)

**Alexander Grigorevitch Kirushenko (Sasha)** – (47) (b.10 January 2216). An archaeologist of galactic renown, he's a man of two faces – the invincible mountain he shows to the world, and the insecure, guilt-ridden boy only his wife knows. At 6'9" and 400 lbs, he's a massive, powerful man. Married 10 June, 2239 to
**Maryana Natasha Fedorovna Kirushenko (Tash)** – (40) (b. 23 May 2222), Sasha's perpetually pregnant wife for 23 years. Diminutive, delicately built, she has never really shed her naïve schoolgirl mentality.

**Their oversized family:**
**Valeria Lin**
**Galina Raisa** – (22), b. Tbilisi, Georgian Russia, 10 June 2240; *The Twins*. 6'0", 150 lbs. Identical on the outside, but not always on the inside. Away at universities for the last five years, they're willing to return home when needed to help.

**Alexei Konstantin** – (20), b. Tbilisi, Georgian Russia, 21 July, 2242; *The Privileged One*. Tall like his father (6'5") but slighter of build, his family position gives him a sadistic power over his younger siblings.

**Viktor Maxim** – (18), b. Moscow, 13 April, 2244; *The Responsible One*. Shorter (5'10") but broad and powerfully built like his father. With his mother's calm, patient nature, he's been in charge of everyone for as long as he can remember.

**Ekaterina Anastasia** – (Katya) (16), b. Moscow, 2 April, 2246; *The Patient One*. Nordic blonde, Katya is 5'4" and 95 lbs. Infinitely patient, motherly toward the younger children, Katya won't cross authority.

**Dmitri Mikhail** – (15), b. Outer Jerusalem, Israel, 18 March 2247; *The Impulsive One*. Not even a year younger than Katya, he's a stringy but boyishly handsome teenager, just 5'6". With his sparkling brown eyes and mother's small build, life is Dmitri's party.

**David Fyodor** – (13), b. Moscow, 9 August 2249; *The Delinquent*. Leader of the 'Fearsome Four' – his 'home gang' with Sergei, Vlad, and Sarah. Thick black hair always hanging in his bright blue eyes, he's already taller than Dmitri and brawny like Viktor. "So much potential if he'd just straighten out."

**Sergei Anton** – (11), b. Kiev, 7 July, 2251; *The Dreamer*. A tall, quiet boy with thick blond curls and brown eyes. Sergei reads anything that holds still, and writes ceaselessly in his journals. Not as brilliant as Sarah, he's still a very gifted student.

**Vladimir Vasily** – (9), b. Kiev, Ukraine, 23 December, 2253; *The Runt*. Tiny and delicate, hopelessly immature, highly emotional, he's riddled by anxiety, with a sensitive stomach just adding to his troubles. Picked on by David because he's easy to make cry, he's been protected by Sarah since she was big enough to make a fist.

**Sarah Irina** – (Sar'ina) (8), b. Kiev, Ukraine, 13 October 2254; *The Brain*. Due to her premature birth, she's only nine months younger than Vladimir, but seems much older. Built like her father, tall and broad, her white-blonde hair and violet-blue eyes are a striking combination. A die-hard tomboy, Sarah counts as one of the boys for everything but rooming – though she tries. With an IQ over 180, she's academically brilliant, but emotionally she's still only eight.

**Elizabyeta Viktoria** (Byeta) – (5), b. Kiev, Ukraine, 4 May 2257; *The Brat*. A breathtaking child with yellow-gold curls to her waist, she's petite like her mother, with long-lashed blue eyes. Sugary sweet, manipulative and bratty, 'Byeta harbors a violent streak of jealousy.

**Nikolai Ivan** (Nikky) – (3), b. Kiev, Ukraine, 14 February, 2260. An energetic preschooler with brown curls and hazel eyes. Born just two days before the move to Navara, he's never known a tree or a rain cloud or a cool autumn breeze. Too young to fear his father, he's been raised by Sarah and Vlad for as long as he can remember.

**Marina Natasha** – b. Outer Kar Ku'umi, Gantankar Province, Ni'nakik, Navara, 20 February 2263.

# Ancient History

Uprooting nine children for a year and moving them halfway across a galaxy was not something to be undertaken lightly, but Archaeology Professor Alexander Kirushenko, of the Kiev Scientific Institute – Sasha off paper, was also someone not to be taken lightly. Forty-two years old, two hundred and five towering centimeters tall, a hundred forty-five kilos stark naked, his size and voice alone were enough to intimidate his children – who were used to him – as well as first-year students, who never really got used to him. His children were seasoned short-term travelers, here for a lecture, there a long vacation that doubled as research, but this was his first year-long sabbatical, paid to play in the dirt with a hand-picked team of students and locals, searching for ancient cities under a grant from the antiquities office in the province of Hantovalle, Emri Sal, Gamma Europa IV. Sasha could not have been happier.

Sasha's wife Maryana – he never called her anything but Tash, for her second name of Natasha – proved the adage that opposites attracted. Sixty centimeters shorter than her husband, 47 kilos when not pregnant, she flitted through life as an *haute couture* social butterfly, her sunshiny hair bouncing down her back with a schoolgirlish charm that made her seem far younger than her 36 years. Maryana, once upon a time an elite debutante and former heiress to the Ivanov Industries empire, was the most seasoned traveler of the family, forever eager to see new places, meet new people, show off her burgeoning family, and push her husband up social ladders he didn't know existed. Whether marshalling her own troops or directing a charity luncheon, Maryana set the standard with a cheerful charisma that made anyone happy just to hear her speak, a fatalistic optimism she relied on far more than anyone – save her husband – knew.

This current gamble was the result of one of her artful pushes, a contact here, a namedrop there, nudging Sasha into writing proposals, and, as always, it had worked like a charm. Sasha's enthusiasm bubbled over like shaken beer, his melancholy self-doubt replaced with a ferocious eagerness that spread to the children. Once a week he'd bring them to see the action, explain what they saw, and even if they didn't understand, they were eager for it. Being stuck away from home in a strange place wasn't always fun, but if Papa was excited, then it must be something really good.

Gamma Europa IV crammed them into a bright blue four-bedroom house in the cool, damp coastal village of Emri Sal, with salty ocean breezes and the calming sounds of endlessly rolling surf hissing into the distance behind them. The rocky, treeless hills were a far cry from the dry flatness of their part of Kiev. Maryana would have preferred somewhere slightly warmer and drier – it hadn't taken long for half the children to become sick with the climate change. Little Sarah, dangerously ill, had to be hospitalized at the mercy of second-world medicine. Now, four months later, the preschooler was sick again, and there were still five months to go. The worst part was being down two pairs of highly capable hands: the oldest children, Valeria and Galina, identical twins, stayed home on Earth, attending university. Maryana never thought she'd miss two children out of the pile, but she did.

Maryana shouted into the handicom she held. "What? Easy, Sash! I can't make out what you're saying. Your finger's blocking the solarcell again. Be careful, okay? I love you, too."

She stood in the room, thinking. Sasha was terribly excited about something. If it was *that* big, she should be there helping him. She ran down the list of *should's* in her head, and realized it would take her a while to get ready.

She checked on Sarah first. The four-year-old lay motionless in bed, wheezing and choking breathlessly on tears, her five-year-old brother Vladimir comforting her.

"Was she up here again?" Maryana asked as she pulled Vladimir away. Just nine months apart in age, the two were as inseparable as twins, though they seemed as opposite as possible. Sarah bore her father's sturdy size and eagerness to learn; Vladimir had his father's coloring but his mother's bird-like frame, appearing two or three years younger than he was.

She flipped up Sarah's pajama shirt. Sure enough, a number of small bruising bite marks covered her middle. Maryana snapped a vial of liquid inhalant onto a face mask and pressed it over the girl's mouth and nose. "You're a smart girl, not a baby. Stop crying. You only make it worse. Breathe!

"Katerina! Viktor!" she called, and the two appeared in the doorway. "Katya, it's your responsibility to keep 'Byeta out of here; she's biting

Sarah again. You're going to have to switch beds and sleep over here. She can't keep getting bit." With so many children squeezed into the temporary house, they'd had to settle for doubling the younger ones up at night. Unfortunately, some of the arrangements just weren't working. Toddler Elizabyeta had the face of a Renaissance angel and the temper of the Devil himself.

"Your father's found something at the dig. He's working straight through the night. I'm going out there with him. You'll have to keep things together here."

Maryana removed the mask. The child gave a gurgle, a long strangling cough, and hacked a lungful of thick goo into a towel in her hands. "Better?"

The blonde head nodded, breathing normally for the moment. Despite Maryana's wary eye, it was the fourteenth time in four short years the child had contracted pneumonia from a simple cold. "Can I go to the Dig, too?"

"When you're better. Viktor, keep an eye on her. If she's having trouble, throw the mask on her for a while. There's still a couple of doses left."

"Yes, Mother."

"I'm going out to the dig," she informed her brood. "Dmitri, David, mind your brother and sister, and stay away from Alexei. Lights out by ten. Sergei, books away at eight. Vladimir, sleep in your own bed! Let Sarah rest. You don't want her back in the hospital, do you? Dmitri, make sure you take him to the sanitary at least twice during the night. Alexei, carry these boxes out to the speedster for me."

Alexei's sneer begged otherwise. "Why me? Can't Viktor do it? He's not doing anything."

Maryana stared fearlessly up at her eldest son, sixteen and towering over her like his father. "Viktor has his tasks, you were given yours. Do it now."

Cursing, Alexei hefted the stack of boxes and brought them outside.

At the Dig, Maryana struggled to carry the heavy boxes to the work tent, one by one. She'd brought only one case of beer. Sasha could be hospitable and celebrate with his crew, but she didn't want him screwing up something important with too much vodka. He could drink that when he got home.

The flood lights blazed down brighter than noon under the weather canopy. Sasha folded low on his knees deep in the massive pit, directing four students armed with laser cutters and brushes, while the others hovered, watching. They were picking at what appeared to be bone.

"Three millimeters, no closer!" he barked at a student. "Don't nick it!" He seized the tool in his massive hand and demonstrated.

Maryana bounded lightly down the ladder. She laid a soft hand on his back.

He smelled her perfume before she touched him. "Tash! What are you doing here?" Backlit by the floodlights, white light shining through the halo of stray hairs on her head, Maryana beamed at him like a heavenly vision, and he smiled.

She brushed the black waves of hair out of his eyes. "You sounded so excited I thought I'd better see for myself. I brought dinner for everyone. You'll need your strength if you're going to work all night."

Sasha shut off his laser. He put an arm around her and gave her a kiss, leaving a trail of dirt down her sweater. "You're too good for me. Break time!" he announced to the twelve-person crew. "Dinner, on me!" A cheer went up from around the dig. Handbeams were shut down, people stood to stretch.

Maryana studied the ground. She'd helped Sasha through enough studies to know what the various indicators meant. "What did you find? Is this still the agora level?"

He pointed out the boundaries. "Underneath. This is what we believe is the temple. The early datings are putting it about 6,000 years old. We've found what appears to be a collapsed altar, three partially intact pieces of pottery, and a huge pile of small bones; we're not sure why. We've got the edges marked, and there are partial walls back there. Scanners show they may go down more than two meters."

She hugged him excitedly. "Fantastic! Maybe that's the break you've been looking for."

"That's *nothing*. Look!" He took her by the hand and moved to the side of the rectangle marked off in front of them. Lengths of bone emerged from the hard yellow soil.

"Look, Tash!" he said with reverence. "It's the find of a lifetime, and I wasn't even looking for it! It's only supposed to be legend! There are a number of paintings, some clay representations, but no one's ever found a single bone, and I've found a *whole* one! See!" He traced the dirt gently with his finger. "Wave scan showed the wings bent backward this way. I'm no paleontologist, but I'm not wrong on this. It's *here*, it's *real*, and *I found it*!"

"That's wonderful!" she gasped. "What is it?"

"The legendary dragon of the Maridionias Cult. By our measure, it's

190 centimeters long, with a wingspan twice that. No one's understood how such an influential animal-based religion could spring up over something that didn't have some basis in fact. The dragon was just thought to be symbolic of power, but here is proof to the contrary, and *I* found it! Tash, this is bigger than I ever could have hoped for! The kind of discovery fewer than one in ten *thousand* archaeologists ever comes across!" Excitement poured off him like so much sweat. "It's the stuff *dreams* are made of! This will turn everything upside down!"

Maryana threw her arms around him. "Oh Sash! I'm so happy for you! I told you this would be a good thing!"

Her handicom beeped while they ate with the crew. Gamma Europa IV had left Maryana with a bit of social isolation; away from a city, with language and cultural barriers and no specific presence of a sponsoring university body where she might find adult interaction, she had turned to Sasha and his crew. The last thing she wanted in the middle of their celebration party was needless interruption. She ignored the chirping for eight or nine squawks, playing with the notion of flinging it into the dirt. She activated it with annoyance.

Viktor's face looked worried on the tiny screen. "Mother? Sarah's awful purply… "

"Find the aerosol with the yellow label," she said, openly irritated at the interruption of their party. "It will expand her lungs. Wait five minutes, then put her over your knees and pound on her back. That should loosen it. If not, there's that suction thing in the closet, but she hates it. Then crush up two of the big blue pills and give them to her in some pudding; she can't swallow them whole." Even Vladimir knew that by now.

Viktor sighed half-heartedly. "We'll try."

\* \* \*

Sarah sat up in the bed, both hands pressing the mask to her face as she struggled to breathe, her violet-blue eyes looking bigger and more purple in her peaked face. Her lips and fingertips were a dark dusky color.

Twelve-year-old Katerina held her up with shaking hands, more panicked than Sarah. It seemed to take forever to attach the new medication to the mask while her little sister clawed her throat, desperate for air. "What do we do if it doesn't work?"

"Then we'll call Mother back!" fourteen-year-old Viktor snapped.

"It'll work. It's got to. Why the hell'd she have to go out?"

Alexei watched from the doorway. "You're a bunch of fucking pussies. Why don't you just call for MedEvac and stick her in a hospital where she belongs? She could die in the middle of the night, and you'd never know it until she was cold and stiff in the morning."

That fear had already crossed Katya's mind. "You are so evil, Alexei! It should be *you* lying here instead of her, except I wouldn't take care of you."

"You're so cute when you're mad. It's not me, and I wouldn't let you, anyway. You're as likely to kill her as cure her. She's probably choking from Vlad puking on her."

Vladimir hung his head. Digestive frailties had plagued him his entire life.

"Why don't you drop dead?" Katya shot back.

"You wish." Alexei laughed, then walked away.

"Save it," Viktor said dismally. "It's not worth arguing with him. Let's try it, Sar'ina." He took the inhaler from her and lay her upside down over his knees. He pounded short little bangs on her back, trying to shake the thick goo loose from her lungs, bottom to top.

After a minute the child began to cough. And cough. And cough. Deep hacking coughs that shook her body and strangled her with the force. When she tried to breathe, they could *hear* the sucking of the fluids shifting in her chest. She coughed up a torrent of thick, frothy slime.

"My God, Viktor! She's so sick!" Katya cried, wiping the spit with a towel. "What do we *do*?"

He shrugged. "Same thing we are doing. What else can we do?"

\* \* \*

Around dawn, Sasha caught a nap on a folded canopy in the supply tent. Dust and hardened foam from immobilizing compound caked him head to toe. Maryana found him an hour later. She brushed his lips with hers.

"I have to go, Sash," she whispered. She swept the thick hair from his eyes with a loving hand. "I'll expect you home for dinner. You'll need your rest to see this through."

"You could give me some energy." He pulled her down on top of him. He covered her rump with his big hands and kissed her, hard.

Maryana fought him off, laughing. "I will not fool with you here at the dig. There's probably a half-dozen students with their ears glued to the tent."

Sasha grinned his endearing half-smile. "About time they learned something. You won't let me sacrifice your chastity on the altar? We can recreate a legend."

Maryana flicked compound from the broad chest and giggled. "I probably should have told you before this, but, I'm not a virgin."

"I'll be the judge of that." He tried to unfasten her clothing with one hand. "It won't take long…"

"No." Maryana kissed him passionately, pulling away with a promise of things to be. "This way you'll be thinking about me all day, and then I *know* you'll be home on time."

### *Earthdate: January, 2260*

Sasha gazed in amazement at the printout from the mail. "Can you imagine? *The Allied Fleet Academy!* An offer from the Space Fleet itself! To *teach* there!"

A dozen people stared at the magical papers trembling in his hand. Sasha was nearly in tears – and he was sober. He'd been sober more than a year, a whirlwind year of awards and interviews and lectures and papers, a year of his face plastered on every Archeology journal in the known galaxy, the granting of his second PhD – a year beyond any dream he could ever imagine.

"Imagine, Tash! *The Space Academy!*" he beamed, trailing her around the kitchen like a small boy promised a big surprise. "It's enough just to be accepted as a student there! Imagine what it must be like to be a professor – to *teach* the best of the very best! You know what they must think of me? An *invitation* to apply? After that, we can write our own ticket anywhere! The entire universe right there at our fingertips!"

Maryana glowed with pride. "Perhaps after all those awards and lectures, they finally realized you're one of the best of the very best. You earned every word. I take it this is the offer you're going after?"

"Like a dream!" Sasha hugged her tightly, despite her advancing state of pregnancy. One too many intoxicated celebrations, a burning indiscretion on the seat of the flyer, and here came number twelve.

Grooming and deportment were never Sasha's strong suits. Left to himself, he wore whatever clothing he grabbed, whether it was dirty, didn't fit, or in poor repair. He combed his hair only if he remembered, and his beard carried crumbs of his previous meal. Maryana scolded him repeatedly for eating peppers and garlic before meetings. His trick of a quick drink to calm his nerves before an event often turned to two or three, fogging him. For every other interview he'd had, Maryana had accompanied him, making certain he looked his best. This time, the interview was far off in western America, too far for a single day's journey. Maryana was in no condition to fly that far, and would not leave the children unsupervised that long. She packed his clothes in pre-matched sets, sent him with a detailed list of things to remember, how to address people, how to shake hands, make sure his beard and nails were clean, and never, never, belch in public, or worse. She crossed her fingers.

He returned three days later, full of stories and small gifts. The interview was merely a formality, the position was his if he wanted it.

"Tell me, Sash," she asked as they got ready for bed. What he'd bragged to the family and what his face said were two different things. "What did they *really* say? What was it *really* like?" She didn't add, *Is it really worth it?*

He sighed heavily, a sound that rumbled on forever like distant thunder. "I was hoping it would be at Seattle. It's a beautiful campus, a beautiful city. The children speak English. But it's not."

Maryana didn't like the disappointment in his voice. He'd turned down a dozen highly prestigious – and profitable – offers to chase this dream. "Where is it?"

Sasha tossed his shirt on the floor. "It's only an assistant professorship. A demotion, when you think about it, but in a more prestigious place. It's at a sub-branch … on Navara."

*"Navara!"* Maryana's nostrils flared as she eased herself into bed. An entire planet of broiling desert sands… and a race of people who never so much as smiled. "That's so far away."

He sat on the bed. "Three days, minimum. And that's in a Davies' drive ship."

"What did you tell them?"

"I said I needed to confirm it with you."

"Did you decide?" *Say no. Say no.* He'd lost his enthusiasm – that wasn't a good sign.

"No," Sasha admitted. "Yes, it's the Allied Space Fleet. Not the center of the glory, but still the Allied Fleet. Navara's a tough sell, so the salary is beyond excellent. It's a new language to learn, a tough one, and the laws for foreigners are strict."

Maryana tried to be optimistic. "If we start Sarah now, she'll be able to translate for us by the time we get there. She's quick like that.

*Quick? The child scared the hell out of Sasha. It was a new family record, being called into school on only the second day of class.*

*"We've never had a student like this before," the teacher said. "She passed a second-form mastery test with a score of 100%. She passed third form with an 85. She managed a 71 on fourth. Eighty would pass her. We want to do a full work up, evaluate all areas, get a firm assessment of her abilities. Right now we estimate her IQ as somewhere between 190 and 230."*

*Sasha didn't even twitch. "So what form will you put her in?"*

*"We can't put her in* **any** *form! She'd have to start halfway through fourth, and we cannot skip students five years. She hasn't turned five yet! We would place her in a self-guided classroom with other students who don't fit the system. She'd work at her own pace for academics, and join the kindergarten for all non-academic programs, such as arts and recreation and lunch."*

*Sasha shook his head. "I don't like that. Isn't the self-guided program for those who can't keep up with regular classes?"*

*Maryana sighed. "It doesn't matter, Sash. It's that or she sits home until she's older, but she'll just be smarter by then and we'll have the same problem. It's not like there's no one at home for her to play with."*

*Sarah was sent into the office. Maryana, four months' pregnant, looked like a model from a fashion ad in a white and navy Pasha Mattei suit. Sasha wore his teaching clothes, and Maryana had made sure his hair was combed. They turned toward her.*

*Sarah stayed by the door. "Did I do something wrong?"*

*"No." Maryana beamed the gentle smile that lit up her face like spring sunshine. "Come sit. The teacher has been telling us about you."*

*Sarah approached with caution, nose out, sniffing. Father just smelled work-nice, so it was okay to come near him. He lifted her effortlessly and balanced her on his knee.*

*Sasha tugged her blonde braids. He gave only a shy half-smile, but his eyes glittered with pride. "You're too smart for this school, Sar'ina. That's my girl!"*

"How long is the contract?"

"Three years, minimum." Sasha lay back on the bed; Maryana shifted closer and put her head on his shoulder.

"When do they want you to start?"

"As soon as possible."

Maryana struggled to sit up with her expanded belly. "I can't do that, Sash. I can't go until the baby comes. I won't give birth on some dirty transport ship. Promise me you won't make me go through that."

He rubbed her arm. "Of course I wouldn't. I told them that might be a complication."

"What do you think? Are you going to take it?" *Say no. No deserts.*

"It's not what I envisioned. Do you think we could stick it out for three years?"

Maryana kissed him lightly. "If that's what you want, then I want it too. Where ever you go, I will be there beside you. Did you ask about housing?"

"There's a house available, I was told. It's 120 kilometers outside Shir P'an, out in the desert. No neighbors, no anything for 13 kilometers. Only three bedrooms, but they're supposed to be big. Two baths, at least."

"Oh Sasha! How would we ever fit?" Maryana wailed. "We have so much here – how can we give it all up?" After twenty years, they'd achieved their dreams – the six-bedroom home outside the city, five lavatories, five computer channels, the fancy furnishings, the housekeeper.

"I know, but I hate to miss what might be a good opportunity. If I can get a foothold, then maybe I can transfer someplace better three years from now. Think of it, Tash! With that on a résumé, we can go anywhere."

Maryana sighed. "If it makes you happy, then do it. The children will learn to live with it. I'm sure we can make it sound adventurous to them." *But how could she make it seem adventurous to herself?*

Sasha ran a hand over the rising belly, a smile hinting at last. "I missed you, these last three days. What do you say we convince this one to come out early?"

Maryana chased the hand away. "No. I fell for that once. Maybe if I'd said 'no' then, Sarah wouldn't have been born so early, and her lungs might not be so messed up. No. Four more weeks, Sash, and then you can do what you will."

\* \* \*

*Heat.* Oppressive heat. Drop-in-your-tracks-and-wish-you-were-dead heat. Worse than running a fever in a burning house in the middle of summer. It had been mid-February in Russia; stepping off the transport ship hit them with a 73-degree temperature difference and a sunburned-red sky to adjust to. The children melted. Six-day-old Nikolai squalled at his first breath of Navaran air.

"Get used to it!" Sasha told his entourage, sweat pouring off him just standing still.

While the city seemed modern and promising, the longer the ride, the more dismal the landscape became. Red sky, coral pink sand, pink-brown stone wavy in the heat, as far as the eye could see. No trees. No houses. No people.

Nothing.

A rusty-brown ridge rose high above them, a mesa sticking up 30 meters as if it were punched up from the other side of the world, creating a shrinking shadow. Before them, the same color as the rock, squatted a long, rambling, shapeless mass of ... *something.* The flat, high roof sprouted an array of dishes, tanks, and electrical equipment. Only three windows were visible in the front. It looked more like a sand castle than a house.

Maryana tried to sound cheerful, sitting on a suitcase and wiping the perspiration from her face for at least the tenth time. The heat outside radiated from every direction, made skin shrivel, eyes squint and water, made noses dry until they bled. Never had 21 degrees felt so blessed cold inside a house. "Well, at least it's cooler in here, and it's clean." The new baby had left her weak, and the slightly higher gravity wasn't helping. *Only one computer channel.* They'd left four; she'd hoped for at least two. It was hard to split one wave among so many inquisitive minds and devices.

*Three bedrooms.* Fitting the three remaining girls in one room would be easy, but seven boys – where to stack them? It would be a few years yet before Nikky would be out of the crib, but meantime...

Sandwiched between the other two bedrooms, the room termed 'office/storage' on the rental sheet was little more than a dead-end corridor, not even 2.4 meters wide and 4.5 long, the last meter carved directly into the mountainside behind them. "What if we give Alexei that little office?" she suggested to Sasha. "If we get two sets of bunks, we should be able to fit the other five in the bigger bedroom, and there's more than enough room for the baby to stay with us."

"We can try it," Sasha agreed.

"Sash, I thought we talked about this."

Maryana climbed onto the bed next to him and ran a hand across the wide chest. They'd brought the custom-length bed with them, one of the few pieces of furniture that made the expensive trip. Import taxes on new goods didn't make the local prices much cheaper. "We agreed the import charge on vodka is too high to be drinking it by the bottle. It's only been two days... " *So good! He'd been so good for so long! Until they'd started to pack.*

Sasha slouched against the pillows, hand balancing his glass on the convex curve of his bare belly. His jaw clenched, and he stared blankly at the stone-pink wall. He didn't answer right away, but sipped his glass. Like everything else on this godforsaken planet, even the vodka was disgustingly warm. The ice maker wasn't working, and he hadn't had time to look into it.

He stirred himself at last. "Tash? Did you ever have the feeling you made a mistake? A very – big – mistake?"

"No. I don't think so."

Sasha took another swallow. "Yesterday I signed away the next three years of our lives, and I don't think I can do this."

"Of course you can." Maryana smiled knowingly. He'd be afraid of failure in the unfamiliar setting, she'd point out his supreme talents and accomplishments, talk him through the fears, and after a week or two he'd settle in and get his confidence back. He always did. "What is it? The heat getting to you?"

"Bah. We'll get used to the heat." He gestured with his drinking hand; the liquid sloshed but didn't quite spill over. "I mean the position. At the Science Academy – at Kiev – there were four of us – six if you counted anthropology. Everyone knew where they stood. Everyone's opinion counted, and we worked as a team. Respect came with merit, not title. This place is so – *regimented*. That snotty shit Anseña..." He sucked his glass dry.

"It's only been two days, Sash. Give it time. You'll make friends," Maryana insisted. "If worse comes to worst, you break the contract and we go home."

"To what!" His voice rose, brows banging together like two black thunderclouds. "I *quit* my job, Tash! We *sold* our house! No one's going to hire a professor who breaks his contracts."

"Then we'll take it one day at a time."

*Earthdate: March, 2261*

12

Maryana stroked his cheek, then shook his shoulder. "Sash? Come on, wake up. It's late. Come to bed. You fell asleep in the chair again."

He picked his head up and tried to focus. An empty liquor bottle rolled from his lap onto the floor, clattering sharply against the stone.

"Come on, darling," she crooned. She left the bottle on the chairside table. "Time for bed. Stand up, Sash. I can't carry you."

Sasha dragged himself up with her prodding. He wobbled, but she did her best to steady him.

She got him to sit on the bed, and proceeded to undress him.

Once in bed, he wasn't as sleepy. Maryana felt a familiar hand snake up her nightshirt as she bent over. She pushed it down. "Not tonight, Sasha. Tomorrow, when you know what you're doing."

Sasha belched loudly, a boiling vapor of hot peppers, beans and *titob,* a local fermented sauce. "I know what I'm doing. I t'ink I know what to do when I'm in bed with a beau –beau'ful woman," he hiccupped. He kissed her lips, sloppy and wet. He wrapped his arms around her and fell backwards on the bed.

He got in position, then stopped.

"Sash, you're crushing me. Up a little. Sasha, I can't breathe!" Maryana almost laughed as she realized he had fallen asleep. *My big baby!* She couldn't get out from under him. He was too heavy; the bed too soft. She couldn't call the boys to help, to see their father so undignified as this – let alone their mother! Holding onto the headboard, she wrestled herself out centimeter by centimeter. She pulled the sheet over him as he snored naked in the middle of the bed. Curling up in the remaining space next to him, she kissed him gently and went to sleep.

* * *

The screams pierced ears at the other end of the house, hair-raising shrieks of rage that stopped only long enough for the screamer to gulp more air. Sasha gave four year old Elizabyeta a final spank and sat her on the chair, but she flung herself to the ground, screaming and kicking in fury. Across the dining room, six year old Sarah glared murderously on an aching bottom, eyes brimming but too stubborn to let the tears fall.

"This will stop now!" he thundered. "No more fighting or else!" Byeta waited until his back was turned, then launched herself at Sarah, yanking the white-blonde braids and trying to bite. Sarah grabbed Byeta's thick honey curls and pulled her head away. She slammed an uppercut into Byeta's ribs several times.

13

"Goddamn you, you little shit!" Sasha picked one up in each arm. "Do I need to use a stick? Tash, take her!" He handed Byeta over.

Maryana struggled to hold the kicking girl. "I swear, Sash. If they stay in the same room, one will kill the other. I don't know what else to do. They can't play outside, so they're always in each other's way."

Sasha wiped the sweat from his face. "Separate them. Sarah's always with Vladya; let the boys watch her. Keep Byeta with you. She can sit in a corner until she learns. I have enough to deal with. I need a drink."

\* \* \*

" ...She's only a *child*, Sasha! What she says doesn't matter one bit. Come." Maryana guided him into the kitchen, out of the shocked stares of the children, and sat him at the table. He breathed heavily, shaking. He crossed his arms on the tabletop and rested his big head, face down. She stepped back out to the screams in the living area.

"Vladimir, stop that noise! Viktor, put her in her bed. There should be a healing cream in the cabinet. Dmitri, clean up floor. Katya, watch the babies. I don't want to hear a sound."

She returned to the kitchen and punched the code on the food replicator. It beeped within 30 seconds. Maryana put a cup of strong coffee before him. This wasn't something sex would fix. This was serious.

"Sash, that's not like you. What's wrong?"

Her towering husband, the invincible intimidator with arms the size of tree trunks and a voice that shook earth, *whimpered*.

"Two more years, Tash. I'm not going to make it. That shit Anseña shot down my second rewrite of the proposal as well. For a hundred credits, I'd beat the bastard's head in. If he just wasn't such a *smug* son of a bitch! He has no right to call himself an archaeologist."

"Shhh. I know. You've got more experience than he's ever dreamed of. It's all jealousy. You have to remember that." She rubbed the mighty shoulders. "It's their game, you have to play it their way, even if you know it's wrong. You must be strong. Keep your dignity. Don't let them see it bothering you. You'll win this, too."

"I know. I know." Melancholia replaced his spent anger. He glanced guiltily at the closed kitchen door. It was bad enough to get disrespect at work, but to get it from a six-year-old had been more than he could bear. "Is she... okay?"

"She'll be fine." Maryana kept up the calming tones as she massaged his worry away. "It's okay. It was just your whip. You didn't use your hands. She'll heal."

*He was scared of his hands. He never told her why.
He'd come home to find one of his mother's male
'friends' taking her bank ID. There wasn't much in the
account – he stole from it himself – but it was all they had.
Mother wore a sliver of underwear and a sheer blouse open
to her navel. She lay in the doorway of their dark apartment,
bruised, drunk and crying, a heavy breast flopping on the
carpet, her thick makeup smeared across her face as the man
kicked her.*

*Sasha didn't care too much about his mother; as far as
he was concerned, she'd gotten a little of what she deserved.
He hated his mother for what she was, but he hated the men
who took advantage of her even more. He attacked the man
with ten years' of buried rage. He knocked him clear across
the hall, pummeling and pounding him with huge, practiced
fists. The man staggered but swung back. In the ensuing
scuffle, the man pushed Sasha down the long third-floor
staircase, falling with him. The man cartwheeled up and
over him, hitting the wall at the turn and landing wrong. The
hall filled with witnesses.*

*"Mama? Mama?" Young Sasha dragged his mother
inside their apartment. "Pull yourself together... Cover
yourself!... The politzia are coming, Mama! Something
happened..."*

*The man was dead. It was the first time Sasha knew the
humiliation of being bound and marched to a detention
center; interrogated, processed, degraded, and left alone in
a cell, his long body aching from his fall. Alone, he cried like
a baby. He was seventeen, and would be tried as an adult.*

*His mother surprised him. She visited him, dressed in
loud clothes and no underwear and her heavy makeup, her
wild natural curls tied back in restraint. She went to court,
presenting herself as a victim being defended by her baby,
her only son. If the situation hadn't been so grave, Sasha
would have laughed. Enough neighbors came forward to
swear the man had pushed the boy and the man was at fault,
but the fact remained the man's liver had been badly injured
by a hard blow before his fall. If the fall hadn't killed him, he
would have bled to death.*

*The final ruling held that the man was alive at the time
of the fall. The injury itself had no bearing on the cause of
death. It was officially an accident, and Sasha walked away
free, forever frightened of his own strength.*

"It's bad this time, isn't it? I'm so sorry, Tash. I don't know what I
... I can't do anything right. I know she's young... She just... pissed me
off at the wrong time. And Vladimir... pissing..." He rubbed his face
irritably.

"Shh. It's just the stress you're under. I know. She sounds older than
she is. It's easy to forget." Maryana kissed him on the ear. "Viktor can
handle it. I'll check on her later. I'd rather not drag in a doctor if we
don't have to."

Sasha nodded. Doctors asked questions. The coffee mixed poorly
with the alcohol and his emotions, and he vomited his troubles into the
sink.

### Earthdate: May 27, 2262

He'd left work at eight, that much she knew, but every page on his
handicom had gone unanswered. Maryana heard the door, ten minutes
after she finally went to bed. He'd never been this late before. He
stomped into the bedroom, piss-eyed drunk.

"What? You don't wait up for me anymore?" he said belligerently,
blood-red eyes glaring at her.

"It's late." *Something must have happened. He was never this nasty.
Not to her.* "I didn't know when you'd be back."

"Well, I'm back now." He stripped off his shirt and threw himself on
the bed next to her. "Stay up with me."

"Only if you wash first. You've been out in the heat all day. You're
a bit fragrant. Come, I'll wash you," she suggested. The cool mist would
relax him, make him sleepy. "Lower your voice, before you wake
everybody."

"Why! Why shouldn't they know I love my wife!"

"You're drunk, Sash." She wouldn't hold it against him. He was too
unhappy here, and his dreadful unhappiness tore at her heart. Drinking
gave him escape, from the heat, from the sand, from his job, from the
crush of children. Sometimes he just overdid it a little. "You need to
sleep some of it off."

"It's not unconsciousness I want." His voice dropped a dangerous
octave. A priceless blonde on a planet of brunettes, and she belonged to

16

him. Twenty-two years, and there'd never been another. He seized her and brought his mouth down forcefully on hers.

She coughed at the pungency under his arms. "Stop, Sash. You're drunk, and you're hurting me."

"Then don't fight me." He kissed her, nipping her neck, her shoulder, her ear, running his brutal hands over her body, yanking her dainty nightwear.

Maryana pushed against him. "I'm not fighting you, you're hurting me. *Ow!* Either go easy, or stop it!" He'd never been violent to her before; she didn't know whether to be angry or frightened. He could be rough with the children, but that was different. How else could he get them to obey?

"Ouch! *Sasha!*" she cried as he nipped her again.

"Oh, for goodness' sake! If it will make you happy and get you to sleep!"

* * *

Twelve-year-old David stirred and rolled over. He made out Dmitri's shadow up on its elbows in bed, listening over the background rush of the enviro fans. David lifted his own head, immediately alert. The younger boys breathed softly, deeply in their sleep. Muffled noises came from the room next door.

"Who is it?" he whispered.

"I think it's *Mother*," Dmitri whispered back.

"He never touches her! Should we go see? Should we wake Vik?" David would never dream of investigating alone. If there was trouble, Viktor would know what to do. If nothing else, Father couldn't chase three at once.

"No," fourteen-year old Dimi decided. "If she needed help, she'd call. We might make things worse. Go back to sleep. No sense in both of us being awake."

David lay down, but he could still hear the low rumbling of Father's voice, mixed with the higher-pitched cries of his mother.

* * *

She was dressing when Sasha woke. "What time is it?" he mumbled, holding his head.

"Ask the clock, not me," she said coldly.

Sasha rubbed leaden eyes that refused to focus. "What's with you?"

17

Maryana took a dress from the closet. "You don't know, do you?" she realized. Not even the Navaran heat thawed her icy stare. "You really don't remember."

"Remember what? Fucking mother, my head hurts." He reached out a hand. "Sit with me. What am I supposed to remember? You had your birthday. We went to dinner. What the Hell is this?" He pulled her over despite her resistance and brushed his fingers over several fresh bruises on her back and arms. There were more on the sides of her neck, some large ones on her breasts. Some looked like groups of fingerprints. Some looked like teeth marks. "What the Hell happened? One of the kids do that? That witch Elizabyeta?"

Maryana's eyes filled with tears of anger. She'd never been a violent person, but now she almost understood the drive for violence. It boiled up, unexpected, choking off her words, trampling her elite etiquette into the dust. Her hand raised before she realized it, and she slapped him sharply in the face, her husband of 22 years.

His hand covered the sting. "Tash...!"

"Don't you 'Tash' me, Alexander Kirushenko!" She jerked the dress over her head and tied a matching scarf over the bite marks on her neck.

She wiped at her eyes with trembling fingers, but it didn't help the loss of precious water. "I'm sorry, Sash. I swear to you, if you are ever that rough with me again, I'll... I'll... I don't know what I'll do, but I guarantee you won't like it!"

The dark, dark eyes grew wide. "*I* did that? *I* did that to *you*? I would never - I swear to you, I don't remember any of it!" he realized. "I must have been out of my mind!"

"I have no doubt of that."

Sasha threw himself to his knees before her, 189 kilos of bloated naked flesh. "God's honor, Tash! I love you! I would never hurt you! You know that..."

"I *used* to know that." She dabbed her eyes again, wanting to believe him with her whole heart. "This stops. Now. This very second."

"Never! Never again! I *swear* to you!" Sasha promised through tears of his own. "I had *no idea*... "

Not a word passed between them at breakfast. It was as if they'd switched roles, Maryana silent and subdued, Sasha softly polite and conversational, with the children frightened into silence by the change. Sasha arrived home exactly fifteen minutes after his last class ended, cold sober. Sweat soaked his clothes. His hands shook. Neither acknowledged the other. At dinner, the children ate silently, then disappeared, keepingeach other out of the way without being told. His food didn't want to go down his throat, and came back to haunt him not long after. After the majority were in bed, he met her in the hall, holding a shipping box. He held it out. Maryana accepted it just as silently. It held eight open bottles of liquor, a thousand credits' worth. She lugged the box outside in the dark and threw the bottles against the ridge, screaming through her tears as they shattered.

It was late when she came in. She shut down the house and entered the bedroom.

He sat on the bed, still dressed. He didn't turn. He didn't speak. He sat without moving, tears creeping down to disappear in the thick beard.

"I forgive you."

The sound of her voice made his tears worse. "I don't deserve it."

She sighed with resignation. "Come here." She pulled the great sweaty head onto her shoulder.

Maryana kissed the dark hair. "It's this awful planet. It makes people crazy. Humans aren't meant to live like this. Twelve months, Sash. Just twelve more, and we're free."

The peace lasted a month.

"It's only beer, Tash. Exactly one per day, no more," he swore. "I'm not drinking at work. I can make it, eleven months."

"I'm not mad about the beer." But she wouldn't say more.

At last Sasha called her on it.

"Five credits cash to the person who can tell me why your mother is mad at me," he announced at dinner.

Ten pairs of eyes glanced around the table. Five credits was a small fortune.

"I'm not mad, Sasha," Maryana insisted.

"You've been a sour fish for a week. Something is wrong."

"This is not the time or the place."

"I want to know!"

Maryana placed her napkin next to her plate. "Very well. It will be obvious soon enough. That night you can't seem to remember? You'd better try a little harder, because I'm about to remind you of it every day for the next eight months." She brought her half-eaten plate to the kitchen.

The words sank in. He followed her.

"For real?"

She nodded without turning. "Beginning of March."

"Contract's up the end of August. Good timing for moving back."

He put his hands – very cautiously – on her shoulders, rubbing her neck with his brutish thumbs.

Maryana trembled. "I'm not happy, Sash. I don't want it! Viktor just *graduated*. That gives us *four* in universities! I'm forty years old! Women my age are *grandmothers*! I've still got a two-year old! I know, I should have put a permanent stop to this when they first advised it. Of course, then we wouldn't have Vlad, or Sarah, or 'Byeta, or Nikky. Now it's too late again. This time I'm not leaving that hospital until there's a complete hysterectomy."

"Then don't do it. I'll go with you this week, and we'll stop it. It's not the best time."

"When *was* it a good time? Having twins when I was 18 and married exactly a year, cut off from all family contact? When Katya was eleven months? When Vladya was nine months and sick? Look Nikky in the eye and tell your son he should have been an abortion. I'd have to go off-planet; it's strictly illegal here. Could you handle them for a week while I'm gone?"

Sasha turned her to face him. "I'm *sorry*," he said with sincerity. "I'm sorry for bringing you to this awful planet, I'm sorry for hurting you, I'm sorry for that goddamned night, I'm sorry for this baby. These last years have been a... a *nightmare*, and I'm sorry about all of it. I should have pulled out of the contract. I probably could have gone back to Kiev with a pay cut, but I would have had a job. *I love you*, Tash! I don't want you to leave me."

Maryana caressed the oversized chest. "Shhh. You know I'll never leave you. What are we going to do, Sash?"

Sasha cuddled her close. "Like you say. We'll take it one day at a time."

# Modern History

# * One *

Deep in space it hung, red, brown and white, one of three planets orbiting the star that was no more than a pin-prick of bright on a dark Terran night. Powerful orbital telescopes could see the planet from Earth, but even then it was only the shadow of the planet as it passed in front of its sun. The Earthmen gave the star a fancy Greek name, but they'd never bothered to give the planet more than a numerical designation. After contact had been established a hundred and twenty years previous, the name of the star changed to Navará, the inhabitants' word for *sun*. The Earthmen had difficulty pronouncing the name for the planet, and simplified things: as there was only one habitable planet in the Navaran system, they called the planet Návara as well. The Navarans accepted the misnomer with typical impassive grace; it was easier to make allowances than hear the sacred name of their world forever mangled by boorish Terrans.

Navara's distance proved annoying to those traveling back and forth. Passenger ships were expensive enough at double-speed; a ship equipped with Davies Warp capabilities, whose powerful engines stretched the laws of quantum physics to bypass time and distance and appear to move faster than light, would push their legal limits and it would still require an average of fifty standard hours to reach Navara from Earth. Without warp, it would not have been possible in a human's lifetime.

Few humans who braved Navara stayed long. Ships kept their environmental controls set for a low of twenty-seven degrees Celsius, increasing the cabin temperature to forty-three by arrival time so passengers didn't collapse on exiting the ship. One in five still did, for the Navaran deserts baked in the draft of a furnace hotter than anything on Earth, an entire planet of burning, blowing sand roasting under a blood-red sky. Forty-three Celsius meant a cool day, fifty-six degrees average, and few humans braved the days that hit seventy-five, for moist lungs withered quickly breathing the super-heated air. Without moisture to form cloud cover, the heat fled every night, dropping temperatures

23

fifty degrees by sunrise.

If a visitor survived the first impact of the heat, he would then be assaulted by the landscape: salmon, red-brown, and brown. Ruffly vegetation grew like fungus under shady rocks; frail spikes imitated bushes, but in shades of tans and yellows and russets, never greens. Even geologists, intrigued by the endless kilometers of rock and sand, soon tired of the scarlet sky and gritty breezes, and moved to greener pastures. And of course, once the visitor recovered from the heat and alien landscape, he discovered the gravity was slightly higher than Earth – six per cent, enough to notice. As a final insult, the oxygen content of the air was less, as if on the peak of a high mountain. If someone had the strength to face the heat and walk across the room, the exertion left him gasping until his body learned to compensate. Half the tourists left on the next flight out.

The Navarans were just as happy to keep it that way. An aloof race of humanoids as steadfast and predictable as the daily weather, they valued their privacy. Founding members of the Planetary Alliance (along with Earth's Sol system, the Altair system, and the Centauri worlds), their understated resentment of other species did as much to discourage tourism as the weather. Tall and strong, with a thick skeleton under their weathered yellow-tan skins, they cloaked themselves in their inhospitable climate and shunned the rest of the galaxy as too intrusive, too warlike, too loud and disruptive to their tranquility.

Rumors circulated about Navarans being touch-telepaths, but Navarans regarded touching others as too intimate, so chances to test the theory were rare. They were said to be deeply emotional by those who managed to understand them, but no one had ever claimed to see a Navaran so much as smile. Perhaps it was because of the hinted telepathic trait that emotions were considered private. It was a far lesser shame to walk the streets naked than to raise a voice in anger, or laugh out loud. Most agreed it was a small price to pay to live on a world with no war, no violence, no alleged crime at all. Peace reigned on Navara before Earth's Christ first preached, before the Egyptians farmed the banks of the Nile, before the dawn of modern man. Navarans sailed their solar system six hundred years before Man first toddled into orbit.

Shir P'an, the great capital of the inhabited territories, blends into the landscape from a distance. It isn't until one travels closer that the stone-colored structures take on form, first as ripples in the sand, then as shapes, finally as artificial construction spread across a wave of sandy sea, the modern city blending the ancient desert culture with the current space-faring one in an aesthetic fusion of stone and glass. But Navara should be left to the Navarans, many say, and certainly there is a strong contingent of Navarans who agree. While Shir P'an profits handsomely from trade, it is not a city that welcomes immigration.

One hundred twenty kilometers past Shir P'an (seventy-five miles to the recalcitrant Americans) lies the city of compromise, Kar Ku'umi, the "Terran City," although the Earth races make up only sixty-eight percent of the 150,000 population. Governed by the United Planetary Alliance, regulated by the Navaran government, it allows those stubborn off-worlders who defy the elements more freedom than the restricted Navaran cities. Anything can be found in Kar Ku'umi, from atomic fusion engineers to xenozoologists.

Thirteen kilometers southeast of Kar Ku'umi (eight miles, if you're recalcitrant), alone in the desert, a house lay sheltered from the blistering sun by a high ridge rising from the sand like the backbone of some long-dead, half-buried monster. The home rambled unevenly in the Navaran style, built half-into the stone to hug the flow of the cliff. It wasn't a particularly large dwelling – tall to allow heat to rise, artificial stone to provide cooling – with three airy rooms and four bedrooms not nearly as large. It had been the largest available property owned by the local branch of the Allied Space Academy – which included a division of the School of Archaeology – when the Kirushenko family, formerly of Kiev, Ukraine, Russian Federation of States, Earth, moved in.

Three years. Renowned archaeologist Sasha Kirushenko had contracted for a three-year position, but he'd spent most of those years locked in classrooms, lecturing or teaching methodology in laboratories, not in the active field work where his heart and real talent lay. The house was far too small for the ten of Sasha's twelve children still at home, but there was nowhere else to live. Navarans averaged two children per couple over a fertile span of seventy Earth years. Housing ten children would have required a hotel. They were too far from the city for the children to partake in many social events, and they had only one hovercraft. The Academy's senseless hierarchy, its endless rules and regulations chafed the free-thinking Sasha, and he clashed with at least one alleged superior. He sent out a dozen applications for positions elsewhere; one by one they fell through. The mood in the house those six months grew black as starless midnight.

Out of options, out of time, their savings too depleted by exorbitant living costs to move everyone back and start over, responsibility strangled Sasha. He worried for his wife. For the first time, her irrepressible cheer seemed forced and resigned. Money or not, job or not, they were leaving at the end of the semester. Sasha would leave teaching if necessary, to do what he didn't know, but they could not, would not, survive another year on Navara.

Sixteen-year-old Katya stood before her mother's bed, her blonde hair braided tight against her scalp to help keep her cool. "Sarah was hacking most of the night. She doesn't sound good."

Maryana sat herself up with a grim sigh. Forty years old, regrettably pregnant for the twelfth time, the incessant heat had left her bedridden these last four months. Katya knew how to judge illnesses, but she could be fooled. Not that Maryana expected Sarah to malinger. Sarah loved school more than life, and would drag herself there on a respirator rather than miss a day. Sarah didn't attend the local schools with her brothers and sisters; her scholastic abilities were so superior, she traveled all the way to Shir P'an to attend a Navaran school. Not this day, however.

Sarah's short life had been a series of breathing difficulties; Maryana knew the tell-tale wheeze all too well. "You're staying in bed. I don't want it to worsen."

Eight-year-old Sarah nodded as a strangling cough shook her entire body. Her lungs were congested, but the burning pain of pneumonia wasn't there yet, nor the fever.

"Good catch, Ekaterina. I'll be back with medicine." Maryana waddled through the door, two hands supporting her back. Three more weeks. Perhaps this baby, too, would come early. She'd been achy all night.

* * *

Young Sarah found pleasure in the day. She had the bed all to herself. She hung over the side, letting gravity drain the congestion from her chest while she studied schoolwork from the glowing screen of her text reader. She couldn't waste a single day, even for sickness. If she worked very hard and pushed herself to the end, she would complete the requirements for a Basic Education Diploma (Galactic Standard Form) next year. She would be nine Earth years and eight months old – a record, as far as she knew. It was a goal she was determined to meet.

She slipped out to retrieve her lunch so as not to disturb Mother, then went back to studying. The quiet made her sleepy, and she dozed in the warm room.

When she awoke, she breathed better, but the heat and coughing had dried her throat. Iced tea would be perfect, Sarah decided, and she climbed out of bed again to see if Mother would like some as well. She wasn't supposed to go near Mother if Mother was pregnant and Sarah sick, but a minute or two in the doorway couldn't hurt.

She knocked lightly, then stepped into the room. "*Mat*?"

No one. Sarah crossed the stone floor to the kitchen, bare feet slapping against the silence. She pushed open the swinging door, and stopped. Her spine crinkled icy-cold, her insides shriveled, and it took a moment or two to remember to breathe. Mother lay sprawled on the floor, a puddle of red around her hips. As if in a bad dream, she turned her head at the sound of the door.

"Sar'ina! I forgot you were home," Mother panted. "Be my smart girl and call for help. The baby's coming."

Sarah's violet-blue eyes grew big, and she froze where she stood. *Baby? Now?* She didn't have a clue how babies were born, but she didn't think it was supposed to involve blood. A moan from her mother spurred her into action. She ran to the comlink desk in the dining room and signaled Emergency Services.

"My mother's having a baby!" she coughed at the dispatcher on the viewer.

"Do you need a hospital transport or MedEvac Team?"

Sarah glanced through the doorway at her mother, the red pool contrasting starkly against the white tile. "MedEvac! She's bleeding. There's blood everywhere."

"Is she giving birth now?"

"That's what she said."

"Can you see the baby?"

Mother looked pained and pale, but her belly still swelled high and Sarah saw no baby anywhere. She wasn't even sure *where* to look, but if what David had told her and Vlad was true, she wasn't about to look there. That was *nasty*. But David was full of fake stories, so she decided, "No."

"Then you should have enough time," the woman replied. "An Evac Team is on the way."

Katya returned as Sarah ended the transmission. "Aren't you supposed to be in bed?"

"The baby's coming! Right in the kitchen!"

Katya ran to the door. "Sarah! Do something!"

Sarah bent double with the force of a coughing fit. "I don't know what to do!"

"Get some towels! Get a blanket!"

Sarah took off for a towel, but the Evac Team was at the door before she returned. Breath rasping in her infected chest, she pointed to the kitchen.

"Hurry!" Katya screeched. "It's coming!"

"There's at least a liter of blood here," the paramedic guessed.

"Grab a hemolyte replacer and a volume expander," the second attendant read off his scanner. "Her pressure's way too low. Get a stasis field ready. What number child?"

"Unlucky thirteen," Maryana said weakly.

Whatever questions Sarah may have had were answered as her newest sister came into the world there on the floor.

Half-way through a late dinner, Father's flyer rattled to a slow stop outside. Minutes dragged before he appeared. He placed his things on the table near the door, his movements deliberate and slow.

Katya braved his silence. "I can get your dinner, Father. How's Mother? Did you name the baby?"

Nikolai banged on the table. "Where's the baby? I wanna see the baby."

"Can I call Mama?" Elizabyeta demanded. "Sarah was mean to me after school, and no one would yell at her." She stuck her tongue at Sarah; Sarah mirrored the act.

Father paused, his back to the room. He breathed deep, exhaling an endless sigh. "The baby… Can be home in a few days. Your mother… Your mother is dead. She… bled to death." He staggered to his room, never looking back.

Viktor froze, fork in his hand. "Did he say what I thought he said?"

"You don't think he was joking, do you?" Katya asked.

Dmitri's face took on the color of his artificial milk. "He didn't sound drunk."

"Freakin' *shit!*" a stunned David whispered. "For real?"

Vladimir put his head on the table. Sergei hugged him, hiding his face on Vlad's bony back.

Alexei shoved his chair back so hard it left marks on the stone. "Just what we need! Another squalling brat, and no one to take care of it." He stormed off to his room.

'Byeta kicked her feet against her chair. "I want Mama!"

"Why? Where's Mama? Kat? Where'd Mama go?" Nikky asked, but no one would answer him.

Katya collapsed into tears. "What will we do?"

A numbing chill washed over Sarah, freezing her blood where it congealed somewhere near her feet. "What did *I* do?"

# * Two *

No one remembered bedtime. Nikky fell asleep on the floor, still in his clothes. Everyone but Alexei gathered in the boys' room, the largest of the children's rooms. They felt a need to be clustered, as if by separating they, too, would disappear. Alexei was twenty and had never been part of the crowd. He took Father's flyer and left.

David jumped to his feet as Viktor entered the room. "You all right? Did he talk to you? What'd he say?"

"What's he doing?" Dmitri asked.

Viktor folded his arms across his chest. "Sitting on his bed, not doing anything. Just sitting and staring. I guess there was something wrong with the placenta. That's why she was supposed to be in bed all the time. She went into labor, got up to get things ready, and it tore or something. She went into shock, and her body just gave out. He was holding her when she died."

The room fell silent, save for 'Byeta and Vlad, who continued to weep, and Sarah, who every so often gave a lung-wrenching cough.

"It's not like she paid that much attention to us," Sarah said, holding Vlad's hand, "but she was all we had."

Katya looked horrified. "Sarah! That's an awful thing to say!"

"It's honest."

"She's right," Dmitri said. He stretched across his bed and rested his head on his arms. "Mother stopped caring about us as soon as we outgrew diapers."

Eleven-year-old Sergei gave a shaky sob. "Yeah, but now that she's gone, I really miss her."

"The funeral's in few days," Viktor said. "We need to call Val and Galina." Their oldest sisters – twins – attended universities back home. It would take two days to make the trip to Navara, providing they could get a hyperspace ship.

"I'll do that right now," Katya said. She stood up and wiped her eyes. "I'll send word to Mother's friends, too. Come, 'Byeta, and I'll put you to bed."

Valeria, oldest of the motherless brood, took over the baby as soon as she arrived, to Katya's great relief. Katerina'd had her fill of babies with Nikky. Father couldn't bring himself to look at the baby, let alone hold her.

"She has to have a name," Valeria pleaded. "We can't just call her Baby. What about Marya? Or Marina? That's close to Maryana. We could give her the same second name, too, in memory of Mother. Would that be okay?"

Father nodded acceptance.

A surprising number of people turned out for the funeral: Mother's friends, Father's coworkers, teachers, parents and friends from the various schools, even a few Navarans. Father held tightly to Galina's hand, but he stared ahead as if not alive. Even cold-hearted Alexei bawled at the service, but not Father. When his supervisor extended his condolences, Sasha pushed past him without a word.

At home, the older girls played host for Father and some of his coworkers. The guests stayed until midnight, though Father drank only enough to be polite. There weren't enough beds with the big girls home, so Sarah crawled into bed with Nikky. She did that often enough, when he wouldn't go to sleep.

Sarah lay still, listening to the soft, even breathing of the boys, enduring Nikky's sleep-squirmy knees and elbows, but she couldn't sleep. She hadn't fully recovered from the virus, and buried her coughing in her pillow lest she wake someone. Over and over for the last three days, she had thought about her mother's last moments, and the blood – the vast lake of blood – puddling under her mother, the great gush of blood from *there* when the icky purple-gray baby slid out. So much blood. She hadn't been frightened, not really; she just had no idea whatsoever how to help Mother. Less than ten minutes had passed between the time she entered the kitchen and the MedEvac team arrived, but what if those ten minutes had been the critical ones? What if she had woke up a half hour earlier? What if she hadn't stayed quiet all day so Mother forgot she was home? *If, if, if!* She hadn't even shed a tear! Her mother was dead, and she felt... nothing. No grief, no sadness, just... indifference. She was a dreadful daughter, with no sorrow for a dead mother who spread herself too thin.

She comforted Vlad, kept Nikky quiet, and no one seemed to notice her lack of remorse. Sarah was serious and sensible to begin with, but inside... Inside she burned with guilt. She was the smartest person in the house – even Father said so – but she failed to help Mother. An ungrateful child who watched her mother die, and did nothing.

She slid out of bed and headed for the kitchen. Father lay passed out across a sofa, giant feet hanging over the arm, one mammoth sandal on the floor below. It was the first 'normal' thing he'd done in four days, and she found it strangely comforting.

Katya and Dmitri had scoured the kitchen floor, removing every trace of blood. Looking at The Spot crinkled her insides, as if ghost blood were waiting to reappear when she least expected.

Galina noticed her. "What are you doing up? It's late."

Sarah sat at the table. "I couldn't sleep."

"A cup of tea for your cold?"

Sarah nodded, and her sister programmed the order on the food replicator. The desert nights were chilly after the broiling days, and the hot drink was welcome. A half minute later, Galina placed tea and toast before her.

"You didn't eat dinner. You're probably just hungry."

Valeria sat next to Sarah. "We're sorry to kick you out of your bed. I hope the boys don't mind too much." The twins looked like clones – same tall height, same faces, same golden wavy hair, but Valeria's hair hung to her shoulders, while Galina kept hers cut in a popular style at ear level. It was hard to mistake one for the other that way, unless on voice alone.

"I can handle them," Sarah said, licking replicated jam from her fingers. She blew on her tea and sipped it, then gave a sticky cough. "What's going to happen now? What will we do?"

"Not much," replied Valeria. The baby let out a cry from the cartabout in the corner, and Galina rose to feed her.

Valeria pushed Sarah's long hair back from the jam-sticky face. "Father is still Father. Galina must return to school, as she'll get her other degree in a few more weeks, but I'll stay to help. We'll manage. Are you worried?"

"No, but Vladimir is." Val and Gal were all grown up; Sarah could hardly remember them ever living at home. She wasn't sure how much she should say to them, whose side they were on. "Mother was a kind of... *regulator* for Father. She knew how to calm him if he got angry. Vlad is afraid with her gone, there won't be anyone to stop Father when he gets mad."

Galina laughed. "I don't think Father's quite that bad." The baby squirmed against her neck as she rubbed her back.

"Think of his side of it," Val explained. "He works long hours to provide for his family, and then comes home to ten – now eleven – children who all have squabbles with each other, and now he doesn't even have Mother to help."

Sarah swallowed her tea quickly to avoid choking on it. "You've been away too long. Two years ago, Father almost killed me."

"Don't exaggerate, Sarah," Galina said. "Father gets mad - "

"I'll show you, but you have to promise not to talk about it."

"Promise," the twins said as one.

Sarah lifted the back of her pajama shirt to show the scars she knew were there. "He did that. Mother had to make him stop."

Galina clutched the baby as if to shield her from the sight.

Valeria shrank back. "*Father* did that?"

Sarah lowered her shirt. "*Da!* And he broke Vladimir's hand – I don't think he meant to, but it still happened – and he gave Dmitri a black eye, and kicked David so hard he broke ribs!" She leaned close to confess, "Of course, he only does that when he's been drinking *liquor*. That's when he gets *really* mad."

"Well, I wouldn't worry about it," Valeria recovered. "I'm sure Gal and I can handle it. Everything will be fine. Tell Vlad I'll be here if he needs me.

Sarah nodded, and finished the last of the sugary tea.

Val gave her a brief hug. "Now get to bed. You're well enough to go back to school tomorrow, if you want."

Nikky lay sideways across his bed, snoring. Sarah climbed to the bunk above him and curled up next to Vladimir, but she didn't sleep.

Having Mother gone was not unusual; she'd disappear for births, or nights out, or short trips with Father, but somehow... nothing seemed right anymore. They arose every morning expecting to greet her, and returned from school forgetting she was gone. Constant disappointment took its toll.

Nikky sat with the Fearsome Four – David's gang name for himself, Sergei, Vlad, and Sarah – in front of the huge holovision. "Where's Mama? Is she done being deaded yet? Don't she want to see our baby?"

"Shah, Nik. We told you already," Vlad said.

"Can we go see her? I wanna see her. When she comin' home?" Nikky leaned over the top of the sofa and kicked the cushion.

Sarah pushed his feet down. "No, Nik. Now stop."

"Why, Sarri? How come? Why doesn't Mama come home? Sarri? Is she at the party with all the peoples cryin' 'cause they couldn't find her? Huh, Sarri?" He jumped up and down on the seat. "Where'd she go?"

David growled from the other sofa. "Shut him the fuck up. Shut up, Nik, if you know what's good for you."

"That's real mature language," Sergei grumbled. "He's three, and so are you."

Nikky sang as he jumped. "I want Ma-ma, I want Ma-ma. Where's my Mama?"

Vlad began to pull Nikky down, but dove out of the way as David stormed across the floor.

David grabbed Nikky in mid-jump and walloped his bottom with unnecessary strength. He shook the shrieking child by his hair.

"SHUT THE GODDAMNED FUCK UP YOU FREAK! She's DEAD! She's NEVER coming back! You're NEVER gonna see her! They burned her up and left her for the worms to eat, and if you don't shut up and stop it, I'm going to put *you* in a box and bury *you* in the sand so the sun can burn *you* up, and no one will hear you scream when the bugs come to eat you! Now *SHUT THE FUCK UP!*"

Nikky ran for his room the second David let go. Neither Sarah nor Vlad could coax him out from under his bed. Only the next morning, after David left for school, could Val convince him it was safe.

Six weeks after his mother's death, Alexei left home.

He heaved his oversized travel case from the bed to the floor. "I can't take this shit anymore! It's a crazy house for preschoolers! We're packed in here like fish in a box. You're crazy if you stay. I'm not going to be held responsible for a woman who allowed herself to be fucked to death. We didn't birth them; it's not our job to raise them."

Valeria gasped. The baby hung over her arm like some favorite toy. "How can you *say* that about Mother! How can you abandon Father like this? Where will you go? What about your classes?"

"I know some people at the colony on Hudson's Planet. They asked me to come out there. I've got a two-year certificate in chemistry; I can start with that. Anything is better than living in this... goddamned orphanage."

A strange flyer came by to pick him up.

Father never moved from his chair. His eyes hardly left the holovision as he mumbled, "Good luck."

Vlad and Sarah watched from the corners, keeping Nikky out of the way.

"What did I tell you?" Sarah warned Vladimir as their eldest brother walked out without so much as a goodbye. "We'll all disappear, one by one. Two down, thirteen more to go."

Following Mother's death, Father's short-tempered violence disappeared, the unpredictable terrorist replaced by an identical-looking android whose soft-spoken, quiet manner made him seem more like a house guest trying to mind his own business. He came home late, ate by himself, then shut himself up in his room, letting the twins handle the chaos, giving his input only when necessary. The sour stink about him disappeared; so did the empty bottles that tripped the unwary and rolled across the floor with a sharp tinkle. What went on behind the closed door remained a mystery.

As weeks passed, old habits relaxed. Older sisters could be fooled by ten younger brothers and sisters, out run, outsmarted, outnumbered. They simply could not be everywhere at once. The rule against running in the house fell by the wayside as David and Dmitri raced through the house in a contest to reach their room, wrestling and laughing without thought.

Father's door flew open. His thick hair stood up in an uncombed mass, his dark, dark eyes glassy and bloodshot as they hadn't been for months. The huge hands closed around the back of the boys' necks, until they twisted on tiptoe to ease the pressure.

*"What the Hell are you doing?"*

Dmitri blanched. "Going to our room, Father."

Father shook them harshly, voice so low it was a threatening whisper. "This is a house, not a gymnasium! Take care you don't forget that fact, or I'll make damned sure you don't."

"Yes, sir!"

As an afterthought, Father cracked their heads together. "Consider that a warning." He turned back to his room and slammed the door.

The boys dove through their door together. They startled Sarah and Vladimir, playing with Nikky on the floor.

Dmitri stared at the door, rubbing his head. "Goddamn that hurts!"

"You're not kidding," David agreed, massaging his jaw. "Even my teeth hurt."

"What happened?" Sarah ventured.

David scowled. "Ol' Booze-breath's back at it."

Galina returned for good, necessitating a shifting of sleeping arrangements. Sarah couldn't sleep with Nikky permanently. Alexei's room had been tiny, once a small office, but he and Viktor had crowded in when Nikky had moved to a bed. That left only five boys in the bigger bedroom. Five would have to become six. There was no way to squeeze six girls into the one room.

"It can't be done," Valeria insisted. "It's too hot to sleep three in a bed. One of us would have to sleep on the floor. With the crib in there, there isn't even room for that."

David shrugged. "Doesn't bother me if you sleep on the floor. We're squished enough."

Viktor moved back into the boys' room. The twins took over the tiny room, jamming the crib against the wall.

Galina elbowed past Valeria to get her clothes. "This is crazy. If we both breathe at once, we'll use up all the air."

"We could take turns," Val suggested. "Stagger our schedules a little, so we're not stepping on each other."

Gal's hand stopped on the drawer as an idea came to her. "That's not as stupid as it sounds."

A week later, she landed a job working nights.

"Don't you even want to play cards?" Vlad pleaded, dropping a deck on the bed. "All you ever do is read that stuff."

Sarah broke away from her homework 'pad, impassive as stone. "I have to, Vlad. All these changes are very distracting. I can't fall behind. You try writing an essay in Navaran." She paused to tear at a fingernail with her teeth, then relented, "You could sit with me and play Solitaire if you want."

It wasn't the answer Vlad wanted, but he climbed onto the bed next to her. "Okay."

But Sarah's quirks wouldn't go away.

The next morning, Sarah entered the crowded kitchen, and for the third day in a row walked conspicuously around the perimeter before stopping at the table.

Katya tripped on her. "Sarah, what are you doing? Can't you walk straight?"

Sarah walked heel to toe around the kitchen, arms waving for balance. "I'm calculating trigonometric tangents. The table and wall are the axes, and I'm walking the curves to measure them."

"That's the stupidest thing I ever heard," David jeered. "Nobody thinks about math *that* much."

"She is not stupid!" Vladimir shot back. "You're stupid!"

"You should talk, dummy."

Elizabyeta sang out, "Stupid Sarah! Stupid Sarah! Sarah is a stupid!"

"Hey!" Sergei yelled as cold juice ran down his shoulder.

Sarah put the empty glass down. "I didn't mean to hit you. I was aiming at *her*." She glared at 'Byeta, who flounced her curly hair and sang smugly, "Missed me! Missed me!"

Sarah grabbed a glass of milk substitute from the table and raised it to throw, but Dmitri seized it from behind. A loud bang shocked everyone into silence.

Viktor brought his chair down hard on the tiles. "Enough!" he hissed. His gentle brown eyes flashed with anger. "Is this how we've ever acted? Is this what we want Father to walk into first thing in the morning? Sarah, leave. 'Byeta, shut up. Sergei, go change. Vlad, sit down and eat. Everyone, eat!"

Sarah hopped the last three steps out of the kitchen. How could she tell them the real reason she couldn't cross the floor? Sure, it seemed perfectly clean, but Sarah knew better. *She* knew where the blood had been. Somewhere, deep down in the flooring, there were no doubt molecules, perhaps even whole specks of her mother's blood. Her mother died, but parts of her still remained in that room. Sarah couldn't stop the bleeding, her mother had died, and she wasn't going to go walking through that ocean of blood again. Someday all that blood might just reappear like long-lost treasure at an archaeology dig, and she'd be damned if her footprints would show up in it, desecrating her poor mother. A thousand years from now someone would sweep away the dunes that would bury their house, and the scientists would prowl around the rooms. They'd come to the kitchen and find the blood like a ghost in a graveyard, and wonder. They'd comb through ancient records, find out about the medical call and the death certificate, and the shameful facts would be made known to their descendants. She couldn't confide such truth to Vladimir; he would just stare at the floor and cry all over again. No, such things she'd best keep to herself.

The baby hit a crabby spell, not sleeping more than two hours at a stretch. The girls dragged themselves like zombies, Father's curses ringing in their ears.

"I'll get up with her if you want," Sarah volunteered.

Valeria shook her head. "You need your sleep, Sarah. We'll manage. It's just a temporary thing."

"Really, Val! I don't mind! I usually wake up the minute she starts crying, anyway. I'm old enough. I know how to feed her. I learned when Nikky was little. *Please?* I want to help."

"You already *do* help," Val insisted. "You and Vlad are wonderful at keeping Nikky out of the way."

"That's regular every-day stuff. It's not *real* help."

"We'll see. I won't wake you. You'll have to beat me to the kitchen."

Sarah met Val in the hall that night almost before the baby finished her first wail. She was long awake, flopping restlessly next to Katya in their bed, like she did every night now. Val's reluctant permission fast became routine. Night after night, Sarah walked her baby sister in endless laps around the quiet rooms, hours after Marina had fallen back asleep. Heavy on Sarah's shoulder, milk-sweet angel breath quick in her ear, the baby was warm and soft and comforting to hold, one more lost soul in the dead of night.

# * Three *

The evening grew late, but the following day was the Navaran Day of Reverence, and only 'Byeta and Nikky were asleep – Nikky in Sarah's bed. Without Nikky in the bedroom, the boys had space to stay out of Father's way. The twins took the baby with them to visit a friend.

Viktor took his turn at the vapor-shower in the hall bath. Dmitri, David, and Sergei spread themselves across the cool floor of the bedroom, deep in a complicated battle-strategy game. Sarah and Vlad grew tired of watching the slow-moving game, and sat on Nikky's bed playing cards instead. Katya chatted with a friend on the commlink in the dining room. Father nursed his nightly bottle in front of the blaring holovision. It was as perfect a night as anyone could wish.

David rolled a ten-sided die. "Your army is hit with food poisoning, Sergei! There's diarrhea all over the battlefield. No one can wear a spacesuit. Lose a turn!"

Sergei grabbed the penalty marker from his brother, who made intestinal noises against his hand. "That's not what it says. It says *ass-*teroid field. You should know what an *ass* is, as you are one yourself."

Vlad nearly fell off the bed, laughing. "How can... you... sit there, Sar?" He squealed again as David groaned and made a louder authentic noise.

Sarah watched with disapproval, though four months ago, she would have giggled, too. "It's your turn."

"Oooh, so proper," David chided her. "Dimi, there's four of us. Why don't we pin Little Miss Navara and tickle her 'til she cracks? She's been an awful hard-ass lately."

Dmitri glanced from brother to brother for the consensus. "That has merit."

Sarah drew a card. "*Ha. Ha.* I am *sooo* frightened." She could hold her own against Vlad and Sergei, or David or Dmitri alone, but not the four boys together.

Vlad bounced on the bed, spilling the cards to the floor. "Let's do it! Let's do it! Sarah hasn't been fun for ages!"

Viktor headed back to the room, toweling his hair, when he heard a noise that just wasn't right. He stopped in the hall and hung the damp towel around his neck, listening. The baby was gone, it wasn't the enviro fans or an electrical noise. A high-pitched shriek came from the boys' room, followed by several voices. The holovision sounded a raucous sports event down the hall. A long moment passed before he heard it again.

"Please, *no!*"

Katya's voice strained with a desperate resonance, and it came from Father's room. Father answered in a murmuring rumble, but Viktor couldn't make out the words.

"Kat?" He tapped a knuckle against the door. As a rule, Father never bothered the older girls, outside of a yell now and then. "Ekaterina? You all right?" A muffled cry answered.

Viktor pounded on the locked door with his fist. "Katya?"

*"Help!"*

Viktor burst through the door of the boys' room with such speed and urgency that all games were immediately forgotten. Dmitri and David let go of Sarah, and the younger boys broke off their painful tickling. All five leapt up, ready to scatter.

"What is it? What's wrong?" Dmitri demanded.

Viktor tore the top drawer from his dresser and dumped the loose contents onto a bed. *There it was!* He grabbed a thin metal bar and a magnet from among the junk and rushed out, followed closely by Dmitri and David. That filled the hall, leaving the remaining three to elbow each other in the doorway.

"What's wrong?" Dmitri repeated.

"Hang on!" Viktor shouted. With a mighty stab, he drove the flat bar into the doorjamb, halfway up. Once in, he stuck the magnet on it, close to the frame.

"Magnetic privacy lock," he explained, wiggling the bar. "Easy to override." The locked popped, and the door slid free. Vik and Dmitri rushed in. Seconds passed before Viktor's eyes realized they were seeing something his brain didn't want to know, couldn't accept as real.

Katya stood against the far wall. Terror twisted her face as she cringed backwards against the stone. Father stood centimeters before her, blocking her escape.

"...so much like Tash," Father finished mumbling, voice heavy with inebriation. Sausage-thick fingers combed her yellow hair. Katya's shirt hung open to her waist, her thin arms trying desperately to cover herself.

*"Noooo,"* Viktor whispered in a long breath, and the disbelief turned to rage. He cleared the room in three steps, jumping onto the extra-long bed before Father could turn around. Taking the towel still hanging from

his neck, he threw it over Father's head and jumped on his back, pulling the ends of the cloth with all his strength. Kilo for kilo he was no match for Father, but he'd been the number two player on the school wrestling team, and he didn't let his shoulder strength go to waste.

Father stumbled from the unexpected weight, stinking of whiskey and two days' sweat.

"Go! Get!" Viktor yelled. Kat ran as far as the end of the bed.

Father lurched and fell to his knees, dropping Viktor to the floor. Vik was slow to anger, but this time his fury went beyond reason. Beating on them was one thing, but not this! There had to be a limit. He slammed Father's head against the floor. Father let out a howl of rage and ripped the towel from his face.

Viktor danced backwards. Father heaved to his feet. The spidery veins on his nose glowed purple. His dark eyes glinted coldly under their blanket of thick black brows.

Vik shoved Katya into Dmitri's arms. "Get her out of here!" he shouted, pushing them toward the door. "All of you, get out!"

"You son of a bitch!" Father hissed. "I'll kill you!"

"No you won't, you King of Shit!" Viktor spat, beckoning. "Who the Hell do you think you are? Come pick on the person who's going to kick your oversized ass around the nearest satellite and back! Come on, you worthless waste of flesh! The only thing you know how to kill is a bottle!" He'd done the unthinkable. He'd crossed the line. He might as well run with it as far as he could before Father *did* kill him.

\* \* \*

Dmitri pushed everyone into the back room in a hurried rush and slammed the door just as Father lunged. They stood, staring at the door, until Katya burst into tears, holding the front of her shirt.

"It'll be okay," Dmitri said awkwardly. Katya leaned into him, crying her heart out.

He patted her back. "It's okay. Vik'll take care of it."

Katya gulped between heaving sobs. "He was going to… He said he … and he squeezed my… so *hard!*"

"Hang on. Here." Dmitri took off his own shirt and pulled it over her gallantly, embarrassed by the glimpses of flesh. It was nothing Kat wanted to show, and nothing the others needed to see. Now her tears flowed on his bare skin, her arms locked around him. His insides fluttered, seeing the purple-red marks on his sister's neck. He'd left marks like that on girls before; they weren't made by hands.

"He's so much ... bigger than me! I couldn't... stop him."

"Of course you couldn't. Not by yourself. No one could have." Dmitri glanced several times at the door. An awful lot of crashing sounded down the hall. He wanted to know what was happening, but he couldn't leave Katya.

"We'll protect you, Kat," David vowed. He smacked a brawny fist against his palm for lack of something better. "Don't worry."

"He's gon-na kill Vik-ik!"

A loud shattering came from the living room.

"Vik's all alone!" Sarah realized, and bolted for the door.

"*No!* Stay here!" Dmitri ordered, but even David's fast grab was too late. She flew into the hall, Sergei and Vladimir right behind.

\* \* \*

Sarah skidded to a stop at the end of the hall, the boys piling into her. The room was destroyed, the heavy furniture overturned, the wall hangings ripped away. At least one of Mother's prized figurines lay smashed, along with various photos and treasures that had once been on the triangular side tables. Broken bits lay scattered across the holovision platform, leaving gaping holes in the projected picture. Bloody footprints followed Viktor, his bare feet shredded by glass.

"What's the matter, you chicken-shit bastard? Who's killing who?" Viktor may have been panting, but Father weighed a hundred and eighty kilos stark naked and freshly shaved; his breath came in heaving gasps. The air was too thin, the household temp down only to twenty-seven degrees. They circled each other, waiting.

"You belong in a street gutter, you goddamned drunk!"

Father attempted a hard punch, but it went wide. Viktor tucked low and rushed him, driving his shoulder into the soft stomach. Father stumbled backwards, but the half-wall of the dining room caught him.

Viktor backed up. "What's the matter, old man? You'll only pick on young women and children? How dare you call yourself a man!"

Sarah moved into the room, ready to help.

Vik glanced at her. "Get out! Now!"

Sarah backed up only a step. Sergei leaned from the alcove and dragged her back to the shadows. Vladimir slid his hand into hers.

"Don't distract him," Sergei whispered. "He knows what he's doing. If he messes up, Father'll kill him! *Dead!*"

"He'll kill Viktor if we *don't* help him!" Sarah hissed. She wrenched away and dashed into the room. *Something to help...* She grabbed a

41

broken display frame and began to scrape some of the glass out of the way. Shards stuck together, gooey with blood.

*Mother's possessions, bloody and broken, just like her...*

Father swayed, but he stood and lurched unevenly toward Viktor. Vik straightened up to meet him, ready, when Father lashed out and pulled his son in close with a choke hold. Viktor pounded and clawed at the massive arm pressing his throat, but he could not break the grip. His shocked face darkened.

"*Now* who is the fool?" Father spat, squeezing the thick arm ever tighter. "Never underestimate an opponent, you ungrateful bastard! *I* am the law in my house!"

Viktor's legs gave out, and he sagged. Vladimir's hysterical screams brought Dmitri running.

"He's killing him! He's killing him!" Vlad shrieked. "*Do* something!"

Dmitri froze. He wasn't nearly as strong as Viktor, not as tall, not as heavy. *What could they do? Who could control such a man?* City Security could. He sprinted for the commlink.

Sarah was quicker. She grabbed one of Mother's decorative statues, a heavy marblesque replica of Sarentall's *Maiden in Morning* nearly the length of her arm. Two hands gripping the maiden's bare middle, she swung the weighted base as hard as she could into the back of Father's supporting knee. He fell hard as the knee buckled, dragging Viktor with him. Father's head hit the stone floor with a sharp crack. He struggled to rise for a moment, then lay still.

Viktor rolled to his knees, gagging. Sarah and Dmitri helped him sit. Sergei joined them, but Vladimir would come no closer to Father than the hall. David appeared behind him, holding onto Katya.

"Thank you, Sarah!" Viktor wheezed. "I didn't think I would make it. That son of a bitch is strong."

Dmitri sent Sergei for some water. "What do we do now?"

"Take him out by the dune walls and dump him," Viktor rasped, half-serious. He took the water from Sergei. "Just a wandering drunk."

Dmitri looked doubtful. "How're we going to get him in the flyer? He weighs as much as five of us put together."

"We cut him into pieces first," Sarah suggested.

Sergei rapped her on the head. "He's not dead, you ninny."

"That can be remedied."

"And David calls *me* weird."

Viktor picked a needle of glass from his foot. "It doesn't matter. I have a better idea. We clean everything up, then call for medical assistance. We tell them our father was drinking heavily – true, fell down – true, and may have injured himself, can they come and get him. *They* will have to move him, *they'll* keep him 'til he wakes up – tomorrow morning if we're lucky – and we'll all sleep easy tonight. Chances are he won't remember it. Sound good? Hurry, then. We don't have much time."

"What about your feet, Vik?" Sarah pointed out.

"Run and get me a pair of sandals," he winced. "I'll deal with them later." Sarah returned with his sandals and a well-used tube of anesthetic healing cream.

Vik ruffled her hair affectionately. "You're a lifesaver!"

With everyone's combined efforts the furniture was soon in place, glass cleared, floor washed. Dmitri cleaned Father carefully. Viktor hunted through the house, searching for bottles. They found six, destroyed all but two, which they left empty by Father's chair. The Fearsome Four were chased, protesting, to bed. Rather than drag Nikky out of her bed, Sarah took his. Katya locked herself in the bathroom. Viktor and Dmitri found a program on the holovision and set out a deck of cards, as if they'd been there all night.

Dmitri waited by the commlink. "Ready?"

Viktor's face darkened. "Let's give him something to wonder about tomorrow. This is for Kat," he spat through clenched teeth, and kicked his father hard in the groin. The unconscious man groaned, but didn't move.

"Nice touch," Dmitri said, and hit the call button.

"So what happened to Katya?" Vlad asked David softly. "What was happening? Nobody'd let me see."

"Nothing you'd understand."

"I would too!" Vlad protested. "I'm nine. I'm not a baby, you know."

"I don't understand either, and I know more than he does," Sarah added. Hidden by darkness, she climbed silently up to Vlad's bed and squeezed between him and the wall, out of reach of most dangers. Vlad shifted over to give her space.

David chickened out. "Sergei'll tell you."

Sergei grinned in the dark. "Uh-uh! I couldn't see anything, either."

"Shit-ass."

David thought for a minute. "It's like this: Father wanted Katya to, um, … have a baby, and, um, Kat didn't want to."

"Oh," Vladimir said in presumed understanding. "That's why he choked her?"

Sarah sat up, indignant. "You are so full of sulfur, David Fyodor! Why would he want to have *another* baby! We have a baby right *now* he doesn't even look at! I don't *want* any more brothers or sisters! Mother died, wasn't that enough? He wants to kill Katya, too?"

*"Shhhhh!"* David hissed. *"Quiet!* Then ask Vik, but don't go bugging Kat about it. You'll just upset her again."

Sarah lay awake most of the night, trying to make sense of the pieces.

The Navaran holiday, and everyone slept late – except Sarah. She picked her way across the spotless kitchen to get Nikky breakfast. She had to admit, the replicator had its purpose. Pour in the nutrient matrix, punch in a pre-programmed number, and a minute later the machine delivered something that resembled what you wanted, more or less. Things like tea were pretty authentic, but fancy things with a hundred ingredients, like duck á l'orange or Navaran twelve-spiced *chitora'c*-root pudding left a bit to the imagination. If you weren't careful, your meat, vegetables, and bread all tasted the same, but it was much quicker and easier than Mother's cooking, and a lot cheaper than importing the actual items.

She and Vlad hung around impatiently, waiting for Viktor to rise, and to catch him alone.

Sarah perched on his knee. "… And then David said to ask you." Viktor was always calm and patient, and he was Sarah's favorite brother – next to Vlad, so his reaction surprised her.

"It's nothing you need to worry about!" he snapped. He raised a finger at them. "Leave Katya alone! I catch anyone discussing last night with *anybody*, even yourselves, and so help me, I'll take Father's whip to you myself! *Is that clear?* Leave her alone."

Unnerved by Viktor's reaction, Sarah and Vlad promised, but it hardly answered anything.

"I'm going to the library in Kar Ku'umi," Sarah informed Val at lunch. "I want to research something."

"You can't do it from the computer here?" Valeria asked. Almost any information available at the public library could be accessed from home. "Who's going with you?"

"I don't want to tie up the computer that long, in case someone else wants it," Sarah said selflessly. "Vlad and Sergei will go with me." It was Viktor's idea that the girls might be better off always being in pairs, and Katya never left alone if Father was home. "We'll be back by fifth-mark. Please?"

Val yawned. "See if Viktor will fly you in. Can you guys take a shuttlecab or something back on your own?"

Sarah nodded.

Life in the Terran City continued on schedule. Schools and government buildings were closed in respect for the alien hosts, ceremonies were held, but leisure and learning facilities did a booming business. A hundred thousand people needed *something* to do with their free time, and the library was more crowded than usual. Within twenty minutes, Sarah found something in the files to suit her purpose, and waited another ten for a temp copy to be printed and bound by the machine.

Dmitri found them at home later that afternoon. To overlook one missing child in a crowded house was easy, but not four. The Fearsome Four crowded whispering in the girls' closet, studying Sarah's printed copy.

"What are you doing in there?" he said. Something that interesting might be interesting to him, too.

"Nothing," Sergei said. "Just a book."

"David doesn't look at a book unless it's been nailed to his eyes. Hand it over."

Dmitri reached for the text. Sarah closed it fast, but his grab was quicker. His thumb held the place; it took several hard tugs to make her release it. He stared at the photo on the page. Blushing, Dmitri looked in shock at the Fearsome Four. David studied his feet. Sergei buried his face in the crook of his arm. Vlad hid behind Sarah, arms protecting his head. Only Sarah had the nerve to keep her chin up. Dmitri flipped the book to read the cover:

*Human Reproductive Anatomy: Function and Dysfunction*
"Valeriaaaaa!"

Val sighed, covering her mouth with her hand. "I guess I won't ask you why."

"Because everyone keeps talking about babies," Sarah said in frustration. "Having them and making them, and no one will ever tell me the first thing about it. Father won't let them teach me it in school until next year, and he blocked the computer. Sergei won't tell, and David lies too much for me to believe him. Vlad and I wanted to know, once and for all. David found us and said he'd see it, too, or he'd tell, which means he doesn't really know, either."

"But Sarah…" Val turned a page with two leery fingers. "Such a technical book! *I* don't even understand half of this. And these – *pictures*! I'm not sure these are the best ones to learn from. Life isn't like this."

"I *don't* understand a lot of it. I was reading about the… ." Sarah flipped to the contents and scanned the sections. "En-do-crin-ology."

"Do you have any questions? I mean, that you… want to ask me?"

Sarah chewed her lip. She turned pages until she found a subject. "This stuff – Is this for *real*?"

Valeria skimmed the pages, answering a couple of questions. "I think Gal and I were eleven; Kat maybe thirteen."

"Not me! Never! I don't want that," Sarah vowed.

Valeria smiled at her sister, so smart and so naïve at the same time. "You don't have a choice. It will happen whether you want it to or not. That's the way nature is. When you're older, you'll feel different about it."

"No I won't!"

"You can't judge everything by what you read in a book, Sar," Valeria said. "I wish you had asked me first. There's a lot this book doesn't cover – like emotion, love, trust, personal experience – The universe isn't cold and clinical. I'm recycling this book. Please *ask* what you want to know. I promise, Galina, Katya, and I will try our best to answer whatever questions you have. And Sarah," Val said firmly, "leave the boys out of it. Viktor will deal with them. It's not their business. Let them figure it out for themselves."

Sarah pouted. "Not fair."

Father showed up at dinner, cross-eyed drunk and madder than a hornet. His first action was to retrieve his whip from its place in the drawer of the table by the door – the gift of a sarcastic student as a comment on the way he sometimes drove them.

"Sons!" he bellowed, cracking the whip. "I want all my sons, right here!"

All six boys, down to little Nikky, scrambled to form a line.

Elizabyeta's curly head popped over the sofa to watch. "Somebody's in trouble. I bet it was Sarah, Papa! Sarah did it!"

"Hush!" Galina said. "You don't know that, 'Byeta. Don't lie."

Val tried to smooth things over the way Mother would have done.

"Father, why don't you let me get you some dinner? If there's something I can help with… "

"*Help?* Like you helped me today? You know I am in a trauma center, but you don't call to see why? You don't want to know how your own father is? No one comes to bring me home? The shame is mine, for spawning such a disloyal wretch!" He flung out a thick finger. "Do not patronize me again! You are in my house and you are still my child and you will respect me or leave!"

Val winced as if she'd been hit herself. "Yes, sir. I'm sorry, sir." She grabbed several dirty plates from the table and ran for the kitchen, helplessly letting things run their course. Galina stayed in the doorway, torn in both directions.

Father limped up and down the row of boys. "The hospital said that two of my sons called to have me hauled away like trash. Dragged away while I slept, to wake up in a medical center with no idea what happened to me or my family. I want to know which of my sons have embarrassed me to this degree, and *I will know now*!"

Nikky leaned forward, peering down the line to see who would answer. Sarah, hovering anxiously in such situations, pulled her baby brother to the side with her.

"Get back in line!" Father barked.

"No, he won't," Sarah replied, cold and brave. "He was asleep last night, and he doesn't know how to work the commlink. You know that."

"Then get him out of here!"

Sarah bent down and whispered something.

"Okay," Nikky agreed. He skipped off to her room.

'Byeta stood on the sofa. "You better not touch my toys! Papa, he's gonna touch my toys! If he breaks something, I want a new one!"

Vlad's skin had a ghostly sheen. He made a quick, hopeful face at Sarah. *What about me?*

*How?* Sarah signaled back.

"I hear *silence*!" Father thundered, cracking the whip. "Sergei!"

"Yes, Father!"

"Who called for medical assistance?"

"I don't know, sir. It must have been after I went to bed." It wasn't a lie, *per se.* Sergei knew it to be one of two, but he didn't know which.

"David! I guarantee it was you, you good for nothing shit!"

David looked through Father to the wall beyond. "No, sir! I really don't know, sir."

"Vladimir!"

Vlad jumped and ducked. "I didn't do it! I didn't!"

"'Not me! Not me! I don't know, sir,' " Father mimicked. "I'm tired of hearing 'I don't know'!" He turned sharply and lashed out with the whip. Sergei flinched; next to him, the tip stung Vlad on the elbow. Vlad tried, but a cry escaped him. Silent tears spilled down his face as he rubbed the spot.

Sarah stepped in front of him. She'd gotten into serious trouble before, defending her brother, but runty Vlad wasn't strong enough to stand up to Father, even when he wasn't to blame. "Leave him alone! He didn't do anything!"

"Enough out of you!" Father roared, catching Sarah's cheek with the back of his hand. She stumbled and sat down hard.

From the sofa, 'Byeta clapped with glee. "Do it again, Papa! Do it again! Sarah's doing back talk, Sarah's doing back talk!" Galina carried her into the kitchen kicking and squealing, a hand over her mouth.

A few stars still dancing in her eyes, Sarah climbed to her feet, undaunted.

"Or is *that* your secret?" Father guessed. "A girl called, and the boys only delivered the goods?"

"No sir! You were sleeping on the floor when we went to bed, and you were gone when we got up. And that's the dead honest truth, so help me Sil'anak!" Sil'anak was the most revered of the ancient Navaran philosophers.

Father nodded, alcohol-fueled gears turning slowly in his mind. "Okay. You were in bed. And you, and you," he pointed to Sarah, Vlad, and Sergei. "Get out." Sarah and the boys nearly trampled each other to get down the hall first, only to creep back and peek from around the corner. A reprieve like that was far too rare. Usually Father started at one end of the line and beat all of them until someone confessed.

David tripped over them moments later where they whispered in the shadows.

"Go! *Go!*" He rushed them into the bedroom and slammed the door.

Vlad's belly cramped with nerves, and he held it with both hands. "What happened?"

"Viktor gave in to get me off the hook," David hushed, ear to the door, "and Dimi gave in so he wouldn't be alone. I wasn't gonna tell, honest! But I sure am glad not to have to go through what they're gonna get." They could hear scuffling in the hall, and Father's door shutting.

They dared not leave the room, but they couldn't hear a thing except for an occasional unintelligible loudness. It seemed forever before Dmitri banged into the room. He shoved David out of his way, stomped over to the corner, crossed his arms over his head, and stayed that way.

"You all right?" Sergei asked. Dimi nodded.

Moments passed before Viktor entered, jaw clenched, walking stiffly. He bent to dig under his bed, and came out with a yellow duffel.

"I don't know about you," he announced to the room, "but I am nineteen years old and I have had my fill of this shit! Alexei was right. I am too old to put up with this. Any other person in the world did that to me, I'd do twice as bad back to him. I don't know why I can't stop him once and for all, but I can't. I just can't."

Vik noticed Dmitri standing alone. He laid a hand on his shoulder.

"Hey man, you okay?"

"Yeah," Dmitri gulped. "I hope that son of a bitch chokes in his sleep." A last deep sniff, and Dimi tipped his head back, blinking. Viktor gave him a final pat, and they pretended not to notice his red eyes.

Sarah's heart fell. If Vik and Dimi lost faith, they were all sunk. With a start, she realized what Viktor was doing.

"You can't do that!" she ordered.

"Yes I can," Viktor said, stuffing clothes into the bag. "I am done. I have endured my last grand humiliation."

Sarah pulled on his arm with one hand and tried to unpack the bag with the other. "You can't! Who will protect us? Protect Katya? You *can't* leave us!"

"You can't leave us!" Vladimir echoed.

"I have to." Viktor pulled the straps of the bag tight and fastened them. "I'll save up and send for Katya as soon as I can get the money. After she's safe, we'll get the rest of you out together. Dmitri's old enough to take care of everyone. I know he can."

"Sure," Dmitri mumbled. "I can't even sit down."

"You know the routines. Just stop and think first."

"Wait!" Sarah begged, and ran from the room. She returned in less than a minute, right behind Katya.

"Viktor, don't do this," Katya pleaded. "We need you here. Without you …."

"It's our only chance." He wiped a tear from her cheek and hugged her. "Come with me now, then. We'll do it in half the time."

"I can't…"

"Here!" Sarah pressed a mass of local coins into his hand. "It's all I have, but it might keep you from starving somewhere. You can exchange them for galactic credits in the city." She wrapped her arms around his waist and held on.

Vik kissed the top of Sarah's head. "Thank you."

Viktor waited until Father entrenched himself in his room for the night, but he wouldn't change his mind. Goodbyes three times around, and he still couldn't get out the door. It took Katya, Dimi, and Valeria to pry Sarah away.

Sarah pointed a despondent finger at Vladimir. "That's three!"

* * *

Another week, another morning. Father left early for work, and the world relaxed. Dmitri and David, now the oldest of the boys, grew bolder without Viktor to curb them. Without Father, no one had authority over them but three sisters.

"She's coming! Get ready." David and Dmitri scrambled into position on either side of the door.

Sarah entered the kitchen and stepped automatically to the right to avoid the center floor Spot, her mind lost in the black thought of the moment, dreading another breakfast without Viktor's cheerful optimism. If Vik had his way, Katya would be leaving soon, and who knew who would be next after that. Katya was better at mothering than Mother. They were losing every person who could possibly protect them from Father. What would happen when Val left? Or Galina? Dmitri took after Mother; he wasn't big enough to fight Father, and David wasn't old enough or smart enough or brave enough. The dark thoughts ended when she found herself swooped upon by two older brothers. Each grabbing an arm, they dragged her to the middle of the room, laughing.

"*Put me down!*" Sarah shrieked. "No! Don't *do* that! Let go of me!"

"Leave her alone!" Galina ordered.

"Drop her!" 'Byeta squealed. "Bonk her head!"

When they reached the center, each boy grabbed a leg as well, swinging the struggling girl before lowering her to the floor on her back.

"NO!" Sarah shrieked, arching away from the floor.

Dmitri laughed. "Say hello to the kitchen, Sarah!"

They were all laughing – David, Nikky, 'Byeta, even Vlad – and then it *happened.*

As Sarah's body touched the forbidden floor, her tortured soul began to scream, and scream Sarah did. All the silent screams of the past five months poured out in a noise so loud and horrible even 'Byeta stopped laughing. And Sarah's little fear that she *knew*, she *knew* was ridiculous, suddenly became real.

All around her, the blood appeared. She *saw* it. A bloody pond on the kitchen floor, a pond of her mother's blood, and she sat in the middle of it, centimeters deep in sticky red blood. Sarah *felt* it soaking through her clothes, warm, slick, and wet, slapping her ankles in small waves as she scuttled backwards, dripping from her hands as she stared, horrified. She scraped at them, wiped them frantically on the knees of her pants, *saw* the great red streaks they left, and yet her hands were still bloody. She backed against the lower cabinetry, and the pool flowed with her, following, filling in wherever she moved. She scrambled to her feet and held her hands out, seeing the blood drip.

In her terror, she heard a voice, Father's voice, no louder than a memory. It was no more than a tickle in the back of her brain, but it whispered

*your fault*

like a breath of air. The words echoed back and forth, rebounding inside her skull, never louder, never softer, always just audible. When Sarah was just about as confused and terrified as she could be, it disappeared.

"Why! Why did you do this to me?" she screeched. She splashed through the puddle, leaving a trail of prints as she fled the kitchen.

David looked ill. "What just happened?"

Dmitri answered, "I don't know."

"I'll go see." Katya ran out of the room, followed by Vladimir.

"I hope you two are happy!" Galina flashed. "You couldn't leave her alone!" But the boys' cheeks already stung with shame.

Katya pounded on the bathroom door while Vladimir lay on the floor, pleading into the crack underneath. "Unlock the door! Sarah?"

"She won't open," Katya told Galina and Dmitri when they followed. "She's not making any sound at all."

Galina stood Vladimir up and hugged him close, while Dmitri tried the door. "I can undo it," he said. "Viktor showed me how. Find me a magnet."

It took several minutes of fumbling before Dmitri popped the lock. Vladimir bolted for the door.

Katya stopped him. "Wait here. She's still a girl in the bathroom."

"Sarah?" Katya tiptoed into the dimly lit bath. She adjusted the brightness. Clothes were strewn about the floor. The door to the vapor shower was shut, and the water misting. No steam fogged the room – Navara being a desert planet, all water, including vapor, had to be reclaimed. The mist shut off automatically when Katya opened the shower door.

"Sarah?"

Sarah sat in the smooth shower capsule, knees pulled up, sobbing tearlessly in the last of the luke-warm fog. She turned her hands over and over, rubbing at them.

"Sarah? Are you okay?"

"Why did they do that?" Sarah asked mournfully, staring at her hands. "Now it won't come off."

"What won't?"

"The blood. Mother's blood. That's where she bled to death."

"Oh my God! So *that's* it! *That's* why you... Oh, *Sarah*! You poor thing! Finding Mother scared the daylights out of you, didn't it. It scared me, too. But Sarah," Katya shook her head, "there's no more blood on the floor."

"I know that. I knew it this morning, and I know it now," Sarah said in a dead voice. She scrubbed at a cuticle with her thumb. "But I can *see* it, and it's *real,* and it *just – won't – come – off.*"

"I'm going to get you some different clothes," Katya said cautiously. "Promise me you won't move. I think you need some rest."

She repeated the information to Galina and Dmitri while she found clothes.

Dimi swore at himself. "It was my idea. We thought she was just thinking too much about school. You know how she gets. We just wanted to lighten her up. Let me talk to her... "

"No. Katya's right. Let her rest for now," Galina said. "I think you've done enough."

# * Four *

When she wasn't in school, Sarah hid in her room. She wouldn't, couldn't, enter the kitchen but picked at her food in the dining room. She felt frightfully numb, and didn't care to speak. Everyone else avoided the Spot now as well. Sarah had stopped looking at her hands. She could see only faint stains now and then, but she didn't like seeing them at all.

Father's mood at dinner one night was especially foul. Outside of the twins' soft reminders to Nikky to hush, no one dared make a sound. Father collapsed in his chair afterwards, the inevitable glass and remaining half-bottle nearby, a soccer game blaring from the holovision. The girls cleared dinner while Sarah, Vlad, and Sergei settled down to schoolwork. The older boys slipped onto a sofa, watching the game. 'Byeta broke the uneasy calm.

"I want the computer," she demanded. She shoved Sarah hard enough to tip her sideways.

Sarah pushed back with an elbow. "When I'm done. It's still my time." The worst thing about their house was the single, solitary main computer interface. Father had his WorkBook, strictly forbidden to all. Viktor had a linked notebook that he left with Dmitri, the twins had their ports from university, and Katya, Dmitri, and David had pocket research 'pads, but each peripheral slowed the signal, and a secondary line meant the personal expense of rewiring a rented house. Children were allowed exactly half an hour per day with the main computer, youngest first. 'Byeta had the first slot after school, and she'd chosen to skip it.

Elizabyeta gripped the edge of the desk and fought the elbow, used to getting what she wanted. "I want to play 'Manny's Monkey Ship' *now!*"

"Goddamned waste of a point!" Father bellowed at the holovision. The Terran Tempest was losing the division finals by one point. "Get him out of there!" He poured himself four more Father-sized fingers of vodka and downed half of it at once. "Jackasses."

"My turn!" 'Byeta whined, stomping. When she got no reaction, she reached out and yanked Sarah's hair.

"OW!" Sarah pushed her away. "I'll be done in a minute! Let me transfer this reference to my homework 'pad."

'Byeta waited impatiently, then wandered over to Father's chair.

"Papa?" 'Byeta leaned over a big knee, sticky-sweet. She twirled a long golden curl around her finger. "Papa, Sarah had her time on the computer and I asked her nice, but she won't..."

"*Sin sukah!*" Father swore, eyes on the holofigures. He shoved 'Byeta off his leg. "What's your problem?"

"Will you make Sarah let me on the computer? It's my turn and she won't..."

Sarah stabbed a glare at her sister. Hate was too nice a word for what she felt toward 'Byeta. Only 'Byeta was bold enough to mess with Father, especially over something so stupid. She'd have to come up with something really good for revenge this time. Maybe she'd drop a sand spider in her hair, let it tangle up good and tight in those obnoxious thick curls.

Father stared at the game, hand on his glass.

"Papa? I want the computer..."

'Byeta leaned over the arm of the chair. "Papa? Make Sarah move so I can play my game...

"Papa, Sarah's being mean to me...

"*Please,* Papa?" 'Byeta pulled at his sleeve, and the glassy eyes swiveled.

The buzzer sounded on the game just as the team from Alpha Prime scored a goal, ending the tie and winning the title. Father swore violently in Russian, downing his glass before turning on 'Byeta.

"*Can't you stop acting like a baby!*"

'Byeta took a step back.

"Can't you see I'm watching this, you little shit! I missed the last play! Stop bothering me with your petty goddamned *bullshit!*" He leaned his bulk forward and lashed his hand out to slap her.

'Byeta wasn't used to being hit, but she saw the hand rise. Her eyes closed as it neared; she turned her head and started to duck.

Father's huge hand, a hand that had caused him problems before, a hand that could grip and lift ninety-kilo pieces of field equipment without the help of an anti-grav carrier, swung upward and caught his daughter full force under her jaw. Elizabyeta's head twisted sideways and snapped backwards before her feet left the ground. She flew backward a meter and a half, catching the pointed edge of Mother's triangular end table just below her head as she came down. 'Byeta slumped to a heap before the table, curls covering her face.

"*Get up,*" Father ordered, and poured himself another glass. He drank some of that, refilled it, and drank another half as well. He changed the program on the holovision, cursing to himself.

No one else moved. Valeria looked at Galina for direction; Galina looked at Katya. Katya was closest. Kat paled, but tiptoed over to comfort the girl. 'Byeta didn't move.

"Father?" Kat said cautiously. "I think Elizabyeta might be hurt."

"She'sh fine," Father slurred, rousing himself. "Shit wants to shulk on floor, leave'r."

No one could contradict Father, no matter how wrong he might be. "Father? Perhaps Valeria and I should move her to her bed. That way ..."

"I shaid leafer!" he mumbled, fighting his eyelids. "Move when she wantsh." Another moment, and he drifted off.

Children appeared in the living area like gophers, sniffing for danger. Valeria, in charge only after Father's authority was gone, sped to her sisters.

"Straighten her out. 'Byeta?" She shook the girl's shoulder. "She's out cold. Her mouth's bleeding; she must have bit her tongue or something. She's awfully dark." Val leaned an ear close. "I don't think she's breathing! Dmitri, call for help – my responsibility!"

"Got it!" He ran, but he rubbed his backside anyway.

The MedEvac team arrived fast, but the Navaran emergency physician packed up his instruments. "Who has authority here?" he asked in lightly accented Standard.

"I guess I do, right now," Valeria said, stepping out of the clustered pack. Father's chin rested on his chest, rising and falling with each slumbering breath.

"There is nothing to be done. She is dead. Her spinal nerves are compromised, and she has been without oxygen for more than ten minutes. I can do nothing further."

Katya sank to the floor, rocking and wailing. Sergei ran for his room. Vladimir plugged his ears and scrunched his eyes shut.

"I must ask how this occurred," the physician said, making notes on a compad.

"I think she fell," Valeria hedged. "She may have hit the table with her head... I was at the other table when it happened."

"He did it!" Sarah blurted, pointing at Father. "He hit her so hard she hit the table."

The assistant looked at the doctor, who gave consideration to the idea. "It is possible. There is remarkable trauma to the jaw. However, this man is asleep, and has not woken despite our presence."

Dmitri's wounded face looked anywhere but at someone. "He's

*drunk,*" he said bitterly. "The bottle next to him was full when he opened it."

"And he becomes violent after the consumption of alcohol?"

Sarah wasn't afraid to lock eyes with the doctor. She answered him in flawless Navaran. //*Do* sifuoti *fly?*//

Murder on Navara was inconceivable, therefore few protocols had ever been devised to address it. After much debate it was decided to be a problem of law (a violation of Elizabyeta's right to life), and a problem of mental health (Father obviously had a mental illness if he could commit murder). Then came the matter of jurisdiction. Navaran laws were ultimately sovereign, and the incident occurred in open territory. However, the building belonged to the university, which was technically a part of the Human quarter, and *that* was sub-governed by Allied Space Fleet authority through a treaty with the Navarans. Officials poured in from everywhere.

Two hours passed before the body was removed, two hours of knowing a *dead body* lay on the floor of their house, that their *sister* lay *dead* under the sheet in the living room, that *Father* had made her dead. The investigators ushered everyone into the kitchen to avoid the scene, but Sarah would not, could not, get past the doorway, and clung to Galina in the dining room instead.

Father slept through it all, snoring, shifting, and breaking wind. A small troop of armed 'Fleet officers arrived, part of the local Kar Ku'umi City Security peace-keeping force. The commander shook Father, poked him, and at last drove a knuckle into the big man's breastbone. Father gave a snort, and opened a bleary red eye.

"Alexander Kirushenko," the commander recited, "You are under detention for the murder of Elizabeth Kirushenko."

Father struggled to clear the cobwebs clouding his brain. His accent rolled thick under the sea of alcohol. *"Shto? Ubistva? Kto? Na koi herr!* Who let you in? Lizbye–? Din' touch her - sleeping...."

"I'm sorry, sir. You'll have to come with us for questioning."

"Not going anywhere." Sasha staggered from the chair, private nightmares rising from his past to haunt him. "This is *my* home. Lying bastards! Who started shit this time? Where's 'Byeta? Get her the fuck out here! Valeria!"

Tears fell from Val's eyes. "Father..."

"Sir, I will need to place you in restraints for transport. If you will please cooperate... "

"Get away from me! Didn't kill anyone!" Sasha turned to the

children huddled in the dining room. "'Byeta! Where in hell is she? 'Mitri! You touch that goddamned 'link again?"

"No sir!"

"*Sir!*" insisted the commander. He seized a massive arm.

"*Leave... me... alone!*" A powerful fist swung at the commander.

A sizzling flash filled the room, followed by the distinctive smell of ozone. Katya screamed, the boys ducked, and Sarah grabbed Vladimir in a surge of panic at the burst of short-ranged EPSAR fire, right there in the house. The stone floor seemed to shudder as Father hit the ground, stunned.

"Papa!" Galina cried. "What did you do that for? We would have calmed him down! You didn't give us a chance!"

"I'm sorry, ma'am. Standard procedure for violent suspects," the commander said. The officers trussed Sasha and dragged him out to a waiting transport.

The Medical Examiner had crawled through the house, measuring and scraping and photographing in the quest for forensic clues. Then the Fleet officers repeated the procedure.

"Can you tell me what happened?" an officer asked the twins. "Did you see or hear anything? Was this an accident?"

"Of course it was an accident," Galina said, numb.

"Someone said the little girl was hit. Now, I took a look myself, and I have to say, that's what it looks like to me. So, what happened?"

"I was over by the table. I really couldn't see. I suppose it's possible..."

Valeria, who had finished a degree in history and had started law school before leaving Earth, stopped her twin. "I think we'd rather wait until we can confer with counsel. In any case, he'll probably need a lawyer, and I don't think we should be saying anything until that lawyer's been appointed and had a chance to counsel us."

The officer swallowed his impatience. "Ma'am, they took a dead child out of here under that sheet, a pretty little girl with a broken neck and smashed face. I need to know what happened. Is your father the one who did that?"

Valeria choked back a sob. "Don't you think I know that? That's my sister under there! I was the one who realized she wasn't breathing! I was probably the last one to touch her alive! But he's also my father, and I know his legal rights. I think we all need to step very carefully here, and that starts by demanding his right to counsel here and now."

The officer scowled. He nodded, eyes scanning the room, from the twins, to the infant paraphernalia, the mental counting of Sarah, Vlad, Katya, Dmitri, David; the spectre of Sergei hiding in the shadows of the hall; the cold clinical eye picking out Nikky hiding among the legs of the chairs under the table.

"Ma'am, Navarans have harsh laws against violence. I have a dead child who has died a violent death in a house full of children, and I need to know who is responsible. You're right. This is kind of delicate. Maybe I need to pull in Child Services to ensure the safety of the other children. They may need to be placed elsewhere until the matter is resolved."

"No!" Galina said quickly. "That won't be necessary."

"Nobody's taking me anywhere," David warned, attitude rising. "Take him, and we can live here just fine."

"There's no need for that," Valeria said. "This was an accident..."

The officer spoke into his handicom. "This is Officer Flitcher responding to the homicide outside the walls; can you send me Child Protection? There's a whole mess of kids out here, babies on up. If we take the suspect, I'm not sure what the situation will be. We may need temporary placements."

"How many?" said the 'com.

"At least seven that I can count."

"Sending now."

The officer closed and pocketed the device. "Let's start this again. Where was everyone when this happened?"

Dmitri glared back. "Why the hell should we cooperate with you when you just threatened to take us all away, when we didn't do anything?"

Sarah lifted her head as the confusing bits of conversation came together in a frightening idea. "We just won't go. You can't catch all of us. We'll run into the desert if we have to."

The officer glanced down at her, but his expression didn't change. "That's why I'm here. To keep anyone else from getting hurt. Now, let's see just how cooperative everyone can be, and maybe the situation won't be as dangerous as it seems..."

They set up the kitchen for private interviews; Valeria stepped in on Sarah's behalf that she not be forced in there. After five separate waves of interrogations, a lawyer appeared at last. The twins went over the facts yet again, voices droning on into the night.

Sarah slouched uncomfortably on one of the hard sofas. Nikky's head rested in her lap, while Vlad leaned heavily asleep on her shoulder. Grains of sand invaded her eyes, invisible pinchers squeezed her head, her mind felt numb, but she couldn't fall asleep. Nothing seemed real anymore. She couldn't sleep, because life was just one long nightmare that kept getting worse, and there was no waking up. If you weren't awake, then you must already be asleep. The big boys slumped in chairs and on the floor, staring into space until one of them would speak. Katya dozed on the cool floor, her head resting on Dimi's leg.

Sarah's mind drifted, until an unfamiliar voice startled her.

*Murderer*

She jolted alert. The voice rustled no louder than a whisper, but seemed to speak directly to her.

"I am not!" she replied, indignant.

"Not what?" Dmitri mumbled sleepily.

"Never mind," Sarah answered, unsure now if it was a dream or a piece of conversation she'd overheard. "Nothing."

A crisis counselor paid a visit early the next morning. A Human woman, she seemed no older than the twins. She scribbled down almost everything they said, even though her voice recorder caught every word. Valeria and Galina had not slept at all and couldn't bear so much enthusiasm; they'd spent the rest of the night trying to track down Viktor.

The counselor, Miss Kellar, glanced at her list of prepared questions. "Do you know what you'll do with your sister's body?"

Galina shook her head. "Not yet. What's happening with Father?"

"Your father will be arraigned today on murder charges. There seems to be enough evidence to bring him to trial. The judge can consider extenuating circumstances."

Sarah's eyes narrowed. "When will he be back?"

"If he's cleared, at least a month or so, sweetie."

Sarah wasn't in any mood for senseless pity. She stood up, angry enough to bite. "I'm not your 'sweetie,' and I never want to see him again! We don't *want* him back!" David pulled her down.

"Let's just say we're not shedding any tears over Father not being here," Dmitri explained.

"I see," said the counselor, taken aback. "Your Father had a recent history of alcohol intoxication, did he not? I have a hospital record here somewhere – ." She grabbed for her portfolio case; it fell to the floor and an avalanche of record cards slid out with a clatter. She tried to grab them all at once; four fell back on the floor. She dumped the pile in the portfolio, searched for a specific one, and stuffed it in her compad on the third try. Any other day, the children would have been hard pressed not to laugh out loud. Today, the woman's overzealous bungling only annoyed them.

She scrolled through the notes on the screen. "Was he intoxicated at the time of the incident?"

"Passed out cold, just the way we like him," David said.

"I can sense your hostility," Miss Kellar said. "I am assigned to your case, either way. I'll call or visit every other day or so. I'll be available to help with financial guidance, support services, grief counseling, and direct you to anything else you may need. I can help you deal with Child Services, too."

"I think we could all benefit from the grief counseling," Valeria admitted. "We've had so much tragedy in the last six months, I think we're all a little on edge. I know Sarah's having some trouble."

Sarah looked up at the mention of her name. The conversation bored her, so she'd been thinking about the conjugation of an irregular Navaran verb. "What? What did you want?"

Galina smiled graciously. "We'd be grateful for any help you could give us."

In her next two visits, Miss Kellar met with everyone alone. Vlad was an easy victory; he poured his heart out with little prompting. Katya, too, seemed much happier. On the second day, Miss Kellar met with Sarah.

"Isn't there *anything* you'd like to talk about?" Miss Kellar said, stymied by the force of the child's indifference.

"No. Unless you want to discuss the reverse microcrystalline helical structures contained in Transium, and how that impacts space-warp physics. That's what I have a test on next week," Sarah challenged, gnawing furiously at a fingernail. "I'm wasting a lot of valuable class time. Can I go back to school tomorrow?"

Miss Kellar tried a different approach. "It can be very hard when a little sister dies so suddenly. Perhaps we could talk about the things that made her special. Tell me something you remember about her. Anything at all."

Sarah lost her patience. "Nothing! I didn't like her. I don't grieve for her. I don't know you, but I don't like you, either. And I'm done with your idiotic questions. Good day." Sarah left without waiting for permission.

Vladimir tagged behind. He followed Sarah into the girls' room, where she dropped on the floor at the foot of her bed. She pulled her knees up and hugged them tightly.

Vlad sat on his heels before her. "You shouldn't have yelled at her like that. She's just trying to help."

Sarah rested her head on her knees and stared at the wall. "I don't care. Who's she, anyway? It's our business, not hers. We're not supposed to talk about those things. She's got no right to pry into our business like that. You know what Father will do if he finds out?"

Vlad grew subdued at the reminder. "Well, it's not like we told Security anything they didn't already know."

"It's still terrible trouble, Vlad! No matter which way you look at it. I'm never going to graduate on time."

"Sure you will. You're the smartest person on the planet. You're smarter than Father, and he's a professor."

Sarah shook her head. "It doesn't matter. It's only going to get worse."

"This *is* the worst thing that could ever happen. It *can't* get worse than this." He reached out and squeezed her hand.

Sarah squeezed it back. She looked close to tears, but crying had never been a part of her behavior. Neither 'Byeta's troublemaking lies nor the subtle taunts of her alien schoolmates had ever broken her. When her brothers had teased her beyond endurance, she'd learned to respond in kind. Not even Father's cruel hand had reduced her to bawling like a sissy. She pulled Vlad in and hugged him, hard.

"But what if it *does,* Vlad? What if it does?"

It took Sarah a long while to fall asleep that night. She slept fitfully, then began to dream.

All around her was blackest night, smooth and dark as an underground cave, yet she could see clearly. Elizabyeta sat in the computer chair in the corner of the dining room. She turned to look at Sarah. Her eyes were dull and half-opened as when she died. Her cheeks were blue, her lips grape-stained purple; blood cascaded over the bottom one. The unnatural sight struck fear into Sarah, crinkling her spine and scalp. Dead people weren't supposed to sit up like this. The purple lips began to speak.

"Why, Sarah?" Elizabyeta asked. "Did you really hate me so bad you had to kill me?"

"*I* didn't kill you." Dream-Sarah shook her head, not denying the hating part. "Father hit you. You didn't duck fast enough. I had nothing to do with it."

"Why wouldn't you let me have the computer? If you just let me use it, I'd still be alive, and no one would be upset. You didn't even try to help me after I'd been hit. You're supposed to! You're older! That's the rule! You don't even care I'm gone.

"*You* killed me, Sarah. *You* did! Don't worry. Your time will come. Father doesn't forget, and *I'm* his favorite. Even the stinky baby knows that." Elizabyeta rose and walked toward Sarah, dragging the medical examiner's biosheet across the floor, though her legs never seemed to move.

Dream-Sarah tried to run, but the room twisted and warped, and she couldn't seem to move her feet. The icy blue fingers reached for her hair.

Sarah awoke with a jolt, wondering if she had really screamed out loud. Her heart pounded in her chest, and she wanted nothing more than to cry.

*I won't cry! I won't!* she commanded herself. *Three years on Navara, I'd better know how not to cry!* But a shuddering sob grabbed her just the same.

"What's th' matter?" Katya muttered next to her. Across the room, 'Byeta's bed lay dark and empty.

"A horrible dream!"

Kat raised an arm. "Com'ere. It's just a dream. Wanna tell me it?"

Sarah dove under the arm. "No," she gulped, shivering. Katya fell asleep again within seconds, but Sarah stared at the inky blackness until daylight, alone with her terrified thoughts.

# * Five *

P *ock. Po-pock. Pock. Pock.*
"Shit!"
"That's game, I believe."
Langley threw his tennis racquet over his shoulder and shook hands across the net.

"Just once, Tomas, couldn't you miss a ball and let me win?"

Tómas Ivanov laughed. "I don't think just one ball would do it. Maybe for your birthday."

"You're such a shit. You know damned well that was last month. I don't suppose you'd play it zero-G?"

"What, and give you a fighting chance? I keep my feet and my business on the ground." They walked together to the locker room.

A young man met them at the door. "Mr. Ivanov? Miss Bellini would like to know what you want to do with the Gorwin account. It bottomed out at forty-five Hydran *Tappos*."

"Ouch!" Langley winced. "That's twenty less than they expected."

Ivanov frowned. "What's that equal to in interstellar?"

The aide calculated in his head. "About twenty-three credits, sir."

"Fine. Buy up any and all shares that become available." He started into the locker room.

"Sir?" The man stopped him again. "Also, the Rurana Corporation has been calling every hour on the hour, requesting to speak with you. Mr. Jaegar tried, but they insist on speaking to you personally, sir."

"Then, tell them I am unavailable. Anything else, before my sweat congeals?"

The aide looked uncertain. "There was a strange inquiry by the Galactic Trade Press, wondering if you were any relation to a Maryana Ivanova, formerly of Byelorus."

Tomas Ivanov froze for the length of a blink. "And what did the service tell them?"

"That we had no such information, and to contact you directly

63

through your mail service."

"Very well, then. Carry on." He fled to the locker room.

Lunch was held in a private dining room at the top of the United Earth Building, overlooking the New York skyline. Off in the distance, behind the clogged air-flight arteries, the five towers of Ivanov Industries stood out against the river, their distinctive solar-black X-shape prominent against the network of bridges criss-crossing the water. Two corner towers for business, two corner towers of residences, and the center tower for power plant and waste treatment. The shape of the building helped channel in the breezes that whipped across Manhattan toward the huge energy turbines of the central tower. Between solar sheathing and wind power, the Ivanov towers were self-sufficient, and relied on no one else for support. It was a widely envied, highly profitable system.

Ivanov hated things that weren't profitable, a philosophy born of efficiency, not greed. He was but one person in charge of his end of an Empire – below Mamá, of course – and more people vied for his attention than there were minutes in a Terran day. He had to draw the line somewhere. By relying on other companies for utilities, he would then have to add those companies to his registry and cater to them. They could then further complicate his life by price wars, strikes, or kickbacks. His buildings were their own entity, controlled by no one else unless he said so. Time was his most valuable commodity, and couldn't be wasted.

Besides, he received credit on his land-use tax if he sold any excess energy produced to the over-burdened metropolis of New York.

Time was money, indeed. Fyodor Ivanov taught his son not to waste time, and Tomas took the idea to a new level. Outside of the lavatory, there was hardly a given activity that wasn't a covert meeting of one sort or another – and even the lavatory wasn't always exempt. Ivanov had seen more insides of board rooms and meeting rooms and offices than he ever cared to see. If he had any chance at all to conduct business elsewhere, even at his expense, he did it. He'd bought companies at race tracks, argued funding on sailboats, negotiated trade deals during an interstellar cruise, navigated the Tritanium mines on Mars, or, like this morning, entertained new merger ideas over sports. Nine times out of ten, if he showed the client a good time, the deal went his way.

Today's lunch brought together the mayor of Manhattan, Governor Pirolam of New Jersey, Senator Marchall of New York (Future Earth party), and the Ambassadors of the United States and the Berenician Tribunal, over the possibility of building an Embassy just outside the city. Ivanov Industries stood poised to win the building contract. Tomas would approve the contract at one hundred million credits below cost, in exchange for a ten-year exclusive deal for building rights on Berenicia – a potential one *billion* credit profit taking. No one else had come close, and the deal looked and felt good.

"Did you see the news report this morning?" Senator Marchall said when the conversation paused.

"You mean the incident on Navara?" Ambassador Giftyis of the United States replied.

Mayor Rinaldi shook his head. "Unbelievable. I can't imagine what that's going to do for the Alliance. If the Navarans pull out, they'll shut down Kar Ku'umi. Can you imagine the exodus of a hundred thousand refugees? The Fleet will be rescuing them from space for months. As it is, they want to ban alcohol entirely. They don't call it The Dry Planet for nothing."

Tomas swallowed his bite of farm-raised lobster. "I must have missed that. What happened?"

*"Murder."* Governor Pirolam drew the word out as if it were a threat by itself. "The Capital of Peace and Harmony had a murder."

"Good Lord!" Ivanov said. "By a Navaran, or to a Navaran?"

Ambassador Giftyis leaned in. "Worse! A human *child*! Some drunken ass beat his child to death."

Ambassador Ki'ai'an of Berenicia wagged his neckless head sadly. "Many of those who live on Navara become insane from the heat. It is a tragedy of diplomatic proportions. I'm sure it will be heavily debated at the next Alliance Assembly."

Ivanov looked ill. "A child? Heat or no heat, how could someone do such a thing?"

"Some Russian professor or something at the Academy there. Like you," Marchall said to Ivanov. "Take you out of those cold latitudes of Russia, drop you in a blast furnace like that for too long, and you'll go insane, too. A little booze, a little too much weather, and snap! They say mirages take on a whole new meaning out there. Ever been there?"

"No, I can't say that I have."

Mayor Rinaldi frowned. "What was his name? Kirolan, Kishman, Karpenko – something with a K."

"You realize that's going to start a whole new wave of galactic expansion protests," Governor Pirolam sighed. "That'll cost a fortune in additional security officers to manage the crowds. I might as well start juggling the budget now and have everything in place ahead of time."

"Talk about out of touch with reality!" Marchall exclaimed. "Like we're suddenly going to roll back three hundred years of technological progress. This is the golden age of Earth! We've never enjoyed such global prosperity as we have right now. Can you imagine, Ivanov, trying to cut contact with the rest of the galaxy? I'll bet that would put a hefty dent in your megafortune."

Ivanov had been lost in deep thought. "Hmm? Oh, yes! Yes, it certainly would hamper things a bit." He tried to return to the conversation, but his mind stayed elsewhere.

The chronometer read ten p.m. by the time Ivanov dragged himself back to his apartment. He didn't live in any of his downtown buildings; he rented a small place on the shores of Long Island. It was a matter of privacy – and business. Culture expected him to live in the luxury residences in his towers, where the press could keep a tight watch. He would lose the substantial income generated by the potential rent, and he would be expected to bring home every Juan, Don, and Kwan who shook his hand. Living on the island was more inconvenient, but much quieter. He lived alone, in a four-room security apartment he sublet from a friend. He'd been in charge of the New York offices for years, but he spent only half his time there now. He lived at least half the year on the fly. The four divisions of Ivanov Corporations were headquartered in Moscow, with major offices in Minsk, New York, and Hellas, Mars, but lately a good portion of the work flowed from the family estate in Minsk. Mamá wasn't as young as she used to be, and didn't care for long commutes merely to shake hands and butter asses, as she'd termed it. That had become Tomas' job.

Ivanov tossed his jacket to its usual spot, the arm of a small sofa. He replicated a bland little supper of vegetable soup and toast, and poured himself a glass of red wine. Years of stress and unpredictably strange meals had left him with chronic indigestion, and he ate lightly whenever possible. The chance of trouble on Navara didn't sit well. Navara constituted a full quarter of the strength behind the Alliance, a major producer of exquisite scientists and mathematicians and artisans, and a budget that never saw red. If they withdrew from the Planetary Alliance, it would rock the entire structure of government right through the financial core. He had to be prepared.

He took his glass of wine and sat down at the pop-up screen. "Computer, scan today's news bulletins. List and load all references for Navara." Within seconds, more than a hundred responses began scrolling. He opened the first, and started to read. By the time he finished, his stomach panged with knots, and he'd switched to a glass of rare brandy.

Sometime after midnight he placed a video call to his twenty-four hour reception service.

"This is Tomas Ivanov. Under no circumstances, I repeat, *no circumstances*, is anyone to give out any information regarding a Maryana Ivanova or Maryana Kirushenko. Such a person does not exist in relation to the Ivanov Corporations. Second, I want a call placed to the Navaran Ambassador, requesting a brief but urgent conversation with him at his earliest convenience. Any response will be forwarded to me immediately on a top priority basis. Is that understood?"

"Absolutely, Mr. Ivanov," the secretary answered.

"Third, I want the event on Navara followed intensely. Send a silent investigator out there, but all news of the incident will be logged in a private file and transferred to my home address. Lastly, anyone trying to contact me from Navara, or with the names Ivanov or Kirushenko in the address, you will download the files into a separate block and immediately encrypt them under my personal ID. Send it to my line here, no outside access, not even Madame Ivanova. Understood?"

Yes, sir, Mr. Ivanov," the secretary said. "It will take effect as of now."

# * Six *

Two endless weeks, another funeral, and the wounded family fell into a new if tenuous routine. Valeria and Galina worked with the counselor, dealing not only with their own grief, but learning how to recognize it in the others.

"You realize that's five?" Sarah counted off to Vladimir, sitting together in the living area. "We've been cut by a full third. The question is, who's next, and how?"

David exploded from his seat. "*Stop it!*" he screamed, millimeters from her face. "Just stop it with your doomsday *bullshit*, Sarah, or I'll knock the shit out of you!" Sergei pulled him back, but David yanked free.

Sarah met the fierce gaze with an unnerving stare of her own. She didn't twitch a muscle, daring him to act first, a skill borrowed from her Navaran classmates. "There is only one person on this world I am afraid of, David Kirushenko, and it is not you."

David swore loudly, kicked the couch, and stalked off.

Dmitri stumbled in an hour late one night, smelling of alcohol. Valeria, who had tried for so long to be so very patient, lost control.

"What were you *thinking*?!" she ranted. "Hasn't alcohol caused enough pain in this family?"

"I'm sixteen, for cryin' out loud! Lighten up! It was only beer. So I needed to get away for a while. After all this shit, I think I'm entitled to some fun for a change."

Valeria hesitated, then slapped his face as hard as she could. "Don't make excuses! If I could, I'd haul you down and have Father flog you himself! There will be no alcohol in this house. If I ever see you with alcohol or utopics or find you in such a condition again, I will throw you out myself! And that goes for David, or anyone else, too! *Do you understand?*"

"You're my goddamned sister, not my parent! I have as much right to make the rules as you do!" Dmitri shouted back. He pushed her out of his way and left her fuming.

Sergei had been quiet all his life, sitting silently in a cubby with his nose buried in a reader screen, or intently scribbling on a little notepad. More than once he'd been forgotten somewhere, and Mother would be in a panic until the museum or taxi service or spaceport could locate him. Sarah, too, was usually serene, used to imitating her impassive schoolmates, or concentrating on a problem. When eight people always spoke at once, no one realized Sarah no longer spoke unless spoken to, not even David's crude antics bringing a sparkle to her eye. She grew fussy about eating, but Valeria chalked it up to stress. Galina knew Sarah rose before the sun, but assumed she went to bed early. Vladimir knew she was upset with the lost days from school, but never spoke of it. Katya spent many a dark night hugging away nightmares, but Sarah wouldn't discuss them. She would not, could not, set foot in the kitchen.

The Fearsome Four studied in the boys' room, Sarah stretched across Sergei's bed. She tapped the inside of her wrist on her temple, writing answers on her homework 'pad.

"Stop it!" she whispered too loudly.

David turned from the desk. "Stop what? Nobody's doing anything."

Sarah looked up in confusion. "Huh? What?"

"You said to stop it," Vlad explained. "We're not making any noise."

"I didn't say anything!"

"Yes, you did. Clear as day," David insisted.

Sarah tore at a fingernail with her teeth, removing a chunk of skin with it. "Did not! I think I know when I'm talking." Blood welled up around the nail; she stuck the finger in her mouth to hide it.

"You did say 'stop it'," Sergei confirmed.

"Maybe if your head wasn't always in a screen, you could hear yourself think," David said. "Cryin' out loud! They ever run your name through a dating service, the only match they're going to get is with the encyclopedia."

"At least I know how to study! You try graduating nine years early when every time you turn around you have to miss a week of school, and see how hard *you* have to work." Sarah grabbed her text reader and homework pad and stormed out of the room, Vladimir five seconds behind.

"She makes a very valid point," Sergei agreed.

To Sarah, school was her last salvation. Brutally exhausted from lack of sleep, her mind confused and preoccupied, only through obsessive concentration could she hope to maintain her level of study. The house could collapse around her, the sun could supernova, but that diploma would be hers in just nine more months, and that one determined vision kept her going.

"Do you feel okay?" Galina inquired after finding her napping at the computer screen. "Maybe you should take a break."

Sarah perked up. "I'm fine! I guess Current Trends in Physics isn't as interesting as I thought."

Valeria broached the subject after she caught Sarah sitting alone in a corner, biting hard on a knuckle. "Sar, have you thought any more about talking with Miss Kellar? She's really very nice. She might be able to help you deal with things."

Sarah twisted the tooth-marked finger in a stray lock of hair, tugging it. "Deal with what? Can she tutor me in astrophysics? Does she understand the reasoning behind the Deniston Treaty of 2152? Can she explain all twelve forms of the Navaran noun *'p'tsuvonak'* and when to use them? That's all I care about right now. If she was the last human on the planet, I still wouldn't have anything to say to her."

Val watched her sister stalk off, out of ideas.

The mysterious fleeting words Sarah heard now zipped through anytime she wasn't focused on something. Perhaps they were bits of dreams slipping through in waking hours, or memories sliding out in her exhaustion. She didn't dare mention them to Vlad. He would never understand. Sarah supposed she loved Vlad more than anyone, but even Vlad knew he could be a little slow. She recognized Father's voice among the whispers, and maybe 'Byeta's, too, muttering nasty words and threats.

What bothered her more was the growing sense of dullness, a swelling emptiness that blotted out life itself. She'd buried her feelings out of habit, maintaining expected etiquette at school, but she'd always relaxed at home. Yet, when her mother died, she could not mourn. When Viktor left, her whole being cried for him, but she stuffed it down. She'd hated 'Byeta, yes, but never truly wished her *dead*. At least, not the way it happened. What had happened in the kitchen frightened her beyond reason, but she didn't cry over it. The tears never came.

*I just need some sleep,* she told herself. *Nine more months.*

Colors disappeared from her eyes, and the flat grays that remained seemed fuzzy. No doubt it was all the reading; this, too, would pass eventually. The replicated food had lost all taste, just the same pasty feeling in her mouth no matter what she ate. But it could be the replicator needed adjustment. Sarah felt like a shadow, dimming fainter every day, until one day she wouldn't exist at all. She wanted to scream, "I'm here! I exist! I want to feel!", but she couldn't keep the nightmares and voices at bay long enough.

Nine months' determination lasted nine days. Sarah sat on the edge of her bed, unable to move.

"What's wrong?" Katya asked, pulling on her ankle-high shoes. No matter how high the shoe or how tightly she laced them, the sand worked its way in.

"Can't do it."

"Do what?"

"Go to school."

Katya felt her sister's face and back, listening for the tell-tale signs of pneumonia. "Are you sick?"

"Don't know. Maybe." Sarah spoke as if in a dream, numb and hazy inside and out.

"I'll get Val." Katya ran from the room fast.

Sarah sat frozen, afraid to move. Every microgram of concentration she had was focused on keeping her little voices to a minimum. If she kept a running thought, she heard only a hushed buzz, like a speech given two rooms away. When she moved around, the words came through. She couldn't possibly get through classes like this. Better shame at home than shame in public.

Valeria rushed in. One look at Sarah, eyes darkly purple and too large in her colorless face, and there was no decision to be made. "That's it. You're going to the medical center."

Sarah spoke without moving her jaw. "'Kay."

"Can you hold on 'til I get everyone off to school? Just ten minutes?"

"I'll try."

Sarah stumbled out to the main rooms, holding her head, listening to the jeers with each step.

*Murderer.*

*Fail!*

*Deliberate waste.*

*Stood by.*

*Die!*

Reading would keep her mind busy. She collapsed into the computer chair.

"There you are." Valeria juggled the baby on one hip and helped Nikky with the tie to his desert robe. "I'm dropping these two off at the learning center, and I'll be right back, fifteen minutes, tops. If you need help, Galina's asleep in the other room. Just give her a yell, okay?"

*"Da,"* Sarah lied.

Exhaustion weighed on Sarah like a blanket of lead, crushing her strength. She would have cried, but rain didn't fall in the Navaran desert, and the desert had crept inside her. Words glowed bright on the vidscreen, but the letters danced and swam, then faded out entirely as the whole room dimmed. As she struggled to focus, the voices swelled in volume.

*Killer,* sang one.

*From this very chair,* whispered another.

*What did you expect.*

*Ungrateful,* snarled a fourth, snatches overheard above the murmur of an invisible cocktail party where she was the only subject of conversation.

*"Stop!"* Sarah whimpered. She jammed her hands over her ears, but the noise was inside, not outside. "Get out! Get out!" she pleaded, banging her fist on her forehead. "Get out of my head!"

Her elbow knocked against Valeria's computerized notepad on the desk. She picked it up and struck her head with it. The stylus clip at the top dug into her scalp, but she scarcely felt it. The voices paused in shock.

*I'll fix you!* Sarah yelled inside her mind. She struck at the voices again; they backed off further. The hit felt like a bee sting, no more, though the clip had cut her scalp. The feeling was so faint, so minimal, but it seemed more than she had felt in weeks. The third forceful blow shattered the delicate circuitry in the writing 'pad, and the metal clip bounced off the bones of her skull.

Every hit dulled the noises, gave her new strength and determination. She could! She would! shed the awful cloak of lifelessness enveloping her. Blood trickled down her face, but it didn't seem to be real, didn't seem to be hers; maybe it belonged to the voices. Her head throbbed weakly, a well of sensation in the desert of her soul. One more whack, and the clip broke off the writing pad.

*No!* She couldn't stop now! She was chiseling away at the shell that separated her from the living world, and she was *winning*.

She tried to repair the clip, but she couldn't see. Blood made one eyelid sticky; the other eye watered. Blood stained her fingers where she'd touched her head, blood snarled her hair where she'd pushed it out of her eyes, blood stained the compad, made the stylus clip slippery and hard to hold. Always blood!

*Was it hers, or was it Mother's?*

Sarah wasn't sure. She needed to wash. She stumbled across the room until she bumped the wall. Her hands slid across the salmon-pink stucco, leaving dark streaks. She knew the space well – Father's preferred whipping spot. The living room walls were made of heat-absorbing Castcrete, to look and feel like natural Navaran stone.

Sarah gave the wall a solid tap with her head, resting her forehead against the coolness. It worked here, too. A new surge of feeling burst over her – not pain, but a hard tingle, as if her head were asleep. She turned and slammed the back of her head against the wall, the part where the voices seemed to live. An explosion of light flashed across her eyes – and the whispers disappeared! There was still no pain, just an itching, as if bugs were crawling under her scalp. Two times, three times – and Sarah relaxed. Four times, and she smiled with relief. She would! She *would* cure herself of this! Val would be relieved to see her feeling better. Once more, and she would see how she felt for a while. She turned and brought her forehead down as hard as she could.

A blinding light sparkled, and the room went dark. The torn skin on her forehead scraped down the wall.

Valeria found her there, just three minutes later.

"Sarah? No! *No!* Galina!" Val screamed. "*GALINA!*"

Galina ran out in her nightwear. "What's the ...? Not again! Is she...?"

"She's still breathing. Call for MedEvac!" Val cried. She cradled her limp sister in her arms, caressing the bloodied cheeks. "Oh, Sarah!"

In the trauma center examination room, a nurse watched the vital sign graphics on the bed monitor. Satisfied, she removed the pressure field generator from Sarah's head and began to clean the wounds. The scanners showed no fractures, just a small chip on the front of her skull where the corner of the stylus clip had bounced.

Sarah came around as the nurse wiped. Her forehead had swelled, making it difficult to open her eyes. She pulled away from the strange hand poking her face.

*Screwed it up* whispered in her head.

"Well, hello there, Hon!" the nurse said. "You're awake! You're at Ku'umi Primary Trauma Center, sweetheart. Do you remember why?"

"I must have hurt myself," Sarah said. "Can I go home now?"

The nurse shook antiseptic from a green bottle. "When I'm done, the doctor is going to repair your head here. That might take a while, but it won't hurt, so don't you worry. Then there's another doctor who wants to talk to you. We won't keep you a minute longer than we have to."

Sarah wrestled her head side to side. There was no time in her life for this nonsense. She had goals to keep. Other nurses were busy moving around the large room. Some brought equipment, others set up trays nearby.

"Is my sister here?"

"You can talk with her as soon as we're done. Hold still for me, sweetheart. Does this hurt too much?"

"No. Just stop."

*Beware* said a voice.

*You'll never leave!* replied a voice that sounded like an angry 'Byeta's.

*One thing at a time!* Sarah screamed back in her mind. *I can't fight them and you!*

"What? I'm almost done, hon. Be a good girl, put your hand down. Okay, that looks good." The nurse stepped away to a cabinet.

Sarah sat up immediately and looked around. On the tray next to her waited the surgeon's instruments; she recognized the laser scalpel. No one was looking. She palmed the scalpel and lay down.

A woman approached the bed. "Hello, Sarah, I'm Dr. Wallace. You've had quite the nasty bump there. Do you remember what happened?"

Sarah squirmed, wishing the voices away. She couldn't afford more lost days from school. "I must have hit it."

"Mmm, there's more than one cut here," Dr. Wallace said, looking and poking. "More than just a fall. Are you sure there's nothing you might want to tell me? Was someone else with you when you hurt yourself? Did someone hit you? Who hit you like that?"

"When can I go home?"

*Not going to let you leave!* a male voice whispered insistently, while a high-pitched female voice laughed.

"... then we... two... I'm not sure... concerned... like you to talk..." The rising and falling of the hysterical laughter blocked out most of what the doctor said. Sarah tried to listen to one and not the other, increasingly agitated.

She closed her eyes and pressed a hand to her temple. *"Ostanovitye yevo, ya skazala!"*

"What was that?"

*Never let you leave* rang her head, and the last thread of Sarah's control came unraveled. Her thumb slid the switch of the hidden microscalpel to *on*. She slashed upwards at the doctor, catching her across the face and forearm in a long, deep gash.

"Leave me alone!" Sarah screamed to the voices.

"Shit!" exclaimed the doctor, jumping back. "Security!"

Sarah wasted no time. She rolled to her knees and slashed twice across one wrist and down her forearm. Someone rushed to tackle her; she slashed him, and he, too, backed off. Switching hands, Sarah sliced her other arm and wrist, up to her elbow. Her arms stung no more than a scratch, but the voices died.

*The feeling!* She didn't feel her battered head or the gaping wounds on her arms, or notice the chaos flying around her. She focused only on the glorious stinging that broke through the deadness of her body like a thousand needles imbedded in her skin. A slower, deeper gash kept the feeling fresh. The whispers faded, chased away by the fiery needlepricks. A jarring shock took her by surprise, a blinding flash that jolted her core and made her drop the scalpel. Her vision faded as she fell forward on the table.

Valeria stared at the doctor. "You had to use *stun* control on an eight year old child with a 200 IQ? You've got the wrong patient. That's not Sarah."

The head of emergency medicine wasn't laughing. "Two nurses, an orderly, and a surgeon. The doctor nearly lost an eye. It's not a joke."

"I don't understand this," Valeria said. "That's ridiculous!"

"We want to see our sister. *Now,*" Galina demanded. "What you're saying is crazy."

"I'm afraid she's still in surgery," said the chief, "but I can take you to recovery. You can wait there."

"When will she be ready to go home? I have to pick up two other children from playcare," Valeria said.

The chief seemed surprised at the question. "She won't be leaving for a while. This is now a psychiatric case."

Reluctantly, Galina left Valeria to wait alone. She would retrieve the youngest children, inform the older, and let Dmitri and Katya handle things while she got some sleep. She also wanted to get the blood off the wall before Vladimir saw it.

Valeria brooded for an hour before Sarah was brought into the ten-bed recovery room. A pressure-relieving gel bandage wrapped her head; shiny clear Nuskin covered her arms. To Valeria's horror, Sarah wore wide black immobilizing bands over her limbs, pinning her to the bed.

The orderly turned to leave.

"Aren't you taking those off?" Valeria asked.

"No, ma'am. Doctor's orders."

Val ran a finger down the slash lines under the clear protectants, shaking her head in disbelief. She stroked the pale hair hanging below the bandages. "Sarah? Sarah, baby –"

Sarah struggled to open her eyes. "Home," she mouthed, trying to find her voice. "Am I done? Can we go home now?"

"You have to wake up first, Sar."

"I am awake." She blinked to focus, strained hard to stay that way. "Undo my arms?"

"I... I think the doctor has to do that, babe. Want me to ask?" Sarah nodded, and Valeria spoke to the nurse, who paged the doctor.

"He's on his way," Val assured her. "We'll get you home as fast as we can."

After a moment of silence, Sarah said, "I'm sorry. I ruined your day, didn't I."

Valeria smiled forgiveness. "Shhh. Don't worry yourself about it. We've all had bad days. Today's your turn. We've lived through worse. We'll make it."

A man with peppered hair approached. "Miss Kirushenko? I'm Dr. Carmichael." To Sarah, he said simply, "I see we're awake."

"Can I go home now?" Sarah tried again. "I rest better in my own bed."

"That's what we need to talk about."

"Can I have my arms back?"

The doctor hesitated. "Let's hold off a few more minutes. You created quite the chaos downstairs."

Sarah turned away, angry he'd mentioned her misbehavior in front of Val.

"Now, even though Sarah here won't discuss it, the consensus is her head injuries are self-inflicted. A fall or a blow is a one-shot injury. Her head shows evidence of repeated trauma, and that doesn't usually happen by accident. You're absolutely sure she was alone when this happened?"

Val nodded.

"It took more than an hour to close her scalp," Dr. Carmichael continued, "including removing a bone chip. I think what she did downstairs speaks for itself. We've never had anything like that happen before. Not here, anyway.

"So, the medical team feels there is a serious risk in releasing her right now. With your permission, we'd like to keep her for 48 hours, run some tests, do some observation, and take it from there."

Val frowned. "Why? What kind of tests? What for?"

"If we find something organic, we can try and correct it. If there's a chemical imbalance, we can treat it with medication. If it's a behavioral problem, we can address that as well."

"It's not a '*behavioral problem*'!" Valeria spat. "Sarah's probably the best behaved of the bunch! I don't think ..."

"We'll take that into consideration," Carmichael interrupted. "Right now, though, I'd like to transfer her upstairs to an observation room. We can take those restraints off up there."

Valeria balked. They'd always taken care of themselves. Doctors were the very last resort. "Forty-eight hours, you say?"

"Forty-eight hours."

Val sighed and nodded permission.

Dr. Carmichael sat on the foot of the bed. "Okay, Sarah, here's the game plan. In a few minutes, we'll transfer you upstairs and take those straps off. We'll see how you do, maybe run a few tests, and if all goes well and you feel better, you'll go home in a day or two."

Sarah's gaze traveled from Val's falsely cheerful face to the doctor's. "I'm going home *now*," she insisted. "I have school."

"We'd like to run some tests first."

Val fumbled with the end of the mesh blanket. "M-maybe it's for the best, Sar. Just for a day or two ..."

Sarah fought to sit up. "No! Take me home, Val! I hate hospitals! Please, Valeria! I *promise* I'll behave! I won't do anything bad! I'm sorry! *Don't leave me here!* I can't miss school!"

Valeria's eyes filled with tears. She tried to pet Sarah's cheek. "I'm sorry, Sar. I'll be here the second they let you out. I promise. I'm so sorry!"

Carmichael ushered Val to the door. "Come. I have some consent releases for you to sign."

"*DON'T LEAVE ME HERE!*" Sarah screamed, bucking against the restraints. She tried to bang her head, but the gel-filled wrap gave only a soft squish. Fear and rage broke loose in a flood, overtaking her.

\* \* \*

Galina and Valeria spoke a dozen times with the doctors via the commlink, exchanging questions. This was the final call; the holding order expired today.

"Neuro screen shows a high level of depression," Dr. Carmichael explained. "However, positron scan found evidence of auditory hallucinations. It's difficult to make an exact diagnosis due to the level of sedation needed to perform the tests. Her level of agitation is extreme. I cannot allow her release. Not like she is."

"Forgive me," Galina interrupted, "but we're having trouble believing any of this. Sarah is the most – intelligent, reserved person I know. What you describe is unimaginable."

"I agree," added Valeria. "It's totally unlike Sarah. I talked to her two days ago. She was scared, but she made perfect sense. I would have to see it for myself."

"We'll be there in a half hour," the twins said in unison.

The four boys blocked their way. Nikky circled them at a gallop, chanting, "Me, too! Me, too!"

"We're going with you," Dmitri said.

"No," Val said. "It's not everyone's business. And if it is true, I don't want Vlad upset any more than he is." Vladimir had collapsed without his other half. All he would say to anyone was a nonsensical, "That's *six!* That's *six!* *She's* number six!" He'd curled up on Sarah's bed, crying until he vomited himself into dehydration. Even David hadn't had the heart to pick on him.

"I'll come," Katya decided as the twins readied to leave. "I'm with her most of the time, anyway."

"Like Hell!" Dmitri said. "Where's it written girls make all the decisions around here? Sarah spends more time in our room than yours. Vik told me to take care of things, and I am. I'm going, like it or not. Someone's gotta tell Vlad the truth."

Val traded exasperated looks with Galina. "Fine! But that's it!"


They crowded together with the doctor in a small booth outside an observation room. The room could have been a staff lounge, except for the mirrored screen and the camera ports that gave a 360-degree view from inside the booth. Cheery motivational posters decorated the walls. Three staff were in the room, an examiner and two aides whose job seemed better described as body guards.

The Kirushenkos hardly recognized their sister. Sarah's long hair had gone unwashed and uncombed for two days. The bandage had been removed; her scalp showed red and purple through her pale hair. The hospital clothing she wore hung loose, meant for adults, not children, and she never stopped moving.

Their ever-logical sister flattened herself against the wall, appeared to speak to the ceiling, vaulted over the low arm of a sofa, squatted on the farthest cushion, hands on her temples, and shouted something in angst.

She jumped up to rip a picture from the wall, threw it, knelt and began to rock on her knees, this time speaking to the floor.

Carmichael touched a button on the side of the observation room window. The sounds of the exam room came through on a speaker.

"The goal is to assemble a simple perception puzzle," he explained. "Shapes on a board, nothing more. At this point, we'd consider the task successful if she sat in the chair and stared at them.

"See that there with her hands? We think that's a response to an auditory hallucination. Watch her face – she isn't happy with it. But until she calms enough to talk with us, we don't know for sure. We can tranquilize her into a coma, but we can't force her to cooperate. We believe there may also be some degree of hysterical blindness, and/or visual hallucinations."

"Blindness?!" Katya exclaimed.

"Not blindness as you're thinking," Carmichael corrected. "There's nothing physically wrong with her eyes. It's in her head. Look." He changed the view on the wallscreen and called up a chart.

"This is the positron scan we obtained yesterday. When presented with a visual image, she doesn't respond, but her brain insists she does see it. Yet, when she *should* be seeing nothing," he touched the picture and it changed, "we get these bright spots here and here, usually a sign that something *is* being registered by the brain."

Sarah continued to move, mumbling a continuous sing-song stream of Russian punctuated by shouts, pleas, and curses.

"When did this start?" Galina said.

"Upon arriving on this floor day before yesterday. Except when heavily sedated, that is – and I mean heavily. She's determined to fight it. She hasn't slept, hasn't eaten, hasn't stopped. We've sedated her seven hours a day, letting her body rest, giving her IV fluids and nutrition. She's doing relatively well on the mood elevators. She's stopped trying to tear herself apart, thus she's not restrained right now. She's a very strong little girl."

"She has to be, with six older brothers," Dmitri said with a hint of pride. He didn't mention Father's training.

The female examiner placed a chair in the middle of the room, away from the aides. "No strings, Sarah," she said, backing up. "Sit on the chair for me. One minute, that's all."

Sarah squinted at the woman from the corner of her eye, reciting or singing under her breath. She crawled to the chair, ran her hands over it. She shrieked, she howled, she punched her fist hard into the chair several times. Springing to her feet, she swung the chair and threw it awkwardly at the watching staff.

" – *tvoyu matz!*" Sarah screamed in Russian, yanking her own hair. A longer string of vulgarities followed, but only her siblings understood.

Dmitri whistled. "Where'd she learn to talk like that?"

Katya crossed her arms. "One guess."

Sarah charged a staff, knocking him to the floor. The other grabbed her hands and spun her around to give the man time to get up. Sarah dropped down and swung a foot over her head to kick the man holding her.

"We had to order that no safety devices be worn in her presence," said the doctor. "We learned the hard way yesterday, when she used a pressure hold on a staff, took their stun weapon and knocked out all the staff. We had to flood the room with tranquilizer gas to get it back. That is one child who should never have studied martial arts."

Free again, Sarah threw herself against the locked door and pounded on it, howling.

"When you sit, Sarah," the examiner said.

"I want to see her," Valeria announced. "I promised her I would be back."

"I don't recommend that at this time," Carmichael said. "She could attack you; it could make her worse."

"Worse than that?" Dmitri asked with animosity. He pointed to the wall screens. "I mean, how do we know that's her scan? How do we know that's what it means? How do we know this isn't all from something *you* did? Sarah doesn't act like that."

"You're welcome to a second opinion, of course," Dr. Carmichael conceded. "The best news is that we found no organic defect or abnormality. That means the cause is most likely chemical, and that can be helped." He sighed. "We'll try it, but I can't guarantee you'll get what you're hoping for. She probably won't recognize you."

The four entered the locked room, followed by the psychiatrist. The examiner left to watch from the observation booth. Sarah spun to her own music in the far corner.

"Sar'ina?" Valeria called. "It's Valeria, Sarah. I came back, just like I promised."

Sarah stopped in mid-spin, hands frozen at ear level, listening intently. She squinted sideways through her tangled hair.

"It's Val, Sarah."

Sarah mouthed the word three times before it came out as a whisper. "Va. Va? Val?"

"Yes, Sarah. It's Valeria."

Still squinting, Sarah toe-walked forward two steps, sideways one, forward one more. Valeria knelt down and held out a hand. Sarah shrieked, "Val!" and ran. She wrapped her arms around Val's neck and hung on.

Valeria hugged back, kissing her. "I'm so glad to see you! We missed you so much! Look who came with me! Galina's here, and Katya and Dimi, too. Let's sit." Val dragged Sarah to the sofa.

With everyone talking to her, petting her, hugging her, with two days' medication flowing in her veins, Sarah gave a strangling gurgle and exploded into rare tears.

"I tried. I tried... to be good... I did try. Please... *please* take me home now... I'm... so... *tired!*"

"Shhh. You're okay." Valeria rocked her side to side, and Sarah melted in, exhausted. Her muscles, strained from her two-day dervish, continued to twitch and jump without her.

"Shhh. Did you know we heard from Viktor last night?" Valeria said with forced excitement. "He's working for a 'Fleet patrol out on the Burin-Jai border, all the way out there. He's being trained as a weapons officer. Isn't that great news?"

Sarah coughed hard on tears, but nodded.

Val rocked hypnotically. "He says he loves you, and he misses you, and not to worry about him."

The psychiatrist squatted near the cluster. "Perhaps this would be a good time for us to talk, while she's calmer. Maybe one of you could stay here, and the rest of us could go next door."

"I'll stay," Katya volunteered. "Will you sit with me, Sarah?"

The arms transferred to Katya's neck.

"I miss you, Sarah," Kat told her after the others had left. "The bed is empty without your sweaty feet. I have an idea. Sit down here." She pulled and pushed Sarah's now-lifeless body down between her knees, fished in her shoulder bag and produced a hairbrush. She picked gingerly at the tangles, careful not to touch the angry scalp.

"There, this is better, isn't it?"

* * *

"Yes, given time, we can help her," Dr. Carmichael explained, "but we're an emergency center, not a long-term care facility. In addition, new regulations have been handed down in the last six weeks. Due to the unfortunate incident the other month, the Navarans have requested that all serious psychiatric cases be moved off-world. They feel that many of the problems we see are a result of stressors caused by the climate itself, and that they can be cured simply by removing the patients from the planet. They feel it is safer for everyone concerned; psychiatric patients are more prone to violence, and they are afraid another murder could occur. I know, she's only a child and that risk is ridiculous, but currently there are no exceptions. We can appeal through the diplomatic council, but it will take time. Unfortunately, there is no pediatric psychiatric facility within a parsec. The closest full-care facility is Rangler Psychiatric and Rehab on Starbase 4, which is only half a light-year."

"Once again, our family screws itself," Dmitri muttered.

Galina looked doubtful. "That's so far. It would make visiting difficult."

"You can't visit, at least for the first few weeks," Carmichael said. "I've been in contact with Rangler, and they're willing to try a 90-day program."

Dmitri stabbed the air with his finger. "Look, I don't pretend to know what's going on. *Nothing* makes Sarah cry, not David, not Father, not *nothing*! And she's in there crying like Vlad on a bad day. But she's just a little kid! You can't go shoving her into a hospital alone for weeks and weeks somewhere far away because you don't want to deal with her. Look how much better she got when she knew we were here for her. You can't do that."

"Dimi, be fair," Valeria said, trying to convince herself. "Two of us are trying to care for eight children. Father has a criminal trial coming up. Not one of us can be spared to babysit Sarah around the clock. It's killing me inside, but I see no other choice."

"She belongs home, with her family, then she'll relax," Dmitri insisted. He crossed his arms and tipped his chair back. "She's not stupid. She's just scared. Anybody'd be scared, all alone in a place like this. She hates hospitals. You really feel like wiping puke off Vlad's chin for the next three months? Of course you don't care," he corrected himself. "You're not the one stuck doing it. I am."

"Dmitri, don't make this harder than it is. Galina?"

Galina looked helpless. She ran a hand through her hair. "I don't see how we could handle that at home. You can't stop that whirling and screaming and juggle a baby, too. I have to side with Val. But only ninety days, not one more! Ready or not, she comes home. And Vlad will visit her as soon as possible."

Valeria reached for the commitment forms with a heavy heart. "That's it, then."

*"Traitors!"* Dmitri jeered. "We take care of our own!" He slammed

the chair legs down and stormed out to the hall.

* * *

"Try to remember the good times," Katya advised Sarah, able to sweep the brush gently through most of the hair. "There were some, once. Remember when you were small, and Father was supposed to be digging for a lost city, but he found some extinct creature instead? Remember how excited he was? Remember how they named it after him? *Kirushenkus* something or other?"

"I re-mem-ber," Sarah gasped. She wiped her nose on the knee of her baggy pants, unable to stop crying and too numb to care. "I had a b-blue Daienar dress with a... shi-iny skirt."

"That's right! Remember that reception? You must have been about four. All those important people shaking Father's hand, all those fancy clothes, all the pictures? Mother was so proud of him. I never saw so much food as I did that night. I wished it would never have ended."

Sarah hiccupped uncontrollably. "And... Mo-Mother... said... she was... pre-pre-preg-nant... with... with Nik-Nik-Nik-Nikky...."

"Yes! See? Think of the good things, Sarah, not the bad. Then you won't have nightmares."

"I'm afraid... to s-s-sleep. Keep moving ... stay awake."

The doors opened, and the group returned. Sarah's hair was smooth and held back with a hair clip Katya took from her own head. Her face was red, though, her eyes swollen nearly shut by tears.

Valeria and Katya lifted her back onto the sofa.

Val searched for the best way to broach the subject. The right word, a rational phrase from her sister, and she would change her mind about the whole thing. "Sarah? We talked with the doctor, and we – We think there's a better hospital for you, one that will help you get better faster. Just for a little while, then you'll be home. You're just – too sick to come home right now. Do you understand? Is that... okay with you?"

Sarah nodded slightly, cuddled against Katya. She'd been sick in hospitals before, and always returned home. She wouldn't like the arrangement, but she would get better and go home. She was sure it meant having to stop crying, but she didn't know if she'd ever have that kind of strength again. She was *tired*, to her very bones. All her energy dripped out with the unfamiliar tears that stung her nose and rasped her throat and blinded her eyes.

She just couldn't fight right now.

# \* Seven \*

From the darkness of space it resembled a fat metal doughnut skewered through the hole by a pretzel rod salted by dozens of communication towers and sensor arrays. The words *United Planetary Alliance Starbase 4 / GA 7481-908* were painted on opposite sides of the doughnut in ten-meter tall black symbols, along with the universal symbol for hospital. A small blue star glowed dimly at a distance; its single lifeless planet circled in tight orbit, no bigger than one of Saturn's moons, but the light from the star was enough to remind the inhabitants of the base they were still part of the universe. While it maintained itself as a fully functional starbase, a place where tired crews could restock, refuel, and take shoreleave, the other half of the structure was known as Rangler Mental Health Center, a modern, top-of-the-line psychiatric rehabilitation hospital. Its strategic placement, hanging in space rather than built on an orbiting body, meant it was not only independent of any local government, but reasonably accessible to more than a dozen star systems. It also meant that the mentally unstable and sometimes dangerous clientele would have greater difficulty attempting escape. In thirty years, only six clients had ever made it to the public side of the facility, and none had ever escaped.

Rangler itself occupied thirty-eight levels of the fifty-four-deck Starbase, with beds, if necessary, for a maximum of three thousand clients. To support this, there existed a small army of psychiatrists, behavioral therapists, counselors, nurses, assistants, technical staff, and a constantly changing number of students. A model teaching hospital, it prided itself on its far-reaching and comprehensive programming. New theories were tested, realistic new treatment methods welcomed. What worked on one species of humanoid might just work on another. While some of the clients lived in temporary apartments and needed only a few weeks' counseling with a therapist, other clients had greater impairments, requiring constant supervision and high-security measures. Even so, Rangler boasted an eighty-one percent success ratio.

It was precisely that open-mindedness of hospital policy that allowed a severely impaired eight-and-three-quarter-year old child to be admitted to an adult facility. The proposal seemed simple. Housing in a low- risk women's ward, a special aide assigned to ensure her safety, a thorough exam to arrive at a detailed diagnosis, and with an appropriate treatment plan, ninety days would be more than enough to solve a crisis in a previously well-adjusted child.

So said the plan.

The starbase personnel were unprepared for a young child; the next youngest patient was seventeen. It was the closest facility, however, and since the director knew Dr. Carmichael, he agreed to try. A treatment team was assembled, with a flurry of meetings to bring everyone up to date on child psychology. After Sarah's first week, the staff promptly forgot their new training and went about their business, lulled into believing they had an easy job.

The wildcat hibernated. Sarah had no memory of her family leaving her. She would not remember changing hospitals, or her entire first week at the new facility. When she'd finally worn herself out physically with activity and emotionally with involuntary tears, Sarah collapsed inward with the gravity of a black hole. She did not sit up unless someone sat her, did not lie down unless someone helped her, or she fell over. She could not walk without assistance. If prodded enough, she would eat if someone fed her, drink if someone held a cup for her. Now and then her lips would move as if speaking, but she made no sound. The thirty-four other patients in Section 23W soon lost interest in the small lump of flesh curled in a chair. The hospital reran tests and tried new ones, formulating a plan.

Sarah felt as if she'd fallen into that black hole. Everything, even breathing, it seemed, required more effort than she could give. Her limbs felt so heavy she was certain the gravity of the hospital must have changed. Her vision disappeared completely; sometimes she saw nothing but darkness, sometimes a gray fog. A few times it lightened until she saw shadows, but little else. Her hearing did the same – sometimes nothing, sometimes voices with no words. When she could see the shadows and hear indistinctly, she'd call for a brother or sister. She couldn't tell if they heard her, but then she couldn't tell if she made any noise, either. Not that it mattered.

One morning the fog lifted, and she saw shades of gray. Noises filtered into her ears, life noises and soft conversations. There were no *Welcome to...* banners on the walls, but nurses lived in hospitals, so she must be at a hospital somewhere. A woman led her on a walk to a door that read:

## Liesel Eisgaard DPM PhD FUPACPM
*Whatever foopacpem meant.*

"Do you know where you are?" the doctor asked.

*No,* shook Sarah's head.

"You are at the Rangler Psychiatric and Rehab Facility, also known as Starbase Four Mental Health Center. You have been here for nine days. Do you know why?"

A pause while Sarah thought, then shrugged.

"Can you tell me?"

A pause. *No,* shook her head. The woman spoke, but Sarah turned away in boredom. She'd heard enough. She inspected her fingernails, which had grown long. She tore at one with her teeth, then proceeded to make the others precisely the same length. Ignoring Father's rantings proved to be a useful skill, for Sarah didn't hear a word the doctor said. She thought about the Periodic Table of the Elements, tried to remember them in alphabetical order, along with their atomic weights. Actinium. Actinium. Goodness Gracious! She couldn't remember Actinium! Sarah ran through her head, but the more she tried, the stronger the blank she drew. She blurted out:

"Actinium!"

Dr. Eisgaard, Fellow of the United Planetary Alliance Consortium of Psychiatric Medicine, looked up from her notes, also having given up on the appointment. "Actinium?"

"Do you know the atomic weight of Actinium?" They were the first words she'd spoken.

"Actinium," the psychiatrist confirmed. "Computer, the atomic weight of Actinium?"

*Two-hundred-twenty-three moles.* Sarah nodded her thanks, visibly relieved. *Of course! She knew that! Why didn't she remember?* She returned to picking her nails and thinking. Another boring hospital stay.

So Sarah thought, until she woke in the night drenched in cold sweat, another gruesome nightmare pounding in her chest. But here there was no Vlad to press against, no baby sister to sit up with for company, no sun to watch rise. The loneliness crushed the breath from her, making her gasp. It *would* be a very long stay.

Sarah woke with a start. Because of her age, she had a room to herself, an observation room next to the nurses' area. She must have dozed at some point, but she felt far from rested. By the sounds outside the room it was morning, but too early for her personal aide. *What did*

86

*it matter?* Time of day was irrelevant when you were locked in a place with no windows. A knot yanked at the pit of her stomach, and she realized with a jolt *they* were back. The voices. They weren't loud enough to understand yet, but she sensed them, like the threat of an itch in a place she couldn't reach to scratch.

*Waiting.* They were playing a waiting game, and the suspense was murderous. She knew they would soon chatter, but when, how loud, how fast, what words? What would the hospital do to her when they did?

She made it to breakfast. Sarah ate fast, every tasteless bite serving to feed her dread of impending doom.

*Worthless.*

Her spoon fell, and she heard it clang distantly on the floor. She stuffed her fingers in her ears and jumped up, rattling her tray.

The aide stretched out a hand. "Talk to me, Sarah. What's wrong?"

"My room," Sarah mumbled with a sense of urgency. "I need my room."

"Come on." The aide took her charge by the elbow and ran down the hall.

Sarah paced laps around her room, tapping her wrists on her head, her fear of the voices worse than the voices themselves. She had no concentration. She could outrun the noises, but it did nothing to alleviate her anxiety.

Doctor time. Sarah didn't want to go. She dragged her feet through the halls, pulling away from the aide's concerned touch.

*Unstable* flashed through her head.

*unstable*, it echoed.

"Sarah, you seem upset since our meeting yesterday," Dr. Eisgaard observed. "Has something happened?"

"No," Sarah muttered. She paced the office like a hummingbird, tapping a thumb on her temple.

"Sarah, you need to calm yourself. Sit down for me."

"No." Sarah's arms writhed now, her whole body involved in activity to chase the voices away.

"Sarah, I'm concerned about you. I want to give you some medication to help stop your upset." The doctor reached into a pocket. With her other hand she pressed a button under the edge of her desk.

Sarah spun around as the aide entered. "No! No drugs!" *Evil doctors, and their drugs, drugs, drugs!*

"It will help you feel better."

*"NO!"* Sarah grabbed her ears and looked to the ceiling in fear as *poisonous* slithered across her head. "Stop it! Stop it!" she shouted,

stomping her foot. From the corner of her eye she saw the doctor raise the airhypo to adjust the dosage. The aide slipped behind Sarah and held her arms.

Panic rose, cold and deadly. Two against one, and they weren't about to believe her. Sarah wasn't a baby; she knew what pain was, and she knew how to save herself. *Run* was the word of the moment.

Arching against the aide, Sarah loosed a powerful kick at the doctor's hand. *"NO!"* Her foot not only hit the hand, but sent the metal airhypo backward. Her heel slammed the doctor's nose; the hypospray handle cut the doctor's cheek. The doctor grabbed her face as blood ran from her nose.

"Computer: Security!" Eisgaard ordered as the aide battled to hold the girl. A muffled alarm rang out in the hall.

*"Code red, office four. Code red, office four,"* the address system repeated calmly.

Sarah saw the blood start between the doctor's fingers, heard her head echo *blood/flood, red/dead,* and flashed back to her mother lying in a red puddle. Terror won. Her head smashed the aide's chin; she dropped her weight downward as the woman recoiled, wrenching free. She bolted out the door and ran blindly down the hall, anywhere, anywhere but where she was, anywhere without blood or invisible voices. She ran right into one of two security guards coming toward her. Two more came from the other direction.

She bit and clawed and kicked and screamed, but the staff were used to restraining adults. Eisgaard applied the hypo with a much stronger medication.

Terror swallowed Sarah alive. When the sedatives abated, the nightmares began. Horrible, gruesome dreams, but she didn't awaken; they just continued until the next dose of tranquilizer so doped her she didn't dream. In her dreams she tried to run, to fight off the attacks, but it never helped.

*Gods only knew what she'd done this time. Father tied her to the chair and splashed her with vodka. Her clothes and hair were soaked, and she shivered. Horror crept into her heart as she realized what Father was about to do.*

*"No!" she pleaded. "Don't do that! I'm sorry! I'm sorry! Please don't do that! I'm sorry!"*

*"You know what you did," Father replied, holding a fire starter. "Catch."*

*Sarah screamed as she burst into flames…*

*They were running lost through endless tunnels, she and Vladimir. Not far behind but always out of sight, Father could be heard thundering.*

*"Come out here now!" Father bellowed in a drunken rage. "You have to obey your father!" His footsteps echoed through the tunnels, his whip cracking every so many steps. "I know where you are, ungrateful brats! I'll go easy if you come to me!"*

*Every gulping breath burned their lungs, every step cramped their aching legs. The tunnels were smooth; there was no place to hide. Vlad and Sarah paused to breathe for an agonized second, but they could see Father's oversized shadow coming around the corner.*

*"I'm going to beat you little fuckers when I catch you!"*

*"Come on," Sarah gasped, grabbing Vlad's hand and hauling him along.*

*His hand ripped suddenly from hers. She turned. Vlad sat on the ground, holding his ankle. "Come on!" she repeated, pulling on him. "Hurry!"*

*Vlad lifted a teary face. "I can't! I can't go on!"*

*"He'll kill you! We've got to go **now**!"*

*"I can't!" Vlad cried. Father's shadow reappeared close by. "Run, Sarah! Save yourself!"*

*"You can do it! I'll help you! I can't leave you!"*

*Father appeared, larger than ever, eyes glowing red with too much drinking-stuff.*

*"Run, Sarah!" Vlad screamed. "Run!"*

*Sarah ran and ran and ran and ran, the slap of the whip and Vladimir's tortured screams ringing in her ears….*

*Sarah recognized yet didn't recognize where she was. One of Father's Big Digs, some archaeological find somewhere. The hard brown walls of the canyon yielded mazes of ruins, a townsite 10,000 years old. She lay naked on a great stone table, an altar of primitive sorts. Many arms reached out – Father's assistants and students. They pinned her to the slab against her will. A robed figure stood by, watching.*

*Father produced a stone knife, and sliced her from neck to groin. When her insides were exposed, he turned to the robed*

*figure and asked, "You would like first pick?"*
*The figure pulled back its hood. It was Elizabyeta, as tall as*
*a grown up. She inspected the incision and said, "That one,*
*right there."*
*"Good choice," said Father. "That's a fine looking liver,"*
*and proceeded to remove her organs one by one. They were*
*passed among the ensemble to be admired. When everything of*
*value had been removed and examined, those holding her*
*dropped her empty body down an endlessly deep garbage pit.*
*Sarah felt herself falling down, down, forever down...*

"I've tried that," Dr. Eisgaard said at the staff meeting. "Nothing's worked. Without sedation, she attacks anyone within range. I'm amazed at the rapidity with which the behaviors are swinging."

"What about play therapy?" suggested Dr. Carver. "She's a young child. Studies have shown it to be highly beneficial in cases of traumatic stress."

"Play?" Eisgaard sneered. "Play what? Wild animal?"

"It doesn't hold much for schizophrenic behavior patterns," Dr. Hepatnesharu agreed. "At this point, we're fairly certain she's hallucinating."

"But *is* it schizophrenia?" Carver countered. "We still don't have a definitive diagnosis. 'Looks like.' 'Resembles.' 'Similar to.' "

"We're running out of time," said Dr. Saluria, the silver-haired Chief of Psychiatry Team 4. He pushed the stack of computer records before him farther into the middle of the conference table. "We should have reached a conclusion last week, and been well into the course of appropriate treatment. Dr. Carver, your specialty is recreational therapy. This case would seem to be designed especially for you. As the newest member of our treatment team, perhaps you would like to try your ideas on Miss Kirushenko. Impress us in person as much as your résumé."

"I'd be glad to," Carver said.

"Dr. Eisgaard, it's your patient, your call."

Eisgaard appeared relieved. "By all means, take her. I've had enough excitement for this year. She's the most uncooperative child I've ever met."

"I want her brought off the Sedistrate over the next 24 hours," Dr. Carver directed the nurses after checking on his new patient. "No restraints save the forcefield on the doorway. Let's keep the Elavixor steady at ten mils; we don't want to up it too fast. And let's try adding

90

five milligrams of Antivox, see where that gets us."

"No restraints?" said the nurse. "What if she starts gouging herself again?"

"I don't think she will. Unless she's doing serious damage or going for her eyes, let her go." He signed off on the orders. "I'll check in every couple hours."

Sarah awoke from the last nightmare surprised. She was really awake! *But where now?* Creamy white dimples covered the walls of the tiny room. She lay on a low bed that was little more than a padded outgrowth of the floor, almost like an – altar? Sarah shuddered and breathed deep to calm herself. She reached out to touch the soft wall, and met invisible resistance seven centimeters from it. Only when her hand moved slowly could it advance.

*Inertia dampeners,* she realized. A high-tech rubber-room. She sat up stiffly. By the level of light in the room and hall, it was still artificial "nighttime." She walked over to the doorway, shimmering with its electrical forcefield, and sat down. A nurse would notice her at some point. She listened for voices, but found none. *They must still be asleep,* she thought, and settled down to wait.

Not long after breakfast, the aide readied her to leave the high-risk ward. The staff here didn't play games. Sarah sported a tight band around her ankle that flashed a green light; green was good. Two meters from the main door and the light changed to red, locking the doors. No patient could pass without an override from the nurse's control board. The seriousness continued in the hall: the new aide wore a stun glove in case of attack. They stopped outside a room labeled Rec Room 17.

"This isn't my doctor's office," Sarah said warily.

"Dr. Eisgaard is no longer your doctor," the aide replied, motioning to the door. "Let's go."

Sarah entered the strange room alone and heard the door shut behind her. She knew from hard experience hospitals were places of deception, full of pain and horror and loneliness and lies designed to make you cooperate. This confinement was a little different – for the first time, Sarah wasn't hospitalized for pneumonia. She hung back against the wall to sort it all out.

*Caution, caution,* she warned herself.

The size of the room surprised her, filled with a chaos of tables, chairs, sofas, carts, and blue-gray walls full of shelves. Story chips, trinkets, toys, puzzles, hologames, and every other plaything Sarah could think of sat on them. A large cage on a countertop held a number of white mice. An upright piano hid under clutter in the back. Over at a table, a lone man sat bent over a puzzle sphere. It was not what Sarah expected to see. *Was he a doctor or a patient?*

The man looked up. "Hello! You must be Sarah." He came toward her with his hand outstretched, but she shrank away. "I'm John Carver. You can call me John if you want. I'm a recreational therapist. I play games with people – the fun kind. Sports, hobbies, crafts, games – whatever you like to do, I can arrange it for you. Do you like games?"

Sarah shrugged. This was not what she expected. *Where was the doctor?* The man before her looked too young. Soft brown hair combed back from a boyish face, and kind brown eyes watched her with amusement. He wore normal clothing, not the uniform jackets or deep-green shirts of the rest of the staff. He came across as pleasant and sincere – a concept so out of place for a hospital she didn't know what to think.

"What if I don't want to play?"

Carver returned to his chair. "That's your choice, but it's rather boring to sit and do nothing. There's an awful lot of stuff to mess with in here. Come in!" He tried to wave her into the room. "Pick a seat, or look around if you like." He went back to his puzzle.

Sarah waited, but he didn't move. She eased over and sat on the dusky purple couch nearest the door. She pulled her knees up under her chin, and watched.

She waited.

And waited.

He worked on the sphere before him, not speaking. She studied the puzzle, working it out in her head.

After a long while, her aide returned. Sarah stood up to leave.

"See you tomorrow," Carver said without looking up. "Think about what you like to do. Anything at all."

Sarah hesitated, unsure what had transpired. She took a couple of steps toward the table. A closer look, and she turned to leave. She stopped at the door.

"B, K, L, C, E, A, M," she said, giving him the sequence to solve the puzzle. She left.

Carver shifted pieces and saw she was correct. He rushed out to the hall. "Hey! How'd you do that?"

Second session, and Sarah still wasn't sure what to do. John Carver sat at the same table, this time building a house of cards. He wasn't having much luck. He greeted her with the same eager pleasantries, the same invitation to look around, and a couple of idle sentences over what he was doing. He asked nothing personal, gave no advice, and not more than brief eye contact. Unlike doctors, he didn't seem bothered that she crouched silently in the corner. After half an hour, Sarah felt bolder. She walked the perimeter of the room, examining items with her eyes, daring a finger to touch something here and there. Always, she tracked the therapist from the corner of her eye. He didn't acknowledge her movement at all.

Her finger trailed lightly down the keys of the piano at the back wall, tinging a few.

Without turning, he said, "There's music in the file box on top."

Sarah shrugged and moved on. A quarter room more and she came to a chess game left in progress. She examined it for several minutes, then moved a piece.

John glanced over. The card house wobbled three stories high. "You play?"

Sarah moved another piece. "*Ya Russkaya.* I'm Russian," she stated flatly, as if it answered everything. Her aide entered; the session was over.

"I'm no great chess player," Carver said, "but if you want, come back this afternoon and I'll play you a round. Aw, damn!" He hit the table with his elbow, and the card house collapsed.

Sarah nodded thoughtfully. Maybe.

By two, Sarah had made up her mind to return. She had nothing else to do. She couldn't concentrate on lessons, the other patients scared her, and she had no interest in any other activities on the high-risk floor. She liked chess. Only Sergei would play her at home, though supposedly Father had once been good at it. She hadn't played in a long while. At least the rec room would be quiet, and she wouldn't have to watch her back.

Carver jotted notes onto a computer pad. "Sarah! I'm glad you came. Have a seat. I'll be with you in a minute." He scribbled several lines, then put his notes aside and carried the chessboard over. Sarah hesitated. Carver noticed, and switched sides of the table, leaving her the chair with unimpeded access to the door.

"Black or white?"

Sarah slid into a seat. She chose white and set up the pieces. For two hours they sat without speaking, playing a waiting game of wills more than chess. At last Sarah braved the risk and knocked the rook out of the way. "Check mate," she said, pulling back to watch the man's reaction.

To the girl's surprise, Carver exclaimed, "Wow! You're really good! That was a long game." He paged the transport aide. "See you tomorrow."

Sarah got as far as the door, gears turning. She didn't look back, but she said "Thank you" loud enough to be heard.

"That's my job, but you're very welcome."

Sarah shook her head. She knew enough to know her win was real; he hadn't played stupid just to make her feel good. "For playing honestly."

Fourth session. She'd behaved enough to move back to her old room on 23W, minus the ankle lock. The voices remained silent, and her fogginess was lifting. Faint colors returned to her vision, and she started to think again – about home, about school, about the hospital. Today she skipped the couch and sat at the table on her own. Carver's workpile sat nearby, a deck of cards on top.

"Cards?" he asked, picking up the hexagonal deck. Her family said it was a favorite activity. "What's your pleasure?"

"Nine Square. Or Poker."

"Poker?" Carver laughed. "Poker's no fun with only two. Do you know Blackjack?"

Sarah nodded.

"An eight year old card shark," he grinned, shuffling. "I'm sorry. Nine. You're nine now, aren't you?"

"I am?!"

"Didn't you have a birthday the other week?" He flipped through the stack next to him and peeked in a file of print-outs. "Here it is. Yes. Last week."

"I forgot it?" Sarah mourned as he dealt her cards. No family, no cake, no wishes... A lost year. The Magic Weeks, when she and Vlad were actually the same age, and she wasn't with him to share it.

"I think you were preoccupied last week."

Sarah played two hands in silence, lost in miserable thought. At last she admitted, "I didn't mean to, you know."

Carver shuffled the cards. "Forget your birthday?"

"Mess up the doctor."

"She'll recover."

Sarah twirled a lock of hair around her finger, then added, "She rushed me. She made up her mind I was just a kid, and she didn't give me time to handle myself."

Carver dealt another hand. "You *are* just a kid."

"Age wise, maybe, but I'm not a baby. I'm in the equivalent of twelfth form at school. I'm used to (hit me) making decisions for myself. Like when I don't want medication. Stay."

"But you take medication every morning, don't you? (house wins)"

"No. They administer it, which so far I've allowed (stay)," she said, as if she had a choice in the matter.

"You win. Do you know what they give you?" Carver asked, shuffling. Sarah shook her head. He flipped open the hard-file once again. "Elavixor, fifteen milligrams – that's a mood regulator, and Antivox, ten milligrams. That's an antipsychotic. Do you know what that means?"

"It means they think I'm psychotic," Sarah said morosely, peeking at her cards. "Stay."

"It's a drug to control hallucinations – voices or visions that aren't real. You sound pretty rational to me. You win."

Sarah pushed the cards away and stood up. "I don't want to play."

Carver dealt himself a hand of Solitaire. She paced the room for several minutes before stopping at the end of the table.

"These drugs – Do they work on dreams as well? *Bad* dreams?" she asked, afraid to say too much. It wasn't like he was a doctor or anything, but he'd been nice so far; she wanted him to stay nice.

Carver chewed his lip. "Nightmares? I suppose they might. You have nightmares?"

"Bad ones," she whispered, sliding into her chair. "Very bad. But not for two or three nights now. So I wondered."

He flipped a card. "Well, there's nothing wrong with a good night's sleep."

"That's why I didn't want the tranquilizers," she confessed, biting a nail and hoping she didn't make a mistake trusting him. "They make it hard to wake up from the nightmares."

"I guess I can understand that. Nightmares can be disturbing. You prefer to be in control of such a situation, no matter how little control that is."

Sarah thought about it while she picked at her fingers. "I guess so." The aide entered the room. Time was up.

"Think about it," Carver told her. "I'll be here this afternoon if you want a rematch on that chess game."

Sarah gave a pensive nod.

Seven days crossed off the calendar in Sarah's head. She knew the daily routine now; it was predictable, and she found the predictability strangely soothing. Today, however, the routine had changed. John had to evaluate a new patient, and canceled their morning session. It left Sarah restless, with nothing to do.

She curled in a fat stuffed chair in her living unit, writing a letter to Vladimir, a beat-up compad on her lap. Patients on the units weren't allowed near the commlinks. Once written, a nurse or aide would feed the letter into the mail system, and Vlad would receive it at home. Sarah missed him terribly, so much sometimes it made her stomach hurt.

*Дорогой Владимир,*
    *How's everything? I feel better, I guess. I hope David's being nice to you while I'm here.*

She sucked on the end of the computer stylus, thinking. How to describe where she was without making him sad... She decided to write about the mice in the Rec Therapy room. Vladimir loved animals, and loved stories about them almost as much. She wrote to him in Russian, even though he couldn't read it well – it wasn't taught on Navara, and he'd had only two years of schooling in Russia – but this way no one on the floor could read it, either. Sergei would help him if he got stuck.

Another patient snatched Sarah's compad from her lap. "Whatcha got here? Who ya writin'?"

"May I have that back, please?" Sarah said.

Llewella walked away, squinting at the screen. "What kind of funny scribblin' is this? I can't read a thing here."

"Llewella, give her back her 'pad," an aide said, taking the letter and returning it to Sarah. "It's not your business. Go back to what you were doing."

Llewella left, but snuck back a minute later. She leaned over the back of Sarah's chair, lisping in baby talk. "Writin' home to Daddy and Mummy? Are you a little daddy's girl, hmm? Do you miss your daddy?"

Sarah's eyes burned with suppressed fire, but she clenched her jaw and waited for the taunting to stop. She missed her father like she'd miss a brain tumor. Llewella played with contraband substances. One overdose too many, and she'd lost some important brain cells.

Llewella saw the slight reaction. "Miss your daddy, honey? Or is that why you hang out with your therapist so much?" She turned her back to Sarah and broke out in laughter.

The compad fell to the floor with a rattle. Sarah stood on the chair and jumped onto the woman's back. She hung on with her knees, arm around the woman's throat, pounding Llewella in the head with her fist, stabbing at her with the dull computer stylus.

Several patients screamed, and staff came running. Llewella whirled around the lounge area, shrieking. Sarah tried gouging her ragged remains of fingernails across the woman's face, then hammered the edge of her hand into the side of the hysterical woman's neck.

Hands pulled at her now, but she clamped down with her teeth. They couldn't pull her off without hurting the woman, couldn't stun one without the other. Llewella fell to her knees, and Sarah saw what she hadn't thought to consider – an airhypo at ten o'clock.

"Don't you *ever* talk about my father! Ever!" She tried to scuttle out of the fray, but found herself grabbed first by an ankle, then by a leg, then several other staff gained a grip.

"Wait a minute!" one of the nurses realized. "Aren't her orders for *no* sedatives?"

"Then you better get a damned good grip on her!" the first nurse snapped.

Six people carried Sarah to her room and put her in restraints.

Sarah fought madly, shouting explicit Russian epithets through lunch time. At one o'clock, a familiar figure appeared.

John Carver leaned against the wall by the door. "Well, well. I heard you missed me. I'd like to take you out of here, but I don't think I can get that bed through the door."

Sarah stopped straining; the rest was welcome.

Carver released the restraints, one by one. "How about some water?" Sarah nodded. He filled her cup at the small lavatory sink and helped her sit up.

He signaled to the person at the door to release the energy field. "Can you walk with me, or should I bring an aide?"

"I can walk," Sarah grumbled.

John walked briskly. He didn't hold onto her like the aide, just glanced back every now and then to make sure she was still there. Sarah had to jog to keep up.

She didn't know whether to be aggravated or anxious, especially when they walked past the hall for the rec room. "The turn's right here …"

"I know. Come on."

Sarah stopped walking. "Where are we going?"

Carver stopped. "I'm trusting you to keep control and stay with me. You trust me, don't you? Have I ever done anything to upset you?"

Sarah thought, then shook her head. "No." That didn't mean he wouldn't, though.

"Then, come on." He resumed his pace.

He stopped before a new door, and they entered. Mind braced for all sorts of deceptive tricks and painful retaliations, Sarah was puzzled by his choice of locations. John Carver had brought her to a large gymnasium. Shock-absorbing flooring and padded mats covered much of the visible space. Three stories of balconies rose above the immense central floor, each level holding a dozen plastiglass-walled rooms and more equipment. A racetrack circled the main floor, three hundred meters around, ringing a host of gymnastics equipment. Weight stations lined the walls in small clusters. In the back, under the balconies, several pairs of people worked with sparring sticks. Sarah stared in awe.

Carver stretched his legs at a nearby bench. "Come on. We'll go for a run." He found space on the track. Sarah followed.

He paced himself to the girl's slower speed. Sarah jogged half-heartedly for a portion of a lap. "I don't like this," she panted, dropping to the ground. "I'm running in some of my nightmares. It makes them real."

"Okay, fair enough. Let's go upstairs."

They caught a lift up two floors, to a long room covered in mats.

"You studied martial arts, didn't you?" He'd been in constant contact with the girl's family, learning the details of her life Sarah had yet to tell him.

Sarah hooked her hair behind her ears and nodded. "I have a green belt in traditional karate, and a first-level badge at Navaran So-tau-kam."

John took off his shoes. "Any good?"

"Depends on the opponent. I dropped my brother David twice."

"I'm no black belt, but I know a little jujitsu. Let's see how far we get, mixing it together."

Butterflies flapped in Sarah's stomach. Any other day, she would have enjoyed the physical challenge, exploring the gym and playing with the equipment, but the last time she'd created a disturbance, she'd been drugged and shipped up to High-Security. Why bring her here this time?

Carver bowed, and she gave the slightest bow in return. "Aren't you going to yell at me?"

"For what?" He spaced himself away from her, measuring the distance with his arm.

Sarah positioned herself defensively. "You know. For what I did this morning."

"No. Am I supposed to? You did what you did. I'm not your father."

Sarah's face darkened. "What's that supposed to mean?" She slapped away the move coming at her, and let an angry leg reply.

"You have some unresolved issues with your father," he said, dodging the weak kick. "A green belt can do better than that! I don't think you're trying very hard. Get your leg up higher, and straighten your knee. You look for control in situations because you had no control over your father. He was violent and unpredictable, and you hated him for that."

"Children don't hate their parents." Sarah gave two better, hard kicks that would have hurt if they'd connected.

"Some do. Your father was a brutal man. You have every right to hate him."

"He could be nice if we were good. He brought us gifts, took us places, taught us things. Ow!" She misjudged timing and hit her wrist on his arm. "I don't want to talk about that."

"But I do," John goaded. "You hate your father, and you hate your mother for leaving you to deal with him all alone. Come on! Your blocks are sloppy. I could have hit you. You're not concentrating."

Sarah threw an impulsive jab toward Carver's ribs. "Shut up! You don't know either of my parents! You have no business talking about them like that!" She rounded a vicious kick, but he caught her foot in his hand and pushed it down.

Sarah stared at him with growing ire. No one at home could stop her kicks! The fact that this starbase-bound baby-sitter could catch her made her all the more furious.

"It's not a secret, Sarah. I've talked with your sisters. I know some of the things that went on. You still live in fear of him right now. He haunts you in your dreams, doesn't he? Am I right? Be honest with yourself." Carver's voice grew angrier as well. "If he were here right now, would you tell him 'I love you, Father,' or, 'I hate you, and I wish you would die.' Which one?"

"He's *not* here!" Her kick went so wild she fell on the mat with a thud. "He will never *be* here!"

*Would he? What weren't they telling her?* She jumped up, unnerved.

Carver's careful thrust made light contact with her shoulder. "Which one, Sarah?"

"Shut up! Just shut up!"

"Answer me!" he demanded, pushing her shoulder more forcefully. "I thought you said you knew karate? Your kicks are weak and your defense is lousy. I could have hit you a dozen times now. Which is it,

Sarah? Would you tell him you love him, or hate his living guts? *Answer!*"

"*Stop it! Stop it! Shut up!*" She sprang and landed a forceful, two-footed kick to his middle, knocking him down. "*Die! Die!* I wished he would die!" Kneeling, she began punching Carver as he tried to rise.

"*I hate you!* I hate you! I hate you! I hate *him,*" she sobbed. She let herself slide face-down into the mat. "I hate him."

"I know," Carver said with sympathy. He sat next to her on the mat, his calm self once more. "You just had to admit that to yourself. There's no law that says you have to love someone, especially if they're mean to you.

"Once you realize that's okay, you'll be a lot more comfortable with yourself, and you won't go getting into battles like you did this morning. You don't have to defend your father. He made an adult decision to do the things he did. Llewella didn't know you have a father. She really meant nothing personal. You took it that way because you were angry with *him*. Do you understand that?" He pushed loose hair off the teary face.

Sarah stared at the comforting blankness of the dark mat under her. "I think so. I want to. But I'm still not going to apologize! She's a... a pain in my ass!"

*So's a cactus,* David would have replied.

Carver raked his hair with his fingers and chuckled. "Sarah, Sarah, Sarah! Let me tell you another secret of the universe." He sat her up next to him and hung an arm around her shoulders.

"Nobody is going to physically punish you for what you say or do here. You curse, you act rudely, you refuse to apologize – that's *your choice*. They're not the nicest things you can do, but it's your choice to do them. You swear and then cringe, waiting for a physical reaction. It's not going to happen, so you can stop trying to antagonize people. You are safe here. It's a very safe place."

Sarah stared dully at her socks. "I didn't know I was doing that. I guess I thought I was just being brave."

"Sure. To you it is bravery. Did you ever get mad at your father? Stand up to him?"

She sniffed and ran her sleeve under her nose. "Sometimes."

"Were you afraid?"

Sarah nodded.

"What did you do?"

"Mostly nothing. Sometimes I yelled back. Once I hit him."

"It took bravery to do that," Carver admitted. "And what happened?"

"Usually I won. Once... Once he beat me within a breath of my life," she dared admit.

"That's what happened to your back?"

Sarah's cheeks burned red. She knew the whip scars were there, even if she couldn't see them, but it wasn't a subject open for discussion. It was one of several family subjects spoken of only through heavy conversational pauses, a knowing glance, or perhaps a '*you* know....' Everyone had at least one 'unmentionable.'

She stared into space for several seconds before nodding very slowly.

"You must be mad about that?"

Sarah gave the same extra-slow nod. Madder than she could explain, but not for the reason he thought.

"My point is," Carver said, "when you're angry like that, like you were this morning, have your staff bring you down here. Run, kick, box, lift weights, whatever you like. Take it out down here, not on the other patients. Remember, they have troubles, too. That's why they're here. You feel better? Look up at me."

Sarah couldn't force herself to look higher than his chin.

"Yeah."

# * Eight *

After six weeks, Sarah enjoyed the Rec Therapy room, practicing piano, playing games, and even attempting school work. Concentration was still an issue, but if she could catch up, she would still get her Basic Education Diploma next spring. Stubborn determination proved a powerful match for her dampened abilities. Carver helped, skimming her lessons and quizzing her on the information.

"I have a surprise for you," John told her one afternoon as he sat at his computer. "You're having visitors tomorrow."

Sarah's head snapped up from the textreader before her. "Visitors? Who?"

"Your family."

*"My family!"* Sarah stood up so fast her chair fell over. She flew to his desk. "Here? For real? To see me? All of them? Please say it's not a joke! Is Vlad coming?"

Carver laughed at her very natural – and very normal – reaction. "I don't know. At least two. How do you feel about that?"

The first real smile in longer than she could remember lit Sarah's face. "Excited!"

The page to Rec Room 17 arrived just after lunch. The aide tried to keep the girl to a jog, but found herself being dragged along. The door slid open, and Sarah threw herself into Valeria, screaming for joy. Val scooped her up with almost as much energy. Sarah was passed around without ever touching the ground. First Valeria, then to Katya, then David, at last Dmitri. They stood together as a cluster before squeezing together on Sarah's favorite sofa. Sarah sat in Val's lap with her legs across Katya.

"Where's Vlad!" she demanded, tapping a fist on Valeria's shoulder. "Why didn't you bring him?"

Valeria hugged her again. "I couldn't. He and Sergei are too young. He wanted to come, though. He misses you so much. Lean back, Sarah; let me look at you. You've gotten bigger!""

"I eat chocolate pudding every day," Sarah whispered. "Sometimes twice!"

Katya tugged her sister's hair playfully. "You've still got my hairclip."

"It's the only one I've got."

"You need your hair cut," Valeria said, pushing Sarah's too-long bangs out of her eyes.

"Will you do it for me?"

"Of course."

Sarah went down the line again, hugging and kissing.

David grinned, scrubbing his face. "Cut it out! You're not like you at all."

Sarah balanced on Dmitri's knees. "I'm just so excited! How long are you staying?"

"Just till tomorrow," Valeria said. "We're staying here tonight."

"They have a suite on the visitor's floor," Carver told Sarah. "Would you like to stay with them?"

"Could I?! Really?!"

"As long as you're back before morning meds," he promised. "I can take care of the paperwork."

"That would be wonderful," Katya said. "I miss you at night, Sarah. I'm all by myself in that room now. It's scary, being alone."

"Sarah, why don't you take your family on a tour?" Carver suggested. "You know where you're allowed to be. Let me talk with Valeria alone for a while."

Sarah bored her gaze into the therapist's eyes, looking for a trap. *To be loose without a transport aide?* Then she winked. Valeria was grown up *and* she was pretty, all polished for the trip.

"Gotcha," she grinned. She pulled at David's arm. "Come on! You've *got* to see the gymnasium!"

"I can't believe that's her," Valeria said when the others left. "She's so – different!"

Carver moved to a closer chair. "How so?"

Val struggled to say what she meant. "She's – *vibrant*, I guess. Sarah's always so quiet, so reserved, so proper. Always watching. Always thinking. Even when playing with the boys. She's the scout of the group, sometimes the mastermind. That's – a totally new Sarah."

"To tell the truth, today's the first I've seen it, myself. Like you said, she's usually very quiet and observant. The medication may be part of it, but mostly I think she's just happy to see you," John explained. "It's not easy for her. She's used to having a lot of people around who support her. I think she's lonely, afraid she'll be forgotten."

"Forgotten? How?" Valeria exclaimed. "All anyone has to do is look at Vlad to know who's missing."

"There're a lot of other children at home without her. It's not far-fetched for her to worry you might resent her returning home. Any institutionalized child fears abandonment."

"Poor kid. How's she doing, really?"

"Honestly? She's made considerable progress, but she's not there yet. She can still be non-compliant, she still has trouble sleeping, though she insists the nightmares have stopped. She's opened up some as to what bothers her, but there are still many things she refuses to discuss. I hoped you might be able to shed light on some of those for me."

"I can try," Valeria said, "but Katya and the boys may be the ones to ask; they spend more time with her than I do. Will she ever be normal again?"

"Sure she will. It will take some time, but she'll get there. Keep her out of the Navaran schools. They give her an excuse to keep everything in," said Carver. "I think she'll do fine tonight, but don't be afraid to use the pager if you have any concerns."

\* \* \*

The visitor's suites were essentially hotel rooms, places where family could stay while patients were being evaluated, treated, or processed. It was a place where families could reintegrate, or a place for clients to regain independence prior to release. Help could be called at the touch of a button, and staff could be paged to answer questions. A weekend pass to the suites was the highest patient privilege, and Sarah had one.

Sarah was soaked, scoured, scrubbed, and shampooed. Katya rubbed her down with perfumed lotions, then Valeria trimmed her hair.

"Look at your nails, Sarah!" Katya cried. "I would have painted them for you, but you've eaten them!"

Sarah looked at her hands. Her nails could not be chewed shorter. The skin at the corners was cracked and peeled where she'd picked at them. Katya's nails were perfectly shaped and smooth, and colored to match her clothing.

"How about my toes?" Sarah offered, wiggling them.

"What color?"

"Mmm, green, maybe? Or how about purple?"

Katya dug in a travel bag. "I'll see what I have. How about glow in the dark pink?"

Sarah wrinkled her nose. "That's a girly color."

Katya held up a sparkling pen. "Here we go! Iridescent opal. Makes a four-color prism every time you move."

"Stellar!"

"Val, if you do her feet, I'll do her hair."

Valeria took the pen, while Katya combed Sarah's hair.

"So what do you think?" Sarah asked.

Val dabbed silvery enamel at a squirming toe. "Of what? Hold still."

"John Carver. Do you think he's nice?" Sarah tried to hold her feet still and see the progress at the same time. She liked hearing her sisters' opinions on things. Someday, when she was old enough to think about boys, she'd have to know what to look for. She'd already decided any future romantic prospects would have to be stronger than herself. She didn't think she could respect a man who wasn't at least her equal at wrestling and spitting. Her brothers certainly wouldn't.

"I think he's *dreamy!*" Kat whispered in her ear.

"He's got to be around your age, Val," Sarah reasoned. "He's nice, he's smart, he has a good job. You should have dinner with him to discuss my leaving, and you could tell him all about you..."

"Stop it, Sarah," Valeria said. "I'm not about to date your medical staff. He's a lot older than me."

Sarah prattled on, planning in her head. "No, he's not. You could marry him, or he could just live with us. Then..." She didn't see the slap coming, but it stung her face just the same.

Katya stared in horror. *"Valeria!* What'd you do that for!" She wrapped her arms around Sarah.

Val waved the polish applicator angrily. "You listen to me, Sarah Irina! I'm not marrying your therapist! Don't even talk to him about me! I have to deal with him professionally. I have to be able to listen to him objectively so I can make decisions about you! I can't do that if you're spreading false ideas so I'm mooning over him. Understand?"

Sarah nodded, daydreams vaporized. "If you did, he could fix my head at home instead of here."

"You'll be home soon enough," Val assured her. "And yes, he is kind of cute."

"That's all you girls think about," Dmitri drawled, lying on the far bed.

Sarah inspected her finished toenails as Katya cemented the braid in place with hair lacquer. "Yeah, right. And which of us was rating every female staff we saw today?" A pillow bounced off her head in reply. She threw it back, grinning.

"What's there to do here?" David asked, bored, bored, and bored. The three-room suite contained only a small desk viewer, not a massive holovision.

"There's a special event almost every night. I think tonight's a dance recital," Sarah said. "The patients perform something on the weekends."

"Boring!"

"You didn't take the dance class?" Valeria asked.

"I tried the ballet a couple of times," Sarah said, "but they don't know what they're doing."

"That's because you're Russian," Katya told her. "It's in your blood. Not everyone is so lucky."

\* \* \*

The dance program was broken up with men's strength and gymnastics exhibitions, sparing teen boys from death by boredom. Doctors were required to attend to show support for their patients, and associates were strongly urged. The auditorium on deck 32 hummed with people.

John Carver couldn't escape duty, either. He sat in the back row, where staff were visible but didn't have to pay attention.

"Hey, John," said a doctor, taking the next seat.

"Hey, Raj. How'd your crisis go?"

"He was faking it. Wasted my time. Isn't that your kid down there?" He pointed to the last row of the first section, where Sarah knelt backwards on the seat, chattering to the boys.

"Mmm, yeah. She's on visitation."

"She looks great. I'd heard she was having a rough time. You seem to reach her better than Liesel did."

Carver gave a short laugh. "She's a tough cookie, that one. All depends. The mother's recently deceased, father's in lock-up pending trial for the murder of another daughter, and the twenty-three-year-old twin sisters are trying to raise the younger eight children."

Raj whistled. "Eight? You're kidding! Colonists?"

"No, just prolific. And there's two more who don't live at home."

"They good with her?"

"Mm. Very close. Almost too close. They've been parenting themselves for too many years, I think."

"You going to approve discharge?"

Carver shifted uncomfortably. "I don't know. Her release comes just a couple of weeks before the father's trial. If he's found guilty, he'll be gone at least ten years, long enough for her to grow up in peace. If he's found innocent, I'd be dropping her back into the Hell that put her here. I'd have to recommend against release, which will destroy her faith in me, and destroy her family as well."

"Tough call. Even with Child Advocacy involved, you'll have to fight to remove her."

Carver nodded. "And she's still going to need at least a year of outpatient. Try and find *that* on Navara. There's an awful lot of anger and suppressed violence throughout the family – a lot of dysfunctional stuff going on. Watch." He gestured toward the group many rows below.

Sarah sat in the middle of the line, talking animatedly across Dmitri to David, her long blonde hair braided and tied with a colorful bow. Although she could choose from several styles of patient clothing and a wide variety of colors, she never wore anything but a simple, loose two-piece white outfit – white had nothing to hide, she claimed. She burst out laughing at David's reply, and the two started a slap-fest in jest. Dmitri play-slapped both of them on the head. David punched him on the arm, while Sarah dug her fingers into Dimi's side, tickling. Valeria leaned across Katya and waved a finger at Dmitri, a no-nonsense look on her face. The trio settled down, repentant. Dmitri looked around, leaned back stretching, laced his fingers behind his head, and managed to whack both Sarah and David in the head with his elbows as he leaned forward again. This set off a giggling shoving match.

Exasperated, Valeria stood up and made Dmitri switch places with her. Mercifully, the lights dimmed, ending the intermission.

"I see what you mean," Raj nodded. "And that's only three."

Carver shook his head as someone entered the stage. "I just don't know."

\* \* \*

Sarah slept well, squished between sisters. How she missed the warmth and comfort of another person in the dark loneliness of night! Nurses just chased you back to bed, and wrote notes in the night log. She awoke early as usual and lay quiet in contentment.

Dmitri dressed first, so he walked Sarah back to her section for her medication, his flashing visitor pass displayed clearly on his shirt. The staring women on the ward unnerved him, and he stayed close to Sarah. She whispered in Russian, explaining each patient to him. The nurse handed her three pills, a cup of water, and made her open her mouth to show they went down. The two walked back to the guest floor.

"*Yilkh!*" Sarah coughed when they were part way down the hall. She dug a finger in her mouth. "You got a pocket?" She looked Dmitri over and stuffed her hand in the front pocket of his pants.

"What are you – *Sarah!* These are your pills!" Dimi dropped his surprise to a whisper. "You're supposed to take these!"

"I hate them! They taste gruesome, they sit like nitric acid in my stomach, and they make me feel funny. I haven't taken them for ages and I'm fine, aren't I?"

He remembered how she'd been at the first hospital. "I guess so."

Sarah patted his pocket. "Just don't throw them out here,"

"Come on, Sar. You promised John you wouldn't do this." Valeria pried the locked fingers from around her waist as she stood at the boarding hatch for their ship home. The aide had Sarah by the middle, waiting for the hands to be freed. The others had already boarded.

Valeria broke the desperate grip and backed out of range. "Six more weeks and you'll be home for good. Work hard! Remember, we love you!" She forced a smile and a wave as the airlock shut. The betrayal in Sarah's face hurt worse than when Val signed her in there.

Sarah sank to the floor, immobile.

The aide pulled at her. "Come on. Let's go back."

The nurse made the call in late afternoon.

"Dr. Carver? I hate to disturb you, but I wanted to check with you on Miss Kirushenko. She's been crying heavily for about five hours now. We can't get her up, and she refuses to eat or drink."

Carver rubbed a finger across his forehead and sighed. "I was afraid of that. Keep an eye on her. As long as she's not self-injurious. If she hasn't stopped by ten or so, I'll order a sedative."

"Thank you, doctor." The nurse signed off.

Sarah wore herself out a little after nine. Her heart had bled for eight hours, so morbidly homesick she couldn't bear it. All that was left was a shell so heavy it pinned her to the bed, and she sobbed herself into a peaceless sleep.

When morning arrived, Sarah's body had turned to lead, her eyes scratchy like a sand storm. To form and hold the simplest thought took more effort than she could give. Only her heart seemed to feel, crushed by emptiness for the joy that had gone. She curled herself up in her preferred chair and spat her morning pills invisibly into her hand, waiting with endless resignation for the long day to finish, for time to bring her one day closer to home. She could wait.

*"Code One, Emergency. Code One, Emergency,"* the computer repeated throughout the hospital. *"Doctor Carver to section 23W, Code One."*

John Carver blew into the women's section at full speed, afraid of what he might find. He had just one patient in 23W. *Had he underestimated Sarah's downswing? Or her self-destructiveness?* Nurses, staff, and patients crowded around the girl's motionless body. The crowd parted to let him through.

"Status?" he panted.

"Two full seizures, three minutes apart," Maura explained rapidly. "First one, a minute and a half, second, four minutes, incontinent and cyanotic on the second."

"Medikit." The nurse had it already in hand. "Sarah, what are you doing to me?"

"There she goes again!" someone observed as the girl's arms and legs stiffened. Her body bent, then began to shake and jerk mercilessly, eyes dull behind fluttering lids, spit bubbling from her trembling lips. Her breath gurgled and choked until her face and lips took on a bluish tinge.

"Narcostat, thirty milligrams," Carver ordered. A nurse laid a hypospray in his hand. The girl's body relaxed and breathed normally as the medication hissed into her system, ending the spasms.

"What started it?"

"She was sitting in the chair, not doing anything," explained the frightened aide. "She just fell over and hit the floor shaking."

Carver chose a sterile vial from the medikit and clipped it into the aeroderm. A quick adjustment and he pressed it against the inside of Sarah's forearm, withdrawing a blood sample.

"Run this," he said, handing the tiny vial to the nurse. "Give me a tox screen, med levels, electrolytes, and a Neuro-Four eval."

"Three minutes," the nurse called from the biocomp behind the nurse's enclosure.

"Let's get a cart over here," Carver directed. "We'll move her down to the infirmary. Talk to me, Baby." He looked down with worry, wiping spit tenderly from her face. Any reaction to the medications would have happened weeks ago. Two aides brought an anti-grav stretcher, and they moved the girl onto it.

A nurse handed a readout to Carver.

He frowned, whistling. "Did she get her medication this morning?"

"I gave it to her myself," the head nurse said.

"Impossible. Her levels are too low – going by this she hasn't been medicated in days. Electrolytes are completely off. The Neuro's – Do you check to make sure she takes them?"

"Absolutely!" Maura insisted. "I make her open her mouth, and there's never anything there. She's been very cooperative about that."

Sarah's aide held out her hand. "Are these familiar?" In her palm lay eight sticky, lint-covered pills; three day's worth. "They were in the cushions of the chair."

"Those would be them," Carver said grimly. "Dammit, Maura! You have to do more than just look! She could hide them in her cheeks. Check her room, and anywhere else she might go right after meds. I don't want someone getting hold of a stash."

"I'm sorry, Doctor," the nurse apologized, shaken. "I didn't realize...."

"Of course you didn't. It's been going on for at least three days, and I didn't catch it, either," Carver admitted. "I suppose we should be thankful she didn't horde them and take them all at once. Let's get her out of here."

Sarah slept, all that day and part of the next. Intravenous fluids rehydrated her ravaged body, computer-guided titration reestablished therapeutic levels of medication and balanced out her body chemistry. The last lines were removed just before noon. Not long after, she blinked and opened her eyes.

"Well hello there, Sleeping Beauty!" said an unfamiliar nurse. "It's about time you woke up."

Sarah looked around in confusion. This wasn't her bed. It wasn't her room, or even the inertia dampening room. Six beds with continuous bioscanners stuck out from the walls. All were vacant save one at the far end.

"Where am I?" she asked softly, afraid she'd switched hospitals again without knowing it.

"You're in the infirmary on deck 30. You gave everyone quite a scare."

"What happened?"

"Dr. Saluria left orders for me to call John Carver, and let him discuss that with you. Are you hungry? I can get you something to eat," the nurse offered, pressing various buttons to record the current numbers from the biobed display. "Anything you like."

"Chocolate pudding?"

The nurse laughed. "I think I can find some of that. I'll be right back."

An hour later Sarah had nibbled at the pudding, and lay resting on the bed. She felt weak, but not very sleepy.

"Hey, my troublemaker's awake!" John greeted her upon entering the room. "I see you're feeling well enough to eat some pudding." He stopped, staring at the fiery colors flickering from Sarah's bare feet. It came from her toenails.

"Your sisters do that?" he asked in amazement.

Sarah wiggled her toes to intensify the effect. "Yeah. Iridescent Opal."

"That's very… eye-catching." Carver gave a last glance, then tapped a finger on Sarah's arm. "But you are still in very big trouble. Doctor Saluria is not happy with you."

"What did *I* do?"

"Do you remember?"

Sarah scrunched her forehead. "I was sleepy. I didn't want breakfast." She shook her head. "That's all."

"That's normal enough. You suffered a couple of seizures," Carver told her. "Your brain tried to short-circuit."

Sarah's eyes went wide, and she sat up fast. "Seizures! Don't they come from brain damage?" She was going to be crazy for ever and ever, and *never* finish school!

"They can, but not in your case," Carver said. He leaned against the bed and crossed his arms. "How long did you do it? How many days?"

"Do what?" Sarah looked the picture of innocence, with her big purple-blue eyes and her pale hair swirling uncombed around her face. Carver's look of disapproval made her uneasy.

He sighed. "It was a nice try, but you didn't have all the facts. You can't stop Antivox cold turkey. It works at the synaptic level. Withdraw it too fast and you screw up the neurotransmitters, resulting in seizures."

"Oh." *That.*

"Why?"

Sarah picked at her fingers. "Pills choke me. They tasted nasty, and one of them was burning a hole in my stomach."

Carver nodded. "Elavixor can do that to some people. If you'd told someone, it could have been taken care of. The pharmacy can coat pills to any flavor you wish. The Elavixor can be buffered. What else?"

Sarah chewed a nail, stalling.

"What else, Sarah?"

"Because." She tore a fresh hangnail, heart rate escalating at the single drop of blood that accompanied its release. She sucked the finger, keeping the blood inside her where it belonged. "I felt really good and I... I thought... If I didn't have to take the medication, I could go home sooner."

"I don't have to tell you how stupid you were. I think you found out for yourself. How'd you do it? Are you one of those people that can bring back things they've swallowed?"

"I hid them under my tongue. No one looked."

"I don't know what to say. You've broken a lot of people's trust," Carver said. "It's back to injections, and unless you're on the pills, the doctors won't let you go home. It's your choice. I'll get you sent back to your room. Think about things today. We'll meet tomorrow."

Sarah had an entire day to do nothing but mope, aching at her loss and furious over John's refusal to take her side against the doctors and their horrid tablets of chemical slavery. *A hostage,* she realized as she lay on her bed, kicking her pillow. *They've got me by the dendrites. I'm nothing but a neurologic hostage, kept here through neurochemical dependency.*

She entered the therapy room the following day and sprawled on the couch, a sour expression on her face. She tapped the arm with her feet.

Carver spread an activity across the table. "Why don't you come over and see what I've got."

"I don't want to."

"Okay. What do you want to do?"

"Nothing. I'm tired of the game."

He sat at the table. "Which game?"

"This game." She walked to the piano. "The game where if I behave and be a good girl, I'll get to do what everyone else wants me to do." She pounded loud minor scales across the keys, preventing further conversation.

Carver waited out the concert. Her aide no longer waited for the session to be over. Time was theirs, and he ran the sessions until they felt finished. "And what is it you want that no one will let you do?"

Sarah spun around, eyes narrowed. *"You know what I want!"* She banged a few more chords.

"Ohhh, I understand now." Carver fought hard not to laugh. He waited for the piano to stop. "So you're angry because your brothers and sisters left, and you couldn't go with them. And, let's see, you're angry because you're stuck here for twelve weeks whether you want to be or not. You're angry because you thought you could speed up some of the process, but you failed."

"I never fail!" Sarah shot back. "I simply did not know enough of the facts."

Carver couldn't help laughing this time. "So who are you angry with, Sarah? Me? You? Valeria? Your father? Who?"

Sarah rose and walked to the farthest corner, examining a shelf of materials. "Just shut up! You talk too much for someone with nothing to say. I'm not talking to you anymore."

"That's too easy a challenge."

She poked through a box of seashells she found, fingering the tiny ridges. She could still remember oceans and beaches on Earth, so long ago. These were too clean; there was no sea-scent left to them. "Fine. I'm not talking to you *today*."

"Good. While you're quiet, come over to the table."

Sarah put the box away and shuffled over, taking time to touch just about everything within her reach on the way. She plopped down in a chair and tried to look extremely bored.

"What's this?" she said, forgetting her vow.

"Finger paint."

"Finger paint! Go away! That's for babies. I've studied Allovsky and Renoir and Dar San of Taurus, and people like that. Show me oils or watercolors or clays or something. How about a nice Grecian fresco?"

"No, not just for babies," John coaxed, pouring paint. "Come on, I'll do it too. Pick a color."

Sarah hesitated.

"Haven't you ever done this?" he asked, drawing his finger through a glob of green. He spread it around, wrote his name in it, then swirled the paint and tried something else.

Sarah shook her head. Red was by far the closest color to her. She stretched past it and chose blue.

Carver dropped several lumps of spearmint-scented paint before her. "I thought every kid finger-painted. Stick your fingers in and see what you can come up with."

*What a stupid, dumb, messy idea!* Sarah pulled a finger through the rubbery slickness. She'd grown rather squeamish about textures, ever since mother's bl...

"I don't like this!" She stood up fast and held her hands out as if they were contaminated. "Get it off!"

"One second. Try this." He sprinkled art sand over the paint. "It will give you a little more texture."

Sarah balanced on the edge of her seat and dragged a reluctant finger through the grit. "Better, but I still don't like it." Now it felt like blood with sand in it, just like the kitchen floor. She made a few short lines on the plastic.

"Done!" she announced, standing up. She lunged across the table for a stack of hand wipes, brushing her arm over Carver's. As she pulled back, she noticed a blue splotch on his sleeve.

In the blink of an eye, Sarah jumped back more than a meter, slamming her chair into the table behind them. "I'm sorry! I'm sorry!" she shouted. Her hands were still slimy with paint.

Carver didn't move. He looked at his arm without turning his head. Two blue dots decorated the elbow of his plum-colored shirtsleeve. "No problem, Sar. It comes off with water. No harm done."

"I'm sorry!"

"Watch." He walked slowly to the room's sink. With a damp wipe, it took less than half a minute to remove the marks.

"See? It comes right off. No damage. Come wash your hands." He backed up behind his desk, giving her wide, safe access to the sink. Sarah stumbled the short distance to the counter, scrubbing her hands for several minutes.

"Sar, when was your last neuro scan?"

"I don't know."

"I think I'm going to ask Dr. Saluria to order bloodwork and a progress neuroscan. I'm a little concerned with your reaction here. What do you think?"

"Whatever."

Carver crossed his arms in aggravation the next morning. "I hope this is just a phase, Sar. Your bloodwork was fine."

"I told you it would be," Sarah interrupted. "I didn't lie. I get my meds every morning."

"I didn't doubt that. I wondered if they shouldn't up the dosage. Tell me about the brain scan."

"I didn't have one."

"I know that. Why?"

Sarah looked over her shoulder as if the answer lay there. "They didn't do it."

Carver sighed. He leaned over the table and slapped a printout before her.

"Here's the report. Have you read it? Maybe I should read it to you. These words don't generally apply to the Sarah I've been working with:

'Extremely uncooperative. Impossible to perform scan. Patient refused to acknowledge ability to speak common language. Patient made frequent use of obscene threats – ' Shall I continue? I'd like an explanation."

"They exaggerate."

"You're not answering my question."

"Do you know what they've done to me!" Sarah shouted. She stood and stared at Carver, nose to nose. "They took away my pudding! They said I've gained three and a half kilos in seven weeks! Now I have to eat low-calorie pudding substitute. Do you know what that tastes like? It isn't enough that I don't taste most foods as it is? They took away one of the few foods I can!"

"That may be a legitimate complaint, but you're still not answering my question."

"Arrgh!" Sarah stomped over to her sofa. She threw herself down, hands gesticulating words her mouth couldn't seem to find. Finally, she let her hands drop. Her forehead rested against her wrists in silent defeat.

"All right, maybe I can't speed up my leaving this place. Maybe being nasty to people isn't as much fun as it should. But maybe I'm sick of living inside a box for two months, walking from 23 to 17, 17 to 23. Maybe I'd like to breathe real air, see grass and trees – not that we have those on Navara. I'd settle for walking on sand, as long as it was somewhere else. Did you ever see a Navaran sunset after a sandstorm? How the light reflects off the particles and intensifies the range and tone of the colors? It doubles the length of the sunset. Absolutely brilliant."

"Can this be honesty I hear, or are you still playing games?"

Sarah scratched at a shadow of dirt on the white knee of her pants. "Honesty, mostly, I guess. You leave the floors. The nurses leave the floors. Valeria left the floors. I'm tired of being caged."

"I take it no one's ever brought you to the gardens up on deck nine?"

Sarah lifted her head. "No. What gardens?"

"Six intensely cultivated hectares, four decks high in places. Jungle, forest, grassland, waterfalls, a half-hectare pond with a tiny beach. It's quite nice," he said, laying the bait. All deep-space facilities contained some sort of botanical gardens. They were expensive to design and implement, but it kept people from going crazy after extended periods in the artificial environment.

"For real?" She slid forward on the edge of the sofa. "Can we go there? Will you take me? Please?"

Carver rested a finger across his lips, lost in thought. "Tell you what. I don't like the way you've been trying to manipulate people all week Wherever you go, whatever you do in your life, there will still be rules.

115

You might not like them, you might not agree with them, but you *will* have to follow them.

"I'll make you a deal," he said, pointing his notepad stylus in her direction. "You think about everything for a couple of days, you get a scan done *without* giving anyone a hassle, stop abusing the staff, and I will talk to the dietician about the pudding thing. Do that, and we will spend a day – you and me, picnic and all – exploring the gardens. Take it or leave it."

Sarah knew when she was cornered. "I'll take it."

# * Nine *

Two days. For two endless days, Sarah didn't meet with Carver. Her aide took her to the gym for several hours, but she didn't do much of anything. It was just somewhere else to be. John had beaten her to the punch: no staff would bring her to the gardens, and she couldn't leave her unit by herself.

The adultness of the situation tormented her. It wasn't as if she were about to play with *toys*, not with her advanced mind, but at least loose toys could be rearranged to academic purposes – finger puppets could represent political figureheads and recite their famous speeches before the roaring crowds, dominoes could be stacked to mimic the ruins of ancient cities aching to be discovered, or magnets could be arranged to represent chemical formulas. All she had to do was *be*, to kill time and do as they told her. Nothing could have been harder.

Sarah shadowed the nurses, asking infinite detailed questions, most of which they weren't allowed to answer. She read through every drug advertisement and reference manual they found for her. She read through procedure manuals, and pointed out where the hospital didn't follow their own rules. The harried nurses and aides, not used to having her on the floor most of the day, tried to keep her out of the patient files. The limited-access patient computers contained mostly entertainment programs, and popular journals were boring. She tried to study, but her thoughts buzzed elsewhere. Sarah chafed, she squirmed, she twisted her hair into hopeless knots, but no one could deny she hadn't kept her promise to behave.

Today's session she could gloat to John, and tomorrow she would see something green! She couldn't wait for morning routine to be over. Brushing her hair wasted time; let it hang loose! *Trees!* She couldn't sit still enough to eat breakfast, and downed only some fruit juice. *A pond!* She couldn't see that at home! *Leaves!*

Time! Her regular aide had the day off; the substitute moved far too slow for Sarah's liking. *Flowers!* Compared to her, the woman moved in slow motion. Sarah wanted to race at a full run. *Mud! Remember mud? There had to be mud around the pond!*

They had almost reached the Rec Therapy room – Sarah could have seen it if it weren't for the corner of the lounge area they had to walk through – when the aide met a friend coming toward them with another patient, a man. After several impatient minutes of chitchat, Sarah moved off a few meters to play on a square of colored floor tiles, her long hair swinging with every hop.

The aides were *still* talking. Sarah gave up, squatting against the lounge wall while she waited. *In another minute,* she promised herself, *I'm going to the room myself, and to hell with her!*

Neither aide noticed the male patient wander her way. Sarah stood up, wary. Men were housed in a different area of the facility, but they shared the office floors. This one wasn't huge like Father, but lean and faded, with deep lines at the corners of his eyes. He came close, making the hair on Sarah's neck rise. Some of the patients here were *really* crazy, and you couldn't always tell at first glance. He glanced comically to each side and leaned down, as if about to tell a secret.

"Are you a kisser?"

"What?" Sarah coughed. His breath made her cringe, worse than Father's after he got sick from drinking.

He took another step, too close. Sarah took a step sideways.

"Are you a kisser?"

*Did he mean a noun or a verb? A face, or one who kisses?* Before she could shake her head, he lifted her off the floor under her arm and pinned her against the wall with his body. His festering mouth clamped over hers.

Fear flooded Sarah so coldly that time itself slowed and stretched. He squished her too hard for her to raise her knees to kick; pressed too close to let her flailing punches do damage. She opened her mouth to scream, only to gag when he stuffed his rancid tongue into her mouth. He crushed her into the wall until she began to wheeze.

With a new shock, she realized his free hand was burrowing under the stretchy fabric of the hospital pants like some malignant spider. She couldn't bend her arms enough to gouge his eyes; pulling his hair and ears had no effect. His knee was between hers, keeping her legs apart, forcing his way through unwilling flesh, brutal and rough. Sarah's smothered screams were clearly audible.

"Where's – Oh *Shit! No!*" cried her aide.

"Security!" The aides fell on the man with little effect. A choke hold released his grip as security ran up.

Sarah slid to the floor. It took five or six seconds of hyperventilating to catch some breath. Once she did, a scream formed somewhere around her feet and rolled its way upward until it reached her head. It burst forth so intense no fewer than five doctors and two aides came running from the adjoining hall, including the Chief of Psychiatry himself.

"What's going on?" Saluria demanded. "What's happened?"

Security held the man to the floor. He jabbered a string of insensible obscene chatter.

Carver was one of the five doctors. His patient stood alone against the wall, screaming blindly, her hands wrapped in her hair, pants halfway down her hips. Carver stepped over the man to get to her, but not before Sarah pulled her hands away, heavy wisps of hair still twisted around her fingers.

"Is that Robison?" Saluria barked. "What the hell was he doing unattended? Get him to lockup!" He pointed to the two aides. "I want both of you in my office, NOW!" He moved toward Carver.

"Sarah?" Carver said gently. "It's John, Sarah. I'm here. You're safe."

As if from a distance, Sarah knew someone was speaking, but she hadn't a clue as to who. The only thing real besides her pain and terror was the foul taste of Robison's breath, coating her mouth like a thick paste. She felt a growing wave swell in her stomach; she almost welcomed it. Her liquid breakfast purged itself, but the dry gagging that followed helped neither her mouth nor her morale. It did stop the screaming.

"Sarah, it's John," Carver tried again, kneeling to her level. "I'm here with you. You're safe with me. Will you take my hand?" He stretched his fingers within millimeters of hers.

Sarah didn't turn, but recognized the voice. Time had frozen, leaving her unable to move or see or think. She grabbed Carver's hand, gripping it until he winced.

"That's my girl. Come on. Other hand now. We'll go to the room, Sarah. You're safe in the room."

Saluria squatted next to him. "How is she?" he said in a whisper.

"Doesn't look good. What happened?"

"I'll find out before I fire two aides," Saluria promised.

"After you do, can you bring me five milligrams of Pentoprine? See if we can get her to relax just a little. Have Georgia meet me in 17."

"I'll do that." Saluria stood up. "Keep me posted."

Carver nodded. "One more hand, Sarah," he urged.

Sarah's vision was cloudy, but she thought she could make out John's face in the cold gray haze. She lunged for him, locking her arms around his neck without a sound.

Carver fought to stand with the added weight. Sarah might have been well-proportioned, but she wasn't a small child. He adjusted her clothing with his free hand. "Let's get you out of here."

Safety had been so close. In the room, Carver parked her on the cabinets near the sink. He rinsed his coffee cup with one hand, then filled it with water and offered it to her.

"Do you hurt anywhere?"

Sarah shook her head slightly, face locked in a look of absolute vacancy, an emptiness of her soul. He didn't need to know about the pain. She accepted the cup with one hand, but held him by the neck with the other. She rinsed her mouth and spat through two cups of water.

"Here, I've got something better." He hefted her back up, took a candy from a cabinet and handed it to her. "It's not chocolate pudding, but the peppermint's better for your stomach."

Sarah slipped it into her mouth and buried her face against his neck. Carver carried her to the couch, and there they sat, Sarah on his lap, until Saluria entered.

Sarah didn't move until she felt and heard the hissing of an aeroderm. She gave a short cry and glanced fearfully at the intruder. Saluria always reminded her of a growling silver bulldog; she trusted him about as much.

"Shh," Carver hushed. "It's not going to make you sleep. It's just a little something to help you stay calm."

"I am calm," she mumbled softly.

"More like in shock. When that wears off, you'll be glad you had the medication. Maybe we can keep it for a day or two."

Saluria nodded.

"Anything?" John asked over the top of Sarah's head.

Saluria nodded again. "When you have a minute."

The door slid open again and a petite woman entered, bubbling with energy. She, too, wore regular clothes, a soft tunic and flowing skirt.

"Hello, Georgia," Saluria said. "Thanks for coming on short notice. I'll leave you three alone." He returned to his office.

The woman took a seat before them. "I heard there was a bit of an incident."

Carver nodded. "I think this might need more of your expertise. I'm not exactly sure what happened, but I think it could be out of my league."

"Always glad to help. We'll work on it together. Who have we got here?"

Carver pried the arms from his neck. "Sarah, this is Georgia Jacobs, a friend of mine. Her specialty is Crisis Intervention." He omitted the word *sexual*. "I'd like you to talk with her for a little while."

Sarah seized fistfuls of his shirt. "No."

"I need to talk with Dr. Saluria. I will join you in one hour, that's a promise. I want you to cooperate for me." He pushed her off him. "You'll be safe with Georgia."

"I promise I won't bite," Dr. Jacobs said. "My office is just down the hall. We can come back here if you're not comfortable."

Sarah's eyes searched the woman for false intent. The unwanted medication dulled her sense of caution. The woman *seemed* honest enough, and John trusted her. "Even if I do nothing?" Everyone here always wanted you to *do* something.

"Even if you never say a word," promised Jacobs. "I might talk to you, though."

Sarah laid down her rules. "No drugs, no tricks, no games, no other people."

"Fair enough, if I can ask the same of you – no tricks, no games."

Sarah held out two fingers, and they shook on the deal.

"I'm more of a teacher, Sarah. I won't pester you with all the deep questions John does. Do you like learning?"

Carver spoke for her. "Sarah will graduate school next spring."

"You can't be old enough!" Jacobs exclaimed. "How old are you?"

Sarah leaned on Carver's chest, feeling as small as little Nikky. "Nine, but I forgot my birthday."

"Maybe you should be teaching me! Will you take my hand, Sarah? I'd at least like to start in my office. We can come back here later if you want."

"Go on," Carver urged. "I'll be along soon."

Sarah uncurled her fingers and allowed her hand to be grasped. "Thank you," Jacobs said. "We're going to room nine."

Sarah hoped it wasn't a trick. For the first time in her life, she was afraid to run.

* * *

"Come," Saluria said at the door page. "Ah! John! Come in. You got her to stay with Georgia? That's something in itself, I would think. If I recall, she's not quick to trust."

"She's not," Carver agreed, taking a chair before the desk. "Georgia's pretty easy-going. She should be able to handle her. I don't know what I'll do when the shock wears off. I was starting to think she might make it. Did you find out what happened?"

Saluria grimaced. He leaned back and scratched the hair behind his ear. "Unfortunately I did, and it doesn't look good from a legal standpoint. Computer, display records, Robison, J.N." An unflattering detainment photo appeared. Saluria rotated the desk's viewscreen.

"Jaroll Robison, age fifty-one. Admitted three days ago for evaluation of competency to stand trial in court. Currently facing forty-one counts of child molestation on Goldin's Colony."

"Forty one?"

"Forty one," Saluria said. "That's just the confirmed ones, mind you. And he just happened to be walking down the same hallway as Miss Kirushenko, the only child on the entire Starbase. According to the aides, they stopped to talk in the waiting area. The next thing they knew, he had her pinned against the wall and his hands under her clothing, second or third degree we won't know without the girl's testimony."

Carver's fist slammed the arm of the chair. "God damn them to Hell! Of all the people – hasn't that kid been through enough? It's taken me almost 300 hours to get her as far as she is! Daniel, there is no way I'll allow her to testify on this – you want information, you take it from the therapy records. I won't put her through that."

"Calm down. I agree with you, it's the worst we could do. Here's a bigger dilemma: legally, she has to be examined to rule out injury. She's also a minor, and we have to notify the family."

"No. Oh, no. First, she'd never allow it while conscious, and she's terrified of sedatives. She doesn't need that kind of stress on top of the incident. Nor would I tell the family. They're just kids themselves, Daniel! Any stigma could have massive repercussions when she returns home. Her father's in lockup himself; can't we just say it was impossible to notify guardian due to legal status?"

"We might be able to stall that way," Saluria considered. "It could buy a little time, at least. As to the exam, does she get an evening medication?"

"Mmhm. A five-milligram booster of Elavixor before bed. It seems to control recurrent nightmares."

"What if we add a short-acting anæsthetic cocktail – knock her out, do the exam right there in the room, use a hypnotic to make her forget anything she might possibly remember. Twenty minutes, start to finish. She'll wake up with no memory of it."

"I don't like it. It's exactly the kind of authoritarian abuse of power she's afraid of. Hypnotics don't always work. If she found out, it would destroy any trust of medical personnel forever. I'm sorry." Carver shook his head. "I can't allow my patient to be examined against her will, regardless of age."

"You realize that unless you gain her consent, you leave yourself open to legal action?"

"Yes. I'm willing to absolve the hospital of that responsibility."

"I hope you know what you're doing. John, given her extreme history, have you considered prior sexual abuse?"

Carver frowned. "There's nothing in the medical records. She's never mentioned it, nor has the family. There's no evidence of precocious behaviors, or other typical symptoms."

"Even a med student would consider that a poor answer, let alone a psychiatrist," Saluria reproved him. "What's the deepest family secret there generally is?"

* * *

"Are you set on that now?" Jacobs asked Sarah. "It's not going to be nearly as bad as you think. Don't believe everything your brothers tell you."

Sarah spoke softly to the table. It was easier than talking to the woman. "I think so. I just haven't been dealing very well with… "

The door opened, stopping her in mid-sentence, and she glanced up in fear.

Carver sat next to her. "You're still here. I'll take that as a good sign. How's everything going?"

Jacobs patted Sarah's hand. "We learned some much-needed answers to a few questions. She's even brighter than you told me."

"Good!" Carver shifted uneasily. "Sarah, there's no easy way for me to say this. Legally, I have to ask you some things … "

Sarah turned her face to the wall. "No." There was no other possible answer. Bad events only resulted in worse questions. She wasn't ever talking to Child Services again, no way, no how.

"It's not my choice, Sarah – "

*"NO!"*

Carver sighed. "Sarah, the man that … upset you… He's done that and worse to forty-one other children. You are now a witness, and could be called to testify in court. I don't want you to have to tell that story to a roomful of strangers. If you tell it here, the record's admissible by law, and that's the end of it."

Sarah's fingers stuffed her ears. "Take me back to my room."

"Sarah?" Georgia asked, "Would it be easier for you to show us what happened, using figures, perhaps? Or maybe write your answers down."

"NO! NO! NO!" Sarah yelled, leaping from the chair. She backed away from the desk. "I'm NOT TALKING to you! I'm not a baby! I don't want dolls! Leave me alone!" She paced the two meters between the couch and the cabinets.

Carver backed off. "Okay. There are other questions I need to ask you. Unfortunately, they may be just as difficult. Please try to answer, Sarah. Even a nod will do."

She hugged her shoulders as if she were cold. "No. I want to go back to 23 *now!*"

"Sarah, has – anything like what happened this morning – ever happened to you before? Your father, or maybe a brother – ?"

*"NO!"* Sarah shrieked, spinning to face him. Her brothers were her life, all for one and one for all. "I TOLD YOU! How could you even *say* – " She stopped in mid-sentence, in mid-stride, as something buried in her memory came flooding forward, suddenly making sense. She could *feel* the pieces click into place. The room wavered and spun.

*Was that what -?*

Her hands rose to her mouth, but could not stifle the scream that poured forth once, twice. She stumbled backward until she hit the wall, unable to run from the memory. Her eyes saw only the images in her mind. *Torn clothes. Bruises. Making babies.* She sank to the floor.

The doctors rushed closer. "Tell me what you see, Sarah," Carver urged. "Who's hurting you?"

Sarah shook her head hard, eyes wide. "It's not me!" She trembled, now understanding what no one would tell them about that night. The more she thought about it, the sicker she felt. The look on the face had the same feeling Sarah felt right now. "It's not me."

"Who, Sarah?" Georgia pressed. "Who's being hurt? Where are they?"

"I can't tell you! I can't I can't I can't! We promised Vik we'd never tell." *She cried and she cried and she cried ...*

"Sarah, if someone is in danger, you shouldn't keep the secret," Jacobs advised. "You need to get that person to safety as soon as possible, so they can't be hurt again. Was 'Vik' the one doing the hurting?"

"NO!" Sarah glanced fearfully at Carver. Right now, the danger *was* gone. She shook her head again, holding in the secret by holding her breath.

*Why did Saluria have to be right?* "Computer," Carver said to the air, "voice lock, Carver, John A., access number 6511460N."

"Acknowledged," replied the computer from speakers hidden about the room. "Voice lock activated."

"Sarah, your secret is safe. No one but me can retrieve what you say from the records. What you say will not leave this room. No one will ever know unless you tell them."

Sarah bit down hard on a knuckle, afraid the words would fall out. *If Viktor found out...* Her eyes glazed with a far-away look as she remembered.

"Katya," she whispered so faintly Carver strained to hear. "It was Katya." She turned away, denying she'd ever spoken.

"Who hurt Katya?" Jacobs asked gently.

Sarah curled herself into a ball, hugging herself. Seconds ticked before she took a shaky breath and spoke. "Father had drunk an awful lot. Viktor had to break open the door to get her. He tore her clothes, and her – her chest there – was all bare. She had big red marks. On her neck, too. Some of them bruised up. She kept crying and crying."

"What happened then, Sarah?"

Sarah took another long, shuddering breath. "Viktor and Father got in a terrible fight, and Vik left home. He made us promise never to talk about it.

"We didn't understand what happened. David said Father wanted Katya to have a baby. It seemed ridiculous, but now –," Sarah gasped, crumbling, " – now – I understand!" The impact of the morning's events plowed into her with the force of an anti-matter explosion. She squeezed her head in distress, then banged it backward into the wall, anything to override the coming storm.

"Don't bang, Sarah," Carver said, taking her hand. With a cry, she threw herself around his neck. Through spasmodic floods of tears, she choked out some of the details of her ordeal. Some of it she couldn't force herself to say. She wore herself into a stupor on Carver's shoulder.

Carver rocked her, seized by compassion. "Firing squad's too good for him."

Sarah woke in her own room sometime after nine. The lavatory called. Only hushed noises drifted in from the unit, but she wanted no part of it. Saluria would have told the nurses what happened. She didn't need their stares or special treatment. Nothing happened today, nothing at all. Parts still hurt underneath, but it wasn't a pain she could ever talk about. Even a hint, and someone would want to look for a reason, and she wasn't about to allow *that* while she had breath to fight it. The pain in her heart, *that* was the unbearable pain. Worse than the time she went to school with a black eye and pretended not to hear the speculative whispers of the students. Worse than the shame when she looked the stone-faced Navaran mistress in the eye and lied as to the cause.

Nausea twisted her middle.

She curled up in the one corner of the room that couldn't be seen from the door and hugged her knees tightly. Nothing here could distract her from the pain; design made sure of that. Nothing sharp, nothing hot, even the sink would sound an alarm if blocked. No heavy strings on her clothes to choke the unwary. Sarah hated the thought of banging her head – the noise might be heard, and it would leave her with a nagging headache that would radiate through her teeth, not the sharp, attention-focusing pain she needed.

"Think!" she commanded herself.

Seeing the bed empty for too long on the monitor, the evening nurse came to check at 2300 hours. A motherly woman who had worked at the starbase for several years, she had seen many bizarre things from patients, so she wasn't particularly shocked by what she found. She merely crossed her arms and sighed.

"You know, you're going to get both of us in trouble for this."

Sarah sat on the floor with her pant legs pushed up past her knees. She nodded, knowing it. She had pulled the blanket from her bed – a durable open-weave fabric interspersed with a fine metallic-filament sensor web that could report to the computers at the nursing station. Using the edge of the blanket, Sarah had sawed back and forth every few centimeters on both legs, from her ankles to her knees, creating great stripes of friction burn across her shins. A few bled in pinpricks; all were raw and oozy. A smaller mark covered the inside of her wrist where she'd first experimented. She'd been going over the lighter burns, scraping them deeper.

"You know I have to take you to get those treated."

Sarah eyed her handiwork. Her legs hurt like hell, each stripe a sharp, flaming pain that she couldn't ignore. Her mind was focused, and would stay that way for at least a week if the wounds were left untreated, enough time for the aching shame to ease.

"Are you going to give me trouble if I walk you down there myself?"

*No,* shook the head. Sarah had succeeded in her intent, blissfully numb on the inside. She had no need to fight.

"Let's go."

Sarah clung to the hand, especially in the halls.

* * *

Carver read the compad report the nurse handed him in the morning. "No, it's my fault. I meant to order an increase in the Elavixor. You should have called me; I was still here filling out forms."

"I think her calmness surprised me more than anything," the nurse explained. "She never said a word, the whole time we were gone. Nothing seemed to bother her."

Carver signed off on the report. "I know. It's not a good sign. Has she had her morning meds yet? Let's try adding three mils of Catechoplex, twice a day for three days. See what that gets us." He signed the order before heading across the hall.

He knocked on the doorframe of her room. Sarah sat on her bed – a bed with no linens – running a finger down the shiny clear mediskin covering her shins. She yanked the pant leg down when she noticed him. John was dressed casually, as if he weren't supposed to be there.

"You ready?" he asked.

"For what?" Morning session wasn't for an hour.

"Did you forget our picnic? I heard you earned it, as per our bargain."

Sarah reflected none of his bright enthusiasm. She nodded and slid off the bed. Today she wore a one-piece white jumpsuit, with a tight, high-necked shirt underneath.

"Get your meds, and we'll go."

The scale of the gardens impressed Sarah far more than she'd expected. John hadn't mentioned the five areas were functioning ecosystems, replete with twenty species of birds, butterflies, and a few dozen species of small mammals, reptiles, and aquatic creatures. They sat half an hour on a rocky ledge ten meters up an artificial hillscape, looking out across the expanse of the gardens, Sarah silent but attentive. She listened to John's one-sided conversation, and pointed to things of her own interest.

They had covered only half the immense space when John broke for lunch on a grassy strip next to the footpath on the back shore of the central pond.

"Just what you ordered," Carver said, removing items from the pack he carried. "Sausage, fresh bread, and sour creamed potatoes. This is really what you wanted for picnic food?"

Sarah nodded. She spoke for the first time since they arrived. "My mother used to buy fresh *kielbasi*. That's more of a salami."

Carver turned the thick sausage over, examining it. "I didn't know there was a difference. Let me guess: when you're in here, you can pretend you're elsewhere, and you want foods from home to go with the illusion. Right?"

Sarah nodded again. It wasn't hard to figure out. She ate half a piece of bread, licked butter off her fingers and spoke again, looking at the trees.

"There are no *beryozi*. I think I saw a gray birch, but no white ones. Back in Kiev we had a yard with a stand of *beryozi* in the back. We'd play out there until it was so dark we couldn't see each other, only the ghostly white trunks."

"You'll have to suggest it to the gardens crew. I'm sure they plant new things now and then. You miss Russia?"

"*Konyechna*. It's a beautiful country. I miss snow. On Navara, it's always hot, brown, and you forever have sand in your shoes. And your clothes. And your hair." Sarah had a sudden brief memory of Mother crying over the demise of her precious oriental-weave carpets. Six months of sharp Navaran sand being ground into the fibers had left them shredded beyond repair. She took another bite of food, chewed, and swallowed.

"I think things were better in Russia. We all had music lessons, and dance lessons, and just about everybody played one sport or another. Father was an important person back then. Going to Navara was supposed to be some great honor or something, but I don't think he liked it very much. It might have been an honor, but he wasn't as important a person."

Carver made a sandwich out of the sausage and bread. "How old were you when you left?"

"I don't know. Five? It was right after Nikky was born. Mother refused to move until then. She didn't want to have the baby on a ship."

"Was your father drinking then?"

Sarah shrugged. "I don't know. Probably." She slid onto her bottom instead of kneeling, rubbing her shins to get the grass impressions out of her skin.

Carver noticed the shift. "Legs hurt?"

"Enough."

"Enough? I don't understand."

"I don't expect you to."

"Try me."

Sarah speared another piece of sausage with her fork. "I don't think I can explain it."

"You may have noticed, I'm a pretty patient person."

"It's – " She wrinkled her brow in thought. "Why am I telling you, anyway?"

"Because I have to explain why you did it in my report, and find a way to prevent you from doing it again. As it is, I'm trying to convince Dr. Saluria why you shouldn't be on the high-security floor."

"Always back to that," she scowled. Sarah thought hard. "It's like a vaccination. I use a little pain to make me forget a big pain. And hopefully, by the time the little pain goes away, the big pain will have gone as well."

Carver nodded. "I can understand that. The little pain – your legs, I take it – distracts you from a bigger pain, which is... ?" He waited, but she didn't answer. "Could it have to do with yesterday's incident?"

Sarah looked away. "That's not open for discussion."

"Is that what you were doing when you hurt yourself on Navara?"

She chased a cold slice of potato around her plate with her finger. "I don't know. Yes. No. Maybe. I don't remember."

"That covers all the bases."

Sarah glared humorlessly. "I mean, I think that might be when I realized the connection. I just felt dead inside, and if I tried hard enough, I could feel pain. Something was better than nothing. It dulled the noises in my head." She looked down at the fine T-shaped line on the inside of her arm. Already it had faded; soon it would disappear.

Carver made a mental note to himself. "Coping skills. We'll concentrate on those for the next three weeks. We'll teach that brain of yours a new trick or two. Maybe I'll split the time with Dr. Jacobs. Do you mind working with her?"

"Is she a hospital doctor, or a university doctor?"

"A Ph.D. doctor. Does it make a difference?"

"I think so. What about you?"

"Me? You're going to question me after all this time?"

Sarah nodded.

"I'm less than a year from my doctoral in Recreational and Play therapy," John told her honestly. Sarah's shoulders slumped in relief, as if she'd been holding her breath against the answer.

"Why don't we pack up if you're done?" he suggested, getting away from the subject. "We've still got two or three more sections to go."

"We can skip the desert part," Sarah offered. "I'll see enough of that on Navara." As she squatted to pick up her things, a small furry animal raced down the footpath. When it saw her, it shifted direction and ran to her, yipping, knocking her backwards to the ground.

The fawn puppy had a black face and shining round black eyes. It jumped and squirmed over Sarah, barking and licking everywhere it

129

could reach. A lead trailed from the collar around its neck. Seconds later, three identical puppies and a mother dog followed, dancing and pulling at their leads. A man in running attire pulled back.

"Oh, good, you got him," the man said. "I've been chasing him for the better part of ten minutes."

Puppies swarmed the picnicking pair. Carver scratched one behind the ears. "Aren't they cute! How old?"

"Four months."

Three puppies mobbed Sarah. No matter where she turned, a puppy managed to be there first with a wet, ready tongue. They were warm and soft and wriggling and alive. Sarah broke into a smile, a meaningful smile that happened without plan or thought. She had eyes for nothing but the puppies, and then the oh-so-serious girl *laughed*.

First a giggle, then a chuckle, then a deep, rolling laugh. Sarah fell backwards on the grass. She tried to grab them all at once, but they were sleek and smooth and hard to hold. She settled for holding the nearest one to her cheek, its tail and tongue wagging madly.

She squealed anew as a nose snuffed her ear. "They're wonderful! I wish Vlad could see them! What are their names?"

"The mother here is Daisy," the man patted the dog, "but I'm not keeping the pups, so I didn't name them. That one really likes you."

"I wish I could keep him!"

Carver watched her with amusement. "Did you ever have a dog, Sarah?"

Sarah scratched the pup's fat belly. "Goodness no! Earth animals can't be imported to Navara. Vlad would have done anything for one, but Father said the last thing we needed was one more mouth. We found a bird once; it had an injured wing and couldn't fly. We were going to keep it until it was better, made it a nest and all, but Father found it. He said it wouldn't survive a night in captivity, so he broke its neck with his fingers."

"Is there *any* part of your life that has a happy ending?" Carver asked, shocked at both the brutality of the act and her casual acceptance of it.

"Happiness is a relative term," Sarah answered, letting a pup chew her fingers with its needle-sharp teeth. "This is the only life I've had; I have nothing to compare it to. Things could be worse."

Carver raised an eyebrow of approval. "That's the first positive thing I've heard you say."

# * Ten *

Bloodwork. She was so *sick* of bloodwork! Sarah sat in a chair at the crowded medical lab, waiting her turn to have her blood drawn. Her meds were being decreased in anticipation of her leaving, and the levels were checked every other day. She didn't mind the procedure; it didn't hurt and took less than a minute, but nothing ever seemed to run on time.

"You're Dr. Carver's patient, aren't you?" asked the Altairan aide next to her.

"He's not a doctor yet, just a rec therapist."

"John Carver? Of course he's a doctor."

Sarah wasn't supposed to correct grown-ups; Mother had taught her that years ago, and you didn't dream of correcting a Navaran elder, but it seemed downright stupid to let people walk around in perpetual ignorance simply because you were younger. "He won't receive his doctorate in therapy for another six months."

"I don't know about that," the woman went on, "but there's a John Carver who's a junior member of the psychiatry team on this starbase. I went to the welcoming party four months ago."

"Could we change the subject?" Sarah said, irritated. It couldn't be true. It *couldn't*. There must be two John Carvers on the staff. It was a simple enough name. Her mind raced in circles, relieved only mildly when her own name was called next. Her thoughts reeled so fast she didn't hear a word said to her.

*Why would he lie to me? Has he lied about anything else? HAS he? I trusted him. He's always been honest, never rushed me, never medicated me – of course not, a therapist couldn't do that. Saluria did that. Saluria's a doctor. If Carver's a doctor, why didn't he? He wouldn't lie to me! She doesn't know what she's talking about. John will explain it later. But what if he's lying?* Sarah twisted her lip, trapped in thought. There had to be an answer.

She could not wait until after lunch. Sarah's aide had a meeting; Sarah was supposed to behave herself within view of the nurse's area until the aide, Rowena, returned. Sarah asked Maura about John, but all she would say was, "Ask him yourself."

"Can I page him?"

Maura laughed, shooing the girl from the 'comm. "Get out of here! I'm not here to relay messages."

Sarah tried to sneak a look at printouts, hunting for signatures, but a nurse chased her away – three times. She sulked on a chair while she formulated a plan. Doing something against the rules could be very dangerous, but her need to know was stronger than her fear. She now had a Mission. At home, as a scout for the Fearsome Four, she was used to Dangerous Missions, requiring skill and planning and occasional acts of daring bravery. David had scratched more marks on the plastic tally card he'd given her than on Sergei's. Vlad had only two marks on his.

She hung around the nurse's area until she felt certain they were used to her presence, going about their business with little regard. As soon as she had a clear chance, Sarah leaned over the low wall of the nurse's area and pressed the door release button. The doors slid open. A three-meter sprint, and she slipped through the doors before they could close.

The happy inspirational murals in the hallways looked the same, but without a staff person by her side, anxiety crippled her. Sarah'd held tightly to her transport aides these last two and a half weeks, no matter how slow they walked. She wanted to run as fast as she could to minimize the danger, but forced herself to a slow jog. Running, especially fast running, would be very suspicious.

Her heart quickened, and she sprinted past *that* corner of the waiting area, feeling Robison's foul breath on the back of her neck with every racing step. Two doors down. Sarah palmed the motion eye and the door opened... to an empty room. Her heart sank in disappointment, but her determination grew.

Back in the hall, hands on her hips. *Which way now?* She had to be careful in the office section; too many people knew her. Laughing voices came from her right; she pressed on. Peering into a staff lounge, she found John joking and chatting with several other doctors.

Carver caught sight of her. "Sarah! What are you doing here? Where's your aide?"

Sarah stretched herself as tall as possible, the Kirushenko temper running true. She looked him straight in the eye. "You lied to me, *Doctor Carver!*"

Carver's smile faded, and he stood up. "I never lied to you, Sarah. There are just some things neither of us has volunteered to discuss."

"So it's *true!*"

"Where's your staff, Sarah?" he asked again, turning her to the hallway. "I'm impressed. It took courage for you to walk here alone."

The intercom interrupted him.

"Doctor Carver?" Maura's voice sounded exasperated.

"I'm here."

"Doctor Carver – um – Miss Kirushenko seems to have left the floor alone. The locator indicates she's in your area."

"She's here. Send a staff to retrieve her, please."

"On their way."

Sarah pulled away. "We need to talk."

"We will, this afternoon."

"No, *now*!"

"I can't do that, Sarah. I have a client to assess in the men's section in ten minutes, then I have a lunch meeting. You know that; we talked about it. I don't have time until our meeting this afternoon. I'll see you then." He turned back toward the lounge.

Sarah's rage burned hotter. She hadn't braved the halls alone to be blown off like this! She wasn't just some dumb kid! She had a legitimate issue to be discussed! Wasn't she supposed to be doing more for herself?

"You want self-expression?" She charged forward and shoved him, making him stumble.

Several doctors stood up, but John waved them off. He walked to the intercom and thumbed the button. "Security escort to staff room three."

Sarah had never seen such a look from him before. Her hands stayed on her hips, but she took a step back, ready to run if necessary. Outnumbered by doctors, she had to keep control.

Security arrived with the aide.

"Escort Miss Kirushenko and her staff to section 23. If she resists or becomes combative, she is to be put in ID seclusion," Carver ordered.

"Understood," said the uniformed woman.

Sarah stared in disbelief. How just like a doctor! She was such a fool for trusting him! And she had considered him a friend!

Rowena tugged on her elbow. "Come on. Maura is hopping mad at you."

Sarah let herself be dragged backwards until the room disappeared from view.

Back on her floor, Sarah endured the head nurse's wrath before she could respond.

"I don't care how mad you are at me!" she stormed at Maura. "*Ya dyesats vremen kak sumashedshikh na tom sinke suki!*" Son of a bitch, indeed! She threw herself into her room to carry on her tirade in private, where she got a devilish idea.

"Will you take me to the gym?" she begged her staff. "It's in my protocol. Better yet, the gardens! It's so peaceful and calm there. I'm all torn up, and I really need to relax. We can wade at the edge of the water and watch the fish. Please?"

"After this morning? Are you kidding?" Rowena said. "All right, but you better behave. Anything's better than watching you sulk."

They walked around the forest area, Sarah forcing herself to be pleasant and casually talkative.

"Let's play a game," she begged, hugging a tree. "Hide and seek! We can take turns."

"You're not supposed to be out of my sight," Rowena reminded her. "I don't feel like losing my job. I'm finally settled in my apartment."

"Come on!" Sarah coaxed, locking her arms around the narrow trunk and swinging herself around. "You can't play it on Navara; there isn't anywhere to hide. You'd have to bury yourself in the sand, and then the worms and sandflies think you're lunch. Come on! It's just a game…"

Rowena eyed her charge. "Don't think I won't call security if you try something funny."

Sarah tried to look innocent. "I'm *supposed* to play, remember? You first."

For twenty minutes they took turns, Sarah being the more creative one at hiding – under bushes, behind rocks, once up a small tree. Each time she pushed further toward the jungle area – and the exit doors between the sections. When she saw her chance, she dashed out.

Sarah found a lift not fifteen meters from the door.

"Deck 17, section O," she told the lift. "Computer?"

"Waiting," agreed the mechanical voice as the lift ascended.

"Location of Doctor Carver?"

"John Carver, DPM, is on deck 25 M, room 36."

"Thank you." *Too good to be true!* The lift opened half a corridor from the Rec Room. Speed mattered now.

Nineteen minutes. Sarah'd allowed fifteen, but she'd forgotten about travel time. Her heart hammered with anticipation. *Did she make it?* The side doors to the gardens swooshed open and she darted over to the jungle, plowing through undergrowth off the side of the path. She honestly tripped on a shallow root, tangling her hair in a branch and leaving dark soil on the knees of her jumpsuit. Enough was enough after she squashed a palm-sized beetle with her hand, running out of the jungle shrieking and rubbing away the crunched-bug feeling.

Rowena ran down the path breathlessly. Two unfamiliar staff were with her. "Sarah! Thank God! I was about to use the locator."

"I got lost!" Sarah locked her arms around the aide and buried her face. "I squished the world's biggest bug!" She showed the staff her dirty palm.

Rowena sighed. "I knew something would happen. You're a mess! Let's get you back and cleaned up for lunch." She thanked the other aides.

"Do you know how long I've been looking for you?" Rowena continued as they walked to the lift. "What ever made you hide in there?"

Sarah hung her head so her smile wouldn't be seen.

\* \* \*

Carver returned to his office, bearing a fresh cup of coffee and his compad. He'd had a productive lunch meeting. One patient was being discharged, two more were being considered for inpatient therapy. His caseload would be expanding. *13:30.* He still had a half hour before Sarah's afternoon session. Not that he looked forward to it. His youngest patient was too smart, too stubborn, too obsessive to accept a simple explanation. He needed to form his arguments now.

The doors to Rec Therapy hissed open; he stopped, awed. Not even an earthquake would have left such damage.

Unrelenting fury had vented itself through the large room. Table legs surrendered to the ceiling. Chairs and sofas hunkered belly- down; a cushion oozed stuffing through gaping wounds. Storage units stood bare, stripped of their contents; wall shelves pulled down or cleared off. One overhead light panel hung open, another lay shattered. Paint raced in stripes down a tipped shelf, yellow puddling on the floor – red the only bottle still capped. A yellow toeprint screamed caution, the smooth slipper print of a smaller patient.

Only the large mouse cage remained untouched, sitting in its place on the cabinets – cabinets whose raided contents were purged onto the floor. The doctor swore something strong and kicked a chair that lay sideways at his feet. Temper rising to unprofessional levels, coffee cup still in hand, John Carver stormed out of his office.

\* \* \*

Bathed and clean, Sarah sat lunching with her aide when Carver blasted through the doors of 23W. He shoved a foot behind the leg of Sarah's chair, trapping her.

"Where's she been since this morning?" he demanded.

Rowena was puzzled by his anger. "We were here for a while, then we went to the gardens. We've been back here since about one."

"She was in visual contact at all times?"

"Yes. Well, all but ten minutes or so, when we got separated. She got lost in the jungle area, and it took a bit to find her. We were playing hide and..." Rowena's dark face fell. "You don't mean she wasn't... *Sarah!*"

"I want a written report in my mail in thirty minutes," Carver ordered. "Quotes, actions, reactions, start to finish. I'll take her now." He hauled Sarah out of her seat and marched her toward the door. He called over his shoulder to the charge nurse, "We'll be in 17. Better send her dinner down. Thirty minutes on that report!"

Sarah's toes barely touched the floor. "I was with Rowena. Ow! You're hurting me, John! What's with you? Why are you doing this? Slow down, at least!"

"Save it," he snapped, and dragged her into the lift.

Carver released her only when they were within the confines of the Rec Room. "Computer, exit door on my voice command only."

"Confirmed," agreed the computer.

Sarah stepped back warily. "That's not safe. You're endangering me."

"The only danger in here is from yourself." He righted a chair and sat down. "You want to talk? We'll talk as soon as you've fixed the mess you've made."

Sarah scanned the destruction. "*I've* made?! I was with my staff all day – How –"

"Computer, list all persons entering this room between 11 a.m. and 1 p.m. today.

"Affirmative. Kirushenko, Sarah I., 12:42 p.m. Exit 12:56 p.m."

"Fourteen minutes. Fourteen minutes to completely destroy my room. Were you trying to break a speed record?"

"No," Sarah said sullenly. *Damned know-it-all computers! Damned patient ID chips!*

Carver crossed his arms. "I don't know what to do with you. By rights, you should be on a high-security floor, tagged so you physically can't exit the living unit. You accuse me of lying to you, but you lied to me at least twice in the last five minutes. I'm very angry, Sarah. Angry and hurt. If that was your intent, you've succeeded."

"I was – "

Carver shook his head. "No. I don't want to hear a word from you unless it's preceded by 'I'm sorry,' and 'I'm done fixing the room'."

"I will not apologize!" *She* was the one wronged! Looking around, she added, "I can't do this myself. It would take a week."

"Then that's how long we'll be in this room."

John dragged the chair over to his desk. The desk attached to the wall, hence it went unscathed. He turned his back and began on the morning's computerwork.

"I can't fix this myself!" Sarah repeated, louder.

Carver didn't respond.

Sarah sat down in the midst of the disaster. *To Hell with this! He couldn't make her do anything!*

Ten minutes, and he hadn't so much as looked in her direction. She lay on the floor. John stayed intent on his computer screen. She rolled onto a sofa cushion and banged her feet, a yellow stain visible on the bottom of her shoe.

Her legs grew tired, and she stopped. She tried going over scientific laws in her head, but couldn't get past the third law of thermodynamics. She tried remembering all the Russian Heads of State backwards, but got lost around Chernenko.

*Insufficient memory available. Circuits not responding. Please come back and try again.*

Nothing. After all, who would forget their own birthday? She ran through the long list of her siblings' birthdays, but mixed up by the time she got to David. *Hopeless!* She couldn't even kill time in her head.

*Time to liven things up*, Sarah thought wickedly. *What couldn't he ignore?* She threw back her head and let forth a scream.

Not a flinch. He was tough. Very tough.

She upped the stakes another notch.

"NOOOO! NOOO! Don't touch me! Owww!" Another long scream followed.

*Ha!* John straightened a little, and rested his chin on his thumb. Another deep breath, another ear-splitting protest.

The intercom sounded. Carver answered, and Saluria's face appeared on the viewer. "I had a report of a disturbance from your room. Just making sure you don't need reinforcements."

Carver didn't seem the least bit ruffled. "If you have a minute, come on down. I'm being entertained by the show of the century."

Two screams and a kicked chair later, Saluria entered. Sarah's scream stopped so fast she choked herself into a coughing fit.

*Outnumbered.*

She flew lightning-fast behind an overturned table to rethink her strategy. Noise was out; she needed to hear what they said. Saluria couldn't be trusted. He was the *Chief* of Psychiatry; he held *all* the power.

"Should I even ask?" he said.

"Someone found out there's a DPM after my name."

Saluria pulled a chair over, facing the room. "Is it safe to sit with your back to her?"

Carver frowned. "She shoved me this morning, but I don't think she'll do much else. I think it's a test to see what I'll do. Now it's a matter of who blinks first. No matter what happens, it can't be me."

"How long do you think that will take?"

"I don't know. I fully expect to be here all night."

Saluria watched her peek at him from the safety of the table blind. "What will happen if you leave?"

"Leave?"

Saluria motioned to the door with his head. "Take a break. Follow up on something. What better means to show contempt than walk away?"

Carver wavered. "I should follow up on this morning's incident. Okay. I'll leave you today's reports to read. You'll be stuck until I get back – door's on voicelock."

"We'll be fine."

Sarah raced John to the exit, but the debris slowed her.

*"No!"* She banged desperately on the door, then caught sight of Saluria watching her. The hair on her neck prickled like ice crystals. She took two steps backward, then clambered to the rear of the room as fast as she could. Cramming herself between the wall and the piano, she stared back with wide, frightened eyes.

Saluria watched her for several minutes, then began reading reports. Every half page or so he would lift his eyes, but she merely sat, hugging her knees and watching him.

"Isn't there something you should be doing?" he barked.

Sarah jumped and began hastily picking up puzzle pieces scattered the length of the back wall.

She had rehung the shelves and was scrubbing the spilled paint when Carver returned more than an hour later. The back half of the room had been restored. Sarah hadn't realized how tense she had been in his absence; the sudden relief made her stumble.

"You seem to have a touch," Carver told his boss. He took a seat, back to the room.

"Nothing I did, I assure you. She was one step from panic the moment you left. Light panel fell and scared her half to death. That's the only time she made a sound."

"What's she doing now?" Carver wondered.

Saluria glanced up, then frowned. "Biting her hand."

Carver shook his head and chuckled. "She's stubborn, I'll grant her that."

"John!" Sarah called, not without a little fear. "I'm bleeding!" She held up her hand. A thin line of red showed bright on a knuckle, ringed by a number of teeth marks.

"I'm sorry to hear that," Carver replied evenly. "Wash it out with the disinfectant by the sink."

Sarah's face clouded over. She gave the hand only the briefest contact with the disinfectant.

Saluria gave Carver a wink. "I need to get back to my office. I'd bet my money you've won."

Another hour, and Sarah struggled to push the furniture right-side up. It took three tries for one table alone. The second table slipped and landed on her foot. Carver didn't ask the computer to translate the angry stream of Russian.

The couch was too heavy; she didn't ask for help, nor did he offer. At last she threw herself at the wrong side of it. The sofa teetered, then fell over into place, dropping her to the floor. A lot of shoving and sweating and it, too, faced the right way.

That was it. She couldn't fix or replace the light panels. She wouldn't mention the piano. Better to provoke that anger only if she must.

Sarah waited silently next to John's chair; he ignored her.

*What now?*

She bit her lip as she realized what he wanted. *Could she really swallow that much pride? Wasn't it enough penance to have straightened the room?* Having him angry at her left her all alone, and Sarah no longer liked being alone.

"I fixed the room," she pointed out.

Nothing.

"*Izvenyayus,*" she admitted grudgingly.

"I'm sorry, I don't understand that language."

Sarah almost growled. *Couldn't he leave her **some** dignity?*

The white flag snapped on high. "I'm sorry. "

Carver smiled as if nothing was ever wrong. "Thank you, Sarah. Pull that chair over, and we can talk. You were full of questions this morning."

Sarah searched his face for false intent. "Why did you lie to me?"

"I never lied to you," he explained. "Call it more of a planned omission. Based on the reports from Ku'umi, you seemed to have a real phobia about doctors. As soon as someone entered a room, you'd attack everyone, including yourself. You were afraid of Dr. Eisgaard, and wound up hurting her when you panicked. The treatment team felt it might be best if we downplayed the whole idea of 'treatment,' and worked therapy into a non-demanding routine of life skills, social development, and recreation. Low-key tactics. My primary goal was to get you comfortable enough to function on your floor. I had to break down some of those damned thick defenses you have. I've called all the shots with your medical treatment – signed all the orders, changed your medications as I saw fit. You never directly asked me if I was a Psychiatrist. I've never denied it."

"Deception is a fine line to lying."

"But it worked, didn't it? Would you have felt more threatened if you knew I was just another doctor?"

Sarah slouched in the chair. She *hated* being wrong! Mistakes were as shameful as a slap in the face, maybe worse.

"Yes," she grumbled.

"Okay, then. Now answer this – yes or no – does it change anything, now that you know?"

"Yes!"

"Does it really? Do I really have any more power, any more ability to influence you than before? Has anything about me changed since you woke up this morning? Or just the way you imagine things to be in your head?"

Sarah squirmed hard in the chair. She tried counting the number of hairs per square centimeter on her finger. John stayed silent.

*"No, "* she whimpered, defeated.

*"No,"* Carver agreed. "If I'd wanted to do that, I would have had you in security when you left the floor alone. I could have had security hold you, and ordered a heavy tranq after you pushed me this morning. I didn't."

"Why not?"

"Because I trust *you*, Sarah. I go further out on a limb trusting you than you do trusting me. If you're wrong, you only have to answer to yourself – and you're pretty hard on yourself – but if I'm wrong, I have to answer to a review board. If I'm wrong, you could get hurt. But I know you're smart, and I know you're unhappy, and I'm trusting that, when I give you the right choices, you'll make the choice that will make you less unhappy. Have I failed you yet?" He tipped her chin up. Sarah dropped her eyes and shook her head.

"I'm not about to start now," he vowed. "Unless you pull another stunt like today. I'm really angry about that. I'm disappointed. Your staff will be lucky if she isn't fired. You owe her an apology, too. Any more garbage like today and I'll have to play hard, and I won't have a choice. Your meds are decreasing, you'll be off the Antivox in another week. You'll have more responsibilities, start seeing me only once a day. Promise me, no more vindictive games like today."

Sarah nodded, her bent head brushing the table. "I promise."

"And no more going anywhere alone! I shouldn't have to tell you how dangerous that is."

"I know."

"Good." He reached over and gave her hand a squeeze. "Let's get you back to your floor."


"You're awfully quiet," Carver said the next afternoon. "Did you know you have mail?"

Sarah sat up quickly from her sprawl on her sofa. "From who?"

"It's your mail, not mine. Do you want to open it here, or back in 23?"

Sarah leapt for the computer screen. "Here! I want it now!"

Carver tapped commands until the hyperspace mail heading appeared.

"It's from Vlad!" she cried as she read the address. A few seconds later Vladimir's face appeared on the screen, Nikky on his lap.

"Hi, Sarah!" he said brightly. "Valeria said we should send you a feed. We miss you. (Nikky leaned into the screen. "We miss you Sarri!"). We can't wait for you to come home. (Nikky took his finger out of his nose and held it up to the transmission recorder. "I cutted my finger wif a knife.") Sergei's been helping me with my homework, but he doesn't know everything the teacher's looking for, either. (Nikky's nose nearly touched the videoscreen. "I tan't see you. Why? Why are you sick? I got sick an' I throweded up on my bed.") Umm…"

The picture broke. When it reappeared, Nikky was gone. "Umm. I'm trying to think of what to tell you. Val made Katya see a doctor because she kept getting sick again, but Kat wouldn't go. Ummm. Oh! *Sarah!*

141

Valeria and Galina are so *mad*! David and Dmitri got into a fight at school, and they might kick David out! Val's trying to get them to let him stay."

"You goddamned little shit!" David's voice growled off screen before he appeared, one eye swollen and blackened clear across his nose. He folded Vlad in half and punched him twice in the back. He leaned into the recorder. "The snitch didn't mention he isn't supposed to be talking about it. Hurry up and come home, Sar. I need you here to help kick ass." He let Vlad up with a shove. Vladimir aimed a wild punch at his brother, but David laughed off screen and walked away. Vlad chattered several minutes more, then signed off.

Sarah giggled. "David and Vlad don't care for each other," she explained. "Vlad's weak enough for David to pick on, and Vlad absolutely *hates* it. David and Dimi fight once in a while, but never like that, and never at school. 'Mitri must have nailed him hard. That's not like him. I guarantee David threw the first punch."

"Your sister's been ill?" Carver asked.

Sarah didn't seem the least bit concerned. "Nah. Sometimes Katya throws up after she eats. Val must have caught her at it. Serves her right. That's repulsive."

Carver sighed and closed his eyes, shaking his head slowly. *Each of them hurting in their own way, none of them able to realize it. How could he let Sarah go back there?*

# * Eleven *

Two weeks. Sarah now studied three hours a day with a tutor. She worked cooperatively with a stress-management counselor. She braved an interview with Doctor Saluria – alone! – to state why she thought she should be released – and Saluria was impressed! Only three days remained until her release, and her family was coming today!

Today she would move into a visitor's suite. She would keep her regular schedule while they – Sarah didn't know who would be coming – attended meetings and inservices to learn how to help her stay well. Sarah could barely restrain herself.

Carver went with her to meet the shuttle. "Excited?"

Sarah jounced up and down on her toes. "I thought you said there were no stupid questions? That's one of the dumbest I've ever heard!"

The shuttle arrived ten minutes late, dragging out the agony until Sarah could leap onto Valeria.

"Sarah!" she cried. "You look wonderful!"

Dmitri clapped her on the shoulder. "Hey, Sar! Vlad's driving us crazy, waiting for you to get home."

Sarah tackled him with both arms. "Not half as much as I will. Only two of you came?"

"Galina wanted to," Val explained, "but Katya couldn't manage everyone on her own, and Dmitri can't be trusted."

"Hey!" Dmitri protested, hurt.

"So you brought him here to babysit him!" Sarah said with delight. "Someone must be in an *awful* lot of trouble!"

Dmitri shot her a dirty look, but kept his mouth shut.

"I'm afraid we've got a tight schedule," Carver interrupted. "There won't be a lot of free time in the next couple of days. I'll show you to the guest quarters. You'll have the rest of the hour to visit, then Sarah has places to be, and we'll start right in with a meeting at eleven. If you'd like, I can send someone for you."

"I'm sure we can find it ourselves," Val said.

Two and a half hours of interrogation by the board of review left Val unnerved. She expected the meetings to be about Sarah, not her, but it made sense. If Val was overburdened or indifferent to Sarah's needs, what was the point of sending her home? The meeting broke, then reconvened for another two hours to hear status reports. Some of the news worried Val. She couldn't picture Sarah doing the things they claimed, and how the hell would they handle her at home if she did them again?

"No problems with self-help skills," Rowena told the panel. "She's self-sufficient in all areas."

Maura Hastings sighed in turn. "I can't say that her stay hasn't been without excitement. Two staff were fired, three put on probation, and two quit. She's bypassed our security system, manipulated staff, and fought with other clients, forcing the relocation of one. She's managed to avoid medication despite inspection. I would say her intelligence definitely worked against us.

"However," Maura changed her tone, "when she wasn't making us dance, we found her sweet, fearful, lonely, and very bored. All she needed was some motherly attention."

"Dr. Carver, can you sum up your work?"

Carver glanced at his notes. "At the time of admission, Miss Kirushenko presented with a severe mood disorder, psychogenic visual disturbances, auditory hallucinations, and traumatic stress reactions, as supported by behavioral observation, neurochemical assays, and brain-function scans. With chemical intervention, we were able to eliminate hallucinatory effects and regulate her mood, which varied from stuporous to extreme agitation. With anxiety and mood levels under control, psychogenic disturbances disappeared. Through various cognitive psychotherapies, Sarah understands the circumstances that have led to her extreme anxieties, and has learned more appropriate measures to handle such stressors in the future.

"Due to past negative experiences, Sarah doesn't trust easily, and her high intelligence allows her to see through most false pretenses. The key to forming a therapeutic relationship of trust was patience on my part, and giving her a sense of control over any and every situation to alleviate anxiety and helplessness. This doesn't mean letting her run the show – not by any means – but giving her two or three choices and giving her the time to choose what she knows is the correct one. Iron discipline was a second key: once Sarah knew I wouldn't back down, she would generally cooperate.

"Self-control is Sarah's area of greatest difficulty – both over-control, such as training herself to overcome the impulse to laugh or cry or smile, and a lack of control, such as jumping into dangerous situations without thinking. For Sarah, it's all or nothing; she cannot regulate herself. Hence, she locks up until she finally explodes. She still resists talking about things that bother her, but she's made steady progress in self-expression, self-management, and releasing stress. I strongly recommend continuing therapy on an outpatient basis for a minimum of nine months, including neurologic medications. I have spoken with Dr. Carmichael at Ku'umi Central, and he has agreed to take over on her current schedule, fifteen to eighteen hours a week."

Valeria fled back to their suite at the dinner break, Dmitri following wearily behind. She didn't think they'd ever remember all the information coming at them, despite the 400-page printout they'd been given. An intense, irritating headache pulsed behind her eyes. After dinner, they still had an hour of personal therapy.

Val sat at the table rubbing her temples. All the talk made everything seem so dismal, no matter how normal Sarah seemed. There were so many if's. *After the trial,* she told herself. *Everything will settle down after the trial.*

She moved over to one of the beds. Sarah eyed her expectantly. "What's that look for? What are you planning?"

Sarah tried to be the picture of innocence. "Me? Nothing. I just had a question…"

Val lay down, yawning. "What? We boarded the shuttle at four this morning. I need a nap."

Sarah pounced down hard next to Dmitri, watching the flatscreen receiver from the other bed.

"Hey! What're ya doing?"

Sarah wriggled with eagerness. "Asking my question! Tell me! Tell me what happened with you and David!"

Dmitri swung a pillow at her. "Aw, for crying out loud! Will you leave that alone?"

"You might as well tell her," Val mumbled sleepily. "She's not going to stop until you do. She'll find out anyway from Vlad."

"It was a misunderstanding," he said, then gave up. "Fine! It's like this: David and Andraen Nulsky got into a big fight out in the quad – you can guess what it was about – "

Sarah nodded. "Andraen's nasty. David hates him."

"Well, I try to break it up before a teacher finds out, but they won't give. Finally Goby Willark grabs Andraen and I grab David. I swing him around by the arm, he trips and hits a rock face first and puts a tiny crack in the bone around his eye. Isn't that just my luck? He gets up and starts hitting on *me* for breaking up the fight. *That's* when Principal Alchulian comes into the courtyard and sees the two of us. I was only defending myself! David almost got expelled, Andraen got suspended for a week, *I* got suspended, and now David and I aren't exactly talking. That's the last time I ever try to save his *sraka*."

"But you can beat him! He's big and all, but even I can ..."

"That's why they're apart," Val said from under the arm she had over her eyes. "There's no way I could have left Katya or Galina to deal with that. No one's going to be avenging anything."

Dimi gave Sarah a wink that promised otherwise.

"Sarah, can I borrow you for a little while?" Carver asked at her door the next morning.

Sarah remembered to look to Valeria for permission – something she hadn't had to do for a long time. "I guess I'll see you at lunch, maybe," she told Val, and stepped out into the hall. "Where are we going?"

"Down to medical."

Sarah's eyes narrowed, and she stopped cold. "Why?"

"Something that may solve both our problems."

Carver patted the exam table as a nurse laid out instruments – away from her possible reach. "Lie down."

"No." There were too many instruments of betrayal in the room for Sarah to put herself in that helpless a position. Trusting a doctor in a rec room was one thing. Trust in a surgical room was another.

"It's a lot easier on both of us if you lie down. I don't want you falling off the table."

"I won't fall."

"Just warn me if you change your mind." John held up an aeroderm and let her examine the drug label. "Local anesthetic – and yes, before you argue, you do need it."

Sarah tensed and held her breath as he applied it high on her left shoulder, but true to his word, only her shoulder became numb. She breathed out with relief.

"Three-angstrom scalpel. Nurse, if she even thinks of turning her head this way, you have my permission to put her in a headlock."

"But not mine!"

Carver leaned close to her ear. "I don't want to cut your nose by accident, so don't turn until I'm done. Okay?"

Sarah rolled her eyes, but kept her head averted. "My nose is not that long."

"A three-centimeter incision – you can look now." Sarah whipped her head around to examine the painless, bloodless slice in her skin.

146

Carver held up six tiny straws, no thicker than spaghetti. "Twenty milligram tubules. Six tubes, six weeks." Using a thin metal instrument, he inserted them into the incision. He made a slight adjustment, then held up one more apparatus.

"Skin sealer." A moment later she would never have noticed the faint line.

"How does that feel?"

Sarah flexed her arm all around, then ran her fingers over the spot. "I can't feel it."

"You shouldn't. Subdermal depot-load Elavixor. Each tube will dissolve slowly, releasing a steady stream of medication for six weeks. No pills, no shots. Next one will be up to Dr. Carmichael."

"How come you didn't do this before?"

"Because we needed the minimal maintenance level. You seem to do okay at this dose."

"What about the Antivox?"

"Discontinued as of last week," Carver congratulated her. "But if you even *think* you hear anything not real, you tell your therapist. Promise?"

Sarah flashed a small smile. "Promise."

Three days, and they were free. Medical training, neurology inservices, behavioral training, family therapy, interview techniques – the list seemed endless. Dmitri liked crisis management training best. He couldn't wait to try the nerve-pressure techniques on David. Let David try and fight him now!

Valeria felt she should be having a graduation ceremony. "Do you remember anything they said?" she asked numbly.

"Just that wrist hold," Dmitri mumbled, dozing in the unyielding shuttle seat. "My brain's burned out. Ask me next week."

"How do *you* feel?" Val asked Sarah, who lay across the middle seat with her head on Val's lap.

"All right, I guess. Tired." They wouldn't arrive home until well after midnight; everyone else would be asleep. *Welcome home* would have to wait until morning.

Val stroked the girl's cheek with the back of her finger. "You gonna miss it?"

Sarah snuggled against her sister. "Maybe. I just want to get home. I don't ever want to leave again."

# \* Twelve \*

Tiram Daamsar pressed the button on the remote in her hand. On the massive wall screen, the blue chart with the glowing yellow line changed to a black chart with a glowing green line.

"Now, as you can see here, the projected output of the platinum vein we're mining on Muphridia II has surpassed our early estimates. We've been processing ore at maximum output for three months. At that rate, current geologic scans show as many as forty-one months left on that vein, with three teams scanning for prospective new ones. Jamison Frine, the director of the project, raised the possibility of building one, if not two, secondary processing plants to deal with the amount of scrap ore. There's a high content of copper in what's being scrapped, and Vega VI is currently crying for copper."

The woman paused when the proposal met with silence. "Sir?"

Tomas Ivanov snapped back to reality, a place he had more and more difficulty staying lately. "Hmm? Yes. Yes, that's a possibility. Tally the numbers and have them on my computer for review by the end of the week. I need to know who's currently supplying Vega, where it's coming from, and what they're charging."

"Yes, sir." Daamsar changed the screen again. "Within the Sol system, the Mars office is reporting that progress on the new visitor's centre is moving ahead on schedule. Original projections were bringing construction to completion two months early, but the inspectors found shortcuts were being taken that could have ultimately weakened the biostructure, so corrections had to be instated."

"Remind me to change early completion bonuses to precision bonuses," Ivanov mumbled.

"In the spaceflight industry," Daamsar continued, "there was a fluctuation in the stock for… "

"May I ask you a question, Ms. Daamsar?"

"Of course, Mr. Ivanov."

"Are you married?"

The trim woman dropped her remote. She hadn't expected that question, though she knew Ivanov was currently single and considered extremely desirable. "Yes, sir. I am."

"Children?"

She retrieved the control wand, blushing. "Yes, sir. Two."

"What ages?"

"I have two boys, twelve and nine."

Ivanov rested his elbows on the table, thinking. "What do they like to do? I take it they're in school at least part of the day. What do children do nowadays in their free time?"

"They... like sports, and watching sports on the vid channels. They go to the holosphere with their friends. They read adventure stories about the big spaceship captains. They like parasailing. My husband bought Rada a hoverboard for his birthday, and he's practically slept on it."

Ivanov smiled to himself. "I'm sorry, Ms. Daamsar. I didn't mean to put you on the spot like that. I asked because I know of a family with children that's facing some very difficult times, and I don't know any children. I would like to find a way to help them, but I'm not sure how."

"Our resource department has virtually limitless employment opportunities on almost any world... ."

Ivanov ran a troubled hand through his hair. "It's not that simple, I'm afraid. I would have to do it in an especially anonymous manner. It can't be traced, or they might refuse the help. You can't send gifts out of the blue when you've never met the people involved. I don't want to insult or anger them with a large financial donation, and I certainly don't want the media getting wind of it and plaguing them. I don't know what to do."

Ms. Daamsar softened. "Is it from a disaster of some sort, sir? Is there a donation fund set up that we could contribute to through buried measures? Spread the money through six or eight different agencies so it doesn't look like it came from here?"

Ivanov shook his head sadly. "No, it's a private crisis within their family, that's the problem. I knew a member of the family many years ago. I feel terrible. All these resources at my command, and not able to openly help."

"Have you had Research dig into it, sir? Sent someone to discover what they might need – medical specialists, transportation, equipment, relief services?"

"I've done some preliminary investigations," Ivanov acknowledged, "but I don't dare pry, lest someone ask questions. How do you let someone know they can rely on you without introducing yourself?"

Daamsar had no answer. "I don't know. Arrange a meeting, or wait for them to make the first move."

Ivanov rubbed his forehead. "That's all I've been able to come up with, too."

# * Thirteen *

Sarah woke before anyone else. After a moment of confused panic to remember where she was, she melted back happily, home, in her own bed, with Katya asleep next to her. No electrical field shimmered over the door, no nurses whispered outside, no bubbly staff person tried to get her moving. Just *Home*. She got up and dressed in her very own clothes. They still fit, and she hugged herself with delight.

She was standing at the window when Galina came home from work.

Gal hugged her off her feet. "Sarah! You look *fantastic!* It's so good to have you home! What are you doing up so early?"

"Watching the sun rise. I missed that on the starbase." Sarah hugged herself again, this time against the chill of the desert night. It would take a bit to reacclimatize herself to planetary weather after the steady temperature of the hospital, the different gravity and air. And she'd forgotten about the unavoidable blood-red sky.

Galina had made breakfast by the time Valeria rose, and not long after came the rest of the crowd. The noise! The shouts! The claps on the back! Nikky climbed on her, sticky with breakfast, until Galina made him sit. Vladimir sat next to her, holding her hand and talking two kilometers a minute. Sarah gave him a hug every so often and let him talk. It would take an awful lot of Vlad to fill up the three-month hole in her heart.

"Enough, Vlad," Valeria said. "Sarah's had quiet all these months. Don't pester her to death her first morning back. And Sarah, don't forget, your tutor will be here at 0900."

"Already?" Not even eight hours, and she'd have school.

"You're supposed to stay on schedule. Do you feel up to it?"

"I guess so. It's my three easiest subjects – literature, Navaran, and geophysics." Sarah pointed at Marina, clinging to the table leg. "Hey! She's standing up! She's just a little baby!"

"Yes, she is," Val agreed, "and you've been gone a full third of her life."

Sarah dragged her feet, but Valeria held her hand firmly as they entered the hospital after lunch. "Do we really have to do this?"

"Come on, Sar. You can't back out now. It's the biggest condition of your release. You don't want to go back to Rangler."

"Maybe?" She wouldn't admit it out loud, but inside Sarah *would* miss John Carver. He was... *nice*. She couldn't see how any other doctor could be that nice – she'd known far too many that weren't. The routine had been boring, but there had been security in the sameness. She didn't remember arriving there, didn't know when she did realize where she was; she was just *there*. She didn't know this building at all. She memorized the count of doors and corridors, just in case.

A large set of doors sealed off their passage, warning

### PSYCHIATRIC
### AUTHORIZED PERSONNEL ONLY

in big orange print.

Sarah fought to breathe. She ripped her hand from Val's and stopped dead before the doors.

Val spun around. "What are you doing? Come on."

Sarah shook her head.

"Sarah, you promised, no games."

Sarah's shoulders scrunched up to her ears, and she whispered to the floor. "I'm not. They can meet me at the door."

"I can't go in there and leave you out here alone. Oh no. Come on."

"I swear, Val! I will be *right here*. I have to ask a question before I go in."

Sarah *always* had a question. "All right," Val relented, "but so help me, Sarah, if you're not right here, I will have you on the next ship to Starbase 4, bound and gagged."

"No games," Sarah promised the floor.

Val returned with the doctor in scarcely two minutes. Sarah not only stood in the same place, but the same position as when she'd left.

"Hello, Sarah, I'm Dr. Carmichael. We met several months ago," the old man said with calculated friendliness. "I'm glad to see you're feeling better. I understand you have a question for me?"

Sarah nodded. "This door – Does it – Is it locked on the inside?"

"Will you come in if it is?"

"No."

"Then come in. It's not locked."

The doctor, then Valeria, stepped through the doors. Sarah followed with tentative steps. As soon as the doors closed, she ran back at them.

"*Sarah!*" Val exclaimed.

Carmichael held up a hand. Sure enough, Sarah didn't move past the open doors. She tried it two more times.

"I didn't lie. It's not locked. Do you remember being here before?" Sarah clung to Valeria and shook her head.

He stopped at the third door of the first corridor. "This is where we'll be meeting." To Valeria, he said, "See you in three hours?"

"Three hours," Val repeated. She kissed Sarah on the top of her head. "Be good. I'll be back." She smiled and gave a little wave as she left.

Carmichael motioned toward the room. "Come in."

Sarah's innards clenched, watching her sister's retreat. All alone, in a strange place, with a strange man with unmentionable power over her. *Three hours.* She knew what she was supposed to do, what Dr. Carver expected of her, but everything inside her screamed to run after Valeria, and not stop until she got home.

*Home!*

Sarah entered with trepidation. Starting over with someone new seemed insurmountable. She just couldn't do it.

The door closed behind her, and she checked it. Carmichael waited. The room bore the office standard – dull floors, long-wearing furniture, and a desk with institutional chairs. It smelled of chemicals and sterility and plastics, and the doctor's sharp cologne. Sarah stayed by the door.

"It's okay," Carmichael assured her. "Where would you like me to sit?"

Sarah pointed to the desk, clear across the room. There was no observation window, but her practiced eye found the tiny camera ports in each corner of the room. She perched stiffly on the arm of the sofa, the quicker to run.

"Did you enjoy your first day home?" He sat and called up her files on his computer.

She laid out her standard rules. "Yes. Don't touch me. No drugs, no games, no lies."

Carmichael nodded. "I'm sure we can avoid most of those. I've gone over your case with Dr. Carver. You're on Sub-dermal Elavixor. Do you know what dosage?"

"Twenty milligram."

"You're cautious with doors. Were you on a locked floor at Rangler?"

Sarah studied her fingers. "You didn't read my file yet. Locked floor, one to one aide twelve hours a day, at least four times in an ID room, restraints and all. I eliminated seven staff in eight weeks. Is that what you want to know? But never in a locked therapy room."

"Good. Bear in mind, we're not used to that kind of approach here.

We're an emergency hospital; this is an emergency psychiatric department. We're used to diagnosing, stabilizing, and shipping out. Your program is through special arrangement with Rangler. I'm sure you won't find our facilities nearly as comprehensive."

Sarah shrugged, picking and chewing a peeling cuticle. Two hours and forty-one minutes to go.

"I wish you would wait there for me," Sarah told Val on their short ride home. "If I ever needed to leave early, I can't."

"If you were sick or something, they could page me," Val offered, "but don't think you're going to start taking off from there. They told me all about your escapes at Rangler."

"I didn't say that at all!" Sarah couldn't explain what she felt.

"And you won't," Val decided.

They returned home to an uproar.

Vlad jumped up and down by the door. "We're rich, Sar! We're rich!" He grabbed her by the hands and tried to get her to spin around. "We got money!"

"What are you talking about?" Valeria asked. "What's happened? What money, Gal?"

Galina held up a fistful of receipts. "It's true! We're off the hook! Look at these!" She handed the stack to her twin.

Val read over the papers, each identical except for the name at the top. "What are they?"

"An insurance policy on Mother," Galina explained. "It arrived twenty minutes ago by courier. It only took them nine months to get here. Each survivor has a cheque for – get this! – *six thousand credits*! *Each* of us! I just got off the comm with the lawyer, and he believes it to be real. I never knew she had a policy."

"The cheques weren't issued too recently." Val held up a pale pink slip whose young owner was also now deceased.

"I know," Galina agreed. "The lawyer's looking into it. He'll handle Viktor and Alexei's, too."

"Can you believe it?" David crowed. He jumped onto Dmitri's back and threw a fist of victory into the air; Dmitri hunched over under the weight. "I already know what I'm doing with mine."

"You'll be doing nothing with it." Val lined the papers up and stuffed them in their plastic envelope. "These will go somewhere safe. Hopefully, we can invest them wisely and live off the return."

"But that's my money!" David protested. "It's got my name on it!"

154

"And I am your guardian precisely to keep you from doing stupid things you'd regret later."

"Come on, Val!" Dmitri begged, straightening up as David slid off him. "How about just some of it? What could that hurt, huh? Just ten percent? *One* percent? We should be able to get *something* out of it!"

Val waved them off. "Enough! I said none, and I meant it!"

Valeria's common sense didn't stop them from dreaming.

Sarah sat in the boys' room, looking over at what used to be Viktor's bed, then Dmitri's, now David's. "It seems so empty in here. We've never had this much space."

"Of course Dmitri got the little room," Sergei said enviously.

Dmitri sat against David's bed, flipping a deck of cards over in his hands. "I should get *something* for being the oldest. It's sure not gonna be cash."

With Father gone for an extended period, they had shuffled rooms again. The twins, along with the baby, took over their parents' room. Sarah and Katya had the girls' room to themselves, and Dmitri took the tiny room. That left only four boys in the larger room.

"Just think of it," Vlad said dreamily next to Sarah. "Six *thousand* credits! I wouldn't know what to buy first!"

"I do!" David exclaimed from his bed. "I'd put a down payment on an S311 Excelsior Groundeffects speed bike, silver with the reflective smoked dome. And dark blue upholstery. That would be *nova*. Those things fly like a demon. There's one on display down on Ve'louak Street."

Dimi flicked a playing card backwards at his brother's head. "You don't even know how to ride one. Besides the fact you're too young for a permit."

"I'd learn! I've piloted more'n you! And you don't need a license if you ride outside the city walls and stay out of the commercial lanes. What would you do with it?"

"Val gave me a money, and I buyed candy," Nikky said. He flew a toy shuttle up the side of his bed. "An' I can buy a Dune Digger like on the holovision." He sang the jingle from the advertisement. "When you're up to your neck and afraid of a wreck, don't rent a rigger, buy a Dune Digger! DUNE DIGGER!"

"I'd travel," Dmitri dreamed. "Anywhere and everywhere. When I'd done it all, I'd pick my favorite place and settle down. I'd have a new girlfriend where ever I went, and if I really liked her, I might even stop back to visit. There'll be a million women dreaming of me all over the galaxy, and I might choose one, maybe even two to settle down with, or maybe not."

Sergei laughed. "Boy, are *you* dreaming! Where in this galaxy would you find two girls who'd want to be with you?"

Dmitri flicked a card towards him. "I got a better chance than you! You'll never find a real girl inside a book."

"No, but a lot of nice ones hang out in libraries, and I know where all the private reading areas are. I could start my own library, or even a book museum, become a dealer in rare books. Or maybe just live near a really big library and spend my time helping girls find what they're looking for. At least I'd know they could read."

David rolled onto his stomach with a groan. "What a waste. I don't know who's worse with all that brain stuff, you or Sarah. You're awful quiet, Sar," he said. "What would you do with all that money?"

Sarah sucked her bottom lip. What didn't she have that she wanted?

"I'd buy an EPSAR," she decided, naming a military energy weapon. "A full working pistol, not just a stun gun, and practice my marksmanship. That way, whenever Father started up, I could make him stop. Then I'd pack up and go home to Russia. I want to see snow. I want to skate again."

Dmitri snorted. "Ice skate? The last time we went skating you spent most of the time sitting on the ice. You almost cracked your head."

"I still had fun," Sarah insisted. "I remember it. It was the day Nikky was born. Father took us to the rink in the park. It started to snow at sunset, the city lights were just coming on, the bells in the cathedral were ringing, Viktor was there, we were all together, and it was beautiful. Then we came here, and it's been nothing but sweat and sand ever since."

Vladimir frowned. "Wasn't somebody bleeding?"

"I was," Sergei started to remember. "David skated like a maniac and shoved me, and I fell and bit my lip. Father made me sit in the snow holding my lip because he didn't want to leave yet. My hand and my butt almost froze."

"I didn't push you," David said.

"Yes you did."

"Father was a good skater," Vlad interrupted nervously. They fell silent, thinking.

"Anyway," said Sarah at last, "I'd go back to Russia."

Four days, four nights, and Sarah backslid when she least expected it. Valeria woke in the black night to a noise that chilled her to the core.

The scream echoed through the house as if the enviro fans had seized and metal was tearing metal. Rushing from her bed, she crashed into Dmitri and David in the hallway. Dmitri gripped a piece of chain Father used when hoisting things at field sites.

"What the hell are you doing with that?" Val had just enough time to ask as she skidded into the girl's room. "Lights!" she commanded the house computer.

"What's she doing?" Katya pleaded, kneeling on the edge of their bed. 'Byeta's bed had been removed; neither Katya nor Sarah would sleep in it. "Why won't she stop?"

Sarah fought something unseen, cowering where the bed met the corner of the room. She couldn't retreat farther, but she tried, fixated on an invisible enemy. Over and over, she slammed her pillow at her kicking feet.

David stared. "What do we do?"

Val climbed onto the bed. "Dimi, get on that side. Sarah? Sarah, it's Val. Come with me, Sar, come – no, Dim, don't touch her yet.

"It's Valeria, sweetheart. Wake up. Take my hand. You're home, you're safe." She grabbed a clawing hand and held it. "Come on, Sar'ina, wake up. It's only Val. *Wake up*. Get her other hand, Dim – "

Sarah took a shuddering breath, and her wild eyes focused. She stared hard, as if seeing Valeria for the first time. The screams turned to little choking whimpers.

Val held her close. "It's okay, Sar. It was just a dream. You're safe. Shhh. Show's over," she ordered the others. "She'll be fine. Back to bed, everyone."

"Won't you need help?" Katya asked.

"I think she'll be all right, now. Take my bed. I'll stay here with her."

Val dozed some, but Sarah couldn't return to sleep. The dream had been so real, so vivid, she still couldn't believe that's all it had been. She felt electrocuted; every nerve in her body burned and pulsed with electric fire. She recited long Navaran meditation chants to calm her racing heart, but soon gave up.

"Get some sleep," Galina told Val in the morning, watching her twin drag herself around the kitchen. "I'll stay up for a while." Val headed back to bed, but Sarah stayed awake.

"Could we skip geophysics today?" she asked her Navaran tutor. "I am not well. I cannot concentrate enough to calculate equations." She worked, but only with the constant prompting of the tutor.

Valeria was up in plenty of time to bring Sarah to therapy.

"Go in the room, Sar," Val shooed her. "I want to talk to Dr. Carmichael."

Sarah wouldn't budge. "No. You're just going to talk about me behind my back."

"That's fair," Carmichael agreed. The objection was more than she'd said in his presence in days. "If it's okay with your sister..."

"I guess," Val said, and they entered the room. Val recounted the long night.

"You had a problem with this before, didn't you?" Carmichael asked. "Did you sleep better at Rangler?"

"Not always," Sarah said, her chair drawn uncomfortably close to her sister's. *Don't leave! Please, Val!* she yelled in her head. Somehow, even if she did manage to learn telepathy, Sarah doubted Val would ever receive the message.

"We should do a quick check of that Elavixor level. I'm sure you know it can be tricky stuff to regulate. Then I'd like to do a sleep study. Did you ever have one of those?"

Sarah shook her head. Not that she knew.

"We can do it in one of the overnight rooms..."

Sarah took to her feet, every nerve poised for flight. "NO! I won't stay here! *Absolutely not!* Val, I won't do it! You won't make me!"

"Calm down." Val asked Carmichael, "Is there a way we could do that at home?"

"I suppose I could see if we have a portable unit," the doctor mused. "You don't need to retrieve the data, just set it up and let it run. Let me see if I can locate one."

He found one, and taught Val to activate it. After she'd left with the device, he tried to get Sarah to cooperate with bloodwork.

"No." It had become Sarah's word of choice where Carmichael was concerned. "Can't they come here to get it? I don't want to leave the room." Here she had a chance in a one-on-one fight. She had no idea what treachery lay elsewhere in the building, and she wasn't up to finding out. Not today. If Val had stayed... but Val always had other things to do.

Carmichael tried to seem upbeat. "I think that could be arranged, this once."

The test results pleased Dr. Carmichael. He prescribed additional medication, but forgot to mention that fact to Sarah.

Sarah frowned at the two pills Valeria placed in her hand before bed. She recognized the yellow triangle – a five-milligram booster dose of Elavixor – but the little round red one was new. "What's this?"

"Dr. Carmichael wants you to try these. He thinks they'll help you with sleeping."

Sarah tried to hand back the tablets. "I won't take sedatives. Dr. Carver knew that."

Valeria pushed the hand back. "I don't think that's what it is. It's to fix some wave during some sleep cycle. I didn't follow exactly,"

Sarah put the pills in her mouth and drank the water Val offered. She turned to leave.

Val caught her by the shoulder. "Not so fast. They warned me about you. Open!"

Sarah gagged and swallowed again. She opened her mouth for inspection, astonished when Val actually ran a finger between her cheek and gums.

"Good girl. Now run and get ready for bed."

Sarah didn't run. She walked slower, cheeks flaming with anger and shame.

The medication proved tolerable, though the thought of biting Valeria's finger during the nightly violation did cross her mind. This night, however, Val had to meet with the lawyer. Inwardly, Sarah hoped the meeting would run late, and she could sneak to bed without the pills. Surely, if she were asleep – or pretending to be – Val wouldn't wake her up.

Val returned long before bed. The older boys were engrossed in a boxing match on the holovision. They sprawled across the furniture, devouring a sack of soft-hulled nuts.

David cracked a nut with his teeth, releasing a shower of dust. "That hadda hurt."

"Don't back off!" Dmitri yelled at the transparent, three-dimensional figures shuffling across the platform. "Get on him!" He threw a shell at the ghostly image. "Go for his face!"

Val hung up the wrap she'd worn. "What's going on?"

Dmitri lounged sideways in Father's chair, bare feet dangling over the arm. "Mighty Martian Anderson versus Hydrax the Invincible for the championship of Cetaxis VI. Look at this guy, Val! He's got four arms!"

"That's not what I meant. *Gd'ye* Ekaterina?"

"She'sh geddin the baby to beb," Sergei said around a mouthful of nuts. There were enough empty shells between him and Vlad to make them both sick.

"Where's Sarah?"

"*Get him! Get him!* Watch that other arm!" Dmitri shouted, spilling the pile of shells on his chest. "I don't know. I think she's giving Nikky a bath."

"Aw, man! Way to *go!*" David yelled as Mighty Martian unleashed a wave of heavy blows, pushing the four-armed Hydrax across the holographic ring right in front of the boys.

"Why is – ?" Valeria ran for the bathroom.

Nikky was pajama'd, Sarah drying his hair when Val burst in with a sigh of relief.

"Thank you, Sarah. I'll take over."

"I've got it," Sarah said cheerfully.

"That's all right, I'll finish up. You weren't supposed to be doing this. You should get ready for bed yourself." Val combed Nikky's hair.

Nikky squirmed. "I want Sarri to put me to bed."

"Sarah's supposed to take it easy. She needs her rest."

"He hasn't rinsed his teeth yet." Sarah slipped dejected out the door and flopped next to David on the sofa. The noise of the room wasn't welcoming, but Val had hurt her feelings, and she didn't feel like obeying.

Several minutes passed before Val reappeared. She stood next to Dmitri and clapped her hands, twice. A glowing menu superimposed itself over the frozen holoimage. "Holo off!" The fight and the menu vanished.

"Hey! What're you doing?" Dmitri made a grab for the hand control on the side table, but Val snatched it first.

"Look at this place!" she growled, pushing Dmitri's legs off the chair. "Look at this mess! Dimi, if Kat's busy, you're supposed to take over! And Vladimir, *you* were supposed to be bathing Nikky, not Sarah."

"Vlad wanted to watch the fight," Sarah said.

"I wanted to watch the fight," Vlad said at the exact same time.

"I *can* do *that* much," Sarah added.

Katya chose the wrong moment to walk into the room.

"Katya, I thought I left you in charge!" Valeria pounced. "Look at this room! And no one watching Sarah? David, have you finished your schoolwork?"

Everyone spoke at once.

"I was putting the baby to bed," Katya apologized.
"Galina woke up and we were talking. Dmitri can watch
the boys just as well as I can..."

Dmitri stood up. "Lay off, Val! We *are* allowed
to have fun once in a while! We weren't doing
anything wrong..."

Sarah glared at Valeria. "I'm not a baby! You keep
treating me like some kind of invalid! I've been bathing
Nikky for more than two years; I think I know how to do
it by now. And I'm not taking any more pills!"

"I still have one more day on that assignment,"
David said. "I finished everything else. Can't I take a
freakin' break?"

"Come on, Val!" Sergei pleaded, taking another
handful of nuts from the depleted bag. "There's only a
couple of rounds left."

Vlad crawled across the floor, turned the
holovision on by the master control on the console,
and locked out the voice control. The noise of the
fight competed with the noise of the argument.

*"I am in charge here!"* Valeria shouted above the din. "And I make
the rules! Vlad, shut that off!"

"...And I don't need you babysitting me all the time!" Sarah vented
in the sudden silence when the holovision cut out. "I can take care of
myself!"

"Like you did the other night?" Val stabbed.

Sarah's cheeks burned dark, and she turned away. She crunched
herself up and hid her face, too angry and ashamed to speak.

"Damn you, Val! That wasn't fair! She just got back!" Dmitri
shouted. "You apologize! Stop riding her. I'd have punched you out long
before this, if I was her."

Galina came from the bedroom, shouting over the mayhem. "Whoa!
Whoa! Hey! Time out! What the hell's going on?"

"Val's being a *bitch*," David spat.

"You stop your mouth, David Fyo-" Val's reprimand was drowned
out by everyone yelling at once.

Galina waved for quiet. "One at a time!"

Sarah tiptoed behind the group and slipped outside. Vlad followed,
grabbing Val's wrap from the top of the pile near the door.

"Dmitri, your turn. Speak!"

* * *

Sarah sat on the step, staring at the starry sky. In the distance, lights from the Terran city glowed softly, a blot on the black horizon. The sweet smell of night-blooming *triti'ak* flowers wafted through the cool air from the ridge behind the house. Insects droned and creaked with steady regularity, free to roam without fear of incinerating themselves. Outside in the Navaran wilderness, the universe was a tranquil place.

Vlad plopped next to her, covering them both with the ends of the wide cloth. Warmth still radiated from the stone step, but the air made them shiver.

"Val's touchy tonight, huh?"

Sarah coughed on the cool air. "She has a right to be. She has a lot on her mind. It must have been a lot easier for her without me here."

Vlad pointed to a meteor streaking the sky. "I don't think so. She was on the comm with the doctor every other day, and she kept talking about when you were coming back."

"Maybe she did it to cheer you up, or convince herself I should come home. She's not a parent, she doesn't know how to deal with all this – *shit,*" Sarah said, feeling delightfully bad for swearing. "None of us do. She doesn't even have any power, really. If everyone decided that David was in charge and we would only listen to him, there's nothing she could do."

Vlad whispered, eyes wide at the thought of mutiny. "You think that's what we should do? Put someone else in charge – not David, that'd be crazy, but, maybe Galina?"

"No. I think she's okay; she just needs to let up. We're not perfect. She's still one of us, she's just the oldest. She needs to stop trying so hard."

They fell silent, until Vlad said, "Do you ever miss them? I mean, you could go an entire day without having Mother talk to you – it's not like she spoiled us or anything – but she was still, *Mother.* Then, when you least expected it, she'd make you realize she knew you were there, and that she cared about you."

"Yeah, she was like that. No one thought twice about her, but boy, did things fall apart without her, huh? It makes me feel kind of bad, like maybe we should have been nicer to her."

Vlad nodded. "And Father – You kind of knew where you stood. You knew what would get him mad. You knew how to behave. Now there's none of that. David's a bigger bully than ever, and Dimi's not in the room to protect me. Dimi's flunking a class again, and he doesn't

162

even care. He wouldn't do that if Father was here."

"Things *are* different," Sarah admitted, "but it sure is nice knowing I can eat a meal without fearing for my life, and that I'll be able to sit down comfortably for it."

"Yeah." Vlad sighed. "Show me home again?"

"You still can't find it?" She'd only shown him a hundred million times. "West by northwest," she pointed. "West by northwest, forty-three degrees from horizon. Topmost star in Sil'anak's Staff. That's Sol. That's home." Sarah could pronounce the alien /'/ sound, but Vlad had given up long ago.

"There you are!" Dmitri called from the doorway. "Val's nearly burst a blood vessel looking for you. You better get in here."

Val looked frazzled and tense. "Damn it, Sarah! What were you thinking, scaring us half to death? You'll be sick for sure, sitting out in the cold!"

"I'll handle it, Val," Galina said, pushing her twin toward the hallway. "Make your plans. Go on. Come with me, Sarah."

The boys were cleaning nutshells from the floor and furniture. Vlad went to help.

In the kitchen, Galina handed Sarah her medication.

"What plan is Val making?" Sarah asked, holding the pills.

"I'm making her take a holiday. Get away for a day or two. She's been doing an awful lot lately. Take your pills."

"I think that would be good for her," Sarah agreed, and put the tablets in her mouth. She drank her water, but Galina'd never given her the medication before. Sarah tucked the pills into her cheek with her tongue.

"All set?"

"Yes."

"Then get to bed – your bed, not Vlad's." Galina swatted her lightly on the rump as she turned to leave. "We're all behind schedule."

Sarah walked to the shower and tossed the pills down the sanitary.

163

# * Fourteen *

Lawyers. Sarah knew doctors, but she'd never met a lawyer before. In less than ten minutes she decided that lawyers weren't much different from doctors; neither could be trusted, but lawyers were more openly hostile. She had to give the prosecutor *some* credit: she'd never seen a doctor so downright enthusiastic about what he wanted to do. Sarah wanted desperately to know his win/loss ratio, but knew Val would get upset if she asked.

Marcus Driskin was the lawyer assigned by the court, a hyperactive man who dressed well, except that his heat robe shed storms of dust and his thin shirts were perpetually wrinkled. As the prosecuting attorney, he insisted on meeting with all of them. Val drew the line at Nikky and the baby. She didn't see a need for Sarah or Vladimir, either, but Sarah wouldn't take no for an answer, and Sarah didn't do anything without Vlad.

"It's our life, too," Sarah argued. "I guess we have just as much right to be there as anybody, maybe more. It's kind of late to hide the facts from us, isn't it?"

Val didn't have an answer for that.

Father would be tried in ten days, and the prosecutor wanted to work out his strategies beforehand. Sarah sat in his office between Katerina and Vladimir, sweating. She had escaped her evening medication three of the last four days. The up and down of the med levels left her dizzy and not a little anxious. She kept herself a bit more locked down, and it helped. Only after listening to the lawyer did the gravity of the trial sink in. The task had seemed easy: sit in a chair and tell sixteen strangers how Father was responsible for Elizabyeta's death, why he shouldn't be released. Now the prosecutor spoke of character witnesses, and visual witnesses, and predisposing factors. He mentioned coroners, professional testimony and psychiatric exams, and establishing patterns of behavior. Nothing seemed simple anymore.

Valeria and Galina would testify, and since Viktor wasn't there, Dmitri, and maybe even Katya, though she didn't like the idea of answering questions about Father's behavior. Driskin had a different approach in mind, a key witness who would tear at the jury's heartstrings and seal the case.

Valeria stared, flabbergasted. "You can't ask her to testify! She's nine years old! She spent three months in a psychiatric hospital because of this! You can't put that kind of pressure on her!"

"I understand," said the lawyer. "But who better to evoke the sympathy of the jury than the poor little girl who was so upset by all the violence she had a nervous breakdown? Make sure you dress her like a little girl – she's on the tall side, you know? Braid her hair, maybe put her in a dress."

Even Dmitri was mortified. "How can you use her like that? That's horrible!"

"More horrible than killing your child over a ball game?"

Dmitri shut up.

"Think of the *power* of such a witness! It's a sure bet." Driskin crouched in front of Sarah, searching for a flicker of understanding in the impassive features.

"You're a smart little girl, aren't you? You understand this. You are a firsthand witness to some of your father's most violent acts. We need every witness we can to testify. If we can't establish a pattern of alcohol abuse and violence, the jury could rule your sister's death accidental. Your father will spend a week or two in an alcohol counseling program here in the city, maybe get ordered to a program for violent offenders, or maybe go free with time served. He can go right back to his ways until someone else gets hurt. Do you understand that? Is that what you want?"

"You are *not* putting Sarah on that stand," Galina insisted. "She has nightmares as it is."

"Is that what you want, sweetheart? Your daddy to come home? Armed with his whip, or maybe a stick this time, ready to show you some new tricks he may have learned in lock-up?"

Valeria rose to the edge of her seat. "I said that's *enough*! Katya, take her out of here."

Next to Sarah, Vladimir exploded in tears. *"No!"* He stared at his wringing hands as two tears splashed his wrist. "I don't ever want him to come home. Never!"

"Aw, crap. There he goes," David muttered in disgust. "Let's hope the other end doesn't start leaking, too."

Sarah put her arms around Vlad and squeezed him, giving him strength. Vlad wiped his face on the collar of his shirt, ashamed of his outburst.

Katya pulled on Sarah's elbow, but she wouldn't budge. "Will they lock him up forever?" she asked Driskin.

"If the jury rules it an accident, he could walk free right there. If we can show intent, based on prior history, we can push the charge up to manslaughter. That would guarantee at least fifteen years in a rehab facility. By then you'd be all grown up. He'll be an old man, with no power over you."

Sarah gave it serious thought. To answer questions about Father's behavior would be embarrassing, even dangerous if Father found out. So many things they could ask her, so many incidents…. Still, it was her fault 'Byeta went and bugged Father in the first place. If anyone knew all the facts that night, it was certainly her. John Carver's voice rose up in her memory, reminding her not to be afraid to take control of her life. Maybe this was such a chance. Someone had to protect Vlad.

"I'll do it," she decided.

*"I expressly forbid it!"* Val ordered.

The lawyer chucked Sarah under the chin. "That's my girl."

Sarah glanced at Vlad, a nervous tic dancing in a corner of his eye. She squeezed his hand. "If it will get rid of Father, I will do it," she said as Val all but carried her from the chair.

The rising sun streaked the sky with orange fire the morning of the trial. Sarah watched the landscape brighten an hour before they had to get up. She'd had a miserable night. Three days on booster meds, two days avoiding them, and now a night with three or four hours sleep at most. So many questions she might get asked, so many ways to answer them. The gravity of the day weighed on her, shrinking her in her skin. She was the Big Witness. It would all depend on her. *One day. She had to survive just one day.* She could do it. It would be over by tonight, and they could rest easy. She paced window to window, rubbing her arms and watching the sky.

Val rushed everyone, wanting to be at the courthouse with an hour to spare. Sarah couldn't choke down more than a single piece of toast. She endured Galina's painfully fast combing of her hair, then practiced breath control exercises to force herself to relax.

She felt bad for Vlad. He'd had no such training. His face glowed ghostly white; his dark eyes seemed larger than ever. The lawyer wouldn't call him as a witness; the strain of practice had left him in tears from his cramping stomach. Sarah hugged him in sympathy whenever she had a free moment, and clenched his hand from the second Valeria pushed them out the door. A half-dozen City Security officers waited for them, a protective escort against the inevitable spectators.

A large quadrangle led to the court, surrounded by covered pedestrian walkways. A sizable group of Navarans lined the path, protesting the very existence of Kar Ku'umi. Sarah translated the silent objections aloud as they passed.

*Murder stains everyone*, read one information board. *Our planet, our law. Request to limit alien settlement. Trade and tourism on Navara's terms*, claimed another. Such acceptance of unregulated self-government by so many aliens would lead to more crimes, more contamination of their culture. Surely, the deliberate, violent death of a child should be a warning? The piercing gray eyes of the Navarans followed the clustered family as security sped them past the news-camera crews into the building.

Inside, they were free. Sarah and Vlad peeked through the decorative metal doors of Courtroom Two. The room was larger than they had imagined, airy and pale, with rows of benches for the audience. Sarah picked out the judge's desk and the witness seat, before Valeria caught them and dragged them away.

"Dmitri, hold on to Sarah. Don't let her go," Valeria said, fluffing Vlad's hair into place. The twins had to appear in firm control, the children had to appear bright, clean and well-behaved, or someone could question if the twins should be given custody of everyone. They were all on their very best behavior, but the twins took no chances. Valeria had charge of Dmitri, Sarah, and Vlad, while Galina kept tabs on David, Katya, and Sergei. Nikky and Marina were spending the day at his preschool.

Marcus Driskin met them in the hall. Even today, dressed in more formal Navaran attire, the bottom of his tunic sported a streak of dust near the hem, as if he'd crossed his legs and wiped his sandal on his knee. "Smile, everyone! Relax! Everyone's so stiff. Everything's going to go fine." He tried to loosen up Sergei by twisting his shoulders. Sergei made a pained face and stepped away. Driskin went on talking with the twins.

Her self guarded safely by two brothers, Sarah's mind wandered. Her gaze roamed the hallway, watching Humans and Navarans going about their business. People filed into the courtroom in spurts, some in loose desert clothing, some in more Earth-traditional shirts and pants.

A small crowd parted, and down the long hall Sarah saw two men walk toward the courtroom, conversing. Both wore traditional clothing, though one seemed better dressed for the heat than the other. With a start, Sarah recognized Dr. Carmichael. *What was he doing here?* He didn't mention coming to court. Then she recognized the other man. She tore free and raced down the hall.

"Sarah!" the boys shouted, running after her.

"John! John Carver!" Sarah shouted, tackling him with a bear hug.

Carver braced for the impact. "Sarah K.! I wondered if I'd see you here. You look great! How are you?"

Her face lost its grin. "Lousy," she declared with overexaggerated irritation. "But it could be an awful lot worse."

Dmitri caught up. "Sar, what are you doing? Get back... ." Vlad was a second behind, slipping his hand into his sister's.

"It's Dr. Carver, Dimi," she explained.

"Dmitri, nice to see you again." Carver shook his hand. He smiled at the smaller boy. "And who is this?"

"This is Vladimir!" Sarah beamed proudly, swinging his arm.

"Vladimir! Nice to meet you at last." Carver shook the small hand as well. "Sarah told me a lot about you."

"Vlad's more upset about this than I am," Sarah shared in a whisper. "Val won't let him testify. We're afraid he'd faint."

Carver glanced at Carmichael. "You're not testifying, are you, Sarah?"

"Of course. I want to."

Carmichael met Carver's stare. "I had no idea. I'm at a distinct disadvantage here. She's said as much to you in three minutes as she's said to me in three weeks."

Carver squatted to look her in the eye. "Sarah, maybe Dr. Carmichael can tell me different, but five weeks ago the *thought* of having to talk about your father left you mute for two days. You think you're ready to handle that?"

Sarah brushed the fear away with a flick of her wrist. "I only have to tell the *jury,* not him. I just have to answer questions – but not think about them too much."

Carver shook his head. "I don't think you understand, Sarah. Your father will be sitting across from that witness stand, watching every testimony, good or bad. That's part of the idea of facing your accusers."

Sarah blanched. "What? No one said he's going to be here."

"They never told us that," Dmitri confirmed.

Vlad pulled at Sarah with both hands. "You can't do that! He'll kill you for real!"

"Maybe we should talk with Valeria," Carver decided. "I can't believe she approved this."

"I certainly don't," Carmichael agreed.

Sarah and Vlad waited in the hall while the adults met with the judge. If she had felt ill before, Sarah's tonsils and stomach had now traded places. She could hardly breathe around the bruising of the butterflies banging against her insides. If she wasn't convincing enough, Father would no doubt make her wish she had died instead of 'Byeta. But now she'd have to describe Father's wrath while he watched. She'd been whipped for less. Still, she had to be strong for Vlad. He had no strength to deal with things on his own. And the big boys... They weren't any better than her! She was a full-fledged member of the Fearsome Four, with her fair share of battle wounds. Certainly she could be as brave as David pretended to be, as proud and strong as Viktor and sometimes even Dmitri could be. She mustn't let them down, either.

The bailiff called Sarah from the doorway. Vlad's eyes begged her not to go. She patted his hand and took a deep breath, compressing the butterflies. "I can do this," she assured him, but she couldn't bring herself to smile.

Her footsteps made a hushed echo in the high-ceilinged courtroom. Valeria didn't look happy; neither did the doctors, whispering back and forth. The lawyer winked at Sarah and smiled.

A man sat at the table in the front of the room. He looked human, but bore strong traces of Centauri in his thick pink skin. His cheeks sagged far down in wattly flaps, as if the Navaran heat had melted slabs of fat from him. Val had chosen a gauzy tan dress for her to wear. Matching embroidery covered the front, and around the neckline and cuffs were several rows of threads in dark desert maroon twisted with a fine metallic gold thread. Her hair was brushed glossy and smooth, pulled back from her face by a maroon ribbon. Long hair wasn't practical for the day's heat, but she did look as young as she suddenly felt – a lot younger and more vulnerable than nine.

"Miss Kirushenko," the judge began, "I have several people here who have very strong reservations about your testifying in today's trial. They worry it will put you under dangerous levels of stress. They are worried that you haven't had enough time to recover from your recent crisis, and that this will complicate your recovery. I would like to hear your opinion. I want to make sure no one is pushing you to do something you don't want to do, or might not be ready for. How do you feel about this?"

Sarah swallowed hard. "Sir, Your Honor. Judge. Sir... " *How* did *one properly address a judge?* She paused, desperate to say something to make the judge believe her, something good enough to stand up to a psychiatrist's argument. In a flash it came to her: *fight psychiatrists with psychiatry.* She hadn't spent three months in rehab without learning *something*! Her butterflies paused in their mad flapping to hear better, and the words flowed out with ease.

"Sir, I appreciate the concern everyone has for my well-being, and I thank them for it, but this is something I must do. Every day, I live with the fact I saw my father kill my sister. Every night when I climb into bed, I see the empty space where hers used to be. Every morning I wake up knowing the fear my father has put me and my brothers and sisters through. In the hospital, they taught me how important it is to share my feelings. If I don't give my side of this story, I'll have once again been made powerless by a fear of my father. Without being able to tell how I feel, I will never have closure, no matter what the outcome of this trial. I'm well aware of the crime that was committed. Sitting at home or sitting silent in the audience won't change anything I've already experienced. Please don't deny me this opportunity for peace of mind."

*"What did you teach her?"* Carmichael whispered. A monster had risen out of the silent, sullen clamshell he'd grown accustomed to. "I had serious doubts about the IQ."

"Don't ever underestimate her," Carver whispered back. "She'll beat you, every time."

Judge Ellmore stared. "Do you understand the words you're using, young lady?"

"Absolutely, your Honor, sir. I'm studying an accelerated academic program and will get my first diploma within a year. If you would like, I will repeat my statement in Terran Russian, Terran French, or modern Navaran. You may check it against the computer," Sarah dared with confidence.

"That won't be necessary. Miss Kirushenko, your argument is lucid, rational, and logical. I reserve the right to change my mind should I feel you to be overly disturbed during testimony, but I will allow it. Court will convene in twenty minutes."

"Thank you, sir." As Sarah left the room, she gave a wink and a smile to Valeria and John.

*No sweat.*


They took their seats with ten minutes to spare, in a long row behind the prosecutor's table; first Valeria, then Katya, Sarah, Vlad, Sergei, Dmitri, Galina, and David. In the second row sat the two psychiatrists – Carver made sure he had a clear view of both Sarah and the witness stand. The Medical Examiner from the trauma center sat with them, along with a former colleague of Father's, the Dean of the Academy branch where Father taught, and the emergency physician who had treated Father the time he'd been knocked out. Across a narrow aisle, the court-appointed defender sat behind his table, absorbed in the spread of compads, color-coded computer chips, loose printouts, and the numerous recording devices before him.

They whispered, anxious and fidgety, until two officers brought in the accused. It was a scene dreamt of dozens of times, but to see it happening slammed home a reality no one could have imagined.

Father, as tall and broad as when they'd last seen him four months ago, was *shackled*. His ankles bore electronic cuffs that limited the length of his step, hobbling the long legs. His arms were clamped at the wrists to a belt around his waist. He wore new, conservative clothing that fit, looking as if he were intercepted on his way to work. His thick black hair lay trimmed and combed, and the wild beard hugged the broad chin with calculated proportion, quite respectable. He didn't glance at the children until after he'd sat. Being accused of killing someone with his bare hands, his wrists remained bound.

A ripple went through the line of Kirushenko children. What were they *doing?* What could they possibly be *thinking* of? How could they make Father be paraded around like a common criminal? Father was a learned man! An important man! He was respected academically! So powerful was his presence, had he beckoned with a twist of his head, at least four of his children would have risen and gone to him. Mercifully, Father's glance was brief.

Valeria paled. Sergei hid his head in his hands. David gazed defiantly ahead, refusing to look at all. Vlad grabbed Sarah and buried his face.

Sarah put her arms around him. His heart hammered in his thin little chest, and she prayed to the Universe he wouldn't do anything embarrassing. If Father looked their way again, if he looked at her, her resolve would disappear. Everyone bragged how they'd punish Father if they ever got the chance, but no one dreamed of saying it to his face. Now they would be doing just that. They would have to. The judge would make them. Sarah's level of misery doubled. They would fail, fail, fail, *fail*.

The judge gave the call to order. Of the children, only Valeria had ever seen a real trial in action. The rules of the court were read, and the jury filed in, eleven men and five women. All wore the long gray robes that the judge wore. They were actually two juries: thirteen local Kar Ku'umi citizens, and a second, three-person Navaran jury. After the first jury made their ruling, the Navarans would decide if further action should be taken to satisfy Navaran law. There was no death penalty on Navara, an idea so horrific they could not comprehend it, but what the

Navarans considered severe punishment no outworlder actually knew. Rumors persisted about mind-tampering and living death.

The bailiff read the charges: "That on Navaran date 33 Tariel 9174, Earthdate 13 August 2263, Alexander Grigorevitch Kirushenko did physically strike his daughter, Elizabyeta Viktoria Kirushenko, causing her neck to fracture and treatment to be delayed until her life functions ceased. How does the defendant plead?"

Father's attorney rose, a slim, weasel-faced man. Next to Father's bulk, he looked like a ventriloquist's puppet. "Alexander Kirushenko pleads 'Not Guilty,' your Honor."

"So be it entered for the record, 9:08 hours, 17 December 2263." The judge sounded a two-tone bell to signal that the court proceedings had officially begun.

The prosecutor had the opening statement. Father had been arrested with enough evidence to warrant a jury; in the eyes of the court he was already guilty. The defender had the harder role – refuting the charges and proving his client's innocence.

Driskin began with a command he'd never shown in his office. He moved to the front of the courtroom, meandering long laps between the judge and the evidence table, across the front, then before the jurors and back.

"What you hear today will not be pleasant. It will bring up behaviors and situations we thought we had eradicated a hundred years ago. A story we will find difficult to believe could happen in our enlightened times. I will tell you a tale of twelve children – twelve – who were so frightened, so ashamed, so embarrassed, that they endured a brutal existence in silence, rather than admit what happened to them. It's a story that slipped through every social service net we ever thought to put in place. Here on a planet renowned for non-violence, I will tell you a story of unremitting abuse. Of indifference. Of cruelty. Of inevitable infanticide. And twelve traumatized children, with nowhere to run."

The lawyer paused before the juries. "We will prove to you today that Alexander Kirushenko is a dangerous man. A violent man. A brutal man. A man who tortured his children both physically and mentally. A man who, *without a doubt*, deliberately and willfully murdered his six-year old daughter. Why? What could drive a man to murder his own child? She asked him a question. That is all, ladies and gentlemen. She died for asking her daddy a simple question.

"But not die *quickly*, gentlepersons! Elizabyeta died slowly. Her spinal fracture might not have killed her, had medical attention arrived promptly. After a time she may have made a full recovery. But despite the pleas of her siblings, Alexander Kirushenko refused to allow anyone to call for aid. He forbade it! Conditioned by a lifetime of fear, the survivors dared not disobey. Nine children had to stand by helplessly and watch their little sister suffocate, minute by agonizing minute." He dragged the last four words out, one by one. "Only when she was dead, her brain irrevocably destroyed, were they allowed a cry for help."

On and on the prosecutor rambled, stretching some truths, padding out others, coming too close to ignoring more. They were not facts the Kirushenko children wanted to hear. Living it once was enough, yet Driskin ground out detail after detail for half an hour before yielding the floor.

Father's attorney, Endron Suarez, stood up.

"Persons of the juries, honored guests: if a person has but one leg, would we blame him for stumbling? If a person had a paralysis, would we prosecute her for moving too slowly? If a person was cursed at conception with a genetic flaw, would he be held guilty of an illness? That's what we are dealing with, my friends – a genetically based illness, a genetically demonstrable inability to produce neurochemicals and process ethyl alcohol. Alexander Kirushenko could not have plotted, deliberated, intended, or otherwise attempted to murder his daughter Elizabeth on the night of thirteen August, as he was incapacitated by psychiatric depression and a copious amount of alcohol at the time of the alleged incident. The death of Elizabeth Kirushenko was an unfortunate accident whose outcome was decided not by any act of her father, no. But by the unwillingness of her siblings to intervene. Her siblings' misguided pact of never asking for help, of always trying to handle crises by themselves, led to the unfortunate delay that caused their sister's death. *By the Kirushenko children's own statements*, their father was unconscious. What could they have feared from an unconscious man? It takes more than ten minutes for a body to die from lack of oxygen; for ten minutes, nine siblings stood by and watched their sister suffocate, and did *nothing*. Six more minutes would pass before help would arrive."

Dmitri caught David's incredulous glance. "He's putting the blame on *us*!"

"Is Mr. Kirushenko a violent man? I don't know. One child can be a handful. Imagine, if you will, trying to raise thirteen. Thirteen children vying for attention, bickering over who has more ice cream, who looked cross-eyed at whom, who got to the lavatory first. Was Mr. Kirushenko a strict disciplinarian? Yes he was. He had to be, to keep order in such a household. Now imagine those thirteen children motherless, relying only on their father for support, and you can begin to understand the pressure on my client. Most children can't wait for their parents to leave them home alone. To eat candy for breakfast, ice cream for lunch, fruit crispies for dinner, staying up all hours, with no one to tell them 'No.' For the last four months, these ten remaining children have been living without a parent's care, without a parent's guidance, without a parent's love. This is a family that needs guidance and care. You will have no choice but to see this death as accidental, and reunite a separated family."

David leaned around Galina. "Dimi, you ever heard such a load of bull? I say we wait around until he leaves the building, and 'accidentally' kick the shit out of him. Show'em what accidental feels like."

"I begin by calling Doctor Kingston Broos, Medical Examiner for Ku'umi Primary Trauma Center," Driskin stated. He waited for the man to be sworn in. "Dr. Broos, you are a licensed Medical Examiner?"

"I am." A heavyset dark-skinned man, his shaved head glistened with perspiration. "I am currently employed by the UPA/Kar Ku'umi Trauma Center as such. I received my medical degree at the University of Johannesburg on Earth, and my Examiner's license from the College for Advanced Anatomical Study on Denebola IV."

"And you have training in homicide forensics? You have experience in examining homicide victims?"

"Well, not here on Navara," Broos admitted. "It's not an issue. But yes, I was well-trained in homicide forensics on Denebola."

"Dr. Broos, you examined the body of Elizabyeta Kirushenko?"

"Yes, I did."

"Were you able to establish a cause of death?"

"Yes. Death was caused by a dislocation of the second cervical vertebra in the neck, resulting in a compression of the spinal cord at the C-2 level."

"And such a dislocation results in instant death?" the lawyer asked.

"Not as we think," Dr. Broos explained. "Such an injury results in a paralysis of the breathing muscles. If help arrives fast enough, say, within one to four minutes, or someone else is able to breathe for the victim, we can often stabilize such injuries. With nerve regeneration and rehabilitative therapies, such patients frequently make a strong recovery."

"And if help doesn't arrive in time?"

"The human brain, without oxygen, starts to die within three minutes. After five, there is damage of varying degrees. After ten minutes, there is not enough surviving brain tissue to maintain autonomic function, even if oxygen is restored under hyperbaric pressure. The patient's life signs cease. He dies."

"Was there any evidence that would suggest a reason for said dislocation?" Driskin asked.

"There was evidence of blunt trauma. Specifically, there was a linear bruise across the area of dislocation. An area of recent bruising was also present along the lower left side of the jaw."

"This bruising on the face – could it have been caused by being struck by a hand?"

Dr. Broos raised his eyebrows. "There is no way to prove absolutely, but the evidence does not rule it out. Not long before the victim's death, there had been a forceful blow upwards and sideways to the jaw. There were two broken teeth, lacerations to the insides of the mouth caused by teeth, and a fracture of the jaw itself. Fragments of teeth were found inside the victim's mouth."

"If I may enter photo exhibits one through eight into the record," the lawyer said, returning to his table in front of the children. "Computer, viewscreen on. Display photorecord number one." A large viewscreen at the front of the room glowed to life. Whispers rippled through the audience. Driskin handed a laser pointer to the coroner. "These photos were taken from your files, Dr. Broos. Could you comment on them for us please…"

The judge took a brief look at the autopsy photo. "Those outside of the jury who wish to leave the courtroom during this testimony may do so." Several in the audience moved to leave.

Sarah froze. The photo showed a close-up of a mouth held open by instruments, revealing cuts to the inside of the lips and fragments of teeth. Thankfully, it was impossible to tell the identity of the subject from the first picture. It might have been Elizabyeta, it might not, though the mix of baby teeth and missing incisors was incriminating. The images were graphic and gory beyond even Sarah's imagination. She jumped at a hand on her shoulder, and turned to see John Carver.

"Maybe you should take Vladimir outside for a while – take a walk in the hall or something."

Vlad slouched low in his seat, fingers in his ears, tears beading on his clenched eyes. Sarah pulled a finger out and whispered in Russian. He shook his head, then leaned on her, hiding.

Sarah shook her head. "He doesn't want to."

Carver motioned with his head. "I'll walk with you. Come on."

Sarah gave him a sad little smile. "It was a nice try. Don't worry. I don't want to look, either." She held Vlad up, keeping her eyes only on him, while a glum Sergei rubbed his brother's back, whispering. Beside her, Sarah could hear Katya sniffing softly. It seemed forever until the medical examiner finished.

Driskin called Valeria next. Val had spent much effort trying to look older and accomplished. She wore a draped white Navaran dress, woven around the edges with tan and gold threads, with a matching head shawl loosely covering her honey-gold hair. An air of serene calm surrounded her, masking the strains of the morning.

"You are the oldest of the Kirushenko children?"

"Yes, sir. By four and a half minutes."

Driskin smiled briefly. "And being the oldest, more or less, you can remember your father longer than anyone else?"

"Yes, sir." Val's hands rested in her lap, feet tucked back under the chair, politely attentive. She appeared cool and collected, and very responsible.

"Has your father always been violent?"

"No. When I was young, Father was quite pleasant. We traveled frequently while he worked at different archaeology sites. Father had many interesting friends – professors, scientists, historians. We had dinner parties Mother would cater herself. For our sixth birthday, he took Galina, Alexei, and me, and some of our friends, to the circus, and somehow arranged a backstage tour. I don't know who had more fun, him or us."

"Was he drinking then?"

"I don't know. If Mother wasn't pregnant, they'd both have wine with dinner. But I don't know if he was ever drunk."

"When do you first remember noticing a change?"

Valeria became thoughtful. "Around nine, perhaps. We hadn't been on a trip in four or five months. We children were pestering if we were going anywhere soon."

"How many of you were there, back then?" Driskin interrupted.

Val counted back in her head. *If she was nine, then there was ...* "Me and Gal, Alexei, Vik, Kat, Dimi, ... If David was born, he was just a small baby. Six or Seven."

"So there were a lot of you already."

"Yes, sir."

"Continue."

"We were naming places we'd like to go, but Father had to teach a new class, and he had a lot of planning to do. He was taking an advanced class himself, so it would be at least a semester before we'd be traveling again. We must have gotten a little noisy, because Father yelled very loud and pounded the table. We quieted down immediately, because

Father had never done that before. I mean, he'd gotten angry before, but this time he was – threatening. We'd never had reason to *fear* Father before."

"Was he drunk?"

"I don't know. I didn't pay attention to such things."

"When did you realize your father had difficulty controlling his alcohol?"

"I became extremely aware of it in the last year, but I think I began to realize it around eleven or twelve."

"So in two or three years your father went from friendly and sober to threatening and drunk," Driskin reiterated.

"No," Valeria clarified. "That's just when I first began to notice my father wasn't a pleasant person after he'd been drinking vodka."

"How does he drink his vodka?"

"Straight, with ice. On a bad day, straight from the bottle."

"And how much does he drink in a day?"

"It depends on the day, whether or not he's been to work, or stopped somewhere on the way home. If he's home all day, I've seen him empty almost two liters."

"That's a lot of vodka. Does he drink until he becomes ill?"

"Yes, sir."

"Until he's unconscious?"

"Yes."

"Does he have blackouts? Forget whole hours, maybe even days?"

"Yes, sir, that has happened," Val agreed reluctantly.

"Did he drink the day your sister died?"

"Yes, sir."

"How much?"

"Half a liter, maybe more."

"So it is possible," Driskin concluded, "that even though your father might *say* he doesn't remember something happening, it may actually have, because he blacked out and can't remember."

"Yes, sir."

"He could have struck Elizabyeta, killed her, and not remember doing it at all."

"It's possible."

"Tell me more about the night your sister died…"

Valeria worked through her memory of that night, and Driskin gave the floor to cross-examination.

"Miss Kirushenko, if you were out of your home for five years, how do you know so much about your Father's drinking habits?" Suarez asked.

"I returned home ten months ago, upon the news of my mother's death."

"And what do you do now?"

"I run the household and care for my brothers and sisters." She brushed a hair off her cheek and hooked it behind her ear under the scarf. "My mother left a newborn to care for."

"So in the prime of your youth, you are caring for eight children. That's a job many experienced parents would find daunting. Do you find that task difficult?"

"At times, yes. I deal with a cranky infant one minute and teenage rebellion the next. But I could do the same job as a hired worker, and no one would think twice."

"You also have a sibling with a mental illness, no?"

"Yes, sir, but she has recovered," Val said in the same assured tone.

"How do you manage that responsibility on top of everything else? Isn't that a strain on you?"

"When we – the doctors and I – felt Sarah could not be managed at home, she was placed in a residential treatment facility where she received excellent care. She is recovered now, and any difficulties have been due to overprotectiveness on my part rather than Sarah. As for stress," Val smiled, "Galina and I were a team long before birth. If I feel stressed, she takes over, and vice versa."

"Did your father ever beat you? Punch you? Strike you?"

"Maybe slapped me once or twice, twisted my arm or such."

"Did you ever fear for your life?"

"Myself? No."

"Did you ever tell anyone about the violence? Confide to a friend? A teacher? A doctor?"

"No."

"Why not? Why choose to live in the shadow of violence?" Suarez pushed.

"I don't know," Val shrugged. "We never thought about it. We loved Father; we accepted him as he was. Everyone gets crabby at times."

"Do you feel the tales of your father's violence are exaggerated?"

"No, I do not."

"You don't remember anything worse than a slap, but you feel your father is capable of murder?"

"Yes. I have to. I saw it happen."

"Do you think your father could have judged the severity of an injury at the time of the incident?"

Driskin stood up. "Objection! The witness is neither a medical or psychological professional, and is not trained to make such a judgment."

"Your Honor, the witness is an expert on the behavior of this one individual, based on a lifetime of observation," Suarez claimed.

The judge leaned back in his seat. "I'll allow it on an opinion basis only, without scientific fact. The witness may answer the question."

Valeria sighed regretfully, looking at her hands in her lap. "No, sir. He – couldn't judge the distance from his glass to his mouth."

"No further questions," Suarez said lightly, and sat down.

"...as you know it to be true?"

"I do," swore Galina.

"You may be seated."

Galina sat. She, like Valeria, wore a white headscarf, but she wore a much more tailored white skirt with a white jacket. She respected the Navarans and their habits, but she wasn't about to blend in with them.

"You are a twin, are you not?" Driskin opened.

"Yes. Valeria and I are identical twins. I'm the unexpected one."

"You were a surprise?"

"Not after the first eight weeks, but we decided long ago that since Valeria was older, I was the surprise."

"I see. Do you agree with your sister that when you were young, your father was not a violent man?"

"Yes. When Father was still assigned to digs, he would come home full of news of things he'd found and done. Sometimes he'd bring something home to show us, teach us how to analyze it. After he started teaching, we were tied to the university's schedule. He didn't have as much to talk about when he came home. We already knew the lecture material."

"You left school to return home."

"I finished two degrees," Galina explained. "I simply put anything else on hold 'til things are straightened out at home."

"So you took employment."

Galina refused to be ashamed. "I work night duty at the Interstellar and Hyperspace Communications Relay Center in Kar Ku'umi. I'm responsible for maintaining satellite communication networks and making sure all incoming and outgoing long-distance communications are correctly routed."

"Is it difficult?" Driskin asked.

"Not generally. Sometimes we get busy, though."

"Why would you take such a job? Wouldn't your father's salary cover expenses?"

"At the start, it did," Galina admitted. "But after two or three months there was less credit available on his account. My employment picked up the extra expenses, and with the Dependent Child Assistance Stipend, we've managed okay the last four months."

"Do you resent having to work while your twin stays home?"

"On the contrary, I feel bad that she can't get out more. I work while everyone sleeps. I come home and help get everyone off to their proper school, then I sleep while the house is quiet. I'm awake in time to help with dinner. Val doesn't have them alone for very long."

"Where do you think your father's money went during those months?" Driskin asked.

Galina tried not to laugh. "Honestly? I believe he drank it. Liquor has to be imported, and it's not cheap. We cleaned at least eight bottles from the house after 'Byeta died. With the import charges being what they are, that's more than 1200 credits right there."

"Do you believe he is a dangerous person?"

Galina tipped her head boldly. "By himself? No. When drinking, yes. I didn't believe the stories at first; I thought they were just the exaggerations of children. Then I saw for myself they weren't."

"When did you first realize your father had a drinking problem?"

"I think I was thirteen before I really hated him for drinking."

"Will you tell the court about that incident, please?"

"It was my – our – thirteenth birthday," Galina said with rehearsed ease. "We hadn't been in Kiev that long, and Mother let us have a party with our new friends. We were having a grand time, except by seven o'clock Father still hadn't come home. At eight, we had our birthday pie without him. He stumbled in at nine, singing a very crude song. Then he remembered the party and became angry that we had gone ahead without him.

"We didn't know what to do. We couldn't exactly pretend it didn't happen. Eventually Mother got him into the kitchen with the promise of pie, but you could still hear him and his drunken mouth. Our friends thought it might be better if they went home, so the party broke up early."

"What did you do then?" asked the prosecutor.

"Ran into the kitchen, told my Father I hated everything to do with him, then cried my heart out with my sister for the next two hours. Father apologized the next day, but it was too late. We never got anyone to come over again, even if Father wasn't home."

"No further questions."

"You say you told your father you hated him," Suarez began. "Did you tell him or shout at him?"

"I'm sure it was more like screaming," Galina said.

"Did he do or say anything back?"

"No, I ran to my room."

"He didn't punish you?"

"No."

"Why not?"

"I think he knew I was right."

"Yet he strikes your sister without provocation?"

"My incident was ten years ago."

"And you believe in the years subsequent, he became capable of murder?"

"Yes. He drinks much more heavily, much more frequently, and becomes enraged much faster than ten years ago."

"Did your father ever hit you, or whip you?"

Galina gave a delicate smile. "I'm sure I had my share of spankings years ago."

"Do you feel your father knew his own strength the night he hit your sister?"

"Probably not."

Judge Ellmore called a five-minute water break – a requirement every few hours, to make sure no one in the courtroom wound up with heatstroke. The witnesses, defendants, and jury were served their water; the audience had to fend for themselves at the water stations. The length of the water line left plenty of time for ogling the children. The judge's bell rang before everyone could squeeze back to their seats. Even though Val knew her last statement had been damning to the prosecution, she'd remained cool and calm. Galina had been rather flippant, refusing to be unnerved. Katya was so nervous that Sarah, sitting next to her, almost believed she could hear Kat's bones rattling in her skin.

"Ekaterina Anastasia Kirushenko."

Sarah gave Katya's hand a final squeeze as she stood up. The clicking of her sandals on the hard floor ticked off the final seconds before she'd have to speak. Katya took the seat, caught sight of Father staring at her with an impassive face, and lost any composure she may have had. Valeria had been perfectly proper, Galina supremely confident. Katya just looked scared.

"Do you swear on your honor to tell the truth of the matter as you know it, above all else, under penalty of law?"

Kat trembled. "I do, sir."

Driskin cleared his throat to begin speaking, and she jumped.

"Nervous, Miss Kirushenko?"

Kat's hands twisted in her lap like dying fish. "A little. This is new to me."

"It's not because you're facing your father? Perhaps saying things he might not want you to say?"

"Objection!" Suarez said. "Speculation, your Honor…"

"I'll rephrase that," the prosecutor replied. "Does it make you nervous sitting up here across from your father?"

Katya flushed a deep crimson. "Yes, sir."

"Was your father ever violent towards you, Miss Kirushenko?"

A visible shudder passed through Katya's slender form. "Yes."

"Slapped?"

"Yes."

"Bruised?"

"Yes."

"Whipped?"

"Not that I remember."

"Could you tell the jury an incident that stands out in your mind? A time you felt your father unjustifiably harsh towards you?"

"Yes." Katya lifted her head, gaining a little confidence. She'd rehearsed this part. She kept her head turned to the judge.

"I – I was going to a school dance, my brothers Viktor and Dmitri and I."

"How old were you then?"

"Fourteen or fifteen."

"And how old are you now?"

"Seventeen."

"How old were your brothers at the time?"

"About … seventeen and fourteen."

"Go on."

"We were going to a dance, a chaperoned dance," Katya recalled. "I was dressed reasonably, no makeup as per Father's rules – he didn't like any of us in heavy makeup. Plain hoop earrings, maybe five or six centimeters across. Nothing wild.

"Father came over as we were about to leave. His eyes were all shiny, like they get when he's been drinking a lot. He asked me where I was going dressed like that. I told him we were just going to a dance. He said no daughter of his was going out of the house dressed like a… a… *joygirl*," Katya blushed.

"I asked him what was wrong, and he reached out with both hands and – *ripped* the earrings out of my ears. He never asked me to take them off, he just *ripped* them. All he said was, my 'damned earrings were too big'," Kat dropped her voice in poor imitation of her father, "and he walked away. My brothers got me out quick. My ears were bleeding. I had to have the holes relocated."

"No further questions."

Suarez jumped up in an instant. "Miss Kirushenko, did you meet any friends when you arrived at this dance?"

"Yes, some."

"And what did you tell them about your torn ears?"

"Nikky was a baby then. I told them the baby had grabbed the earrings."

"Not your father?"

"No."

"Why not?"

"It wasn't anybody's business," Kat answered. "If I told, someone might have mentioned it to Father, and that would anger him, and he'd come back at me and accuse me of lying."

"Did you ever do that? Tell anyone of any time your father harmed you or someone else?"

"No."

"Then how can you know there'd be a retaliation?"

"Because there would have been. I know it." Katya looked to Driskin, at a loss for the best answer, but he couldn't help.

"But you don't know that for a fact, because the circumstances never occurred."

"No, not that way," she had to admit, "but I still know it."

"So you allowed such violence to continue rather than stop it."

Katya flushed. "It wasn't that simple! He was still my father. We were taught to obey him. You don't go ratting on your family. Even the Navarans have a custom about that."

"Even if it means one of you must die?"

*"No!"* Katya nearly shouted. "I *tried!* I *tried* to help 'Byeta! He wouldn't let me."

"Let me ask you this," posed the defense attorney. "If you *had* told someone, and there *was* an investigation, do you think your father would have been forced to stop drinking?"

"Objection," Driskin said. "Speculation…"

"Sustained," agreed the judge.

"What did your mother have to say about the incident you spoke of?"

"Mother felt it was our job to keep each other out of Father's way. She would distract him if she felt he was being too harsh, but discipline was his decision."

"The night your sister died, would your mother have prevented him from striking her?"

Katya thought a minute. "Probably yes. If he seemed upset, she would have made sure nothing disturbed him. She loved him."

"Do you love your father?"

Katya glanced at Father with a look of panic. "I don't know."

Dmitri took the stand without hesitation. His determined manner eased some of Sarah's anxiety. He looked a bit heroic to her, answering questions so easily under such pressure. He'd spent at least a half hour that morning combing his hair, and it had actually stayed in place. Sarah decided that, given time, scrawny Dmitri might turn out to be handsome someday, after all.

"Would you say you and your father got along, Dmitri?" Driskin asked.

"No sir, I would not say that. Not at all." He sat straight and attentive, trying his best to look grown up.

"Your sister said that your father whipped only the boys. Do you think that's true?"

Dmitri shrugged. "There's four of us between the older and younger girls. The older ones were too old to hit; even Father didn't treat girls like that. Elizabyeta was his favorite; I don't think he ever hit her – except that night, you know? Nikky's too little, and Alexei was too old. That left five of us and Sarah to take most of the trouble."

"Does that bother you? Knowing the girls could get off easier?"

"I don't think anybody got off easy, except 'Byeta, usually."

"Do feel your father acted unjustifiably harsh at times?"

"Yes, sir, I do."

"Could you explain to the court what you consider to be unfair?"

Dmitri sighed and leaned back, inevitably starting to slouch. "Just my personal experience?" Some of the worst things he'd only witnessed.

"Just to you personally," Driskin agreed.

"Shaving my head because he didn't like my haircut comes to mind."

"That hardly qualifies as a violent event, but go on."

"Knocking my head into a wall so hard it cracked the paint, because I made too much noise playing. Holding me to a wall and leaving bruises on my throat for being out with a girl eight minutes past curfew. I was thirteen! It's not like I was doing anything, you know? Whipping me for less than a ninety grade in history, whipping me for ripping my clothes, whipping me for calling MedEvac ..."

Driskin stopped him with a raised hand. "Calling MedEvac? When did you need to call for MedEvac?" That would put a hole in Suarez' theory of never seeking help.

Dmitri stuck like glue to the story they'd worked out so many months ago. Viktor had made them practice it so much he could hardly remember anything different. "Father passed out on the floor. We weren't sure he was breathing, so we called for assistance. He came home the next day madder than Hell, and made sure we knew it."

Driskin oozed incredulousness. "Your father whipped you for getting him medical attention when he needed it?"

Dmitri's face burned with unforgotten shame. "Viktor and me, on bare skin."

"How long was that before your sister died?

Dmitri slouched farther. "I don't know. Maybe a month?"

Driskin nodded in sympathy. "And such a negative experience would make you less likely to go against your father's wishes on future calls for assistance, no?"

"Objection!" shouted the defense attorney. "Speculation!"

"If it pleases the court," Driskin explained, "I'm talking about a simple matter of behavioral science fact. Any first-year university student knows that a severe negative experience has been shown to make someone much less likely to repeat an action, from insects to hominids."

"I'll allow it," Ellmore ruled.

"Did this first experience make you hesitant to disobey your father the next time you needed medical assistance?"

"Yes sir. Very hesitant. Valeria promised it would be her responsibility if Father got upset."

"Yet your mother used to make you care for your father when he was incapacitated, did she not?" Driskin led into the part they'd practiced.

"Yeah. Sometimes, when she couldn't," Dmitri admitted. "Me and Viktor."

"How did you feel about that?"

"I hated it!" Dmitri said forcefully, pushing himself up straight again. "It was bad enough to always have to babysit this one, or bathe that one, or feed these two, but Father was supposed to take care of *us*, not the other way around! It was like he wasn't doing his job or something."

"How did you have to care for him?"

"I'll tell you it was goddamned disgusting, that's what!" Dmitri snapped, then apologized, "Pardoning my word choice, sir.

"One time, after we'd been here awhile, Mother sent me and Vik out to get Father. He'd been at a place he liked here in the city, passed out, and they wanted someone to get him before a Security Officer found him. Mother sent us."

"Did you have any difficulty?"

"No, he was out of it. Some people in the bar helped us lay him across one of the seats. We get about half way home and he starts pu – I mean, um, vomiting, while he's asleep, you know? It – the *stink!*" Dimi wrinkled his nose in disgust, remembering. "He eats pickled eggs, for crying out loud! The smell was so bad Vik had to stop the flyer. I got sick, and Vik walked around choking a while. We kept the air intakes wide open, but we stopped a couple more times to walk around and breathe. Mother met us at the door, and we were able to get him awake enough to shuffle if we held him. Mother cleaned him, but we had to clean the flyer. I don't think I've ever had to do something that disgusting before or since. We left the flyer open all night, but it still stunk for a while."

"How old were you, Dmitri?"

"Fourteen, maybe."

"Was that the first time you retrieved your father?"

"Me, yes. Viktor had gotten him a couple other times. But that was the worst."

"Was your father that drunk the night of your sister's death?"

Dmitri chewed his lip for a moment. "No," he decided. "He was pretty well shot, but he was awake and talking. He still made sense, and you could understand him."

"Did he know what he was doing?"

"Absolutely. Father never hits accidentally. If she got hit, then that's what he meant to do. I have no doubt about that."

"Thank you. No more questions," Driskin relented, taking his seat.

Suarez fell upon him instantly. "Dmitri, you state that you were fourteen at the time of the incident you describe. How old was your brother Viktor?"

"Maybe seventeen."

"How did you get to the city? Walk?"

"Hell no!" Dmitri grinned, the twisty little half-smile he used to charm girls. "It's thirteen kilometers! We'd have had to drag him all that way. Mother told Vik to take the flyer."

"Thirteen, fourteen, sixteen, seventeen – that's not old enough for a license to pilot a craft within city limits," Suarez pointed out.

"No sir, it's not," Dmitri had to admit.

"Had your brother ever piloted the flyer before?"

"I don't think so. Possibly."

"But he was not what you would call an experienced pilot?"

"No sir! Not in the least." Dmitri grinned. Viktor didn't know much more than he did. The second-hand flyer had a heavy vibration to start with, and the up and down motion as Vik fought to coordinate the old, manual altitude control with the directional readout and forward velocity made it more like a zero-G amusement ride. "It was probably Vik's flying that made him sick in the first place. At least we never fully bottomed out."

"So a young boy and an inexperienced pilot managed to fly thirteen kilometers into city limits, park a flyer, and fly home again thirteen kilometers, without incident?"

"Yeah, pretty much," Dmitri  agreed. They'd tried to be careful. It had taken fifteen minutes, three times longer than normal. "There's not much to hit in the desert, even in the dark. We had the scanners on."

"Your sister felt your father was impaired enough that he was, quote, 'Unable to judge the distance between his glass and his mouth,' unquote. Yet you feel your father was coordinated enough to aim a fist and deliver a strong punch. How do you account for that difference of opinion?"

Dmitri gave a short laugh and another half-smile. "I'd say Father was so good at hitting he didn't need to aim, but I don't think that's the answer you want." He grew somber as he worked on a better one.

"Val's good, and her opinion's probably right, but she's been gone five years. She doesn't know Father – *this* Father –," he jabbed his thumb in Father's direction, "like we do. She's dealt with him for ten months, and he hasn't hit her once. Vodka might make Father drunk, but mostly it just makes him *mean*. He can aim pretty damned good when you think he's too drunk to walk. Val wasn't there the night he almost killed Viktor, or the time he nearly killed Sarah. I was. Sometimes being drunk makes him even stronger. He doesn't know when to quit."

"So you would agree with the statement that your father may not have known his own strength the night he hit Elizabyeta?"

"I guess that's possible," Dmitri had to admit.

David couldn't wait to get to the witness stand, eager to "fix Father's ass." Valeria closed her eyes and breathed deeply in angst when the judge had to explain that 'You bet!' was not an appropriate response to being sworn in. David was their loose cannon. As with Sarah, Val never wanted him on the stand in the first place.

Valeria had tried to make sure everyone looked their absolute best for the trial, but there sat fourteen year old David on the edge of his seat, in tan pants, sandals, a deep purple vest – and a small tear in his shirt. He had escaped a haircut, and flipped his head repeatedly to get his hair out of his eyes. No matter how often he washed it, his thick hair always looked unkempt in the blasted heat. Galina claimed it was just his age, but more likely it was the luck of the draw, inheriting Father's sweat glands along with his big frame. David never had much respect for authority in the first place; the formality of the court didn't faze him a micron. The fact that Father sat behind a table in restraints, unable to touch him, made him antagonistic. He glared at Father, taunting him.

"David, did you ever have to retrieve your father?"

"*Hell* no! I wouldn't have, anyway." David leaned back, knees far apart. His elbows rested loosely on the arms of the chair, and he watched Driskin from under his long bangs with contempt.

"Why not? He's your father."

"He's also a drunk and a bully and likes to beat on people. Why would I want to help someone like that? Maybe if he'd rotted in the street a couple times, he'd've thought twice."

"Those are strong words."

"Not strong enough."

"Has your father ever beaten you?"

David snorted. "I probably hold the family record."

Driskin raised an eyebrow. "Can you give us some examples of what might provoke him to do that?"

David leaned forward, lip curled in a perfect sneer. "Am I breathing? That's all the excuse he ever needed. I've had my tooth repaired – see?" He pushed his lip up to show the lawyer a faint line. "You get a fist in the mouth when you talk out of turn. It's a goddamned big fist, too, and he punches hard. I hope you measured it for evidence. You get your ass kicked by a work boot so hard you can hardly walk for three days, for blocking the view of the holovision. He makes you drop your pants and take the whip on your bare ass at *thirteen* for getting a seventy-five grade in class. You get the shit beat out of you with fists and feet until you crack ribs if you get caught trying to dump his glass when you think he's passed out."

David twisted the strap to his Chronolog around his wrist. "Is that enough, or you want more?"

"That will do." Driskin had heard enough sarcasm for one witness. "Can you tell us the one incident that stands out most in your mind?"

This was his cue, but David was more of an independent type. He thought for a minute, and chose a different, unrehearsed story.

He became serious, remembering. "It's not just one incident. Father did it every year. When we lived in Russia, Father would take us on holiday somewhere – the Caspian, the Black Sea, the Mediterranean – and we'd always go swimming.

"At first it would be fun, playing in the water. But after Father had a couple of belts, he'd come into the water himself. He'd swim up silently behind you, and he'd pull you under the water with him. He could hold his breath forever, but when you're a kid, you can't, and just when you thought you were absolutely going to drown, he'd let you up, then do it again. We loved to go away, but we hated going anywhere with water because it always happened."

Driskin didn't like surprises on the stand. He asked cautiously, "What did your mother do?"

David shrugged. "I don't know. She always had a baby with her. Sometimes she'd tell him to go easy. But that's the only time Mother ever yelled at him, too," he realized.

"Your mother yelled at him?"

"Just once. Sarah was little, and she was in the hospital a lot with bad lungs. The sea air was supposed to be good for her, but one time Father dunked her, too, and she choked. Mother yelled until she looked about to stroke out. She was afraid Sarah would wind up back in the hospital."

"What did your father do then?"

"He swung her around by her ankles to get the water out. It must have worked, because she didn't get sick, but Mother made him sit out the rest of the day."

"The night your sister died, could your father have simply been trying to scare her, like he did when you went swimming?" the prosecutor tried.

"No way," David said. "I think Father's tried to kill us a dozen times at least. He came real close to killing Sarah, Viktor, probably me, too. 'Byeta just wasn't lucky that night, that's all."

"We will talk to Sarah later, but your brother Viktor isn't here," Driskin inquired. "What happened to Viktor?"

From her seat, Katya tried to catch David's eye. He treaded dangerously close to forbidden territory.

"He and Father had a fight. I didn't come in until Father had Vik

189

around the throat, yelling at him." That much was true. "Vik was purple, and his eyes were bugging out of his head. Father wouldn't let go."

"What stopped him?"

"I think Sarah threw something, and it broke. It distracted him."

"What did he do to Sarah?" Driskin wanted to know.

"Nothing. He turned to go after her, caught his foot on the sofa, fell, and went down for the count."

"No further questions, your Honor." Driskin winked at David. That story was better than the one they'd planned.

Suarez feigned confusion. "I'm unable to understand this. You say that your brother was being choked to death, but not one of you calls for help? Weren't you *afraid*? If not for yourselves, for your *brother*?"

David shook his head. "No. Once Father passed out, he wasn't a threat. When he woke up, he wouldn't remember. Sometimes Val and Galina could wake him enough to drag him to his room, but the problem had passed."

"But what about the next time?"

"We'd deal with it when it happened. It's not like he tried to kill every day. More like once a year or so," David rationalized.

"But that day did come," Suarez insisted, "and someone did die."

"Yeah, the son of a bitch got his way after all."

"Do you feel that death was deliberate?"

David stared into Father's stony face. "Not the hit, maybe. 'Byeta just landed bad. But not letting us call for Emergency? That's as deliberate as it gets."

Sergei looked young sitting before the court. He would have Father's height, too, but his face gave away his twelve years. Driskin made him read a poem he had written, a mournful thing about conflicting emotions where Father was concerned. He never mentioned Father by name, but even Vlad could figure out who he meant. Whether it moved the jury was difficult to tell. It certainly had its effect on his siblings.

"Tell me, Sergei," the prosecutor asked. "When your father got upset, what would you and your brothers and sisters do? Would you sit still and hope he didn't pick you? Or would you steer him toward something else?"

"If we had the chance – like if Father came home in a bad mood, or if his team lost a game, we would stay out of his way, hide the best we could. Under beds, in closets, stuff like that. Once we hid behind towels in the bathroom closet. Father opened the door, but he missed us. We were pretty good at hiding."

"Who's 'we'?"

"Me, Vlad, and Sarah. Once David thought he could outsmart Father by hiding under Father's bed, but then Father went in to lie down and trapped him there. When David thought Father was asleep, he tried to slip out, and Father caught him. David kept quiet until he got ready for bed. Viktor saw his back, and boy, did Vik get mad! He had big puffy bruises all over. He wouldn't talk about it, but Vik said they looked like hanger prints to him – you know, the heavy kind you keep your robe on."

"Viktor took care of you and your brothers and sisters when you were hurt?" Driskin asked.

"He was kind of in charge of all of us," Sergei answered. "Katya helped, too. Like when Sarah's lungs were bad. If she lay down, she couldn't breathe at all. Vik used to sleep holding her against him, sitting up, so she could breathe."

"Did your Father ever 'catch' you, Sergei?"

"Sure. Lots of times."

"Because you were the closest at hand? Or was there something specific you did to set your father off?"

"Sometimes I'd get into writing something, and I wouldn't hear him call. Or I'd waste time in classes I didn't care for, like science and math and stuff, and my grades would slip. It didn't matter. He just wanted you to get upset and cry. Especially if you were getting hit. If you cried and begged for mercy, you got off a lot easier."

"Did you ever cry?"

"Of course." Sergei wasn't proud, but it was the truth. "I think we all have. Except maybe Viktor. He was tough. Sarah's the toughest, though. She drove Father mad."

"Crazy mad, or angry mad?"

Sergei shook his head in respectful admiration. "Both. She'd get mad and yell back sometimes, and then she'd *really* get it, and no matter what Father did, she'd do her best not to give in. That's how he nearly killed her. She refused to cry, and he wouldn't quit until she did."

"Who won?"

Sergei shrugged, eyes downcast. "I don't know. I guess it was a draw. Mother made him stop, and Sarah couldn't get out of bed for a week. She wasn't supposed to eat unless she came to dinner, but we –," Sergei glanced at Father before confessing, "we snuck her food anyway. She was hurt pretty bad."

"And she didn't see a doctor?"

"No. She couldn't have moved that far. We took care of her."

"Not your mother?"

Sergei pursed his lips, thinking. "Not that I know of. Maybe while we were at school."

"One last question, Sergei," Driskin told him softly. "What's the worst thing your father did to you?"

Sergei's young features darkened into an unusually foul expression. "I still don't forgive him for throwing a whole book of my papers into a campfire while we were on holiday two years ago, because he thought I wasn't paying enough attention to the family.

"But the worst was this." He slid around in the chair and turned his back to the jury. He wore his curly blond hair short on the top and sides, but in long ringlets to his shoulders in the back. He pulled the curls up on the left side to reveal an uneven, shiny area of skin, from his ear backwards and down his neck.

"This is what happens when you get mad over losing your papers and you turn your back to Father at breakfast while he's talking to you. You get a bowl of scalding cereal thrown at your head, where it sticks and burns as you run around screaming, trying to get it off. Then the skin blisters up in big huge bubbles that make your hair wet so it sticks to the skin and you have to keep pulling the hairs out of the scab every hour until it heals." He turned back to the court, his anguished face searching Father's with accusing eyes, looking for some faint sign of remorse, some glimmer of shame or sorrow, anything to bolster the boy's hope of ever reconciling the event, but all he found were the penetrating dark eyes and impassive face.

"No more questions," Driskin finished.

The defense had little to ask Sergei, and he answered each question perfectly. It was a relief to hear Judge Ellmore bang his bell and declare a one-hour recess for lunch.

A relief for everyone but Sarah. They pushed four tables together in the crowded court cafeteria. Dr. Carver and Dr. Carmichael joined them. Sarah's nerves had wavered with the building anticipation of hearing her name called. She'd been on edge, stomach churning, ears ringing, a thousand thoughts and responses flying in circles inside her head – and now, just when she'd thought it would all be over, she had to wait another hour. Tension suffocated her.

Galina leaned across David to tap her plate. "Eat something, Sarah. You'll feel better."

"I *can't*," Sarah whined in defeat. She poked the cold purple *inkido* root – a long-time favorite. She put another morsel on her tongue, where it sat wilting to mush until she managed to swallow it. She poked the remainder again, wishing it and the rest of the day would simply disappear.

Vlad was worse. Valeria sat him next to her, hand-feeding him tiny pieces of her own lunch, but all he would swallow was water.

"My stomach hurts," he pleaded, rocking in the plastic chair. "Did you see him look at us? He's gonna be so mad!"

"The truth is the truth," Dmitri said, biting into a fried-vegetable sandwich and talking around it as he chewed. "None of us have to worry about it. It's Father who should be worried."

"No chocolate pudding?" Carver played with Sarah, but she pushed her plate away and put her head down.

"Sarah, you don't have to testify if you don't feel up to it," Valeria said with concern.

"I *want* to testify," Sarah insisted from the tabletop. "I just want to get it over with. I'll be okay."

She didn't add, *I hope*.

# * Fifteen *

*a* half hour, three trips to the lavatory for Vlad, and the court reconvened. Sarah's stomach did another somersault with a half twist, making her butterflies flap to keep their balance on top of the *inkido* root. As if from a great distance, she heard the bailiff call: "Sarah Irina Kirushenko."

She vaulted from her seat as if propelled. *I am strong*, she coached herself as she walked to the front, the room filled to capacity with staring strangers watching her every move. Driskin said she was the Star Witness. She had to make the jury feel bad for her, so they would believe her and not Father.

*I can do this. I have no fear. Fear is a creation of the mind. Control the mind, control the fear. Breath slows, heart slows, thoughts focused, no fear.* The Navaran chants echoed in her head. A year ago she could separate her mind from her body even during a whipping.

She felt oddly small sitting before the crowd – all the seats were filled, and a double row of people stood against the back wall: Humans, Navarans, Arcturans, and other assorted bipedal humanoid-types. Scanning the room, she drew strength from the supportive faces of her siblings. She'd do her best not to let them down. She twitched a smile at Vlad's frightened face.

*I'm okay.*

In the process, however, she caught sight of Father. She knew where he sat, but had avoided looking at him. His eyes met hers. With a start, Sarah realized his eyes were clear and deep and so dark they looked black – not glazed and yellowed and wildly bloodshot. She couldn't ever remember seeing his eyes this clear. His gaze seemed to penetrate her very soul, sifted through it emotionless and unwavering, looking for weakness. Several times she tried to break away, but his stare would draw her back, hypnotic.

She couldn't hide, sitting alone in the chair – unless she turned sideways, but she knew he would still be staring. It was a blessing to be sworn in, tearing her attention away. Driskin finished a glass of water and stood up. Sarah kept her eyes riveted on him, as he'd instructed.

"How old are you, Sarah?"

"Nine Earth years and eight weeks, or six Navaran years and 39 weeks."

"And you're pretty smart for nine, aren't you?"

"Smarter than some." Neither of her parents had ever allowed Sarah to brag about her abilities.

"In fact, the local school sends you all the way to Shir P'an to a Navaran school, because you're so advanced."

"That is correct." *Factual statement/no emotional content. Breath can be controlled,* she repeated in her head, still unable to slow her heart as much as she wished.

"So far ahead that you will finish your basic diploma program eight years early ..."

Sarah shook her head. "I'll be three classes short. I won't graduate until the end of the following trimester."

"Why three classes short?"

"I spent time in a hospital and I lost class time. I'm trying to catch up now," she explained. Her fingers wrestled in her lap without her knowing it.

"That was a mental health hospital, wasn't it?"

"Yes." A fact was a fact. She couldn't fake that one.

"How do you feel now?"

"I'm better," she nodded, knowing it to be true. "I had a stress reaction."

"How can someone as young as nine..."

"Eight," Sarah interrupted, as she often did when nervous. The facts had to be correct. If the facts weren't correct, then the conclusions would be erroneous and the results invalid. If the facts weren't correct, then she would be lying on the stand, and that was perjury, and perjury was Big Trouble. You weren't supposed to correct grown-ups, especially in front of other grown-ups, but he didn't have his facts right! She laced her fingers together in her lap and let the thumbs battle each other alone. "I was eight at the start. I turned nine in the hospital. I forgot my birthday."

Driskin bowed his head in her direction. "I beg your pardon. How can someone as young as *eight* have enough stress to precipitate a crisis?"

Sarah sighed hard, and spoke to her toes. "I watched my mother bleed to death on our kitchen floor and I couldn't help her, and I saw my Father murder my sister."

"You saw this with your own eyes?"

"Yes, sir. Every minute of it."

"Several of your brothers have said your father once tried to kill you. Is that true?"

Sarah glanced at Father watching her like a snake. "I can't testify to his exact intent. You'd have to ask him. But, it sure felt that way to me."

"I wish to enter exhibit number nine." Driskin placed a thick, thirty-centimeter black disk on the exhibit table. He touched a button, and a three-quarter scale holographic photo display rose up before the court.

Sarah realized in utter horror the figure it displayed was *her*, naked but for a privacy band in the front. At least the eyes were closed. A whisper ran through the courtroom as the image revolved. *A holo of her bare* zhopa *right in front of all those people! In front of her brothers!*

"This is a medical hologram taken at the Ku'umi Trauma Center," Driskin explained. "Taken only four months ago. As you can see," he paused the rotation for the jury's benefit, "Miss Kirushenko still bears the scars of her father's temper. Sarah, were these created the night you thought your father meant to kill you?"

Sarah stared in awe at the image. *Where did he get this? How could he surprise her with such a thing?* She knew there were scars on her back; she could feel them. Some itched now and then, a few pulled if she stretched the wrong way, one or two got sore sometimes. She could see some of them on the backs and sides of her legs, but they were smooth and thin and pale, like the fading marks on her arms. But this image! This image turned her insides out, made her skin crawl, made her want to run from it. Marks criss-crossed the hologram's back; some ran together, too hard to separate and count. Some were thin, many wide from multiple cuts in the same spot. Some were white and hard to see, others angry pink and raised and wavy. There were so many marks, so many. Sarah had never seen her back in a mirror. No one ever had mentioned her appearance, though certainly her brothers and sisters had seen them, let alone the original wounds. Now, with this sudden revelation in front of so many strangers, she felt revolted.

"Is that – really me?"

"That's really you," Driskin confirmed. He directed her back to the hologram. "Were all these from one beating?"

Sarah's breath stopped, as if she had fallen off a cliff. "I-I-I... A lot of them?"

"Can you tell us what caused these scars, Sarah?"

"Father's whip."

"How old were you when this took place?"

"Six." Her feet still touched the floor, but her clothes felt too big, as if she were shrinking inside them.

"There are more than thirty-seven scars on your back alone, Sarah. Did you know that?"

"No."

"Your sister Elizabyeta was six, wasn't she? A coincidence? Why would anyone beat a six year old – a *smart* six year old – that severely? What could you possibly have done to make your father that angry?"

Sarah made the mistake of looking at Father. His unwavering stare tore at her resolve. He didn't look mad, he didn't look sad, he didn't look ashamed; just steady and unyielding as a Let's-Pretend mask. She shrank even smaller in the chair, watching her toes flex inside her sandals, knowing that, underneath it all, she'd sort of deserved it.

"Sarah?"

Driskin's voice brought her back. "I – I yelled at Father. I might have pushed him."

"And that deserved such a brutal beating?"

"Yes," Sarah said, truly believing her statement. She had known better, no doubt about it.

Driskin sighed at the brief answer, and tried not to look annoyed. "Can you tell the jury the whole incident? Why would you push your father, when you knew it would upset him?"

"I – I was angry. I acted without thinking."

Driskin waited, then prompted, "Had your father been drinking?"

"I think so," Sarah answered without conviction. "Probably."

"What made you so angry?"

"He was picking on my brother Vladimir."

"Just for the fun of it, or did something start it?"

"Father wasn't very happy that evening," Sarah remembered, pushing herself higher in the chair with her toes. "During dinner, Vlad spilled his water, and it ran across the table into Father's lap. Father screamed that he did it on purpose, but it really was an accident."

"That made you angry?"

"N-no, that was just Father being Father. But Vlad was – is – really afraid of him."

"What made *you* mad, Sarah?"

Sarah hesitated, cornered. "I can't talk about that."

Judge Ellmore leaned toward her. "Please remember, Miss Kirushenko, you swore an oath to answer the questions truthfully. If you know the answer, you *must* answer the question, no matter what."

Sarah looked desperately to Vladimir, palms raised, shoulders up near her ears. *What do I do?* It was Vlad's Unmentionable. It was up to him. She wouldn't do it, punishment or not, if he said no. His wan face nodded.

"Okay," Sarah gave in, "but this is under protest! It's not fair to make me break an oath I made before I took your oath."

"So noted," the judge agreed. "The jury may take that fact into account."

Sarah watched her hands fumbling in her lap, remembering the details of the night not three years ago.

*Vlad turned white as a ghost and shrank small as Father rose to his feet, bellowing. He seized the boy by the ear, dragging him to the table whose drawer held the much-dreaded whip – two meters of five-strand braided black leather with a knotted tip.*

*"Get over there," Father growled, shoving the 17-kilogram boy toward the rough wall so harshly Vlad stumbled, scraping his cheek.*

*"Please, sir!" Vlad begged. "I didn't mean it! It was an accident! Please! I'll clean it!"*

*The air at the table was morbid. It was an unspoken rule not to watch another's humiliation, never to pick on someone for what they did or said during punishment. There but for the grace of God... No one ate save Alexei and Mother, each of the other children braced for the familiar sharp snap! of the whip.*

*"You dare to question me?" Father screamed, cracking the whip close to Vlad's ear. Vlad shrieked, twisting away.*

*"Stand still!" Father ordered, once again flicking the whip so close to Vlad's head he could feel the rush of air past his cheek.*

*The terrified boy began to cry, and then it happened.*

Here Sarah stumbled in the narration, ashamed. Even David, who took such pride in torturing Vlad, never mentioned it.

"He – He wet his pants."

*Seven-year-old Vlad didn't realize it at first. Father noticed the darkening of the boy's shorts, the spreading puddle on the floor. It took several seconds for his inebriated mind to comprehend.*

*Father's voice dropped fifty decibels. "You – you pissed on my floor! You goddamned little baby! You pissed your pants right here on my floor!"*

*Vlad burst into hard tears, paralyzed with shame and fear. Sarah, knowing the tone, lifted her head. Her brother was in more trouble than he could handle.*

Father grabbed Vladimir by his shirt. *"You are no son of mine!"*

Anger overwhelmed Sarah. No one could pick on her brother like that, not even Father. In a flash, she was out of her seat.

*"No, Sarah!"* Viktor hissed.

*"Sar'ina, it's not your business,"* Mother said quietly. *"Sit down."*

*"Stop it!"* Sarah yelled. She shoved into Father with both hands, pounded on him with her fists. *"Stop it! Stop scaring him, you big monster!"*

That got Father's attention!

*"Run, Vlad!"* she whispered, waving him out. *"Go!"*

Vlad stared, sobbing, then sidled out and ran down the hall.

*"What the hell do you think you're doing?"* Father whispered. *"How dare you strike me!"*

Sarah parked her hands on her hips. *"You're nothing but a mean old bully, scaring him like that! He's little!"*

*"You goddamned brat! You think you can save your piss-assed brother from his punishment?"*

She stared back at the bloodshot eyes. *"I'm not afraid of you!"*

Father grabbed her up by the shirt in wordless fury, far off the ground. Sarah's heart pounded in fear, but she would never let Father know it. Eye to eye, she screwed her face up into the meanest look she could muster.

Father's rage went beyond anything she'd seen before. He threw her to the wet floor. She sprang up quickly.

*"Fine! You don't want your brother to take his punishment? You can take it for him! When I finish, I will then punish you for your unforgivable insolence!"*

*"Fine!"* Oh, she was in deep trouble now! She turned her back and braced herself against the wall of the living room, like the boys did.

*"I'm not afraid of you!"* she called over her shoulder, more to convince herself than anything else. She shook hard inside, knowing what was about to happen. It happened to the big boys a lot. She scrunched her eyes, tucked her head, and prayed, 'Please, please let me be strong for Vlad! Please don't let me cry!'

*The first lash knocked the breath from her, and she jumped hard. On the second, she sank her teeth into her lip to keep from shrieking. At three, she repeated to herself, 'Keep standing. Keep standing.' At eight, she couldn't breathe through the pain. At twelve, she was dazed and numb.*

*"I'll teach you to talk back to me!" Father snarled.*

*Vlad, in clean clothes, cried trembling in the shadows of the hallway.*

*"Do you know to fear me now, bastard?"*

*"No," Sarah wheezed, beyond fright.*

*"What?" Father whispered.*

*"Nyet!"*

*The rage unleashed on the girl's back curled her on the floor – but she didn't make a noise.*

"You will fear me!" *Father screamed.*

*"No!" Sarah cried at last, unable to stand or think or speak more than the one word. The room turned black.*

*"Sasha!" The voice caught Sarah's fading attention. "Sasha! That's enough! She's only a child! What she says doesn't matter to you one bit. Come into the kitchen and finish your dinner. Come."*

*Mother? Mother's voice? Sarah couldn't focus, but she could smell Mother's soft perfume. Father's footsteps receded.*

*It was the last thing Sarah remembered for a day and a half. She didn't remember Katya vomit into her napkin, never saw Sergei run crying and shut himself in his room, didn't see Viktor holding back his shaking fist, didn't hear Alexei's typically rude comment, "He really taught her a lesson this time. Think she learned?"*

*She never heard Mother ask Viktor to put her to bed, or tell Katya to look in the cabinet for healing cream. Sarah never knew Dmitri got stuck cleaning the floor. She never knew it was the tough and torturing David who tried to comfort Vladimir, who knelt next to his sister, crying hysterically, convinced she was dead.*

"Weren't you *afraid?*" Driskin asked, unnerved at the story.

Sarah shrugged. "I knew I'd get whipped, and I knew it would hurt, but I wasn't afraid then. I was too mad."

"How many times were you hit?"

"I don't know. I didn't count."

"Were you afraid he would kill you?"

"Objection!" shouted Father's attorney. "Leading the witness, your honor!"

"Sustained," agreed the judge.

Driskin changed questions. "Did you cry?"

Sarah fought the shrinking feeling again. "No. I knew that's what Father wanted, and I didn't want him to win. By the time I wanted to cry, nothing came out."

"What happened next?"

"I don't know. I woke up in bed a day or so later."

"Those wounds must have bled. Did you see a doctor?"

Sarah frowned as if such an idea were uncouth. "No. They were only cuts. Viktor and Katya and everybody took care of me. They kept everything clean and put stuff on them. That helped. It took a couple of days before everything scabbed over enough so I could wear clothes again."

Driskin eyed her strangely. "Weren't you in *pain*?"

"A lot of pain," Sarah agreed. "Aspirins didn't always help. I stayed in bed for four days. The sheet stuck to the cuts, and Katya had to wet it to peel it off. That hurt, but I had to keep covered or I'd get sand in them. Katya'd cry, and I tried not to make any noise over it, but sometimes I couldn't help it. I just tried to – separate myself – from it." That part of the experience was spotty. She'd worked hard to forget it, and digging the memories back up wasn't easy. She caught sight of John Carver sitting behind Katya with his eyes closed. *Had he fallen asleep? He'd always wanted to know that story.*

"Did you go to school during this time?"

"No. Everyone took turns reading my work to me, and I'd do it in my head and have them write the answers. It wasn't as if I were sick or something."

"And your parents never checked on you? Never helped you? Never looked in to see you?" Abuse was one thing, but such utter neglect was another. The mother was as guilty as the father.

Sarah glanced at Father, head bent. "No sir. Not that I can remember. Just my brothers and sisters. We take care of each other."

"I see. Sarah, were you home the night your sister Elizabyeta died?"

"Yes, sir."

"Did you see what happened?"

"Most of it."

"Can you tell us what happened, from the beginning, as much as you can remember?"

Sarah began, acutely aware of the dark eagle's eyes watching her. *If only she could tell what Father was thinking!* The blankness on his face made her back crinkle up into her hair. Slowly, with back-ups for clarity, she told what she had seen and heard that night.

Sarah breathed a sigh of relief when Driskin finished. With Vlad's permission, she'd told one of their deepest, darkest secrets, but she'd held herself together. In her head, she visualized ripping the wings off the black-hearted butterflies banging holes in her stomach. Mistakenly, she stood up before she remembered the cross-examination. Suarez tore into her with particular fervor. The wingless butterflies in her stomach grew not one, but two new sets of wings.

"Miss Kirushenko," the defending attorney began as she sat, "you've just finished three months in a psychiatric hospital, haven't you?"

"Yessir."

"You tried to kill *yourself*, didn't you?"

"No, sir."

"No? You didn't try to shatter your skull, slice your wrists, or otherwise destroy yourself?"

"No – yes," she stuttered. "I did do those things, but I was made to understand they were the outward manifestation of internal chaos, not a desire to terminate myself."

Suarez looked at her as hard as Father. "Could you explain that statement to the jury, please?"

Sarah hunted through the row of witnesses until she found Carver again. He *was* awake. He nodded and winked. She had it right. Morale boosted, she explained, "It means, when I felt really bad on the inside, I would beat myself up on the outside, not necessarily with the intent to die."

Suarez accepted the answer. "Do you remember any details of your stay?"

"Bits and pieces."

"Not all of it?"

"No sir."

"Were you restrained?"

"Yes."

"Were you medicated?"

"Yes."

"Were you violent?"

"If I wasn't, I don't think they would have restrained me," Sarah said. A twitter of laughter erupted in the audience.

Suarez tapped a finger against his lip. "Tell me, how is it you can't remember details from two months ago, but you can remember small details from four months ago, even three years?"

Driskin rose. "Objection! The witness was ill at the time in question. There is no evidence the witness was ill during the previous incidents."

"Sustained," the judge agreed.

Sarah eyed Suarez warily. *Of course she was ill – she was hospitalized! Was that the basis of his defense – her entire testimony, all her experiences, were to be discredited because she'd had a breakdown? Where was he leading? What was he after?* She chewed a fingernail without realizing it. *Beware*, she warned herself.

"Very well. Is it true, Miss Kirushenko," Suarez said, "that you also hear voices in your head? And that these voices tell you to do things? To injure yourself?"

The hair on the back of Sarah's neck rose, and her stomach gave a hard flop. Acid washed up to her mouth, burning her throat, making her cough. *That wasn't true at all!* How did he know? She hadn't even shared that with Vladimir!

"No! Yes, but – I – I *thought* I heard voices. That *is* true. But they never told me to kill myself. Never! *I never wanted to kill myself.* I think I've said that enough, now."

Fear stole her breath. She couldn't panic. She must keep control. He *wanted* her to panic, to fall apart in front of everyone so he could discredit her testimony as the words of a crazy child. Whatever she did, she *must keep control.* If only she could have a moment to pull herself together.

"You and your sister Elizabeth were not friends, were you?" Suarez pointed out.

"No, Eliza*byeta* and I were not," Sarah emphasized, aggravated by his refusal to say 'Byeta's name correctly.

"Would you say you hated each other?"

Sarah pressed her lips together into a line. "That could be accurate."

"Did you ever wish Elizabeth would just – disappear? Be out of your hair, your life, leave you alone?"

Sarah paused, smelling a psychological trap. "If wishes were spaceships, children would fly."

Suarez held his hand out, as if to point out her irrationality. "I'm afraid I don't understand."

"I mean that if everything you wished for came true, no one would ever be around. Father would have disappeared a hundred times over. Just because you wish for something doesn't mean you can make it happen. I don't think anyone believes that."

"That doesn't answer my question. *Did* you ever wish she would go away?"

Reluctantly, she admitted, "Yes, sometimes I did."

"You were present the night your sister died. In fact, you admit to having a fight with your sister just prior to the incident in question. Had you fought with her before?"

"Yes."

"Ever hit her?"

"Yes." 'Byeta was an easy hit; there was no pride to be gained in fighting her. She was a slapper and a scratcher, not a puncher, and most of her attacks occurred when you weren't looking.

"Punch her? Kick her? Pull her hair? Call her names?"

"We fought like babies," Sarah said with annoyance. "And she did the same to me."

"Your father has no memory of this incident. He admits to drinking heavily and being asleep at the time in question. Is it possible then, that *you* were the one who hit your sister and caused the fall that resulted in her death? Could it be that you, in a fit of anger, pushed your sister so she fell, not realizing she needed help until it was too late? Could it be that seven brothers and sisters, all of whom admit to having reasons to dislike their father, banded together to cover up the incident? To protect a sister who was a favored pet? Wasn't it easier to blame your father? He couldn't deny it. Did you blame him to get even for hurting you? Could this unspoken guilt be part of the reason for your breakdown?"

Sarah heard the words, but couldn't begin to comprehend. A great hole seemed to have opened beneath her, and she was falling, falling fast through the center of the planet. Molten terror surged upwards, thick, searing, unchecked. For the first time in months, her peripheral vision grayed and closed in. A hissing sizzled faintly in her ears. She lost track of everything but the words frozen in her head.

*Could she have heard him right? How? How could he say such lies in a courtroom? He wasn't on the stand, he wasn't sworn in, of course he could lie. How – What – How?* Her brain locked, unable to accept the accusations. She didn't see Dmitri and David on their feet, moving to tackle the lawyer, or Galina and Sergei struggling to get them to sit down. A rumble of whispers rolled through the courtroom.

Even Sarah's violet eyes seemed to pale. She sat bolt upright in the chair. Her first *"No!"* was barely audible. The second "No!" was loud. The third was a semi-hysterical shout, "No that's not true not a word of it!"

"Objection!" Driskin roared at the same time. "Your Honor, this is fantasy! There is no physical way a child her size would have the strength necessary to create such an injury. He is deliberately intimidating my client."

"Sustained!" the judge shouted above the noise. "Quiet in the court! Mr. Suarez, please stick to the facts at hand."

"Withdrawn," agreed the defense, as if it magically erased everything.

He was winning. The room and all its staring eyes spun lopsided before her. Even her butterflies shivered in a holding pattern, waiting to see what happened next. How *could* he! Sarah's throat went dry, and she coughed. She tugged at a lock of hair, twisting until the strands tore.

"You said your father was cruel."

"Yes." She let the extracted hairs fall from her fingers and put her hand in her lap, shoulders scrunched, head down, pulling herself in.

"You said your father physically disciplined you."

"Yes."

"Your brothers claim to have been hit on bare flesh. Did your father ever ask you to undress, Sarah? Perhaps... touch you, in ways you disliked. Something you might have said anything to get back at him for?"

A memory flashed through Sarah's mind – *terror, hands, screaming* – but that was in a hospital hallway, not Father. Another memory of Father, only a year or so ago, blubbering drunk and holding her on his lap, crying for some unknown reason and hugging her too tightly. *No.* He was just plain melancholy drunk, and the fear was over seeing Father cry, not his touch.

"No!" she said emphatically.

"If not you, what about the other children?"

Sarah stood up, fists clenched. "NO, I said! *Never!*" She lapsed into Russian, not waiting for the court computer to translate. "We are *children!* He's our *Father!* He hits too hard and he drinks too much, but he's not some monster unattended in a mental hospital!"

*Uh oh!* Sarah's heart sank as she realized what she'd said. *Did she almost give away a secret? Did she just* defend *him?* She sat down, twisting, twitching, breathing too fast. Her shaking hands hugged the back of her neck. *Not good. Not good at all.*

"Has it occurred to you and your siblings, Miss Kirushenko," Suarez said coolly, "what will happen to all of you should your father be incarcerated? Your mother is dead. If a suitable relative cannot be found, your family could be split up and placed with foster families until such time as your father is released. Have you considered that?"

*"Yes,"* Sarah whimpered, strangling in her dissolution. She stopped listening and paid more attention to the rising dread, the helplessness of what had seemed like a good idea gone brutally wrong. Her body shook, her breath came in gasps, the heat of the room swelled to suffocating proportions, the butterflies pushed her stomach halfway to her throat. Suarez talked, but she didn't hear. She mumbled something unintelligible.

"I'm afraid I missed that, Miss Kirushenko. Could you repeat that louder, for the jury?"

Sarah's eyes were wide and she swallowed hard at the sudden rush of saliva in her mouth. "I feel really sick," she warned.

Judge Ellmore motioned to one of the court staff. "Could we have some water up here, please?"

*Too late.* Sarah jumped up and took three steps toward the side entrance before what little lunch she'd swallowed hit the floor.

"Twenty minute recess," banged the judge.

# * Sixteen *

Galina raised a warning finger to Dmitri in the hallway outside the men's restroom. "I'm trusting you. If I think you're fooling around in there, I'll pull you out myself. And leave Vlad alone!"

Dmitri rolled his eyes. "I *know!*"

"I'll keep an eye on them, if you want," John Carver said from the crowd behind Galina.

"I'd appreciate that," she said with relief. "I'll be in the women's room if you need me."

"I can handle it."

The lavatory jammed with people of various races during the break, all lingering longer than polite to watch the poor parentless girls at the washing station. Sarah sat on the edge of the stone basin, shoeless. Katya's arms circled her, sheltering her from the stares and questions.

Valeria gave Sarah's sandal a final wave under the sanitizer, then held it under the moisture recovery vacuum. "There, that should do it."

"I can't believe I did that," Sarah wailed. "What will the Navarans think, when I can't even control my own stomach?" She scraped her nose on the back of her hand.

Valeria turned the tear-stained face to hers. "Listen to me! Nobody gives a damn what the Navarans think. They're not the ones you need to impress. I knew I shouldn't have let you up there. Here. This should be okay." She slipped the sandal over the bare foot. "Wipe your face. You can't go back looking like that."

In the hall, Carver amused the boys with moderately off-color humor. Sergei and Vlad were red with giggles, thrilled to be included in 'adult' conversation.

Dmitri smoothed his hair. "I didn't know doctors knew stories like that."

"We're still people," Carver said. He leaned against the wall between the entrances of the courtroom, a cafeteria cup in his hand. "I spent four summers working with kids with problems. I learned a lot from them."

"People like us," David said sourly. He scraped a toe in an arc on the floor and looked up from under the dark hair that hung across his eyes –

the only one of the boys with blue eyes.

"Worse than yours." Carver swung the cup to include the group of them. "Refugees, slavery, bizarre cults, chemical dependency, debilitating illnesses. You'd be surprised how limited your life gets with a chronic illness."

"I never thought about that," Dmitri said, reflecting. "We used to worry about Sarah's lungs all the time when she was little. Now she hasn't been sick more than twice in the last – two years, maybe."

"There they are." Carver straightened up as the girls emerged. Vlad flew over to slide his hand into Sarah's. To Sarah, Carver said, "You look a bit better. Here." He offered her the cup.

Sarah shook her head.

"Give it a try," he urged. "I had them make it special. It should help your stomach. Go on. There's nothing funny in it, it's just not carbonated. You're going to doubt me?"

Sarah sighed and accepted the cup. It was cold and black and very sweet. She took a second sip.

"She's done," Valeria announced. "I don't want her back up there."

"I'm going back," Sarah said stubbornly over the rim of the drink. Vlad eyed the cup with interest; she gave him a taste. No doubt his stomach was worse than hers.

"Sarah, don't make me send you home," Valeria threatened. "I won't hear another word about it."

"No, Val, *you* listen!" Sarah's eyes had the same look she got when she dared stand up to Father. She stomped her foot.

"I will finish my turn! I will *not* fail. I said I would do it, and I will. You're not going to stop me. I'm sorry for getting sick, but I'm better now, and I *will* go back up there!"

Valeria stared back in surprise. "Sarah, I don't appreciate your tone with me."

"I mean it, Val!" Sarah snapped, still terrible. "I *am* going back!"

Val crossed her arms. All eyes were on her, waiting, watching. It was not the time or place for a big scene.

"Okay," she conceded. "Go back in there. But if I think you look that upset again, I will take you off the stand myself. And we will discuss this at home."

*"Fine!"* Sarah backed down, crisis averted.

David broke the tension, clapping a strong arm across her shoulders. "I gotta give you credit, Sar. That was a bold statement you made in there. If I were you, though, I would have aimed for the lawyer, the son of a bitch."

"Grow *up!*" Sarah snarled, shoving David hard with both hands. She pushed past him and stalked into the courtroom. Vlad, still holding their cup, ran after her.

The court reconvened, and Sarah retook the stand without saying a word to anyone but Vlad.

"One last question, Miss Kirushenko," Suarez said, standing next to her so self-assured. "You stated you were seated at your computer console the night your sister died, and your father was in an adjoining room, correct?"

"That is correct." No fear now. Anger held sway.

"Is there a wall between the two rooms?"

"There's a half-wall, about this high," Sarah said, holding a hand more than a meter from the floor.

"And while seated behind this wall, you were able to see your father strike your sister?"

"Yes, I did," Sarah said with absolute certainty.

"And how high is the table your sister allegedly fell on?"

"About this high," Sarah said, holding her hand sixty centimeters up.

Suarez nodded. He activated the viewscreen to show visuals of the interior of their house, a dead-center photo of the wall divide, with the comm desk and the table and sofa flanking it. "Let the record show the witness has stated that the table in question is lower than the height of the wall separating the rooms. *While seated*, Miss Kirushenko, you were able to see your sister land on the edge of a table *below* the level of the wall?"

Sarah searched her memory. *He was right!* She *couldn't* have seen Elizabyeta hit the table! It was physically impossible. "I – I guess I must have just *heard* her hit the table."

"So you don't know for a fact if she even *hit* the table? It could have been the wall, or the floor, or a pillow, for all you know."

"No," Sarah whispered.

"No further questions, your Honor."

That was it. She was done. She'd wanted this moment for so long, yet she felt no release. Her last statements were crippling. *How could she have been so stupid!* Even Vlad should have been able to spot the error in logic. Her Navaran classmates would have, but she hadn't seen them in four months. She took her seat and put her head on her knees.

"You were terrific!" Katya whispered in her ear, but Sarah shook her head. They were sunk.

Driskin called Dr. Carver to the stand next, to give evidence as to the damage Alexander Kirushenko had wrought, as well as testify to Sarah's mental competence. His testimony was professional and to the point.

"Did you ever discuss the beating Miss Kirushenko received that resulted in the scarring we have seen today?"

"No. We touched on it once or twice," Carver admitted, "but she didn't wish to talk about it."

"Will those scars ever fade?"

"The physical ones? They'll fade, but it will take several plastic surgeries to remove them now."

"If Miss Kirushenko had received prompt medical attention, would the scarring have been as severe?"

"No. In fact, there shouldn't have been any scarring," Carver explained. "It's much easier to prevent a scar than to correct one."

"Did you ever mention surgery to your patient?" Driskin asked.

"I did discuss that with her. However, as I explained to Sarah, such surgery should best wait until she's a bit older, when she's reached adult height."

Carver's testimony went smoothly until Suarez began to cross-examine.

"What's your clinical opinion of the current family grouping, such as it is?"

John rested his elbow on the arm of the chair, and his chin on his thumb, as if bored. "Could you be more specific, please?"

"What, in your professional opinion, are the chances these children can raise themselves successfully? Statistically, wouldn't it be better for them to have the supervision and guidance of an experienced adult?"

Carver's face wasn't overly optimistic. "It's not impossible. Given some support services for a while, some family therapy, I think they should do well. They're very committed to each other."

"But you recommend family therapy?"

"I would recommend it for any family that has been through the string of incidents this family's been through in the past year. As I think has been demonstrated today, they each have some unresolved issues that should be examined."

"Have you discussed any of these – issues – with any other of the Kirushenko children?"

"Some."

"We've heard testimony today of a number of alleged physical assaults, yet we've only been presented with physical evidence of two or three. Do you feel these stories may be exaggerations? Perhaps vengeful falsifications?"

"No. It's unlikely to find five people that can tell the same story of a falsified experience."

"Miss Kirushenko – Sarah – seemed to become agitated at the suggestion of sexual abuse. During her months at Rangler, did you uncover any evidence that would suggest such an occurrence?"

"There was no such evidence," Carver stated with authority.

"And there was no mention of such abuse with other family members?" If one type of abuse was confirmed negative, it cast mental doubt on any subsequent charges.

In the front row, Sarah gnawed painfully at an already too-short fingernail.

A shadow crossed Carver's face. "I can't answer that question."

Suarez stopped his pacing. By his client's sworn statements, it should have been a straightforward negative answer. "Why not?"

"Any information of that sort would be contained in sealed records."

"What kind of sealed records?" the judge wanted to know. "Sealed under what court?"

"Sealed under my security code," Dr. Carver told him. "Sealed under the laws of psychiatric confidentiality and the fact that most of the Kirushenko children are considered minors under current law."

"Doctor Carver, your security lock is not binding in a court of law unless sealed in a court of law," the judge said. "The confidentiality law is admissible only in cases where such information would be crippling to the person involved."

"Your Honor, permission to approach the bench?" Ellmore nodded. In a low voice, Carver explained, "Your Honor, that information is under lock because it was the only way to gain the trust necessary to obtain other pertinent information during a crisis situation. To break that trust – to reveal such privileged information to the public – would have grave consequences at best. I strongly urge, in my professional opinion, that such information be kept strictly confidential."

"This is a murder trial, Dr. Carver. Does such information shed light on the case at hand? Could it potentially damage or clear the defendant?"

"Yes, sir," Carver said reluctantly.

"Then I'll have to allow it…"

"What about putting it through a patient advocate first?"

"Dr. Carver, this is not a medical review board." To the court, the judge said, "I will waive the law of confidentiality as is allowed. I want to hear the evidence in question."

Carver raised his voice, but stopped short of yelling. "Your honor, I *strongly* urge the court – !"

"Dr. Carver, need I remind you, you are under the oath of the court." The judge's pink wattles jiggled in mocking emphasis. "If you will not answer the question, you will be held in contempt and will be incarcerated until such time as you will testify. *Is that understood?*"

"*Understood!*" Carver barked. He slammed himself into the witness chair.

"Will you repeat the question, please, Mr. Suarez?" the judge asked.

Suarez hesitated, trapped by the same law. "Was there any implication of sexual abuse among other family members?"

Katya faced straight ahead, but watched Sarah from the corner of her eye.

John Carver rested his mouth on his fist, wavering. He locked eyes with Sarah, whose frightened face almost imperceptibly shook 'no.'

"Please answer the question," the judge called.

He put his hand down in defeat. To the family in the front row, he said, "I am truly sorry. Please understand I'm being forced." To the court he said, "Yes."

Suarez stopped cold. "Could you repeat that?" He was supposed to be saving his client, not destroying him.

"It was reported to me that there was one such incident involving another family member."

Sarah's jaw dropped in disbelief. *He'd lied! He'd lied to her!* She tried to catch his eye, but Carver stared at Father with a look fiercer than she'd ever seen. He looked ready to kill in his own right.

"And, who would that allegedly have been?" Suarez said slowly.

Carver continued his staring contest. Father didn't look happy, either, accused of something dreadful by a person he'd never met.

"Answer the question, Dr. Carver," said the judge.

Cracks appeared in the stone façade – Father looked downright uncomfortable, almost defensive.

"Dr. Carver!" Ellmore warned.

"Doctor Carver, I find you in contempt of court!" The judge banged angrily on the proceeding's bell. "Bailiff…"

John broke off. "Katerina Kirushenko." The courtroom grumbled, amplified by the high ceiling.

"*You told!*" Katya hissed. "*You backstabbing little shit! You told!*" She slammed her fist on Sarah's shoulder before turning with a cry, pushing past Valeria, and fleeing the room.

"*Sarah!*" Vlad whispered in disbelief. Even *he* had kept that secret.

"Wait'll we get home!" Dmitri threatened across Sergei.

"That's a *lie!*" Father bellowed, standing up but unable to raise a hand to point. "I never touched her like that! *Any* of them! I wouldn't do that!"

The judge banged his bell. "Mr. Kirushenko, restrain yourself, or be removed from this court."

Sarah pressed her wrists to her temples, physically holding herself together. *Layer upon layer upon layer – would the betrayals ever stop?* First priority? Katya. She had to come clean to Katya. She darted past Valeria and ran after her sister.

The hall was empty. Sarah glanced about. It was too hot to run outside; Kat knew better than that. If she wanted privacy, Sarah herself would run… She took off down the hall.

Katya wept against a wall in the women's lavatory. She saw Sarah, and came at her furiously.

"I hate you! I hate you!" she spat, slapping at the younger girl. Sarah backed up until cornered, but made no attempt to defend herself. Katya had every right.

"How *could* you! How could you do that to me! Now everyone on the planet will know! How could you *do* that?"

Sarah loved Kat like a mother; she'd only meant to protect her. She had to explain. She confessed in a shaking whisper the biggest secret she'd ever had. "I only told them because it happened to *me*, Kat. It happened to me, too! I only mentioned you because they promised it would be an absolute secret and couldn't be told. I'm sorry! Please don't be mad at me."

Katya paused. "What do you mean, *'It'* happened to you? Father - ?"

Tears welled up at the memory. "Not Father. A man at the hospital, the – the same way you were. I only stepped away for a minute, that's all. He … ." She couldn't finish the sentence. "I was never so scared in my life, Kat. Not ever. Not even of Father. I'd rather he come home today and whip me every day of my life than go through that again."

"Oh my God! *Sarah!* They never told us that!" Katya forgot her own grief, pulling her sister into a protective embrace. "You kept that a secret?"

Sarah sniffed tears. "I didn't want the boys to know I was stupid. They felt bad for you, but they'd just laugh at me. Please, please don't tell! Not even Val! She'd never leave me alone. I'm sorry I told your secret, but *please* don't tell mine."

"I forgive you!" Katya cried anew. "You should have at least told *me*, Sarah! How horrible!" She wiped her eyes on the back of her hand.

"I won't tell. It's none of the boys' business, anyway. But I wish you'd told me. I sat there at lunch talking with Dr. Carver, and he knew all that awful stuff about me."

"I'm *sorry*," Sarah repeated. "I would never have if... I *never* would have."

Valeria ran in the lavatory door. "Are you all right? They want you both in there."

"We're okay now." Katya smiled wanly at Sarah, sniffing and wiping her eyes one more time. "We'll be fine."

The lawyers demanded a fifteen-minute recess to discuss the information. Driskin resorted to threats, but Katya refused to retake the stand. She submitted a written statement admitting something to that degree happened, but she would have rather sat in a holding cell than relate that incident to a public courtroom. It was a single incident, under alcoholic influence, and it stopped short of becoming a serious crime. She would not, under any circumstances, discuss it further. Suarez was happy to accept the written statement; he didn't want her on the stand, either.

Sarah found herself recalled instead, face still blotchy. *What now?*

Suarez no longer pretended to be pleasant. "Miss Kirushenko, we've been led to believe you're an intelligent little girl. Do you understand what it means to be sworn in as a witness? To tell the truth and only the truth?"

"Yes," Sarah said, shrinking small again.

"Tell us, please, what it means to you."

"It means if I don't tell you the truth, I'm in an awful lot of trouble, and you won't believe anything else I've said, and none of it will count. I'll be labeled a liar all my life."

"That's right," Suarez said. "But you told this court that your father never touched any of you inappropriately, yet you told Dr. Carver he did. Which one of these statements is false?"

Sarah felt trapped. *Would they really put her in jail if she didn't answer? Would it be in the same cell as Father?*

"Neither," she stalled, thinking fast against the rolling chaos in her head.

"They can't both be true."

Sarah grabbed at straws. "Your definition of touch was open to interpretation, and – " She racked her brain to remember what he'd said.

"You asked about *children*. Katya's seventeen, she's a grown-up. Elizabyeta and I were children, and I stand by that answer." A couple of loud coughs sounded from the rear of the room. Suarez looked angry.

"Then let me rephrase the question, so there is no misunderstanding," he said with measured patience. "Did – at any time, ever – your father, present here in this room, touch you, your brothers, or *any* of your sisters in a sexual manner that made them uncomfortable? Do you understand the term 'sexual manner'?"

"Yes, I do," Sarah said seriously. "Yes, he did."

"And who was that?"

"My sister Katya."

"That's a lie," Father rumbled again.

"It's not, Father." Sarah beseeched him, apologetic. She felt as small as Nikky, accusing him of such a heinous act in front of a crowd of strangers. She started out softly, but grew more frenetic the longer she spoke, ignoring Driskin's wild motions to stop. "You drank so much that night you don't remember, but we do! You tore her clothes, and she had red marks on her arms and neck and – and front – and Viktor picked the lock on your door and rescued her and *that's* when you tried to kill him and I hit you in the leg – I hit you, I'm sorry – but Viktor was really *dying* and we couldn't make you let go and we were really scared – and I hit you and you fell and you hit your head on the floor and went out and *that's* when Dimi and Viktor had you taken away, and then you beat them for it and Vik left home because of that, and then 'Byeta died and I freaked out over everything and I came home and came here today and they ripped my deepest secrets from me and made everybody *mad*!" she rattled off in a breathless burst.

Sarah stamped her foot. "That's *it*! That's *everything*! I can't say another thing!"

"No further questions," Suarez relented with a smile.

Sarah took her seat once more. She had done things her way and won – sort of. Katya, sitting with her head high and calmer than she'd been all day, put an arm around her and kissed the top of her head.

Suarez glanced at his notes. "Your Honor, I request a mistrial, based on conflicting testimony and possible perjury by David Kirushenko." The courtroom erupted in noise yet again.

David slammed himself back in his seat, jaw hanging open before silently mouthing a torrent of strong expletives. He heard his name called, ordering him back to the chair.

*Screwed! By a single sentence, a* minor *detail!* He had to admit, his facts from that night were a little shaky – Sarah's version was probably more correct.

The lawyers spoke with the judge, and reached a mutually

acceptable decision.

"I agree." The judge banged his bell once more. "All previous testimony by David Kirushenko will be stricken from the record. The jury will disregard all statements made by him when reviewing this case for their decision. His testimony shall have no bearing on this case whatsoever. Mr. Driskin, if you will call your next witness, please."

Sarah was glad to be off one hook, only to find herself stuck on another. The boys smoldered, throwing foul glances her way every time she looked at them. Even Vlad refused to hold hands; he held Sergei's instead. Dmitri and David would be trouble if they ganged up. Sarah didn't think they'd be too cruel, but, after all, no one else had ever broken a secret, even under Father's crushing thumb, and she'd broken a Big One. Then she'd made David a liar in front of a courtroom. Val wouldn't be too happy with them over *that* mess-up. Somehow, Sarah didn't think they'd accept the excuse of insanity…. She frowned when the judge called for recess.

"We're not done?" she asked Katya.

"It would run too late," Kat explained. "We'll continue tomorrow."

"Just what we need; another sleepless night," Sarah grumbled.

They gathered at the side of the room while the crowd straggled out.

"What do you think?" Carver asked Valeria.

Vladimir stood next to her, lost without Sarah by his side. Val put an arm around him and held him close. "I have no idea. I think it could still go either way. David's testimony being thrown out didn't help matters, I'm sure. We've certainly established a pattern, though.

"Listen," she told Carver and Carmichael, "if you don't have plans, we'd like to invite you to dinner. You've both been such a help to us."

"I thank you for the invitation," Carmichael said, "but I need to check in at the hospital, and my wife is expecting me."

Valeria blushed. "I'm sorry, I didn't realize…"

"Of course not. This has been – interesting, to say the least. I will have to revamp my expectations of a certain someone next week. I think in non-professional terms we'd just say, 'I've been had,' in a very grand fashion. I will see you all in the morning." He left with a wave.

"How about you?" Val asked Carver. "If you don't have a place to stay yet, we have extra room right now. It's crowded, but it's cool and clean. I feel like we owe you *something,* having done so much for Sarah."

"I think I'd like that," Carver said. "Maybe we can make it social and professional. Dr. Carmichael couldn't tell me anything inspiring. I have a feeling there might be some trouble after my testimony."

"The trouble's already started. Hear the silence?"

"Dr. Carver?" Katya spoke up shyly. "Can I talk to you?" She glanced around at all the interested ears. "Privately?"

"Sure. Come over here." He walked to an empty corner of the big room.

Sarah felt a finger jab her hard in the back. David's voice made a high-pitched whirring noise, like that of an EPSAR weapon on a holoprogram. She didn't flinch, accustomed to brotherly harassment.

"You're under house arrest," David whispered in one ear.

From behind, Dmitri's hand grasped her above the elbow. "Soon as we get home, you're dry sand," he whispered in her other ear. "We're going to have a little trial of our own…"

David whispered savagely, "Tattletale!"

John Carver touched Katya's arm with concern. "I want to apologize again. I tried. I wish there was some way I could have gotten around it, but I can't ignore my other patients while I sit in a cell. I never meant for that to be made public. I promised Sarah more than once. Please, don't blame her."

Katya shrugged awkwardly. "It's okay, I guess. Sarah told me some of what happened. If I'd known that before, I wouldn't have gotten so angry with her. I just – I wanted to know, but I didn't want to ask in case it would upset her. I don't know if you'll answer, but – I care about her, and I want to help."

"Of course. What can I do for you?"

Katya flushed, afraid of the answer. "When Sarah was – *attacked* –. When that man attacked her, did he, you know – How far did he – I mean, did he actually… ?"

Technically it was a breach of confidentiality, but Carver knew the girl meant well, and was the closest thing to a peer counselor Sarah would likely ever have. The fact Sarah'd mentioned it at all to her sister said volumes. And obviously the courts didn't give an intragalactic damn about confidentiality.

"No. She was just badly groped."

A dark cloud seemed to lift from Katya's shoulders. "Same as me. Thank you. Now I won't feel so weird talking to her about it."

"I think that's a great idea," Carver said. "Don't push her, though. Don't force her to talk about anything she doesn't want to."

"I wouldn't," she said. "Thank you."

The boys surrounded Sarah like a fence. Katya shooed them away. "Leave her alone, guys."

"We're just protecting you, Kat," Dmitri sneered. "Unlike some who shall be nameless."

Katya pulled a smoking Sarah away from them. "Lay off her! I forgave her already. You leave her alone, you hear! Don't you go messing with her, or you'll have to deal with me!"

David waited until Katya looked away, then aimed and fired his finger ray again.

Sarah crossed her eyes in reply.

Val pushed the group along. "Let's get out of here."

Getting in the flyer took extra time. Loyalties had shifted. Now Dmitri and David were best friends. Now Sarah would sit only between Katya and a window. Now Vlad wanted to sit with Sergei.

"This is ridiculous!" Val said at last, in a hurry to get the youngest ones from the preschool. "It's a five minute ride. Just get in!"

# * Seventeen *

I t felt good to be home, the long pressures of the day left back in the city. They exploded out of the flyer with a battlecry of freedom, racing over the scorching sand into the house.

"Everyone change clothes!" Galina reminded, setting the baby loose on the floor. "You too, Sarah."

"In a minute," Sarah replied. She sat at the dusty grand piano that took up the other half of the dining room and practiced an odd Navaran tune.

"I can't believe the temperature difference," Carver said to Valeria. "It must be thirty degrees cooler in here. You're sure there's no envirosystem boosters?"

"Nothing," Val insisted. "Just geothermics and fans. It's all done within the design of the rooms." She pointed to the seven-and-a-half meter ceiling. "At night, we open the vents, put on the fans, and it pulls the night air in. It stays pleasant enough until about sunset, then we start over again. It's amazing what can be done when there's so little humidity."

The boys ran whooping back into the room, clothed now in loose shirts and shorts, all of them barefoot. Nikky rode atop Dmitri's shoulders, laughing.

Val stopped him. "Dimi, why don't you show Dr. Carver to your room? He can stay there tonight."

Carver blushed despite being pink with the heat. "I didn't mean to put you out. You said you had room."

"We do," Val insisted. "Dmitri has a room to himself. There's an empty bunk in the boys' room. There's no reason he can't go back for a night. A private room is a big luxury around here."

"I don't mind," Dmitri said as he swung Nikky to the floor. "We haven't had guests in a long time. Come on."

Carver whistled in disbelief. "There were two of you in this room? For how long?" He leaned against the side of the bunks. The narrow room left not much more than a meter between the wall and the stacked beds.

"Vik and Alexei shared it for a year or so, after Nikky moved to a bed," Dmitri said. "It kept us from having six in the other room."

219

"I haven't seen a room this small since Med School."

"You should have seen our house in Russia," Dmitri said proudly. "Now *that* was something."

"Nice?"

"We had a beautiful *dacha* outside Kiev. Twelve rooms – six of them bedrooms. Alexei had his own room, but I only had to share with Viktor. We get along really good. He's the best! After the twins left for school, 'Byeta had her own room, too. It was supposed to be Katya's, but not even Father could stop the Sarah and 'Byeta fight, so they had to be separated. They spent one night together – must have stayed up the whole night torturing each other. In the morning they were covered with bruises and missing half their hair. What they hadn't pulled out, they'd used scissors on." Dmitri sighed longingly. "Those were the days."

Carver scanned the tiny room again, twice as high as it was long. The back of the room was dug into the ridge wall outside; there were no windows, but two angled skylights let in light without much heat. Dmitri had done his best to dress it up with holoflats of popular musicians and banners of several local and Earth sports teams, but the rough walls and cramped space still gave the impression of a monk's cell, or an old wine cellar. "You must have hated to leave it for this."

"Mother cried the day we left. She loved that house. She'd grown up in one something like it. It sure was nicer than this," Dmitri agreed.

When they returned, Sarah had moved on to practicing Rachmaninov from memory, making frequent errors and corrections. David and Vlad – an unusual combination – were playing catch with an electronic toy that screeched various signals now and then. Every so often, David would lean toward Sarah and whisper something no one else could hear.

Carver watched the interactions from the sofa. Sarah's mistakes coincided mostly with the whispers. She didn't acknowledge her brother's words, but Carver knew the set of the jaw. He spoke with Dmitri, but kept his eye on the younger group.

David grew bolder. "Hey, Sergei!" he called across the room. "Who does this remind you of?"

Sergei looked up from his textreader. David staggered, holding his stomach. "Judge! Judge!" he called in a high-pitched voice. "Know what I think? Lawyers – make me – sick! Blechh!" He bent over and made gagging noises.

*That did it.* Sarah slammed into him with the force of an ore freighter. They tore into each other with unexpected fury, punching, kicking, and trying to flip the other down.

"Go Sarah!" Vlad shouted with delight.

"She can do it," Sergei agreed.

Dmitri grinned. "Go for it, Dave! Third time's the charm!"

Carver was alarmed by the ferocity of the battle. "Don't you stop them? Someone's going to get hurt."

Dmitri waved a hand. "Nah. Sarah's good. She's licked him twice already."

David had at least twenty centimeters and thirty kilos over Sarah, but he didn't have a great advantage. She was quicker, with trained moves against his street throws, and he spent most of his efforts defending himself.

Valeria flew out of the kitchen at the sound of the fight. "Sarah! David! Stop this instant! Dmitri, don't just sit there! Get him off her!"

"She started it."

Val screamed as the baby crawled behind the grappling pair. Sarah saw her, wrenched the other way, and the two of them fell to the floor.

Val tried to get between them, and got an elbow in her face. "David! Sarah! Stop it!" Carver came over to help.

Rolling on the floor, Sarah's legs tangled in the skirt of her dress. David straddled her, kneeling on the fabric, pulling it tight against her legs so she couldn't kick, hands struggling to hold her wrists. Sarah realized sadly that three months in a hospital had stolen her advantage. She was pinned – unless she tore the new dress, in which case she'd have to deal with Val.

"I did it! I did it!" David hooted. "I got her!"

*"Get up,"* Carver said, pulling the teen by the arm.

A streak shot across the room and knocked David clean out of Carver's grasp before he could stand. David's shouts of triumph turned into a shriek of pain.

Sarah sat up to see Carver lift Vladimir off David with one hand.

David took his hand from his ear, fingers bloody. *"What the fuck d'ja do?"* he screamed. "I'll pound you flatter than paper, you little shit!"

Sarah shrank back at the sight of blood. *"Vlad?! You bit him!"* A tiny smile turned up one side of her mouth. "And they called *me* crazy!"

"He deserved it. He was picking on you," Vlad sulked.

*"What is with you people tonight?"* cried Valeria. "Even Vlad is acting up! Get up, all of you. Now! Apologize to each other!" She pulled Sarah and David from the floor.

They glared venomously, waiting for the other to speak.

Sarah broke off first. "I'm sorry, Val. I forgot we should make allowances for those of low morals and limited wit."

David lashed out with a hard kick. Sarah twisted out of the way, and went to change her dress.

"Come, David, let me see your ear," Valeria sighed. "Vladimir, you have something to say to your brother?"

"No," Vlad pouted, knowing David would punish him soon enough.

"Go sit in my room until I have time to get to you."

The twins made a fancier dinner in honor of their guest, but it tasted pretty much the same. Textured vegetable protein shaped like meat still didn't feel or taste like meat. At least the vegetables were 'real.'

"One time," Dmitri began, "Father, somehow, somewhere, got hold of two steaks – real beef! Not just any steak; these things were nearly two kilos a piece, and as thick as your wrist. After dark, when it cooled down, Father himself cooked them over a flame, and you could smell that meat clear out into the desert. We were lucky to be so far out, or someone would have come sniffing – not exactly a legal meal here. Father ate an entire one himself. The whole thing. Mother split the other one among the rest of us, and I can *still* remember how good that meat tasted."

"Meat meat, meat meat," Nikky sang, mashing his food with his fork.

"A lot better than this stuff," David remarked, leaning across the table near Sarah to grab a dish of fruit relish.

*"Traitor,"* he whispered.

Sarah slid down in her seat to kick him under the table.

"Val! Sarah's kicking me!" he called out, spooning a mountain of relish on his plate.

"Sarah, stop it," Galina said around a mouthful of food.

"He said something to her," Katya frowned. "What did you say?"

David pretended not to hear.

"He called her a traitor," Sergei said.

"Which is what *you* are," David pointed back.

"Traitor? Why is she a traitor?" Katya asked.

Sergei lifted his head long enough to throw David a smug grin. "Because she said stuff she wasn't supposed to talk about."

Katya swore something awful in Russian. She threw her fork on the table so hard it bounced and almost hit Dmitri. She leaned far over the table toward David.

*"I told you to leave her alone!"* Katya stormed fierce and terrible, not at all like her gentle self. Even Nikky watched her with a new respect.

"I'm glad she told! You know why? Because now I don't have to hide! I feel *free* of that secret! I *know* I did nothing wrong! Viktor was in the bathroom, so I used the one in Father's room. When I came out, I found out Father'd followed me, and wouldn't let me leave. None of that was my fault! I couldn't fight a man whose arms were thicker than my legs, and I won't feel guilty about it anymore! And I *will not* have you picking on Sarah for that! Do you understand?" Katya looked ready to explode.

"Yeah," David grumbled. "If you say so."

"I *mean* it! No more insults, and don't you dare lay a finger on her!"

"*Okay!* I get the point!"

"Good! Don't forget it." Katya sat down. She pushed her half-eaten dinner forward and let her head rest in her hand.

Sarah saw her sister's fragile state and gave her a silent squeeze of thanks. The contact had its desired effect; Katya relaxed and returned the hug.

"Gee, Kat," Dmitri mumbled, "remind me to stay on your good side."

"David, I will speak to you after dinner," Val said seriously. "Eat, Katya." Katya pulled her plate back, but ignored the cold food.

John Carver played with his water glass. "It's not my place to say so, but I think today's business dredged up a lot of stuff that's still hanging around. I feel responsible for some of that. If you'd like, I know a couple of group activities that might ease things a little."

"I don't think we've ever been this out of control before," Galina said. "I never thought I'd live to see the day Vlad and Sarah stopped speaking. Even when she was in the hospital, he still sat on her bed to do his homework, just as if she was there. Sergei's taking sides in a fight, and Katya's standing up for herself. This isn't how we normally are," she admitted. "We'd appreciate any ideas you could give us."

They sat on the floor in a circle, in the large foyer between the piano and the back half of the living room, after Nikky and Marina had been put to bed. David's ears still rang from his "talk" with Valeria.

Valeria placed Mother's big soup tureen in the middle of the circle, and sat between David and Sergei.

Carver sat in the circle holding two decks of cards, which he placed together. He passed the double-deck to Galina. "Everyone take eight cards and pass the deck. The rules are simple: Toss a card. If it lands in the bowl, your turn is over, if you want. If you miss, you get one sentence, and only one, to say whatever comes to mind, good or bad, no more, no less. You can comment on something someone else says, but only during your turn. No talking out of turn."

"Not fair!" Vladimir wailed immediately. "I'm no good at targets. Dimi knows how to flip cards real good. He'll never have to say anything."

"Then maybe Val could pick on him instead of me," David needled.

"This isn't a free-for-all," Carver said. "It's to say something that's on your mind where you won't get stepped on for it. Look at yourselves! Nobody's talking to anyone. Katya's not talking to David; David's not talking to Valeria, Vlad's not talking to Sarah, Sarah's not talking to me – Don't look like that, I know when you're avoiding me. You all have a lot to say, you just need to come out and say it. This can open up some of those blocked channels. The rest will fall into place once you start talking. Just say the first thing that comes into your head. I'll go first."

Carver took aim and flipped a card to the pot, a meter and a half away. The card bounced off the rim and hit the floor. "I can honestly say I have never seen hotter weather, and this gravity is killing me. I don't know how you live with it."

Galina flung a card, but it went long and landed on Dmitri. "Anything? Um. I'm really proud of everyone in court today, I think we did really well. I…"

"One sentence," Carver reminded her. "Sarah's turn."

Sarah eyed the pot carefully. Physics wasn't always her best subject. She rose to her knees, took aim, judged distance, and let the card go. It skimmed the rim and fell in. Sarah's arms went up in silent victory, and she allowed herself a self-satisfied smile.

"You can still say something if you want," Carver encouraged.

Sarah shook her head, happy.

"Figures!" David griped before Val whacked his knee with her hand.

Vladimir made a half-hearted toss that went part way. "What ever's most on my mind? I wish Sarah wasn't so mad at me, 'cause I'm not really that mad at her." David would have pounded him if he hadn't played along.

"Good, Vladimir," Carver praised. "That's great! That's honest."

Vlad sucked up the approval, but was happier by far when Sarah reached out and took his hand in hers. All was forgiven.

Katya's card fell short. "I think I'm still mad at David, because I thought I could trust him to do what I asked, but he couldn't."

"Good," Carver said. "Honest and direct, but not derogatory."

Sergei's throw called for a ruling. It caught on the handle, neither in nor on the floor.

"That's outside!" David yelled.

"It's not inside," Dmitri agreed. "Spill your guts, Serg."

Sergei studied the floor. "We all said some really nasty things about Father to his face, and I just wondered, sitting in whatever cell he's in, if he regrets anything he's done."

"Hah!" David choked. "That's stupid! Does a Sirian frog regret giving you acid burns?"

"Please wait your turn, David," Carver said patiently. "There are no 'stupid' thoughts. Sergei brought up an interesting point. I don't know if we'll ever know the answer. We can only hope it's yes."

Valeria leaned over and kissed the top of Sergei's head. Sometimes Sergei seemed to run deeper than Sarah. Where Sarah got lost in cold facts and analogies and her own obsessions, Sergei lost himself in silent emotions and shyly caring about people.

Val's card bounced off the side. "David's had an awful time today, and I'd like to know what's eating him."

David flung his card over his shoulder, unable to resist such an open invitation. "Maybe because we used to have rules around here, but now it seems like anyone can change them whenever they want, and the girls around here are getting awful pushy and know-it-all and I'm getting sick of being bossed around every time I fucking breathe!"

"That's honest," Carver said. "It's a good start. Dmitri?"

Dmitri took aim. He often resorted to tossing cards when he was bored and no one wanted to play. His card, too, went in. "Yes!" he shouted.

The second round seemed harder than the first.

Sarah looked around almost in fright when her card missed the pot. It took a full minute to come up with something she could say. "I think Dr. Carver knows why I'm not speaking to him, if he thinks hard enough."

"I know a secret," Vlad confessed, "and it's bothering me."

"Do you want to share it?" Carver suggested. This family had too many secrets.

"I can't."

"Could you whisper it to anyone here?"

Vlad crawled across the circle and whispered in Val's ear. Val glanced with alarm at Galina, then at Dmitri and David. "Don't worry, Vlad. I'll take care of it. You tell Sarah not to worry, too."

"Vik always knew the right thing to do," Dmitri said in turn, "and I wish he was here, because I'd sure like to know what he would say."

David stood on the fourth round and threw his remaining cards in.

"I've had enough of this shit. I'm done."

"That's probably a good idea," Val agreed. "It's late. Vlad, Sarah, Sergei, bed! Katya, will you play hostess for a few minutes? Galina and I have some 'legal' business to attend to." The circle broke up.

Hardly five minutes passed before Sarah reappeared in pajamas and sat next to Carver. Katya placed two cups of coffee on the table.

"You're supposed to be in bed, Sarah."

Sarah crossed her arms on the table and put her head down. "I know."

Carver took one of the cups. "Talking to me yet?"

"I suppose so," she sighed. "I'm still mad, but I'll get over it twenty years from now."

"I'm glad." He bent forward until his face lay even with hers. "It wasn't my choice, believe me. If you were still my only patient, I would have stayed in contempt. I'm glad you and Katya were able to settle things."

Sarah nodded as best she could with her head down. "Did I ever tell you why I don't trust doctors?"

"I don't think so. I assumed it was from the hospital here."

"I can't even remember that." Sarah sat up; John followed suit. "It was long before then. Have you ever had pneumonia?"

"No, I can't say I have."

"I have. Lots of times. If it got really bad, I had to go to a hospital. Then, one time, on Gamma Europa IV, I was in the hospital and one of my lungs collapsed."

"That's very painful. You must have been very scared."

"I couldn't breathe. But even that wasn't so bad. Once the nurse realized what happened, a whole team of people came flying in. They claimed there wasn't time for anesthesia. They didn't even give me time to brace myself. I was fighting them, fighting to breathe, but they moved in, held me down, then stabbed me in the side with something. That *really* hurt, more than the lung. *Then* they gave me the painkillers and took me for surgery. After that, I never trusted them again. It wasn't even the stabbing me without medicine first, it was the holding me down and not telling me what they were going to do. That was the worst part. I might have only been four or so, but I still would have liked to know."

"That's horrible!" Katya exclaimed. "How could they do that?"

Carver sighed, rubbing tired eyes. He'd boarded the shuttle at one that morning, and hadn't slept much on the flight. "Unfortunately, doctors sometimes get so caught up in the medicine, they forget they're dealing with people. I can't imagine in this day and age the crisis was so bad they couldn't take fifteen seconds for a shot of local. Especially on a child. I wish you'd told me that story before. I would have revamped your program to eliminate all forms of restraint. No hands on."

"You never asked. It's okay," Sarah reassured him. "They didn't use them that often. Nobody hurt me, and if nothing else, I wore myself out fighting them."

"So why tell me this now?"

Sarah traced invisible shapes on the table with her finger. "I don't know. Maybe to show that I still trust you, and I know you really believed in that law of confidentiality."

"I did until today."

Vladimir came out and sat next to Sarah, chin on his hand.

"What happened to bed?" Katya asked. "Is Sergei coming out next?"

"Valeria and Galina are drilling Dmitri and David a new set of ears," Vlad explained. "I kind of told Val about something they were planning."

"That was stupid," Sarah said. "Now they'll be after you, too."

"I don't think so," Vlad replied with an unusual sense of certainty. "Val hasn't been that mad since they tried to kick David out of school. It's a good thing the whip's gone, 'cause I think she's mad enough to use it." At Miss Kellar's suggestion, they had destroyed the dreaded whip, each taking turns cutting a piece until nothing remained. It had been nerve-wracking at the start, as if Father would appear and catch them, but it didn't match the relief they felt afterwards.

As if on cue, the twins and the older boys appeared, none of them looking happy. Dmitri had grown ten centimeters in the past year, but he still lacked twelve or fifteen more against the girls. He looked downright silly, twisting his head to ease Galina's hold on the back of his neck, a trick she must have learned from Father. They stopped in front of the table.

"Sarah, the boys have something to say to you," Valeria announced with disgust. "It seems they were preparing their own game of crime and punishment." She poked David in the back. "Go on! Tell her what you had planned."

David squirmed. "We wouldn't have hurt you."

Galina used her fingernails to make Dmitri writhe. "Tell her! Tell her your idea of just a *game*."

"I can't believe you two," Katya said. "Didn't you hear *anything* I said before?"

"Honest, Sar, we wouldn'a hurt you," Dmitri confessed. "We just wanted to scare you a little."

"Of course not!" Valeria said with a cold savageness no one had seen before. "Their 'game' was going to start by grabbing her out of bed and tying her up. Tell her!"

Dmitri burned red. "You make it sound worse than we meant."

"Tell her what you were going to do after that – after you 'tried' her without defense."

Dmitri hung his head. He was older; by rights, their 'law' said he had to take the blame. "We hadn't figured that out yet. David wanted to make you eat a couple hot peppers, I thought maybe making you drink soap or something. Honest! That's as bad as we were thinking. I know, the whole thing was really, really dumb. We're sorry if we scared you. We were just upset about – you know – everything you said."

"We're really sorry," David echoed.

Sarah stood up, mouth compressed into an unhappy line. "Sometimes sorry isn't enough." She stalked past them without a second glance and went to bed. Her shadow Vlad followed.

Katya also stood up. "That's the kind of shit I would've expected out of Alexei, not you, Dmitri. I never thought you were like that. I hope you guys rot from the inside out," she spat as she walked by.

# * Eighteen *

They knew what to expect on the second day. After a brief glance, Father's presence wasn't as intimidating. Today Dmitri and David each sat next to a twin, as far apart as possible. Val didn't want them close enough to plan anything else.

The morning passed slowly. More witnesses waited to be called: Father's friends, the emergency physician who had treated Father the night they'd shipped him out – and again in prison when Father went through alcohol withdrawal, the court-appointed psychiatrist, and Father himself.

The emergency physician testified as to just how drunk Father was the night of Katya's attack, his blood levels almost three times the legal definition of intoxication. Now he understood the strange bruise on the back of the man's knee. He described the effects of severe alcohol withdrawal.

David's "Serves him right!" could be heard for two rows before Galina stabbed him with her elbow.

The physician spoke for an hour, explaining the effects of alcohol on the brain receptors, of depression, of dependency, and repressed anger.

"Yeah. We were pressed, *de*-pressed, and *re*-pressed by it all the time," David said clearly before Galina whispered a threat.

Listening to the testimony was interesting at first. No one ever imagined Father as having friends, or being witty and social. Since arriving on Navara, he never seemed to talk to anyone, but here were people he spoke with daily, shared thoughts with, joked with, took advice from. How could anyone describe Father as having a sense of humor? Brilliant? Maybe once upon a time, but there was nothing brilliant about a drunken stupor, five or more nights a week. Slowly, the novelty of Father's "secret" life wore off, and the thumb wrestling began. Soon Sergei's little notepad did double duty for wordgames. He and Vlad made Sarah wait out several rounds, as she knew too many long words with 'X' in them.

"There's no such word as 'xenophily'!" Sergei objected in a whisper.

"Sure there is!" Sarah whispered back. "Think of the Greek roots; it's a love of the unknown."

"No fair using words I can't spell!" said Vlad. "I Rule it! Sarah can't use any word over five letters."

"That's fair," Sergei agreed. He wouldn't have Ruled it for himself, of course, but Vlad didn't have a chance otherwise.

"Babies," Sarah grumbled.

The information given by the court psychiatrist should have been interesting, but Sarah shuddered. She'd heard enough of that kind of talk to last a lifetime. Father's IQ of 151, growing up abused by his own drunken mother, his stress reaction patterns, repressed anger at his parents, poor self-image, depression – all the more reasons he should have known better, as far as Sarah could see. She spent the time writing a caustic note to Dmitri and David, full of flowery speech and formal intent.

Sarah was rather pleased with the note. It sounded formal and forbidding, and would probably take David just as long to figure out.

*Мой Дорогой Брат,* she wrote in her perfect Russian script,

*My Dear Brother,*

*How kind of you to bestow such careful thought and attention on me yesterday when my spirits were so low. I am touched by your persistence and dedication. While your plans may have lacked ingenious creativity, they made up for it in sincerity. It is only proper that I return such a display of despicable vengeance.*

*As Valeria is infinitely distracted and has limited time to ponder an appropriate disciplinary action, I have taken unto myself the liberty of doing so. I promise, my action will be swift, personal, and unmistakable.*

*Following said action, I will consider all matters to be null, void, and buried, and I will once again be happy to entertain your company.*

*Sincerely,*

*Your very pissed off sister,*

*S. I. K.*

She wrote it out once for each, then folded them and passed the notes down. Today she could dare to write *pissed off*. David and Dmitri wouldn't dare rat on her right now.

Dmitri read his with affront, then raised an eyebrow and nodded his acceptance of the terms. One swift shot and all would be forgiven.

David reread his several times. He tried to catch Dmitri with a *'What the hell is this?'* look, but sitting six people apart limited communication. He balled up the paper, scowling, and passed it back. Sarah met his gaze and winked, the better to keep him on his guard.

Father was the last one called. The small, all-purpose witness seat only made him seem larger, bound like a circus animal outside its cage. He appeared serious and composed, but from nerves, temper control, or contempt?

"Did you strike your children, Mr. Kirushenko?"

Father spoke softly, but the cavernous room amplified his deep voice. "I maintained discipline."

"With your fists?" Driskin accused.

"With my *hands*," Father corrected. "Sometimes, yes."

"You whipped your children, Mr. Kirushenko. Navara or Earth, that isn't allowed. It's considered brutality."

"The definition of brutality varies from era to era and culture to culture," Father reminded the court, a learned university professor once more. "Here on Navara, it is brutality to feed your children animal flesh. In the Marrosan system, it is a privilege to have your child chosen for ritual sacrifice. Not two hundred years ago on Earth, children were sold as slaves. My children were born into loving arms. They are well fed, clothed, housed, and educated. They are widely traveled, have been exposed to many cultures, spared hard labor; they never lacked companionship. They're exceptionally intelligent, well-mannered, and caring. There isn't a bad seed among them."

"That may be well and true," Driskin allowed, "but we're not in the Marrosan system. The law is here and now. Do you admit that at times you may have been overly harsh in your disciplinary practices?"

Father's eyes scanned down the row of children, lingering on Sarah, but his features never changed. "It is possible, on occasion."

"You admit to being an alcoholic?"

"Yes."

"Have you been drinking today?"

"No."

"Did you ever try to stop drinking before?"

Father bent over to reach his hand so he could scratch his cheek. "Yes. A number of times. I last tried when Tash – Maryana – my wife – died. I knew my family would need me sober, more involved, more in charge. I stayed sober for almost eight weeks, but – without my wife – I couldn't stay that way."

"You admit to blackouts," Driskin reminded him.

"Yes."

"How long did your blackouts last?"

Father shifted his bulk on the undersized chair. The electronic cuffs weren't adjusted properly, and wouldn't allow him to cross his long legs. "Several hours. Up to two days, once."

"You disagree with your children as to the accuracy of some of the incidents they seem to remember. Is it possible that these incidents occurred during your memory lapses?"

"It is possible," Father admitted reluctantly. "I can't confirm or deny it."

Suarez seemed confident dealing with his client. "Tell me, Mr. Kirushenko: how old were you when you started drinking?"

Father shook his big head. "I'm not sure. Teens – perhaps thirteen or fourteen."

"Your parents approved?"

"They didn't know. My mother had divorced by then."

"Did she drink?"

"Yes."

"Was she an alcoholic?"

"Yes."

"Did you steal alcohol from her?"

"No. My friends had a steady supply."

"Did your wife drink with you?"

"No!" Father answered quickly. "Tash never touched hard liquor. She liked wine with dinner, sometimes before bed, that's all."

"Did you ever hit your wife, Mr. Kirushenko?"

Father's invincibility faded in response to the insinuation. "Never! Not even once. Not even in jest! I loved my wife more than life itself. I think even my children will attest to that." He looked to Galina sitting on the end of the aisle, seeming to plead with her to back him up. Gal melted in his gaze, nodding, and gave him a sympathetic smile in return.

Suarez caught the exchange, hoped the jury had as well. "Have you ever been charged with assault before, Mr. Kirushenko?"

"Not since my youth," Father answered honestly, though he looked tense.

"So, assuming you had yourself declared an adult at seventeen, for the last thirty years you have no criminal record, no run-ins with the law, no history of violence on any planet, member of the UPA or not?"

"No, sir. I do not."

Father's testimony went extremely well. He came off almost a stranger to the younger children – a polished, intelligent, university professor who had messed up one night, not the vicious, raving, bloodthirsty lunatic they had tried their best to describe. To the older children, he brought back forgotten memories. As Father left the stand, Sarah stretched forward, tired of sitting. She looked down the row, seeing everyone else do the same, except for Valeria, who sat with her head bowed.

With a start, Sarah realized Val was crying. Seeing Katya's eyes wet wasn't a shock; Katya was emotional to start with, but *Val*? Val was a *rock*!

Following summations, Judge Ellmore dismissed the jury with their instructions in time for a late lunch.

"This court is in recess until such time as the jury reaches a verdict," he announced, banging his desk as if building it. The final waiting began.

"Are our chances that bad?" Sarah asked.

Valeria gave her nose a last wipe. "Huh? Oh, no, no, Sarah. I really have no idea. It's just – I feel so rotten about all this! Father, up there – that's the Father I remember. The one who could speak to a crowd so eloquently. The one who would let Alexei and Viktor and us all ride on his back at once. The one who got more excited about vacations than we did. Without alcohol, he is that same person. I didn't realize he still grieved Mother that much. I'm not putting some nameless monster into prison, I'm putting away my *Father!*" she sobbed.

"I was right," Sergei said. "Did you hear him admit he hit too hard? He does regret it." Dmitri bent over, his hand on Katya's back, whispering to her. Even David stood subdued.

Sarah looked at the maudlin group and crossed her arms.

"I think you're all crazy!" she declared. "You're being suckered by an act. You'd be surprised how well you could act if your life was on the line."

Val stroked the girl's cheek with the back of her finger, much to Sarah's irritation. "No, Sar. You're just too young to remember Father before he drank."

"Hmph!" Sarah replied with contempt. "You just never paid attention."

They ate a slow lunch, edgy with anticipation. They could have walked around the city, but no one wanted to risk missing the jury call. A tour of the building killed all of ten minutes. Time wouldn't move.

The cafeteria seating was more comfortable than the courtroom. Dmitri put his head on the table and took a nap. Katya dug through her shoulder bag, took out an enamel pen, and touched up her nails. Sergei and David kept busy with a pocket game, while Sarah and Vlad, tired of sitting, wandered the room, watching people come and go.

Out of the way of the worst of the crowd, Sarah in the lead, they spied Dr. Carmichael and Dr. Carver lunching together. Sarah turned around and started back, but they'd been spotted. Dr. Carver called them over, too clearly to be overlooked.

Dr. Carmichael gestured to a chair. "Hello, Sarah. Come, sit down with us."

Sarah looked at Vlad, who shrugged. She sighed and sat.

"What's up?" Carver said casually. "After lunch walk?"

"We're bored," Vlad explained. "We have to stay here until the jury comes back, and there's nothing to do."

"Well, hopefully this will all be finished today, and then you can get back to school."

Vlad shot him a nasty look. "I'd rather sit here bored."

"Sarah," Dr. Carmichael said, "Dr. Carver and I were discussing your daily sessions – "

Sarah's guard flew up. Nothing good ever came from people talking about her. "Are you that bored, or am I such a bizarre case you can't stop talking about me?"

"You happen to be one of the things we have in common," Carver humored her.

"I'm just a thing?"

"We were discussing how unhappy you seem to be with the current arrangement," Carmichael said.

"I never said anything like that."

"You don't have to. It's fairly obvious. Dr. Carver and I – "

"Two against one isn't very fair!" Sarah blurted, horrendously uncomfortable with the fact she sat between *two* psychiatrists.

"I've never known you to be at a disadvantage with only two to one," said John. "For you, Sarah, I wouldn't bet my money unless the odds were at least three to one. Now stop interrupting, and hear us out."

"Dr. Carver and I feel that since you seem to be adjusting well enough at home, perhaps you would be happier if we cut things back to one hour a day."

Sarah perked up. "I'd like that. Then Valeria could wait for me, and I wouldn't be so trapped."

Understanding dawned on Carmichael. "Is that the problem? The office makes you feel trapped?"

Sarah looked at the table, but nodded. "At Rangler, I could have gone back to my room. I don't think I ever did, but I could have if I wanted to."

"If you'd told me, I would have called your sister to come and get you."

Sarah slouched until she was eye-level to the table. "Val would never understand. She said only if I were sick or something."

"If it would make you feel more at ease," Carmichael offered, "perhaps, once a week, you could bring someone with you. We could work as a group."

Vlad sprang up straight. "Me? Me? Could you bring me, Sar?"

The more she considered the idea, the more Sarah liked it. Except for three months, she'd shared all her experiences with her family. With someone else there, the unbearable pressure of expectation would be lifted. Vlad was her best friend in the world. And a little therapy certainly wouldn't hurt him.

"Vlad could come with me?"

"Sure, if that's who you'd like."

"I *would* like that. I think that'd be much better." She allowed herself a smile. Maybe she *could* get used to Carmichael.

Carmichael smiled back. "Good. That's what we'll do, then. I'll talk with Valeria today, and we'll start tomorrow." To Vladimir he said, "Can you come tomorrow?"

Vlad's eyes lit up with excitement. "That's in the afternoon, isn't it? I can leave school early!"

"No, no, we don't want that. We'll move the time to after school."

"Does that mean I can go back to school?" Sarah asked with a tremor of hope.

Carver hesitated. "Back to the Navaran school? I still don't think that's such a good idea... "

"Even half a day?" she pleaded. "I can do it! I'm fine now! It's not a problem! I *hate* sitting around the house all day."

Carmichael waved a hand. "We can talk about that."

Sarah wasn't about to give in. "'*We can talk about that,*' always means 'No, you can't, you don't know what you're talking about, you're too young, go away.'"

Carmichael chuckled. "No, I promise, but you have to convince me."

Galina came up behind Sarah. "So this is where you disappeared to. Are they pestering you?" she asked the men.

"Not at all," Carver said. "In fact, we asked them to join us. If they're in trouble, it's our fault."

"Just keeping tabs." Galina smoothed Sarah's hair with her fingers until the girl twisted away.

Mercifully, the address system signaled, calling everyone to return to the courtroom.

They flew back to their seats, hearts pounding. Vladimir and Sarah locked hands, sick with nerves. Father entered with his guards and took his seat. The jury trickled in, as if speed didn't matter.

"Have you reached a verdict?" Judge Ellmore asked the jury.

"Yes, we have, your Honor," a juror announced, standing. She handed a sealed computer card to the judge.

"Very well." Ellmore broke the seal and inserted the card in a reader on his table. "You may read your findings to the court."

The juror read from a print of the file passed to the judge.

Sarah scarcely breathed.

"In the case of Government of Kar Ku'umi for Elizabyeta Kirushenko versus Alexander Grigorevitch Kirushenko, on the charge of willful and deliberate homicide, the jury finds the defendant, not guilty."

Sarah grabbed Katya's hand with her free one; Vlad did the same to Sergei, and seconds later they all held hands down the row.

"On the second charge, assault and battery of a juvenile, the jury finds the defendant guilty, as charged."

Sarah remembered to breathe.

"On the alternate charge of negligent homicide, we find the defendant,"

The pause was hardly more than a fraction of a second, but with so much riding on the next word it seemed to last minutes.

"Guilty, as charged."

A wave of relief rolled through the line of siblings, and the hands released. Vlad hugged Sarah, overjoyed, but Sarah froze, watching Father's reaction. Even with the restraints, she half-expected him to come after her.

"Alexander Kirushenko, please rise," the judge ordered. Father rolled slowly to his feet.

"Alexander Kirushenko, you have been found guilty in a court of law of the charges of assault of a juvenile and negligent homicide in the death of your daughter, Elizabyeta Kirushenko. As per the guidelines given me by the laws of the United Planetary Alliance, I hearby sentence you to be incarcerated in a penal rehabilitation facility for a period of not less than seven years, not to exceed fifteen years inclusive of time served." With a bang of his desk, Judge Ellmore sealed Father's fate.

Father's head dropped forward and he closed his eyes momentarily, but the face that rose looked the same. He glanced at his children one last time, but they were busy with each other. Only one looked in his direction.

Sarah caught his eye. A brief look of pain seemed to flash across Father's face, a momentary glimmer of sadness in the eyes, and his shoulders sagged. Then he was gone.

The courtroom swelled with conversation and footsteps as the crowd rose and filed out. Galina and Valeria spoke with Driskin. Dmitri and David slapped hands in undisguised elation.

John Carver clapped Sarah on the back as she stood. "Congratulations! Are you happy?"

Sarah looked at him with a seriousness forged by experience. "He *will* be back, and he won't be pleased."

"Yes," Carver agreed, "but you'll be as much as twenty-four years old by then. He'll be a much older, hopefully much wiser man, and there's no guarantee you'll ever see him again."

"Maybe."

Sarah wanted nothing more than to get the Hell out of there, but the twins were speaking with the judge, and soon Valeria left with the bailiff through the side door. Carver hung around, talking with the group. Sergei jotted thoughts in his notebook, listening now and then to the bits of conversation. Sarah hung out next to him, too sullen and self-absorbed to desire conversation.

"I thought you'd be happier?" Sergei said after a while.

"I didn't see you jump for joy."

"No. I wish 'Byeta was still alive, and the court just had to make him stop drinking. I never wanted him to leave, just be nicer is all. Maybe if we had told someone, it wouldn't have come to this. What's going to happen now? Val is in charge for good. David won't listen to her now; what's she going to do when he gets bigger? And who's going to watch us? We can't live on Galina's income much longer. Katya'll want to go to university next year. Can you see Dmitri and David in charge if Val's out working, too? You'll be stuck with the baby, because you're the next oldest girl."

"If I get my diploma, I'll be at university next year, too," Sarah said indignantly. "Then *you'd* be stuck with the baby."

"You'd have to take classes at a local program," Sergei pointed out. "No school is going to let a kid board with adults."

"I know. It kind of limits my choices. You don't think Val will split us up, do you? To make it easier on her?"

Now Sergei looked uneasy. "Not if she can help it. You don't think that's what they're talking to the judge about?"

"Don't even think it!"

\* \* \*

Valeria's stomach twisted tight as she walked the corridor of the men's detention wing, hearing an occasional whistle. Non-judicial personnel weren't allowed in here, but the judge granted special permission.

"Ho! Big Boy!" called the security officer as he dropped the force field over the doorway to the cell. "You got a visitor. Ten minutes! Don't do anything stupid."

Valeria looked at the officer with affront. "You are speaking to my father! You will address him with respect."

"Not in here, Ma'am."

Val crossed into the cell; the field activated behind her. "Father?"

Sasha's broad back was to her. "You don't belong here," he said loudly, but the voice wasn't harsh enough, wasn't angry. "Leave!"

"Father, please? I have to ask you some questions. You're the only one who can help."

The giant turned around. "Help? How can you bear to look at me after everything I've done?"

"I'm sorry we had to say those things; it wasn't my choice. I didn't know what to do. We were all alone. They hounded us with questions day after day; we didn't know if we had the right to refuse. We were told we would be called as witnesses whether we wanted to or not, that it was a political case and the government was pushing it. They threatened to take the younger ones away if we didn't cooperate. I was afraid. I didn't want us broken up."

Val's tears returned. "I'm so sorry! I'm so sorry, Papa! I never meant for it to happen. I wasn't in the room. I would have stopped her. I should have watched her better. I'm sorry. I didn't know she was hurt that bad."

Sasha held out a long arm, and Valeria lunged for him like a little girl. "So it's true?" he whispered hollowly, holding her to him like an oversized comfy toy. "I did kill her?"

"You never meant to," Val cried onto his shoulder. "I should have stopped it from happening, and I didn't."

Sasha looked ill, cold sweat saturating his court-appointed dress shirt despite the heavy layer of anti-perspirants. "What about Ekaterina? Tell me! I must know the truth! What did I do to her?"

"Not much," Val sniffed. "You were very drunk, and Viktor stopped you before it got really ugly. You just kissed her a bit. She's okay. She knows it was just the vodka, that you would never have hurt her otherwise."

Kirushenko staggered under the news, willing to believe the truth when it came from his daughter. He leaned on the too-short prison bunk, then sat himself down.

Agony welled up in the dark eyes. "Tash, forgive me! Tell them I'm sorry! I'm so very sorry! I have destroyed everything. My wife, my career, my children. Your mother was the success in my life. It is only right that I sink back to the bottom without her," he said as a tear spilled over. It crossed the small scar on his cheek and disappeared into the dark beard. "I'm so sorry!"

Valeria sat next to him. Father was supposed to be invincible; to see him cry frightened her. "Don't talk like that, Papa! We're not destroyed! I'm going to get us through this. That's why I need your help. Is there anyone you know of who can possibly help us? Anywhere we can go? Are there any relatives or friends that could give us advice?"

Father shook his head, then let it fall into his murderous hand, weeping.

Val remembered her father ecstatic with success, desperate with worry, enraged as a bull, senseless with drink, paralyzed by grief. She'd never seen him cry, not even once. Never seen him... hopeless.

"What about the person Katerina's named after?"

"I don't know where my sister is. If you can find her, she might help you. She always helped me before. Anastasia Groliak, somewhere near Piatagorsk. I'm so sorry, for everything!"

"What about Mother's brother?"

Sasha snorted. "She has no brother."

"Please, Papa! I know Mother sent him letters; she told me. Does he still live where she grew up? Could you at least tell me his name? Please, Papa, I beg you! We have nothing left!"

"And nothing is the *best* they will give you! Those people want nothing more than to see me dead, and you as well! They would not let you clean shit from their shoes."

"Please, Father! I have to try," Val pleaded. "I have to at least try. Please, tell me his name."

There was a long pause. "Tómas. Tomas Fedorovitch Ivanov. But he'll never reply. He's forbidden."

"In Minsk?"

*Nod.*

"Do you know the address?"

"It was a long time ago. I wasn't exactly a guest."

Valeria sighed. "Well, that's something, at least."

"Time's up, Big Boy!" the officer called from the doorway.

"I'm sorry," Sasha repeated forlornly. "I deserve this, but I'm sorry the rest of it had to fall on all of you." The meekness seemed ridiculous on someone so huge, so powerful; he seemed to wither into a lost little boy before his daughter's eyes, and she felt nothing but pity for him.

"No, you don't, Papa," Val said as she walked backwards out of the cell. "You'll make it! You will be wonderful again; I know it. Thank you for your help. We do love you, and we'll be waiting for you!"

She fled the detention wing as fast as she could.

* * *

Whatever the subject had been, neither twin brought it up. Valeria returned as mysteriously as she'd left. Any questions were wiped out by the chaos of leaving the courtroom. More than twenty teams of news reporters had camped outside the building, hoping to glean exclusive information and interviews with the Kirushenkos. With the crime being so sensational for the planet, and the family situation so precarious, the court had instituted rigorous restrictions immediately, resulting in a black-out of coverage. All media were forbidden to contact the family before the trial. No one could follow them, image them, or run speculative stories about them. The media were not allowed near the court until after the trial finished, and the names of the minors could not be published in any form. Communication, however, moved faster than light, and now that the trial had ended, the rules were off. Reporters choked the hallways, elbowing each other for an exclusive live soundbite with any of the surviving siblings. The recording lights of a dozen live-news cameras blinded them.

"What's your opinion of the verdict?" one reporter asked, centimeters from Valeria's face.

"What was your motive for testifying as you did?"

"What will you do, now that you are legally orphaned?"

"Can you tell the people what it was like, growing up in fear for your lives?"

"What kinds of things were you beat with?" A reporter shoved a commercial recorder in Sarah's face, almost hitting her nose.

240

Overwhelmed by the crush of people, the boldness of the questions, she buried her face in Katya's back.

John Carver shoved his way in, shielding the girls. "That's not your concern."

"Please, no questions!" Galina begged. "Just let us pass! This has been difficult enough, please leave us alone." They struggled through the crowd until they were outside.

The late afternoon heat battered the family, but the sun had dimmed and a hot breeze blew from the east; a sandstorm was rising. Dr. Carmichael had left to attend to an emergency, so they bade goodbye once more to Dr. Carver, who was quickly losing his professional status and becoming the first family friend anyone could remember.

Galina slammed the flyer door. "Let's go home,"

# Future
# Shock

# * Nineteen *

Valeria and Galina absorbed themselves in various problems connected with the trial, filling out forms, making notes, and alternating turns with the commlink.

Val read over a computerized copy of one of the documents they'd signed at the courthouse. She had planned on a career in law, finished nearly half her courses before she'd left. She scrutinized every page, learning everything she could. She gave herself a new mission in her education: study with a vengeance, finish her degree, learn every trick and learn it well. She would become her father's legal counsel and free him as soon as possible, a small price to pay for helping to incarcerate him behind his back. Val would not let him suffer alone. Family was family. They took care of their own.

"Did they let you see him?" Galina asked Val once they were alone.

"Yeah."

"How was he?"

"Sad. Quiet. Scared to death. He didn't say so, but you could tell. He kept apologizing. Great Gods, Galina! You should have seen him!" Valeria's voice broke.

Galina held her. "He'll be okay. He will."

Val nodded against her twin's neck. After a minute, she sat up. "I've never seen him remotely like that. He gave me some leads, though. He doesn't think it will work, but I'll start tracking them tonight after everything's quiet. It's worth a shot. The worst that can happen is they'll say no."

Katya stepped in to free up the twins, taking over the household tasks. She drafted Sarah and Vlad to help with dinner.

"Did'ja figure out a payback yet?" Vlad whispered to Sarah.

"I have a couple of ideas," Sarah admitted, removing a bowl of cold noodles from the replicator. "Nothing definite yet. If I do, it will be tonight."

"Tell me!" He walked backwards to the dining room with a pitcher of water in each hand, splashing himself in his excitement. "I'll help you."

Sarah really did hate to leave him out of what might be fun, but it

245

was for his own good. "You can't. I can't get both of them on the same night, and I don't want them torturing you for information."

"I wouldn't tell!"

Sarah eyed him doubtfully. "You crack like glass if David even threatens to drop a sand spider on you."

"Okay," Vlad buckled. "But tell me just before it happens."

A devious smile crossed her lips. "You'll know."

Sarah dozed next to Vlad in his bed. She shook him awake when Dmitri yelled from the next room, and they ran to the door to hear better. Seconds later came a more irate howl: *"Saraaah!"*

She stepped fearlessly into the hall. Dmitri yanked her into his room. He held her with one hand, brushing and picking at his flank with the other.

"Did you put that thing in my bed?" he scowled.

As she studied her brother, an awful phrase came to her. Sarah bit her lip to keep from laughing. Finally, she had to say it.

"You're awful prickly tonight, Dimi." He let loose a string of vile curses.

"Don't let Val hear you."

"That goddamned hurt, Sar! It's not funny! Get that thing out of my bed."

Sarah squeezed past him to the bed, the light blanket already tossed aside. In the middle of the bed lay a section of bristly desert vine. Holding one of the larger spines, she removed the offending vegetation and dropped it in Dmitri's trash bin.

"Now get over here and pick the rest of these prickers out of my leg."

"Are we even?"

Dmitri's attitude softened. "Yeah. You got me, fair and square. Even."

"Come over by the light," she squinted. "You weren't supposed to sit on it."

"You're damned lucky I only brushed it."

She found three needle-sharp spines embedded in the back of his hip, and pulled them. "That's all I see. Do you feel any others?"

He rubbed the spot. "No. It just stings." He sat down – carefully – on the lower bed. "So tell me, did you do the same to David? Or have you got something else planned? He's really been out for you lately."

Sarah sat next to him. "I know. That's why I haven't decided yet. I have one idea, a really really bad one, but I'm not sure I can do it.

He just might kill me. I have to think it out."

Dmitri loved a good prank. "Tell me! You know I'll help if I can."

"No. I said it would be personal. I already told Vlad no."

"And he didn't cry?"

"Not funny. You guys shouldn't pick on him all the time. He doesn't like being left out any more than you."

"Maybe, but it's still fun."

Sarah stood up to leave. *One down, one to go.*

He feinted a punch to her arm. "You know, you're all right, kid. We missed you while you were gone."

Sarah allowed herself half a smile at the compliment. She liked Dimi. He was a lot older, but his mean streak wasn't half as bad as David's, and he'd protected her from David more than once – if she did his homework for him.

"Man, I could have punched you for that," he laughed. "'I'm prickly'…!"

The next day flew for Sarah. She didn't know her lessons as she should have, but for the first time since returning she was happily excited. Carmichael had talked to Valeria, and although Val couldn't see how shortening Sarah's sessions would speed things up, she agreed to the change. And today Vlad would come, too!

Sarah had never been so relaxed in this office, saying as many as four sentences at a time. Dr. Carmichael seemed to have gained some insight as well, making a real effort to connect. On Carver's suggestion, he abandoned the formal furniture, and the three sat on the floor playing a three-dimensional board game. Sarah was surprised, to say the least. Carmichael seemed too stiff to sit folded like that.

"You said we could discuss my going to school," she dared remind him.

"Yes, I did promise that." He moved a playing piece up one square and over four. "If you feel able, I have no problem extending your day, but let's go slowly. Maybe move up to five hours instead of three. And we'll have to set up a new program for you at the local school. No more Navaran schools."

Sarah hid her mouth in her palm, physically holding in her reaction. She looked away and refused her turn at the game.

Vlad tried to find a bright side. "You can ride in with us again."

Carmichael continued to play as if nothing was wrong. "You're not happy with that idea. Tell me what you don't like about it."

Sarah was afraid to open her mouth, lest the words refuse to stop.

She clenched her jaws and played with her fingers, rubbing them in set order, three or four times around.

"Everything!" she blurted.

"The five hours?"

"No."

"The local school?"

"Yes! I don't want any part of that ignorant, useless baby school!" She hugged her knees and rocked herself.

Vlad looked hurt. "It's not *that* bad."

"You don't like the local school, and you want to go back to the Navaran school," Carmichael interpreted.

"Yes!

"They're my friends," she explained, digging at a small sandy scab on her ankle. "I go back to school here, I sit in a room with tutors all day. If I'm lucky, I have a gym class with Vlad. I might even eat lunch with them, but no one cares because I'm not part of their group. I can't talk to anyone. Anything I say to Vlad's friends, they don't understand. And no one in Katya's group wants to discuss homework with a kid. I'm just a freak to them.

"In my school, I sit in with people my own size; we talk about things that interest me, like chemical compounds or quantum theory. We try to stump each other with theoretical maths. Listening to them, I increase my proficiency at a difficult language. I don't fit in perfectly, there's still classes I need a tutor in, but I fit in better than I do at Vlad's school." She pulled her knees under her chin and held the toes of her shoes. "Not that *you* care."

"I do care, or I wouldn't have asked. But the basis of fitting in with the Navarans is adopting their stoicism, and *that*, Miss, is a good part of what sunk you in the first place."

"So I was right all along! My opinion never counted from the start. You already had that plan."

"I never said you could have anything you wanted, but I meant what I said," Carmichael disagreed. "I'm trying to come up with a compromise."

*"Bullshit!"*

"Sarah!" Vlad whispered in disbelief.

Sarah didn't care if he told Valeria she swore. It was worth the vile taste of disinfectant. She rose with an irate flounce of her shoulders and paced the room. *Typical, typical, typical. Couldn't ever believe a doctor.*

Carmichael had heard far worse in his career. "How about this: take your three hours of class at your Navaran school, *but,* if and only if, you find two hours of afterschool activities with human children your own age, and I don't mean family members. If you're only being known for swimming or track or art, then that's how you'll be accepted. No one will question your academic level."

"I'm lousy at sports and art," Sarah sulked.

"Then either you'll find activities that you like," Carmichael said, "or you'll become more proficient at sports and art. That's the best I can offer. Give me a week to set it up."

It was hard to be defiant in such a small room, and Sarah didn't care – too much – if Vlad saw her acting so wickedly. She did the worst thing she could think of at the moment: she parked herself in the doctor's chair and put her feet on his desk, shoes and all.

"I'll consider it," she growled.

Sarah still steamed after they returned home. She and Vlad sat in the space between her bed and the closet, Vlad struggling through homework his sister could have finished with her eyes closed at the age of five, and Sarah stewing wordlessly, not seeing the textreader in her lap. She would accept Carmichael's terms, of course, but it wasn't fair that he turned around and did the right thing after she'd already judged him. How could she save face out of *this* mess? She'd rather be drugged than apologize.

Vlad distracted her. "Did you figure out what you're gonna do to David yet?"

Sarah brightened. "I forgot all about it! Oh *Vlad*! I came up with something so terrible, so positively awful I'm actually afraid to do it! If he finds me out before I finish, he'll *kill* me!"

Vlad's dark eyes grew even bigger. "Tell me! *Please* let me help! Please?"

Dmitri would be better, but Vlad was her best friend, and he was so eager...

"Okay. I just hope it works, or I'm in a *lot* of trouble. All you have to do," she whispered in his ear, "is take your bath right before David's. Just *make sure* you leave fresh towels out for him, and tell me the second you're done. Don't forget!"

Vlad's face wrinkled, disappointed. Leaving out towels was courtesy, not conspiracy. "That's *it*?"

Sarah nodded. "That's all you can do. If you want, once David's in there, warn Dmitri to stand by. I might need protection. I have to do the rest..."

*So far, so good.* Sarah suffocated in the towel closet of the bathroom, heart palpitating so hard she feared it would be heard. This would require absolute timing; she couldn't freeze up. She couldn't see anything in the dark stuffiness;  it took  all her efforts to hear over the banging of her heart. The arrangement of the bathroom didn't allow for a sliding door; the closet door swung on hinges. Sometimes the baked air made them stick, and sometimes sand made them grind. She'd doused them with powdered lubricant in preparation. There wasn't a doubt in her mind that her life hung on the element of total surprise, but her faith in quantum physics assured her it could indeed be done. Sarah waited, one hand on the inside latch of the door.

*There it was. The click of the shower door opening. Now or never.* She almost didn't do it.

But she did.

Flinging open the closet, she leaped out as David, water from his misted hair running down his face, reached for a towel. Blinding light flashed through the room.

"Gotcha!" Sarah screeched, halfway out the bathroom door before the light faded.

David took a second or two to realize what had happened. *"SARAH!"* he screamed, thrusting his wet legs into his pajama shorts and running out after her. "You are so DEAD!"

He burst into the girl's room, splattering water, his wet feet leaving brief duck-prints on the parched floor. Sarah and Vlad sat innocently on her bed, his homework pad between them.

"Girl or no girl, I'm gonna punch the *FUCK* out of you!" he roared as Sarah slid backward on the bed. "Where is it!"

Sarah kept a straight face, but her eyes looked far from innocent. "Where's what?"

Forewarned, Dmitri entered the room. "You keep yelling like that and you're gonna have Val down here. What's going on?"

David lunged around Vladimir. "I'm gonna *kill* her, that's what! Gimme it!"

"What'd she do now?"

"She took a picture of me getting out of the shower, that's what!"

Dmitri's jaw dropped. "You didn't!"

All eyes on her, Sarah got that funny shrinking feeling again.

"She did! She's got to be sitting on it." David threw himself across Sarah, shoving his hands under her bottom. "Where is it?"

"I don't even *own* a camera!" Sarah protested.

"Got it!" David crowed, pulling a wafer-thin EyeSpy from behind the mattress.

It was Sarah's turn to be frantic. "Give it back! Don't break it! Katya doesn't know I took it!"

David held it away. "Take it, 'Mitya!"

Dmitri opened the case. "It's empty. The chip's gone."

"Dammit, Sarah! What'dja do with the recording chip?" David dragged her to the edge of the bed by her hair before Dmitri made him stop.

"That's not funny, Sar," Dmitri agreed, handing back the unloaded camera. "What did you do with the chip?"

Sarah rubbed her aching scalp. "Who says it had one to start with? All I did was test the strobe."

"Yeah, right!" David scoffed, holding her by the shirt this time. He held his other fist high.

"I mean it! It was empty the entire time."

Dmitri laughed. "She got you good, Dave. Admit it. Let her go."

"Dimi! She was *in the bathroom* while I *got out of the shower!*"

"Honest, David, I didn't see a thing," Sarah told him. "All I wanted to do was get out of there alive. I only looked at the door. I flashed it as I ran."

"See? Now admit she got you, and shake hands."

"No fucking way!"

"Bury it!" Dmitri ordered, and pressed David's hand into Sarah's. "It's ended. We don't need Val in on this, too." David shook on it, but said nothing.

"Good." Dmitri slid next to Sarah and put an arm around her shoulders. "I'll admit, Kid, that took guts, but listen close: if we ever – *ever!* – catch you in the bathroom again when one of us guys is in there – including Vlad – "

"I'm *never* in the bathroom with Vlad!"

"She's *never* in the bathroom with me anymore!" Vlad echoed from the back corner.

" – then, as a group, we will strip you naked, and… shave your head," Dmitri vowed, coming up with something reasonably awful but not permanent. "Do you understand?"

"Yes," Sarah agreed, contrite. She wrapped a lock of her hair around a finger, just in case.

"Shake on it."

Sarah started, then pulled away. "No throwing me in there just so you can do it."

"No, no foul play," Dmitri agreed, shaking her hand. He made David and Vlad shake on it as well.

"Put your clothes in the moisture recovery," he told David as he went to leave. "You're wasting water."

David scissored his fingers over his head threateningly, then stalked out in a trail of footprints.

Sarah turned to Vlad, hiding behind his schoolwork. "Some help you were."

"You're quiet today, Dimi," Valeria noticed during lunch the following weekend.

"He's lovesick over Sharinna Hubbard," David giggled. "And he's never even talked to her."

Dmitri flicked an imitation cucumber slice at his brother. "I'm not the one who cried for two days when Tami Kichu broke up with him. At least I keep a girlfriend more than two days at a time."

"Stop it," Val warned. "Gal and I want to talk to everyone, anyway. We want to fill you in on what's going on."

The table grew quiet. The twins had been preoccupied with computer trails since the trial, but no one knew exactly what they were doing.

"You know that Father worked through the Allied Fleet," Galina said, wiping her mouth, "and that the Fleet owns the rights to this house. Well, Father doesn't work for the Fleet anymore. They've been quite understanding, waiting until the trial was over."

"They're throwing us out?" Katya exclaimed.

"Actually, they're being rather nice about it. We've got eight weeks to pack up and find someplace else."

Valeria hushed the wave of questions. "We couldn't afford the rent anyway. There's more: I had a call from the Navaran Relations Bureau. They realize we are not at fault over Father, and they aren't formally *asking* us to leave, but, with the notoriety and all, they would greatly prefer we found another planet. So much so they're willing to grant us spacefare."

"So where do we go?" Dmitri asked.

Sarah's hope blossomed. "Back to Russia?"

"Val's working on a couple of leads," Galina said. "Maybe, Sarah."

Vlad's face wrinkled in worry. "What about my birthday?" Valeria had promised him a big party for turning ten. He'd never had a formal party before.

"It's still next week," Val assured him. "We won't change that."

Sarah realized a new horror: "But I'm going back to school!"

"For a couple of weeks," Val promised. "We'll set you up again somewhere else."

"We also have to go back to court," Galina added. "Val and I have shared temporary custody of everyone while Father's been away, but now he's not coming back. There has to be a permanent transfer of custody." She looked down the cheerless table. "Unless anybody objects?"

The new information sat heavy on everyone's mind. *Where would they go? What would they need? How would they live? What would happen?* Life had finally started to seem ... *normal.* The threat of further upheaval brought fears surging back. For every previous move, they'd had a specific destination – and housing – and parents – already in place.

Vlad and Sarah sprawled on the floor in the girls' room, minding Nikky and half-heartedly playing cards. Vlad's thoughts centered around his upcoming birthday, scarcely two days away. After the trial, only four boys were attending. Who wanted their child in a house where children had been tortured and killed? He'd be leaving his friends soon anyway. It wasn't fair.

Sarah's thoughts turned blackly to school. She'd fought so hard to get back there, and now where was she? Nowhere. Where would they wind up? What kind of schools would there be? Would she be stuck in the back of a Fourth-form baby class, doing completely different work and bearing the taunts of *teacher's pet, teacher's pet*? Or would she be stuck in the back of a senior class, completely out of place except for academics, watching teens cheating off each other and passing love notes and treating her like the class mascot? There were a lot of things Sarah hated about Navara, but she'd always been comfortable academically. She'd never get her diploma next year. So much for breaking the age record. She'd be lucky to graduate by eleven at this rate.

"Sarah?" Nikky jumped on her bed like a trampoline, his brown curls plastered with sweat. "Sarri? Are we gonna go somewheres with a lake or a ocean? Somewheres we can see boats? Huh, Sarri? Tell me about swimmin' in a lake, and the part about fishes in the water."

"It's wet," Sarah answered heartlessly. "It's cold and muddy, and slimy plants grab your ankles and great big fish come up and bite you. The biggest ones can swallow you whole."

Nikky stopped jumping. "Why does fishies bite you? Why, Sarri? Vladya, how comes they bite?"

"Because it's their water," Sarah replied. "Nik, go see if the computer's free." He bounced out of the room to check. She couldn't handle his endless energy today. He didn't look anywhere near ready to nap.

"Nobody's there," he ran back to report.

Sarah packed up their stuff and went out to the computer, Vlad, as always, three steps behind. Perhaps things were better out here.

Valeria's printouts were spread across the desk top. Sarah stacked them neatly before any could be lost, but one page caught her eye. It had their names, broken into columns, with different configurations.

| Gal | Val | Gal | Val | Gal | Val |
|-----|-----|-----|-----|-----|-----|
| Dmitri | David | Dmitri | David | Dimi | David |
| Vlad | Sergei | Vlad | Nikky | Serg | Vlad |
| Sarah | Marina | Sarah | Marina | Sarah | Nikky |
| Nikky | | Sergei | | | Marina |

"What's that for?" Vlad asked, reading over her shoulder.

*"Bozhemoi!"* Sarah gasped. "They *are* going to split us up!"

*"Nyet!"*

"Look for yourself! They're trying to find the best way to break us up. Look here – They split *us* up in this one!" Sarah stared at the paper as if it had sneezed.

Vlad's stomach scalded with acid. "They can't do that! It's not fair! I'm not going anywhere with David!"

"I can understand Val wants to keep the baby," Sarah reasoned, scanning the lists, "but every place, I'm put with Galina. I like Galina fine, but, like I told you, Val doesn't like me."

"Where's Katya?" Vlad asked. "Katya's not there. What happens to Kat?"

A chill shivered Sarah's spine. *What* were *they going to do with Katya? Did Katya know?*

Valeria came out of the kitchen, carrying the baby. Sarah stuffed the paper in the stack before Val noticed.

"Let me move those for you," Valeria offered, putting Marina down. "That'll give you more room." She didn't say a word about the lists.

*When was she going to tell them?*

The pair sat down wordlessly, locking hands. Sarah called up a game, but they couldn't concentrate.

Splitting up. It was incomprehensible. There had to be another way. There *had* to be.

# * Twenty *

Sarah sank into a grand funk. *As if the school thing weren't bad enough.* She and Vlad couldn't be any closer without being surgically attached. How could Val think of separating them? They made sure Valeria saw they were together every waking minute, and more. Katya went to bed, only to find Vlad asleep in her place. Val retrieved Sarah the following night from high atop Vlad's bunk, sandwiched between him and the wall. They kept their secret to themselves, but Sarah couldn't stop the little digs.

"Vlad and I will set the table *together,*" she emphasized.

"Vlad and I will *both* watch Nikky. He likes to be with *both* of us."

"Vlad and I are a *team,*" she reminded Valeria coolly. "Like hydrogen and oxygen. We work best covalently bonded *together.*"

"I'm waiting for Sarah," Vladimir said to Galina, standing in the hall outside the lavatory door. "We stick together, no matter what."

David noticed. "Gee, Vlad, she still washing your ass for you, too?"

Sarah backed off for Vlad's birthday, however. She insisted it was his day, his party, his friends. She didn't need to be in the way. Vlad was confused and hurt; he had thoroughly expected to include her in the group, but his excitement didn't let him sulk long. Sarah stayed visible to placate him, but didn't really participate.

She didn't tell him why. She felt lousy again. She'd managed to avoid her pills the night before, and thus lay awake half the night, the impending split and lack of educational prospects working at her thoughts. How could the twins even *dream* of such a thing? Well, if push came to shove, she just wouldn't do it! She wouldn't go! What she'd do instead she had no clue. Her thoughts spun away from her again.

Val stayed for a therapy session the following week. Sarah's heart sank. *Was this where Val wanted to break the news?* At least Sarah knew she'd made the list, not like poor abandoned Katya. Maybe there wasn't enough money for passage for everyone, and Katya would have to wait because she was the oldest, after the twins. Maybe Katya would go out to be with Viktor, like he'd planned. That could be.

"Sarah, come and sit." Valeria patted the sofa as Sarah started to pace her daily path. "We want to talk to you."

She perched nervously next to Val.

Carmichael sat across from them. "Sarah, we've run into a... *complication* with your school plans."

"What do you mean?!"

Valeria played with Sarah's braided hair, unaware how much Sarah hated that. "Master Jinariam has asked that you apply for class space elsewhere, sweetheart. They don't want you back there."

Sarah leapt up. *"What! Why?* They can't do that! I worked hard there! I did everything they asked! I did everything *right.* No! *No!"* She stomped her foot.

Val reached out with sympathy. "I'm sorry, Sar'ina. I know how much you were counting on this."

Sarah pressed her temples with her wrists, trying to think with a brain screaming to shut down. "It's a lie! You're just saying that to keep me out of there!"

"It's not a lie, Sarah," Carmichael insisted. "They won't consider it, even on a temporary basis."

*What to do, what to do...* Anger, confusion, disbelief, frustration, mistrust – everything churned inside her. *It couldn't be. There was no reason for it to be.* She'd find the truth out for herself.

*"No!"* Sarah cried, and fled out the door as fast as she could run.

"Sarah!" Val called, but in the extra seconds it took to rise from the sofa and reach the door, Sarah disappeared down the hall and out of the department.

"I've got security," said Carmichael, punching buttons on his desk comm. "She was wearing purple, wasn't she?"

"Lavender," Val corrected, gazing down the corridor. "Lavender tunic and white pants. Don't let them hurt her."

Sarah ran the maze of hallway as fast as her legs would take her. The lift. She had to go down three floors. She couldn't wait for the lift. Where, where – *there!* The sign for the emergency stairs. She slipped through the door and went down.

Only someone stupid would run to the city. School was 120 kilometers away; she couldn't walk there, but she needed to get there just the same. The lobby! The lobby had a row of public communications booths. She would call the Master and hear such nonsense for herself. Somewhere, someone made a mistake. Perhaps it was due to a minor nuance in language translation.

*Slow down!* she forced herself as she reached the last set of steps, breath heaving. *Never run in a hospital. You know what you're doing, just do it.*

She opened the exit to the first floor, lungs on fire for the thin Navaran air. No panic, coast clear.

She eased into the wide corridor and followed the orange 'L' strip on the wall to the lobby. The lobby crawled with people gathered around on flower-bright furniture. The bank of commbooths lined the wall near the great glass doors, and near the doors were... a whole slew of security guards, looking around with interest.

*You can do this,* Sarah coached herself. *You're not an inpatient. You're free to leave if you want. You're not doing anything wrong.* She walked steadily toward the commbooths.

One guard nudged another. He in turn spoke to another, who spoke into a handicom.

*Almost there ...*

A guard cut her off. "Can I see some identification, Miss?"

Sarah stared up at him with her big violet eyes. The fear in them wasn't an act, by any means. She did what had always worked in the past: feigned ignorance.

"*Izvenitye, ya vas ni ponimayu.*"

"Grassi, you want to bring a translator? I have no idea what she's saying."

Sarah stepped the other way, but he stopped her. "Just wait, Miss. Waaaait heeeere," he said slowly, as if it would help. "Grassi, hurry up!"

Another guard approached with a translator cube. There went that plan. *When all else fails – run!* She made a dive past the man just as Valeria and Carmichael hurried into the lobby.

"Oh, no you don't." The guard hooked her around the waist.

*Strange hands, man's hands, holding, restraining...* The world closed in. Sarah jabbed the guard in the chest with her elbows, crushed his toes, then kicked hard at his knees, feeding her frenzy with the sound of her own shrieking.

"Shit! You little... !" The guard hobbled on his aching knees, but he held her wrist.

Val rushed up. "Sarah, stop! Stop, now! Can we get her to a chair?" The guard shuffled and dragged the squirming girl to a set of orange seats. Val and Carmichael moved in on either side.

"Let her go," Val instructed, taking Sarah's hand.

"You'll need the translator. She doesn't speak Standard," he warned, trying to hand Val the cube.

Carmichael waved it away. "Of course she does. It's a trick."

"*Sarah, stop, right now,*" Val asked again in Russian. "*Look at me. Stop.*"

Sarah was so tense her joints were stiff. She dug the insides of her wrists into the sides of her head and shut her eyes. They wouldn't – shouldn't – drug her if she calmed down.

"Relax, Sarah. Where were you going?" asked Val. "You can't run all the way to Shir P'an, Sar. Not in the daytime. Not without survival gear."

"Talk to us, Sarah," urged Carmichael, "so we'll know what you were trying to do. We can help if you tell us."

"Call," she forced out. "I just… wanted… to call…"

Val sighed, not without sympathy. "You never stop fighting, do you? I don't know why you won't talk to *me*, Sarah. If you want to ask for yourself, I'll fly you out to the school. You just had to ask. I *am* on your side."

Sarah lowered her arms. "You'd do that?"

Val brushed a tender hand over Sarah's cheek. "Of course, sweetheart! I know how much you miss your school. I wish the boys cared half as much as you."

"Could we go right now?"

"I guess Galina can manage until we get back. No more running from me, even if you're upset?" Sarah promised. "Let's go, then."

Carmichael motioned Val aside. "You know what their answer will be. Will you be able to handle her when she hears it from the source?"

"Sarah won't crack in front of the Navarans," Valeria gambled. "She's worked too hard to be accepted. I think she just needs to hear it for herself."

"You have my emergency code?" Carmichael made sure. "Good luck."


Valeria tried to be supportive during the forty-five-minute trip, but Sarah had no desire to be social. A mumble here, a nod there, and she didn't hear most of what Val said. Just when life felt really good, the blackness, the unstoppable bleakness, pushed up again. Back at home – joy! No more fear of violence – joy! Friends with all the boys again – joy! But now an uncertain future – worry. They were splitting up – disaster! But no more school, after everyone had finally agreed yes? Unbearable misery. Vlad was right – nothing ever *was* fair.

Shir-Tal Nin's receptionist forwarded their request when they arrived. It had been almost four months since Sarah'd last walked the amber-glazed halls. School had finished for the day, but the sights and smells and echoes of the building brought an agony of longing. The acrid bite of the chemistry lab. The language hall. The muffled tinkle of *tilumi'it* practice in the music room. It was here she rightfully belonged.

The Master agreed to see her. Sarah waited in meditation, pushing down the turmoil raging inside. She must be impressive and cool, lest she insult him with overzealous passion.

*//I do not understand the rationale,//* Sarah said, speaking in the strange Navaran tongue. *//Have I failed to progress in my studies? Have I caused offense?//*

*//No,//* Jenariam informed her with the typical tinge of Navaran arrogance. *//You have exceeded our expectations. However, you are not Navaran. The constraint of long exposure to Navaran culture in such a young Terran has no doubt played a partial role in your recent illness. It is irrational to continue a behavior that puts one unnecessarily at risk. You cannot be allowed to pursue such actions.//*

*//I have reduced that risk to an acceptable level,//* Sarah stated, standing at attention. The position was familiar enough, but here there would never be a whip in her back, just an icy blade of words. *//My physician has proposed a plan that ...//*

*//I am aware of the plan. Such a program is irrelevant when one's time is limited,//* the Master interrupted. *//I am aware you will leave Navara soon. It is most certain you will not attend a school such as this. We will provide a tutor for your current study as long as required, but that is all.//*

*//Great Master, such a decision forces me into social isolation.//*

*//Perhaps,//* he agreed, steepling his long fingers. *//But perhaps, also, it is time for you to return to your own people, since in all probability they are the ones from whom you will study eight weeks from now. You will receive a favorable recommendation.//*

*//I am most honored,//* Sarah replied, gestures and all, but she wasn't sure if she'd been insulted or not. Her disappointment showed shamefully on her face, but she limited it to that. She could not fight stone with fists. She would leave with dignity and honor. Three long years she had endured shaded insults from her fellow students and teachers, met daily challenges, proved herself not as good as, but good enough for the other Navaran students. She wouldn't throw that work away with a self-defeating display. She would flaunt her success to the end. *To Hell with them and their awful dried-up planet anyway!*

That was it. Sarah'd done her best and lost, but she'd done it her way. Deceit was not a Navaran characteristic; she believed the master thought he acted in her best interest, even if she disagreed. One did not argue with Navaran elders, not ever, for any reason. Sarah left the school silently, dying inside.

Valeria tried to console her, but Sarah allowed the blackness to take over. Halfway home, she shrugged out of the restraints, folded herself in half, and pressed her face to her knees. Tears of misery rose, crushing her heart, but she held on. She would wait until they got home. The second Val settled the flyer and killed the engine, releasing the doorlocks, Sarah burst from the craft and ran inside.

"What happened?" Galina asked, picking dinner from Nikky's hair.

"She had to hear it straight from the horse's backside," her twin replied, disheartened. "They won't let her return."

"Poor kid. She was counting on that. How'd she take it?"

"Fine until we left the building. Then she just – shut herself off. I'm worried." After hugging Nikky and the baby, she went to Sarah's room.

Vladimir sat by the door. "She locked it," he explained. "She won't even let me in, and we don't split apart for *nothing*!"

Val tried the door, then knocked. "Sarah, it's Valeria. Please unlock the door.

"Sarah, I'm worried about you. I just want to talk. Please let me in."

"Sarah!" Val barked. "Unlock this door or I will break it down!"

Silence, but the next time Val tried the door, it yielded. She entered in time to see a shoe disappear under the bed.

Val sat down on the corner. "Sarah, I know how disappointed you are. Dr. Carmichael and I tried everything we could think of. I'm sorry. Please come out. I just want to make sure you're all right, then you can go back to hiding.

"Sarah… If I have to, I'll move the bed and drag you out. It's up to you."

*Nothing.*

Exasperated, Val dropped to the floor and dug under the bed. Behind three travel bags and a lost sock, Sarah pressed against the wall, hugging a pillow to her face.

"Sarah, I can't fit under here. Are you okay?"

*"Da,"* came a muffled reply. "Top of the world!"

Val gazed sadly at the pillow. "Okay. Leave the door unlocked, all right? I'll check on you in a little bit." She stood up, noticing Vlad's concerned face. He might be ten now, but he still looked more like seven.

"You gonna stay with her, Vlad?"

Vlad nodded. "Sarah 'n' me are *Best Friends*. We stay *together*, always."

Valeria smiled at his seriousness. "I'm glad you are," she said, ruffling his hair. "Keep an eye on her for me, okay?"

Val returned an hour later to an empty room. Neither child had come out front, but there were windows elsewhere if they wanted to do something stupid.

"Vladimir, are you under there with her?"

To her relief, Vlad's head appeared from under the bed. "Yeah."

"Sarah, will you come out now, please? Come have some dinner.

Vlad crawled out halfway to rest on his elbows. "She won't come out. She doesn't want anyone to know she's crying."

"I don't hear her," Val frowned. Sarah *never* cried at home. Not that Val could remember.

"She's got the pillow stuffed in her mouth."

*Enough was enough.* "Stay with her, Vlad. I'll be right back."

Galina and Valeria dragged the bed sideways on the count of three, Vlad blocked from underneath, and Dmitri grabbed from behind. Sarah struggled like a wildcat, but he didn't have to move her far. She held the pillow with her teeth, face and pillow glistening with tears and snot and spit. Cornered, Sarah melted into the bed, motionless but for the sobs and coughs that shook her.

"I'll sit with her," Galina offered. "Take a break."

Two hours, and Sarah still wept, tears oozing from closed lids. Galina worked to get her into pajamas, for Sarah didn't move a muscle on her own. Val came in with a dish of beloved chocolate pudding, but even that wasn't enough. They pushed and pulled the girl to a sitting position, Galina holding her upright.

"Come on, Sar. One spoonful, then I'll leave you alone," Val promised, holding the spoon to Sarah's lips.

Sarah strained to open her tear-swollen eyes. Val stabbed her mouth with the damned spoon. She opened it at last, just to stop the annoyance.

She tried to swallow, but there were lumps in the pudding. The swallow got caught up in a hard sob, and she gagged. Too late to stop it, the pudding slid down.

"You tricked me!" she cried, coughing. "You put... my pills... in the pudding!"

"Yes, I did." Valeria kissed her forehead, and the twins tucked her into the bed. "Sleep now, Sarah. You'll feel better in the morning."

Sarah still wept miserably when Katya tiptoed to bed. When Val went to bed, she had stopped crying, but sobbed hard enough to shake the bed. Only when Galina came home in the morning did exhaustion win.

Sarah didn't remember being this badly off, not even in the hospital.

She suffocated from sobs, each gasp a fiery tug on belly muscles cramped from overuse. Her throat and mouth stung from dryness, her eyes too swollen to open. All her energy had left with the tears; to move even a finger took tremulous effort. And once again she lived only in the present. She could not think a single thought. Each breath seemed separate from the one before it; each hiccupping sob a new experience in pain. There was nothing to think about, just a black, bottomless void.

Galina canceled the tutor. "I put in a call to Dr. Carmichael," she told Valeria when Val got up. "He was on rounds, but he's supposed to call back."

Val sighed. "I don't know what to do. I expected this from the trial, but she did so well. How many kids fall apart when told they *don't* have to go to school?"

"Should we hide the knives?"

Val shot her twin a dirty look. "That's not funny."

Sarah slipped into a restless sleep for three short hours, but it didn't help her mood.

"Want some lunch?" Val asked. "Anything you want."

"*Nyet*," Sarah grunted, rolled up in her blanket despite the warmth of the room.

An hour later Val tried again. Sarah hadn't budged a millimeter. Eyes blinked now and then in the blank face, her chest rose and fell as she breathed, but she gave no voluntary sign of life.

"Come on. A cool soak in the bath, a change of clothes, some pretty powder, and you'll feel a bit brighter," Val offered, grabbing the blanket and pulling.

Sarah pulled back hard. "No!"

"Sarah, be reasonable. You haven't had a bath in two days, and you're all sweaty, wrapped up like that. You need a bath." They wrestled for control of the blankets until Sarah kicked Val hard in the stomach.

"Fine!" Val gave in angrily. "I'll wait for Galina, and we'll do it together. Or maybe I'll get the big boys to help."

"They wouldn't do that!" Sarah yelled after her.

*Would they?*

Valeria was glad to hear the buzz of the commlink.

"We may have misjudged the absorption rate of the Elavixor," Carmichael hypothesized. "I had planned on replacing her pack next week. Run your fingers on her shoulder, and see if you feel anything."

Val returned to the screen a moment later. "Nothing. Not even a tiny bump."

"We'll replace it this afternoon when you bring her in," Carmichael said. "That should take care of it."

Sarah had other plans. After two more hours, she gave in to the idea of a bath – or at least letting Val do all the work while she slouched morosely in the cool water. She slid down until her head submerged, but Val didn't take kindly to that. Sarah was a poor swimmer, but if she wasn't sick she could hold her breath a rather long time. She allowed herself to be dressed and combed, never speaking, but the moment Val turned, Sarah sped back to her cocoon.

"Sarah!" Val wailed. "You're all clean! Come out and lie on the sofa."

Sarah pulled the blankets over her head and lay still.

When Vlad came home, he went straight to the girls' room. Sarah uncovered her head.

He sat elf-like by her pillow. "Aren't you gonna get up, ever?"

"What's the point? It's not like I've got anywhere to go. I just sit in the house and watch everyone else go about their lives. After they split us up, there won't even be anyone to watch. I had more fun in the hospital."

Vlad dropped his voice to a whisper. "I started collecting that stuff. Like we talked about? It's in the black bag under my bed. Even if we make it, though, we'll still need money. We'll never get that out of Valeria."

Sarah adjusted the blanket under her chin. "Dimi keeps his money in the left pocket of his robe in his closet. Start there."

Vlad was amazed. "How do you know?!"

"I hid there one day. I got bored and started looking through pockets for candy, and I found his money."

They fell silent for several minutes. "Want me to get a card game together?" Vlad asked. Sarah shook her head. "I'd read one of your books to you, but heck, I can't say half the words, let alone read them. Want me to get Sergei?"

Sarah shook her head. She couldn't follow a paragraph if she tried. "I wish Viktor were here," she sighed. "I miss him."

Vlad nodded. "Me too."

Valeria and Galina walked in. "Let's go, Sarah," Val said. "Time for Dr. Carmichael."

Sarah rolled over to face the wall. "I'm not going."

"Oh, yes you are. Go, Vlad." Valeria pulled him down from the bed.

"Give me the blanket, Sarah," Galina said, but Sarah stayed

wrapped.

"Okay," Val warned, pulling the last corner of the blanket free from the mattress. The two dragged Sarah forward on the bed, blanket and all. Galina hefted the swaddled form onto her shoulder.

Valeria stepped on Vlad as she helped her twin. "*Move,* Vlad! Get out of the way."

Sarah wriggled. "No! I'm not going!"

"Yes, you are. Dr. Carmichael's replacing your med pack."

"No!" Sarah struggled harder, making it difficult for Galina to walk. By the time they cleared the hall, Sarah was free of the blanket, Vlad following anxiously.

"Sarah, stop! I don't want to drop…," Galina started, but with a mighty push Sarah broke the grip and fell hard on the floor. She scrabbled backwards, then stood up.

"I'm not going!" Panic rose. Right or wrong, she'd made up her mind. If they got her in the flyer and got it in motion, the doors would lock, trapping her there. The hospital would remove her, and never let her home again.

The twins moved to surround her. Sarah plowed between them, but Gal was quicker and caught an arm. Sarah whirled, dropped low, and pulled, but Gal had her tight. She clawed at Galina's hand with her rough stubs of nails. Valeria grabbed the hand, then Galina struggled to hold both hands while Valeria tried to snatch the kicking feet.

"Some help would be nice!" Val snapped at the boys.

The big boys had replicated a six-layer pistachio torte and were busy devouring it. Nikky's face and hair were smeared with pastel frosting.

Dmitri pushed a falling piece of cake into his mouth. "Can't she shkip a day? I don't think she wantsh to go."

Galina struggled. "No."

"Five credits on Sarah," David called.

"I'll help." Katya threw the boys a look of disgust, but before she could cross the room, Sarah nipped Galina's fingers with her teeth and pulled free.

Sarah dove under the grand piano, emerging in the gap behind. Back to the corner, panting, she watched for the next move.

Val stalked over. "Sarah, I'm losing patience. This isn't something you have a choice in. Come out of there."

Sarah hugged her knees and rocked back and forth. "No! I'm not going anywhere! Leave me alone!"

The girls put their heads together, whispering. Galina called the boys over.

"She doesn't want to go. Can't you just leave her alone? At least 'til she feels better? You're making her sadder!" Vlad pleaded. He hung around the piano, protecting his sister by being under foot and in the way.

Dmitri licked icing from the corner of his mouth as he listened. "If you say so, but I think you're making too big a deal out of it. Did you look at all those chart things they gave us?"

"I think I can handle a simple tantrum without professional help," Val said, heading for the piano. "*Move it,* Vlad!"

"Whatever." Dmitri took position on one corner of the piano, while David took the other.

The three girls trapped Sarah as the boys pulled the heavy piano away from the wall, but Sarah had other ideas. Jumping, she scrambled up and over the closed piano before she could be caught. She tried to leap from the end, but Dmitri made a grab and caught her – almost. Too much weight went over his shoulder, and he fell.

As soon as she hit the floor, Sarah wormed free and ran for the kitchen, not minding where she stepped. The utility room, perpetually locked against Nikky, made the kitchen a dead end. *The knives – Where the Hell were Mother's kitchen knives? The razor-sharp ones they weren't allowed to touch?* The wall rack hung empty.

Feet followed fast behind her. Five to one. She couldn't win on those odds, not without a weapon. She backed herself into the far corner, choked with terror, and tapped her head against the wall. It was the second battle in two days she couldn't win, and it wasn't in a school, or a hospital, or at Father's whim; it was at the mercy of her beloved siblings.

Val reached for her hand. "Sarah, you're making this a hundred times worse than it is."

A small figure pushed its way through the crowd and shoved Valeria back. Vladimir, brandishing a long, pointed carving fork, moved in front of Sarah, his delicate features angry and determined. He raised the oversized fork ominously.

"Leave her alone, Val! Just leave her alone!"

David doubled over laughing, and even Dmitri grinned. Vlad, the boy afraid of his own shadow, Mighty Warrior of the Meat Fork!

Valeria reached her limit. "Vladimir, so help me Heaven, give me that before you hurt yourself!" She grabbed for the fork, and was stunned when timid little Vlad poked her with it. *"Ow!* Vlad! What are you *doing?*"

"Sarah's always stood up for me, and now I'm standin' up for her! Lay off her, Val! It's your fault she's sad to start with! We know what you're trying to do!"

"What do you mean, Valeria's fault?" Katya asked.

"How is this *my* fault?" Val puzzled. "Can you please tell me just what I'm doing?"

Vlad spilled the dreaded secret, waving the fork. "Breaking us up! We saw your papers! I don't know where you're sending Katya, but you're not breaking me and Sarah up! We'll run off in the desert first!"

"Vlad, what are you talking about?" Galina said, perplexed. "No one's going anywhere! *Nobody's* breaking us up!"

"You made lists! We saw them. It's bad enough Val hates Sarah, but on one list you put me with Val and Sarah with you. Poor Katya doesn't even get to come with us right away; she's gotta go out with Viktor. Me and Sarah won't have it!" He thrust his hand out for emphasis, prongs pointed at Val's face. Vlad was so small and frail and fearful, the sight of him trying to be ferocious was sadly comical.

"I don't hate Sarah! Vlad, I don't know what you think you saw..."

Galina touched her sister's arm. "Val! The guardianship! We made lists trying to figure out the guardianship."

Valeria paled, remembering all the odd things Vladimir and Sarah had been saying.

"Vladya!" Valeria's frustration turned to sorrow for the misguided pair. "Nobody's splitting up! Oh, Vlad! How could you two – ? *That's*-? Those lists were for the *guardianship*! It doesn't mean a thing! It's only to satisfy the court. It's like this," Val explained. "The judge doesn't want us both to have custody of everyone. If we did, and say for some reason I decided to leave, then Galina would be legally stuck with everyone. It's too much for one person. The court wants some of you assigned to each of us, so that legally, if one of us gets up and walks out, the other person has some legal recourse to demand money to raise the ones left behind. It's a way of protecting you.

"Now, because Sarah takes more responsibility right now, they don't want the same person responsible for the baby to be responsible for Sarah as well. Galina and I were trying to come up with an arrangement that would please the court. It's just a legal thing, Vlad. It doesn't change a thing at home. We're all sticking together, just like always. I promise."

Vlad wavered. "What about Katya? She's not on the list."

"Katerina isn't on the list because she's three months from being eighteen," Galina explained. "She's being declared a liberated adult, and therefore doesn't need a formal guardian."

"I am?" Katya exclaimed. "I thought they wouldn't allow that here?"

"No way!" cried Dmitri. "Not fair! I'm not taking orders from somebody eleven months older than me! That's three *girls* in charge! We need male representation."

"Is that what's been bothering you, Sarah?" Val ventured.

Sarah sat on the floor behind Vlad, knees pulled up, fists hiding her tears. She squeaked on a shuddering sob. "Ya!"

"Goodness gracious! The two of you, torturing yourselves over nothing. Put the fork down and come sit."

Vlad put a hand out to Sarah. She took it without looking, chin glued to her chest. He guided her to a chair, putting himself between her and Val. He laid the fork on the table; truce. Val pulled a chair out, and everyone else found a seat.

Sergei poked his head in the kitchen. "Val, Dr. Carmichael's on the comm. He wants to know how you're doing."

Val glanced over at Sarah, so bent over that her nose almost touched the table, hiccupping with the effort of keeping tears at bay. They were a half-hour late. She took a chance.

"Tell him we're okay, but we won't make it today," she told Sergei, who relayed the information. "Is that okay with you, Sarah?"

Sarah nodded.

"Val?" Sergei called from the doorway. "Baby's up; I got her for you. Dr. Carmichael said if you're not coming in, give her five of the yellow booster pills instead."

"*Spasiba.*" Val rubbed a hand across Vladimir's bony shoulders. "Do you understand now, Vlad? You never had anything to worry about in the first place. You misunderstood. I would never separate you two. You've always kept each other out of trouble – until now."

Vlad smiled sheepishly. "Guess we should have asked you when we saw the paper."

"Do you understand now, Sarah? Are you set with this?"

Sarah nodded without lifting her head.

Valeria poked Vladimir in the arm. "And what do you mean, 'I hate Sarah'? How could you even *think* that!"

"You *don't* like her," Vlad said, still brave. "You always want her to do something she doesn't want to, or stuff pills in her, or want to know where she is every second. She can't be herself anymore. You don't leave her alone for a minute."

"You do hound her, Val," Dmitri agreed, sitting back to back with Katya on the table. "Look at this afternoon…"

"I'm doing my best to keep her together! That's my *job. I'm* the one responsible for her, medically. *I'm* the one who has to drag her to appointments, who fights her to take medication that she really needs. If anything, Sarah doesn't like *me!*"

A wave of tears welled up in Sarah's eyes. She rolled her head from Katya's knee to rest her face in the crook of her arm.

"Do you know what it's like, Sarah," Val continued with pain, "knowing you won't talk to me? Look here – I have to go through Vlad to find out I hate you. You won't talk to *me.* You talk to Vlad, you talk to Katya, you talk to the boys, but I make an hour and a half flight to Shir P'an and back, and you hardly say six words to me! How do you think that makes *me* feel? I've *tried*, Sarah, but you have to meet me half way."

"You try too hard," David said. "She's no different than the rest of us. We're not used to being bossed. Mother never butted in on anything. You're always ordering us around and trying to see what we're doing. Let up."

"Someone has to," said Galina. "Look at the messes we've had – David, if it wasn't for Val, you'd have been kicked out of school. I finished two degrees in Comm Tech before coming home. Val *quit* law school to take care of everyone. She's made the biggest sacrifices of anyone, and I think you're all forgetting that. Do you have any idea how hard it was for her to sign Sarah into that hospital? Or how happy she was when we could finally visit?"

"No," Dmitri said, "but if Val doesn't have a hand in every single thing going on, she thinks everything will fall apart. She's so busy running around making sure everyone is doing the right thing, she doesn't actually let us do it. So what if David and I don't talk for a week? We'll get over it. We always have. It's not up to Val to decide when we call it quits. So what if Sarah doesn't want to be interrogated by some doctor? Like you never had a day when you'd do just about anything not to have to get out of bed."

"How about you, Katya?" Val asked bitterly. "Is there anything I do wrong for you?"

The question seemed heavier than Katya would admit. "I think everybody has a valid point. You do try to do too much yourself. You rush around so fast, you don't always have time to finish what you start, and Galina just sort of follows you around, picking up the pieces.

"When Mother was alive, we had a system. Mother watched 'Byeta, Sarah and Vlad were in charge of Nikky, David and Sergei were supposed to watch Sarah and Vlad, Dimi and I watched Sergei and David, and Viktor was sort of in charge of everybody. If there was a problem, we took it to him, and he handled it."

*"Vik!"* Sarah hiccupped between tears.

"Sarah misses Viktor," Vlad translated.

"We all do," Katya said gently, and gave the girl's shoulder a squeeze. "I think the court might have the right idea. Maybe all together *is* too much. If we divide up the responsibilities more, like we used to, everything should run smoother. We all know how each of us operates. Instead of one person having all the say, we could vote as a group on some of the bigger decisions. Dimi and I aren't exactly children... "

"What the hell am I?" demanded David. He flicked a contemptuous hand toward his brother. "You're gonna lump me in the same class as... *Vlad?*"

Katya nodded concession. "And David's up and coming. Val will have more time to deal with the baby, and we won't be at each other's throats all the time. We'd all have a say again. It really worked."

"Then let's do it," Galina agreed. "It's worth a try."

Val raised a hand. "Wait a minute. How can you put Sergei and David in charge of Sarah? Didn't David beat her up the other week? That's like no supervision at all."

"That's not true!" David objected. "Sergei gets along with Sarah because they both speak Brain. I guess I could let up on Vlad a little."

"I'm right there as backup," Katya pointed out. "Before you two came back, I did it all myself."

Val gave up, irritated and outnumbered. "Fine. But only if Sarah promises – and I *mean* it! – to keep talking to at least Vlad, and Vlad to tell me if something is really upsetting her. No more of this secret guessing-game. And I expect Dmitri and Katya to tell me when something's up – not this 'I don't tell on anybody' vendettas and crap."

Promises went around the table, including Sergei, who listened from the doorway, watching Nikky and baby Marina playing in the big rooms at the same time.

Val stood up. "One last thing, before I forget. Sarah's pills." She retrieved the bottle and some fruit juice, and counted out five of the small yellow triangles that Sarah took at night. She put the cup of juice on the table and held out the pills. "Take these, Sarah, and you're free to do whatever. David thinks he can watch you better than me. Who knows? Maybe he'll surprise me."

Sarah wiped her face on the hem of her shirt. She put the pills willingly in her mouth and tried to drink the juice, but she couldn't coordinate it with the sobbing. She choked, Val banging on her back, until she caught a large mouthful of pills and juice and thick spit in her cupped hands. Worn down with only three hours sleep, Sarah collapsed into heavy tears.

"Sergei, get me a wipe," Val ordered. "Katya, grab the other side."

Hoisting Sarah by the elbows, they walked her to the sink and washed her face and hands.

Val sighed. "We have to try again."

"Let me do it," Kat volunteered. "I know to make sure she swallows them."

"Let her try, Val," Galina urged. "She's got more patience, anyway."

"Fine. Dmitri, help Katya get her to bed." Val gave him the side she held. Vlad followed behind, Sarah's shadow to the end.

David dropped an arm around his brother's neck as they walked. "Hey, Fork Man, I'm impressed! That was pretty bold! Looks like you might be growing some brass ones after all."

Valeria came into the girls' room a while later. The lighting glowed dimly at quarter-power. Katya sat on the bed, Sarah's sleeping head in her lap.

"You want me to save your dinner, or bring it in?" Val asked.

Katya stroked Sarah's sweat-dampened hair. "I'll be out in a minute or two."

Val sat on the foot of the bed. "You get her pills in?"

"Yeah." Katya tossed her the bottle of Elavixor. "I broke them in half and gave her one every few minutes or so. She's never been great at swallowing pills. We used to have to crush them. She drank two cups of juice, too. She fell asleep about fifteen minutes ago."

"I forgot about that. I would have kept stuffing them in and blaming her for throwing them up on purpose. No wonder she told Vlad I hate her. She *should* hate me."

"It's not your fault. You've got too much to worry about, between us and court and moving. Before the... accident, when 'Byeta had the other bed, Sarah and I had been sharing this bed for three years. We're used to each other. What was she when you guys left for school? Three? Four? She doesn't know you, that's all.

"And as for hating you," Katya continued, "of course she doesn't. Remember when we visited her in the hospital? She was all over you. She's just upset now. Give her time. She feels really guilty over making you worry so much."

"She's one messed up kid."

Katya noticed Vlad moping in the doorway. "You can come in," she offered. "She's sleeping."

Vlad, once more his timid self, slipped in and sat on the bed. Being in the room with the big girls wasn't the same as hanging out with Sarah.

Katya smiled at him. "You're sweet, Vlad, caring about her the way you do."

Vladimir's cheeks pinked. "Nothin' big," he grumbled. "We just stick up for each other, is all."

"You want to sleep over there on the floor tonight?"

Vlad perked up, then shook his head. "Nah. David would never leave me alone if I did. He actually talked nice to me today. I better not push it. As long as you're with her."

"I wouldn't be anywhere else."

# * Twenty-one *

Sarah slept. And slept. All night, all the next morning. Three times Val checked on her, finally shaking her awake. After a semi-conscious sentence, Sarah rolled over and slept straight through the afternoon.

Twenty minutes after everyone else arrived home, a flyer stopped before the house. Dmitri burst in, an unstoppable grin splitting his face.

"Where have you been?" David demanded, suspicious. "You've been up to something!"

Dmitri shook his head in disbelief. "Oh, man! Man, oh *man*! I did it! I did it! You are looking at one freakin' lucky guy!"

"What!"

"*I* have a date with Sharinna Hubbard!"

"No way!" David shouted. "You dog! You finally asked her out?"

"Not exactly. A bunch of us were standing around talking, and she was one of them, and John Martigan said he and Jenni were going to the races tonight, and did me and Sharinna want to go with them and make it a double. He set it all up for me! And *she – said – yes*!"

David circled his brother. "Super nova! I've seen her at school. She's freakin' gorgeous, Dim! I wish I could go with you, just to watch the races."

Dmitri polished his nails on his shirt. "This is not a night for beginners. If all goes right, no one will see much of the races anyway. I have to hit the shower. John's picking me up at seven."

Galina listened to the chatter. "Tonight, Dimi? Yesterday you said you'd stay with Sarah tonight."

Dmitri's heart stopped beating. "*Shit*! Will you switch with me, Gal? Please? I *have* to go tonight!"

"Please, Gal? His life depends on it," David begged for him.

"I made plans," Galina said firmly. "When we set this up, you guys swore up and down you were serious about making it work. Now live with it."

"I'll stay with her," David offered. "I can do it."

"House rule, no one under sixteen left in charge with Sarah. Dmitri trained at the hospital how to handle her."

"That's not fair! Let's take a revote… "

Dmitri pounced on Valeria as she sat at the comp screen. "Val, I'm begging you." He hung on the back of her chair, then threw himself on his knees. "You name it, I'll do it!"

Val didn't look up. "No. I've got her during the day, not at night. Group decision, remember?"

Dmitri rolled on the floor theatrically. "Arrgh! My life is OVER! *Please?*" He sat up, lacing his hands together. "Just this once?"

"No."

Katya, having changed clothes and checked on her sleeping sister, let Vlad back into the bedroom and walked to the kitchen.

Dmitri sprang, shuffling after her on his knees. "Katya! Dear, sweet, understanding, lifesaving Katya, my favoritest sister, my almost-twin who loves me to death… "

"Any more bull and you'll have to shovel the room before dinner," Katya said as he hugged her knees. "What do you think I would ever do for you?"

"You're going to swap nights with Sarah for me so I can go on a really *really* big date tonight."

"I had her last night."

"Name it, Kat! I'm *desperate*! Anything! I've *got* to go out tonight!"

"He means it, Kat," David joined in. "This girl's a goddess. He's *got* to go!"

Katya prolonged his agony with a wicked smile. "I'll think about it, and get back to you."

Dmitri's heart nearly tore in half with the strain. "No! Kat! I need to know *now*! Name your price. My blood is yours."

"You take my next two nights, and give me that new music card you got."

Dmitri's face fell. "Neutronix? I just got that! I've barely had time to listen to it twice."

Katya shrugged cheerfully. "That's my offer."

"I'll take it." He jumped up and lifted Katya off the ground in a bear hug. "Thank you! Thank you, Kat! You saved my life!" He grabbed her and dropped a fast kiss on her cheek.

"Your love life, at least," she laughed as he made a fool of himself. "Don't forget, two nights and the card."

"Midnight, Dimi, or I'll come get you," Val reminded him. "Look at the time! I've got to get Sarah ready."

"I'll take her, Val," Galina offered. "That way you can keep working."

Valeria hesitated. "If you want. Third floor, first corridor on right, third office on the left."

"Kat, you want to come with me?"

"Sure," Katya said. "I'm with her tonight, anyway."

They chased Vlad out to get Sarah dressed, dragged her to the bathroom, chased Vlad out, and washed her up. Back in the hall, they tripped over Vlad.

"Can I come too?" he asked. "I know where the office is. "

"No, Vlad," Galina began.

"Sure you can!" Katya beamed at the same time. "Sarah, do you want Vlad to come with us?"

Sarah had been rather inert. She moved with great effort, eyes dull in her expressionless face. Now she gave a slow, brief nod.

Vlad ran down the hall. "I'll get my shoes."

"You weren't exaggerating," said Carmichael, seeing Sarah practically carried in by her sisters. He ran a scanner over her upper arm. "It's completely gone. My fault. I should have checked on it sooner. Children have a higher metabolism; they absorb some chemicals faster. I'm surprised she fell apart this fast; usually there's at least a week before Elavixor clears a system like that. We can fix that right now."

He knelt in front of Sarah so they were eye to eye. She looked through him, not at him.

"Sarah? Do you remember when Dr. Carver put the medicine in your arm? I want to take you to an exam room and put another set in. I'll adjust it so you won't need the extra pill every night, too."

A whine began in the back of Sarah's throat, and her face contorted in a mix of fear and despair. Her hands slid from her lap to the sides of the chair. She gripped the seat until her knuckles turned white.

Katya rubbed her back. "Shhh."

"I can't do it here, Sarah," Carmichael insisted. "It's a surgical procedure, not a blood test. Come with me. Your family can come too, if they want."

Vladimir pried the rigid fingers loose. "It's okay, I'll go with you." He pulled on her arm. "Come on. Then you'll feel better again, and we can go back to doin' stuff."

Sarah raised her eyes to meet Vlad's. If he could be that brave, then she could be strong for him. She closed her eyes and stood up.

"We'll start with the bloodwork," Carmichael informed her in the exam room, but Sarah didn't blink. Blood tests weren't threatening. "We'll find out where we stand."

When the hemocomp beeped completion, Carmichael studied the results. "I'll up it to twenty-five milligrams; that way, you won't have to bother with the evening tablets. Do you remember the procedure?"

Sarah nodded with disinterest.

"Are you going to stay still for me?"

Another nod.

After a short struggle over Carmichael's insistence on Sarah lying down, and Sarah's distrust of loaded airhypos, he started the incision.

Vladimir, holding her hand as part of the deal to keep her lying down, happened to glance over as Carmichael began the incision. Though the surgery was bloodless, Vlad turned unnaturally white. His eyes rolled, and he sank to his knees.

Galina grabbed for him. "Vlad!"

Sarah twisted over the side of the table, still holding his hand. Unfortunately, Carmichael hadn't finished the incision. The surface he was cutting rolled under the scalpel, flaying a simple two-centimeter slice into a ten-centimeter gaping wound across the girl's upper arm.

Carmichael said something Sarah and Vlad weren't ever allowed to repeat, angrier than a Casseiopean sea slug in a bucket of salt. Slamming the scalpel on the tray, he fished through a drawer in the equipment cart and withdrew a restraint strap.

"Is he all right?" he snapped.

"I think so," Gal replied. She knelt on the floor, Vlad half on, half off her lap. "He's coming around."

Sarah saw the strap, but Carmichael, used to dealing with crisis management much more than the slow dance of psychotherapy, was far quicker. In mere seconds, he had her arm pinned above the elbow, and with three deft moves had it secured under the strap.

"Touch it and I'll strap the other one just as fast. I can't operate with you moving all over. Now I have to repair your shoulder."

Sarah stared, dumbfounded by the severity of his anger. Just when she thought he might be trustworthy after all. No. This man posed a danger she'd come to expect from his profession. She could never, ever trust him. Katya stepped in to hold her hand, but Sarah hardly breathed as the doctor repaired the extended incision and inserted six more weeks' worth of slow-release medication.

"That will take three days for full effect," he reminded Galina, removing the strap. "I'll replace it again just before you leave."

Freed, Sarah didn't waste time hopping down, but the room wobbled and spun. She grabbed the edge of the table before she could fall

Carmichael saw it. "That's not from the surgery. Has she been.

getting enough water? When did she last eat?"

"Yesterday, maybe?" said Katya.

Carmichael waved a finger. "I'm not playing today, Sarah. You're jeopardizing your health now. I can have a nurse bring you something and you eat it, you can lie back down for an hour and I'll set up some IV nutrition, or I can call for assistance, strap you down, and feed you through a stomach tube, but you're not leaving until you've gotten something in you. What's your choice?"

Sarah clung to Katya as if her life depended on it. "No."

"I'm sure Sarah will eat something for us," Galina said curtly.

"What will she eat?"

"Maybe some toast?" Katya suggested. "Or, she likes that weird Navaran soup – what do you call it? The one with the weird name. It's yellow, with brown bits. With the lumpy noodly-things."

"*L'rke?*" Carmichael guessed. "I'll send something in."

Katya and Galina forced two pieces of toast and a cup of cold yellow soup into Sarah, all under the watchful eye of the nurse, whose job was to make sure Sarah did the actual consuming.

The nurse paged Carmichael back. He handed Galina a pharmacy order. "If she won't eat, get at least two of these supplements into her instead, and water, every other hour at least, or she'll dehydrate. Understand?"

Galina nodded. "We can do that."

"See you next week, then."

Sarah didn't make a sound on the short ride home, head on her knees. Vlad held her hand, silent in his own embarrassment.

"How'd it go?" asked Val.

"Sarah was fine," Galina said. "It was Vlad we had to pick up off the floor."

"You had to tell," Vlad grumbled as he headed for the hall.

Sarah left Katya's arm and approached Val.

"I'm glad you're up, Sar," Val said. "Are you going to eat with us?"

Sarah looked up, intensely sad. "I don't care what you do to me. I don't care if you punish me. I don't care if you send me away. But I will not – *ever* – go back to *that doctor* again. Just… thought you'd like to know."

*There. She'd 'talked' to Val. Now Val didn't have to hate her so much.*

Sarah dropped her clothes where she stood, slid into her pajamas, and rolled herself up in the bed. Never had she been threatened like that by a doctor. Not that had frightened her. She'd butted heads with Carver, but she'd never feared him. She deserved a Hell of a beating after trashing his room, but he didn't even yell. Carmichael'd seen the last of her, as long as she had breath to say so. After four or five hours of obsessing, she relaxed enough to sleep.

Valeria was up and waiting when a light speeder buzzed to a stop outside the door two minutes after midnight. Dmitri bounded in, overflowing with excitement.

Val smiled. "Good night?"

"I can't tell you how good! She's been watching me for a month! She thinks I'm cute! She's a fantastic ki–... Uh, you don't need to know that," Dmitri rattled, close to hyperventilating. He rushed to hang up his desert robe, hands gesturing everywhere.

"John got seats down at the front of the stands and we got to go down on the field and check out a couple of the flyers and they had this *incredible* light show with about a dozen small craft flying between the bursts and... "

Val laughed. "Slow down! You're moving at light speed." Thinking further, she said, "You haven't been drinking again, have you?"

Dmitri made a snide face. *"Noooo.* John had a case of Boxwood's."

*Boxwood's Butt-Kickin' Non-Alcoholic Brew*, a vile-tasting concoction popular with the teen crowd for its punch – a burst of caffeine equal to three cups of strong coffee. Val put a hand on his chest. "Your heart's pounding! How many did you have?"

"I dunno – three or four."

"That much caffeine isn't good for you. You know that. You'll be up for days."

"Yeah, but you should have – "

A prolonged scream interrupted him. He followed Val at a run.

Katya pulled on Sarah, who fought to bang her head on the hard wall. With Val's help, Sarah slid to the floor. She tucked her feet under her, covered her ears, and rocked back and forth, breathing a droning monotony of pain.

"No no no no ...."

It took several minutes for Val to break through the panic. She sat on the floor against the bed, Sarah wrapped stiff and silent around her neck.

"It's my fault," said Katya. "I was reading, and she got really restless. I should have woken her then, before she got worse."

"No proof that would have – uh! – helped," Val yawned.

"How do you do it, Val?" Dmitri asked.

"Do what?"

"Know what to do with her. I'd have just sat back and tried to figure out what the hell she was doing."

"Pppffft!" Valeria breathed out, rolling her eyes. "I have no *clue* what I'm doing! I make it up as I go. I studied government and history and law. I had one required course in psychology. We built mazes and raced rats. We never studied any of the crazy stuff. You probably know more about it than I do." She scrunched her eyes in the wake of another monumentous yawn. "Ugh. Think you'll go back to bed, Sarah?"

Sarah buried her face in Val's shoulder and shook her head violently. The nightmare had been a repeat, but in the dream she heard a hundred jeering voices, the party-conversation buzz of the voices that had plagued her. They'd been gone for months, yet here came a special-delivery message they were back in town. She'd do anything to get rid of them – short of telling Dr. Carmichael. Now that she was awake, her head was quiet, but she could feel the threat settle over her like an invisible web. She didn't dare sleep.

"I'll sit with her," Dmitri volunteered. "It's not like I'm going to bed any time soon, and I owe Kat a favor."

Val weighed the idea. Dmitri jittered with caffeine, but no one else was awake to distract him. She put the choice to Sarah. "Will you sit up with Dmitri?"

Sarah looked him over, then climbed next to him and linked her arm in his.

"Thank you, Dmitri. I'm exhausted. Call if you need help."

Dmitri dragged Sarah to the kitchen. "Come on. I'm starving." He checked the list of replicator codes and punched up a gooey conglomeration of bread and fake meat and cheese in a creamy sauce, a mounded dish of fried vegetables and spicy sauce, and a large fruit pie with whipped topping. Looking at the stack of liquid supplements, he picked one up and examined it. "Want one?"

Sarah watched him from a chair at the table. She shook her head.

Dmitri opened one of the supplements. He took a swig and rolled it around his tongue before swallowing. "Not bad. I've tasted better, but not bad. Val should keep them in the cooler, though. They'd taste better cold." He drank another swallow, then piled the dishes precariously, took the opened drink plus another between his fingers, and headed back to the main room. Sarah jumped from the table to hold the back of his shirt.

He unloaded the food onto one of the deadly triangular tables and flopped down on a sofa, grabbing the control for the holovision. Sarah plastered herself to his side as he scanned for a program that looked interesting. He opened the second drink and handed it to her.

Sarah shook her head.

"If I can drink one, so can you. It's strawberry or *oknat* or something, I'm not sure which." Navaran *oknat* fruit was also reddish-pink.

Sarah tried a small taste. It *wasn't* bad, she just wasn't in the mood. She took a second sip and accepted the can. Dmitri settled on a program and began to devour the pile of food.

The holovision had been a sticky point with Mother, but a battle she knew she couldn't win. She didn't mind the *idea*, just the *size* of it. For his birthday the other year, she let Father spend a sizable fortune – and a whole lot more – to buy the largest non-commercial holovision he could find, so he could feel as if he were ringside at sporting events. The black projection platform stood two meters square and a half meter high, usurping a considerable amount of space. The receiver/processor stood against the wall behind it, the size of a credenza. Mother hated the ugly metal casing, and kept it covered with a bright red and gold scarf. If nothing else, it made a place to display her various treasures. The device gave off an incredible picture, larger than life. It was too big to take with them, however. They'd have to sell it or leave it.

An hour later, and Dmitri pushed aside the half of pie he just couldn't finish. With his constant nagging, Sarah had finished three-quarters of her drink.

He belched long and loud twice. "Well, I'm full! I'm never going to get to sleep at this rate, though. I am *wide* awake. Come on." He slapped her knee and stood up. He carried the dishes to the kitchen, Sarah's hand clamped to the waistband of his pants, since his hands were full. Dropping the remaining pie in the reclamation unit, he took Sarah by the hand and led her down the hall.

He turned at the bathroom. Sarah dug her feet in at the doorway and yanked her hand free.

"You can come in. I'm not doing anything important."

Sarah shook her head, eyes purply big.

"Well, wait there, then." He touched the switch that opened the wall cabinet and rifled through it, reading labels. He chose a prescription, double-checked the label, shook two tablets out, tossed them in his mouth, and washed them down.

Sarah sucked her lip, watching.

"What're you looking at?" he glared, pocketing the small blue bottle of pills.

Sarah shook her head. Whatever he was doing, she wouldn't tell.

"Then don't look at me like that." He took her hand once more. "They're just some of Father's sleeping pills. I had way too much caffeine. I'll never get to sleep without them." They reinstalled themselves on the sofa, Sarah's head in his lap and his arm across her, staring at the flickering 3-D forms of the holovision.

Galina found them when she sneaked in sometime after three.

"What are you doing up?" she whispered, pulling off her shoes.

"Sarah couldn't sleep," a glassy-eyed Dmitri forced himself to answer. "I sat up with her."

"To bed, both of you," Galina insisted, though Sarah didn't look the least bit sleepy.

# * Twenty-two *

*Dear Mr. Ivanov,*
*My name is Valeria-Lin Alexandrovna Kirushenko. I am searching for the family of Maryana Natasha Fedorovna Ivanova, born in Minsk, Byelorussia, 23 May, 2222. Maryana was my mother. She died unexpectedly on 20 February, 2263. I know she was disowned from her family for marrying my father, but I am seeking to locate her older brother, Tomas S. Fedorovitch Ivanov, with whom she was known to maintain contact. If you are that person, please contact me immediately at the stated address. I am in need of answers to several questions.*

Tomas heaved a heavy sigh. He'd been staring at the message for two days. Rarely was he so indecisive. There were only two choices: respond, or not respond. Either would start an avalanche of aggravation. The note confirmed what he'd gleaned from his investigators: Maryana was gone. His heart grieved for his sister, but it put to final rest a mystery of his own. He had always sent Maryana secret birthday greetings to a neutral mail address at a server somewhere in South Africa. She always sent a reply. She'd do the same for his birthday six months later; he'd reply to that. Her videoletters were always vague, never giving much personal information, a habit from early in her marriage when she feared their irate father would hunt her down. She hadn't responded to his last message, and none had appeared two months ago. He'd hoped it was just an oversight from a busy life.

Should he or shouldn't he?
Should he or shouldn't he?
Should he or shouldn't he?

He'd done the research. It cost him a pittance in grants to have his blood tested anonymously against known samples of the poor little girl who'd been hospitalized. The genetic inclusion rate was ninety-nine percent certain. It was indeed his sister's child. He listened to hours of heart-breaking public-record testimony from his brother-in-law's murder trial, and he blamed himself, a twelve-fold grief.

He could have gone against his father's wishes, admitted publicly his sister was indeed a member of the family. But he never did. He could have told his father what he could do to himself. But he never did. If Tomas had acknowledged his sister, helped her, perhaps the tragedy would never have happened. His father would have kicked him out of the house, out of his job, perhaps he'd have been excluded from his inheritance, too, but some innocent little girl might still be alive for it. Was an empire worth the price of a child's life? What about twelve others? Nieces and nephews, nonetheless. Cousins of his own belated son. Children who shared his DNA.

Five months, and he still hadn't informed his mother what he knew.

Should he or shouldn't he?
Should he or shouldn't he?
*Twelve* children.

Tomas ordered the computer to take a letter.

# * Twenty-three *

Sarah made slight gains. She nibbled the lunch Val brought her, and managed to give herself a bath. Galina dragged her to dinner for half an hour, though she ate little and ran immediately back to bed.

Valeria, scanning the computer for an uncounted number of hours over the last three weeks, sat up abruptly.

"My God! I did it! I really did it!"

"What? What'd you do?" A group formed around the vidscreen.

Galina rushed over. "You got a reply?"

"We did! We got a text letter from Uncle Tomas!"

*"Who?"* Katya asked.

"Who the hell's Uncle Tomas?" David said.

"Mother's older brother," said Valeria triumphantly. "She kept in touch with him, I knew that much, but I couldn't find an address. Father couldn't remember, and it wasn't listed on any residential file I could find. I've been trying to locate him all this time, with no luck. I was down to my last possibilities, but I sent a hyperspace message anyway. I got a reply, and he's really our Uncle Tomas.

"... He's very sorry to hear of Mother's passing. He wishes he could have spoken with her. Her father – our grandfather – died a year ago himself," Val read off the screen.

Sergei wrinkled his face, bewildered. "We have a grandfather?"

"We did, now we just have a grandmother and an uncle."

"Why didn't we know about them?" he demanded. "How could Mother withhold relatives from us?"

"Because," Galina said. "When Mother married Father, they eloped, and her family wouldn't speak to her anymore."

"Father has that effect on people," David agreed.

Val shook her head, reading. "No, it was our Grandfather's idea. He never wanted them to marry." She faced the crowd behind her. "I have no guarantees, but I'm going to ask if we could visit for a short time while we find a place to live, or if he could find us an apartment we could move into. I'll send him another message tonight."

"Where does he live?" Vlad asked.

"He has a house in Minsk, where Mother grew up, but he works in

283

New York City, so chances are he might have a place in New York, too. Maybe we'll move there. How does everyone feel about America?"

Vlad headed for the bedroom. "It snows there, too, doesn't it? I gotta tell Sarah!"

Val tried to get Sarah back to therapy. Sarah clung to the bedframe, kicking anyone who came near.

"Maybe Dr. Carmichael will make a housecall," Val mused.

Sarah's face paled as white as her knuckles wrapped around the frame. "You wouldn't!" But Val did give him a call.

After a two-day standoff, they reached a compromise: Sarah agreed to meet him on a bench outside the hospital. She perched angry and ready to run.

Carmichael played to her intelligence. "I'm sorry, Sarah. I'm not used to having my patients dictate treatment terms, and I have many reservations about the way we've handled this so far. I'm not used to children, I admit that. I have a grown son; my first wife and I divorced when he was five, and I haven't seen him enough since. Outside of those five years, I've never been around children. We may not be the best match, but I'm what's available, and we need to work together.

"Given the choice, I'd like to put you in for a weekend of inpatient therapy. You need bloodwork, Sarah. You need a repeat brainscan. You know as well as I do, the Elavixor isn't working. You're nearing the maximum dose. You may need a second, or even third medication, and I know you don't want any of it. The question is, who is going to put up the longer, stronger fight, and should we be fighting in the first place? We're supposed to be on the same side."

"You won't get me through those doors while I'm still alive," Sarah decided, and ended their session by walking back to the flyer.

"That's exactly what I'm worried about!" he called after her.

If Val wasn't happy with Sarah, Sarah wasn't happy with Sarah, either. The morning's stress added to her feeling of impending disaster. All morning she'd heard faint whispers, unintelligible bursts flying through her head at lightspeed. The more she heard, the less she concentrated on anything, straining to separate real noise from imagined. The less she concentrated, the clearer the noises became, until the noises were voices. What had taken days before had now taken hours.

Sarah lost herself by lunchtime. She sat frozen, fork in hand, unable to eat.

*Never.*

*Ha ha hahaha.*
*Stupid.*

Val's concerned touch startled her. Val's mouth moved, but the inside voices were louder than the outside ones, and Sarah couldn't make out a thing. She shook her head and rested her forehead on the table. Biting her knuckles didn't help. She needed a bigger pain than that. *Not good. Not good. Not good at all.*

*What* was the problem. Sarah wandered the house, searching. All the sharp knives had disappeared.

*Some confidence,* she thought blackly. Two-handed methods were unwieldy and slow. She didn't have time for something like that. Afternoons had too many people around, and no place to hide.

She left Vlad absorbed in the holovision after school and slipped into the kitchen to poke through the drawers. Forks – not sharp enough, but if nothing else... Vlad's now-legendary meat-fork – that was a possibility. Ah! A corkscrew! Small enough to hold in one hand, with a tip sharp enough to pierce flesh.

Slouched in the corner behind the kitchen table, she pushed the tip into the skin near her wrist, dragging it down the flesh to her elbow. A thin red line appeared over the ragged skin, bringing with it a dull burning sensation. This numbness was stubborn. It would take a while.

Six lines bled down the inside of her left arm, drying in streaks against her skin. She was deep in concentration, voices dulled, completing the fifth stripe on her right arm, when a hand crossed her field of vision and made a snatch for the corkscrew. Sarah shrieked in surprise and stabbed at the invader. She tried to flee by pushing the long table out of her way, chairs and all, making a loud commotion.

"Ow!" David yelled. *"Val! Val!* Get in here, quick!"

The cumbersome table slowed the girl sufficiently that Valeria beat her to the doorway.

*Trapped.* Sarah flattened against the wall, screaming. So many people, people that seemed to be moving too fast for her confused mind to follow, so many screams she didn't think they all could be her own.

*If they'd just let her finish!* Couldn't they understand, she *had* to do this! Just two more stripes!

Uncountable hands reached for her, outnumbering, overpowering. One hand grabbed her wrist, squeezing until she released the corkscrew. Sarah raised her empty hands to cover her face. Grabbing her cheeks, she dug her short nails into the skin and dragged them downward.

They pinned her to the bathroom floor. David knelt across Sarah's hand and put his weight into holding her upper arm; it took Dmitri's full strength to counteract the other. Galina lay across the thrashing legs. Val straddled the bucking middle, dodging teeth as she wiped the gouges on Sarah's face, Sergei fetching whatever she needed at the moment. Katya comforted a crying Vlad while trying to keep the baby out of the way. Nikky clung to Kat's legs, unwilling to leave despite Valeria's orders.

Valeria dabbed Kleerpatch on the arm wounds, ignoring Sarah's straining screams. "Thank God they're superficial. At least we have her cornered in a smaller place. Let her go, and see what she does. We can't hold her forever."

On the count of three, they let go. Sarah leapt up, pressing herself into the back corner of the bathroom, eyes shut, ears covered, out of breath. Between the panting she mumbled a steady stream of unintelligible whispers.

Val sighed sadly. "I'll call Dr. Carver. Maybe he can take her back for a couple of weeks. Can you see us doing that on a two-day flight to Earth? They'd drop us off at the first planet."

"Don't," Dmitri objected as he stood up. "Every time you go messing with her doctors and drugs and threats of hospitals, she goes bad again. She was okay until you made her see Carmichael this morning. What happened to handling our problems ourselves?"

"This is out of our hands, Dimi! We can't handle this anymore. Look at her! *We've tried!* We can't be awake 26 hours a day. She'll wind up killing herself, and *that* blood *will* be on our hands." Val turned to leave.

Dmitri grabbed her elbow and turned her back. "I'm telling you, you're wrong about this. You said yourself the cuts weren't that deep. If she really meant to do something bad, she would have done it. She's just upset. She'll come back around."

Valeria eyed him with suspicion. "And you happen to know what's bothering her?"

"No, but you said yourself you figure out how to deal with her as you go. I went back and read those papers. I started figuring things out, too, and a lot of it makes sense. I'm telling you, all we need to do is get out of her face and give her some room to breathe."

Val crossed her arms. "And I'm supposed to take the word of a sixteen-year-old who had to accompany me to a hospital because he couldn't be left near his brother? The same one who plotted revenge on a nine-year old? It's my decision to make, and I've made it."

"That was then. Things are different now ..."

Val turned away. He slid in front of her.

"Dmitri, I'm getting angry. Move."

"Val, you're just plain wrong on this, and I'll fight you if they come to get her."

"And I could call Public Safety and have an officer hold you until she's gone," Val snapped. "Health issues are *my* business, and *I'm* making the decision. You want to put it to a vote? Fine!

"Vlad!" Valeria barked. "You're her living shadow. What do you think? Should we get Sarah help, or just let her beat herself to death?"

Vlad smeared his face on Katya's shirt. "She hates the hospital. If you send her away and then we move, how will she ever know where we went? I won't go without her."

"Sergei?"

"I don't know," he answered gravely. "She's really upset, but sending her away again might make her feel like we don't want her anymore."

"David?"

"I think Dmitri's right," David said with unusual seriousness. "I think she just needs to get out of the house. I go crazy sitting here for a weekend, and she's been stuck here every day for weeks and weeks. What's she got to feel good about?"

"Katya?"

Kat's gaze never left the floor. "Val's probably right. Sarah likes Dr. Carver, and he helped her once. Maybe it won't take so long this time. Maybe we're making it worse not sending her."

"Galina, you're going to have custody of her. It's your call."

Galina still sat on the bathroom floor. She took a deep breath and blew it out. "I don't know. I'd get her treated here again for three or four days, but I'm afraid she'll either come back worse, or they won't let her back at all. Maybe if we seek help right now, so close to the hearing, they'll say we can't handle her, and deny custody. Then what do we do? She needs help, but I wish we could find a way to hold off just 'til the court stuff is settled."

Valeria flung a hand in Sarah's direction. "And take her into court like this? *There's* the risk." She looked around at the expectant faces.

"All right, Dr. Know-It-All," she told Dmitri. "You think you understand this? I'll give you twenty-six hours. If she's not better a day from now, I'm asking Dr. Carver for a readmit. She's not to be out of your sight for a second. Anything happens to her, anything at all, and I'm holding you responsible. Deal?"

Dimi choked. "Me? I can't... What if something really happens?"

"You're the self-proclaimed miracle worker. Twenty-six hours." She ducked around him and walked out. Galina and Katya followed.

Dmitri looked to David next to him, then at Sarah off in the corner, still pretending she didn't exist.

"What are you gonna do?" David asked. "She's really blown her gaskets."

Dmitri was more afraid of the situation than he wanted to admit. "You had a good point, Dave. We all go places, and Sarah used to, too. All she does is go to the doctor, and now she won't even do that. Her files said she'd behave to earn special events. Let's see if Val will let us take her into the city. She likes museums and plays and smartsy stuff like that. Maybe if she goes somewhere she likes, she'll pull herself back together. Come on, I'm gonna need your help."

He waited, but Sarah didn't acknowledge his presence. At last he tapped her shoulder. Her eyes flew open in fright, but her mouth never stopped its silent oratory. He beckoned with a finger.

"Come on," he said, putting his whole hand into the wave.

Sarah took her hands off her head, watching him. As he backed up, she followed.

"My room, Sar," he gestured.

She hesitated, then ran to his room and squatted in the narrow space between his desk and drawers.

Vlad had been waiting for the chance to reach Sarah. He followed right along, but Dmitri stopped him at the bedroom. "Sorry Vlad. Not this time. Top Secret."

"But we're a team!" Vlad cried as the door shut in his face.

Dmitri locked the door. He pulled out the desk chair and patted the seat, but Sarah stayed wedged, whispering and rocking and hugging herself.

Dmitri sat on the chair instead. "I'm sorry we had to hold you like that. I hope we didn't hurt you."

Sarah shook her head ever so slightly.

"You can hear me?!"

Sarah whacked her head hard into the wall, twice. She appeared to listen, then nodded, no longer whispering.

"Don't *do* that!" David hissed.

Something Dmitri had read rang a bell in his mind. "Sar? Are you hearing voices?"

Sarah pressed a fist to her mouth, keeping the secret in.

"You are, aren't you!" Dmitri said, thrilled he guessed right.

"Don't tell."

David eyed her strangely. "You mean, like, you hear *other* people talking right now besides *us*? Who are they? What do they say?"

"I can't always make out the words. They've stopped now." In what she considered a brave move, Sarah added, "Sometimes I can talk over them, or pain can override them, or sometimes if I just keep moving."

"That's why you just hit your head, and chopped yourself up?" David said. He sat down cross-legged on the floor.

"It makes them stop," Sarah repeated, "but it doesn't last long."

"Sar, Val's about to send you back to the hospital," Dmitri said. "You've got to tell her. You've got to let her get you some medicine or something, or tomorrow you're on a MedEvac out of here. I practically had to punch her not to do it now."

Sarah grabbed his arm with both hands. "Don't let her! *Please* don't let her! I can't go back! I *won't*! I want to stay here! I want to be with you guys!" She let go of him and squeezed her head in frustration.

Dmitri pulled her hands down. "Shhh. It's okay. I think I might have an idea. I don't know if it could ever work, but I can try. If it does, you'll never have to go back to a hospital. If it doesn't... I hope they don't put me in the same cell as Father."

David stared. "*Shit*, man! What the hell are you thinking?"

"I won't tell you unless I know it'll work. I have to think. Will you trust me, Sar?" Dimi gave her his best look of good will.

"I have to." The word *wrong!* rebounded inside her head in a stranger's voice, while another voice chuckled briefly. *What else could she do? Obviously she couldn't trust Val. Val couldn't wait to get rid of her.*

"We'll take it step by step, see how far I get. We're gonna have to beat Val at being Val. Right now you have to show her you're trying, anything to change her mind. I know it won't work if you're not here. We – David and me – want to take you out for a while, into town, but you can't go doing the crazy stuff, okay? You can't go digging yourself up and screaming. If it's pain you need, David here'll pinch you every few minutes. He's good at that."

David twisted a pinch of his brother's skin just for the insinuation, and they scuffled a bit. "Maybe you'll show me that damned wrist thing, and I could use that." He'd been trying hard to figure out the maneuver, but Vlad was so scared of him David couldn't tell if it worked or if Vlad let go just to make him stop.

Dmitri grinned, shaking David off. "That's why I won't. Will you come out with everyone, Sar? Just for fun?"

"Can we leave if I need to?"

"Sure! I promise. Just let me know."

A hard knock at the door made them all jump. "Why is this door locked?" Val's voice demanded. "What are you doing with Sarah? Why can't Vlad be in there, too?"

*"Shit!"*

The three siblings jumped up. Dmitri grabbed his music player off the desk and stuffed the receivers in Sarah's ears. He jammed the player into her hands. "Listen!"

"Damned crybaby!" David swore as Dmitri released the door to face a pissed-off Valeria and a teary, snuffling Vlad.

Val scanned the tiny room, sniffing the air for deceit. Sarah rocked to the music, lips moving silently. "What are you doing?"

"You wanted me to keep an eye on her, I'm doing it," Dmitri said. "She's okay right now. Can't I talk to David without Vlad butting in? It *is* my room."

Valeria looked from one to the other several times. Her mouth pressed into a hard line of mistrust. "Keep the door unlocked. Come on, Vlad." She dragged him along despite his protests.

Dmitri shut the door. Sarah seemed happy enough with the music, so he left her alone.

"Who's that kid you hang out with?" he asked David in a hushed voice. "The one whose brother got caught selling fake ID's?"

"Jeff Romano?"

"Yeah. What's his brother's name?"

"He's got two – Terry and Sid," said David. "I think Terry's the one that got in trouble."

"Can you call Jeff and see if we can set up a place to meet? I want to talk to his brother." Dmitri's thoughts started to roll. It just *might* work...

"I guess. Why?"

"I don't want to tell you. If I go down, I'm gonna fall hard, and I don't want you in trouble, too. I need you here to take my place and keep things going. I need to age a year real quick."

Valeria stared at Dmitri. "You want to *what*? In *public*? With her arms and face like that?"

"David had a good point. Sarah never goes anywhere anymore. Maybe if she goes out and has a good time, she'll lighten up." Dmitri tried to look as calm and reasonable as possible.

"You're not taking her anywhere alone. I wouldn't let her out without at least four of you. You saw what it took to hold her."

"Galina'd have to fly us out anyway," David reasoned.

"It could be fun," Galina shrugged. "Go to dinner, catch a holofilm or something, maybe hit a couple shops. We haven't been out at night in ages. She was really good when Kat and I took her to the hospital. If not, we come back. It's a five-minute flight."

Nikky climbed her leg. "Me too, 'Lina? I'm goin', too?"

"We'll all go."

"Not me," Val declined. "I'll keep the baby here. There's too much to get done."

Eight of them set out for Kar Ku'umi as the sun set over the ShirapNi cliffs, far in the distance. Sarah said hardly a word, but she nibbled half of Vlad's salad *and* a fruit jelly at dinner. She kept pace with everyone, clinging to Dmitri and holding Vlad's hand with her other. She remembered to keep her head up, doing her best to ignore the low rumble of chaos in the back of her mind. Now and then David would notice her biting a knuckle, and give her a painful, discreet pinch. At first he was afraid of hurting her, but Sarah shook her head and pinched him back with brutal force.

"Like that," she whispered as he rubbed his arm.

It was easy under the table at the restaurant, but harder on the street under Vlad's wary eye. The first time David did it right, Sarah jumped in surprise, then nodded and never acknowledged it again.

A ribbon of glowing crimson banded the western edge of the evening sky by the time they left the restaurant. Most everything in the city stayed open late, to take advantage of the cooler night air. Galina stopped to buy Nikky a pair of closed shoes for the upcoming trip. If they did wind up back in Russia, it would be early February – not the time for sandals and mesh. They passed a stand selling printed and electronic copies of various trade and special-interest publications. Galina slowed to browse, then spotted a thick volume in the back of a display.

"This looks like something Sarah would like."

Katya peered over her sister's shoulder. *Ott's Study Guide to the Basic Education Exams.* "Only if I can use it, too. I have to take it in six months, too, you know."

"That decides it, then. What do you think, Sarah? Would you share it with Kat?"

Sarah read the title, looked away, and gave a nod. It was a waste, as she'd never graduate any time in the next ten years, but the more she thought about it, the more she liked the idea. Maybe she was ready to take the exam now, without the last six months of school. At the very least, she could correct any weak areas in advance. Perhaps her educational situation wasn't so dismal, after all.

David checked his Chronolog. "Hey, Galina? They got a ball game going on over at Admiral Min Park. That's only two blocks from here. We could watch the game, and Nikky could play on the climber. It's the Photon Phase versus the East End Electrix."

"That's a possibility," Galina considered. "What's the group vote?"

Five boys were unanimous. Sarah gave a disinterested nod.

"Fine with me," Katya shrugged.

"Lead on, Dave."

The park huddled under five expansive open domes, allowing for light and air and ventilation, but cutting the brutal sun and slowing evaporation enough that coarse red-black grass grew up thickly from the sand. It wasn't soft, it wasn't lush, and it wasn't even *green*, but it was the closest thing to an outdoor lawn for six thousand kilometers. The playing fields under the night lights, however, were artificial turf. A few hundred people had gathered to watch the game as the group found seats near the playground.

Nikky ran to join the crowd of children on the climbing forms, and Vlad and Sergei joined a group playing koball.

Twenty minutes had passed when David noticed friends of his nearby. He waved.

"Gal, I'm going to go talk with Jeff for a bit, okay? I'll be right over there. Come with me, Dima?"

"I guess," Dmitri answered casually. "Kat, will you watch Sarah for me? She won't go anywhere." Sarah sat on the grass, flipping through the study guide, biting her thumb.

Kat moved next to her. "Yeah, but don't get lost."


Terry Romano watched the game sourly. "So? I don't do that anymore. I'm a law-abiding rehabbed citizen, whatever that's supposed to mean. What're you looking for?"

"Just a birth record card, moved up one year."

"One year's not much," the older boy said, running his eyes over Dmitri, toe to head. "Doesn't even make you legal for anything." Dmitri took after Mother, short and small-boned. At sixteen, he brushed 167 centimeters, and no matter how much he ate, he never gained weight. He certainly didn't look older than he was.

"That's all I need," Dmitri insisted, "but it's got to be good enough to stand up in court."

"No problem. You got the original?"

"I can get it. When and how much?"

"Three days after I get the original. Twenty-five."

"Twenty-five *credits*? Man!" Dimi's heart sank. If he counted everything he had, and picked the local coins out of David's drawer, he might have all of ten.

"No credit don't get it."

"I can get it," Dmitri insisted, ignoring David's look of disbelief. "It's just gonna wipe me clean for a while, that's all."

"Meet me on the west side of the school when it lets out tomorrow, and we'll deal."

"Done."

* * *

Valeria didn't waste any time with the house empty. As soon as the flyer disappeared, she placed a call to Carver.

"This is Dr. Carver's answering service," said the man on the viewer. "May I ask your name and business?"

"Valeria Kirushenko, and I need advice on a crisis. He'll know."

"Please hold."

Not three minutes passed before Carver appeared on the screen. "Valeria! It wouldn't be good news, would it?"

"I don't know what else to do. She's scaring the daylights out of me. I think I'm over my head." Val went into detail about the last several weeks.

"Up the meds," Carver suggested. "Don't pay too much attention to the self-destruction. Up the meds, and she should work it out by herself."

"They already upped them," Valeria reemphasized. "I can't just let her slice herself up."

"Sometimes you have to. Unless the bleeding doesn't stop in five minutes, or she knocks herself out, or there are edges to a wound you have to pull together to close, ignore it. Keep it clean. Scars can be removed later. Something's bothering her, and she has to work it out in her head before she can talk about it. I mean, prevent it if you can, of course, but you can't always do that. Let her know you're there when she's ready to talk. I'd do more, but I couldn't get there 'til at least the day after tomorrow. Do you still have booster tabs?"

"Some, yes."

"Try them first, and keep me updated."

"Thanks." Val signed off, not as happy as she'd hoped.

*　*　*

It was after ten when the flyer settled outside the door. David carried in a sleeping Nikky. Katya had an arm around Sarah, who held onto Vlad with one hand and clutched the study guide with the other.

Valeria watched the parade. "You survived?"

"You should have come with us. We had a great time," Galina said. "Sarah even ate some dinner. Dimi was really terrific with her. I bought her a book, and she seems to like it."

Sarah nodded at Galina. She didn't smile, but her face had lost its end-of-the-world cataclysm look of despair. She gave Galina a brief hug before heading to her room.

Val watched her go. "Maybe the boys were right. Let's hope it's a turning point."

She expected at least a small battle when she handed Sarah the familiar yellow pill, but Sarah accepted her fate and took it willingly, much to Val's surprise. Nor did Val expect to see the ghostly figure, clad in a gauzy white nightshirt of Katya's two sizes too big, flow out to the dining room a half hour after everything quieted.

Val watched from the kitchen doorway, a cup of iced tea in her hands. Paying no attention to anything but her mission, Sarah stole over and placed a small folded paper by the computer, where Val had been spending so much time. The ghost slipped back to the hall.

Intrigued, Val retrieved the note. A single word lay on the sheet in Sarah's computer-perfect print:

## Antívox

Val jammed her thumb on the commlink switch so hard she broke the nail.

# * Twenty-four *

The dreaded black spirit faded. Sarah got out of bed. She ate. Her face and arms healed. She wasn't the life of the party – never had been – but she spoke when she had something worth saying. Strings of words made sense again, and she could read. She clutched the study guide day and night, analyzing the questions until she understood. It renewed her hope of graduation, with or without the damned Navarans. Liquid Antivox was disgustingly syrupy, but the fruit flavor was tolerable, far better than pills. It was nice to be alone with her thoughts once again.

The great push of packing began. Valeria sorted out what they were taking, selling off what she could and giving away the rest. She let everyone pick their favorite from Mother's collection of famous reproductions, and got rid of the rest. She saved some of Father's archaeological finds, the ones she knew to be of value, and gave the remainder to the schools.

With two weeks to go, the saddest day came: Val sold the holovision. She got little more than half its value, less than it would have cost to insure, ship, and store it.

Dmitri slouched on a sofa in the empty living area. "This is the worst yet! What are we gonna do for two weeks?"

"Move the wallscreen out of the bedroom," Val suggested. "Gal and I never use it."

David sulked on the floor with Sergei where the base unit had been. "That's boring! Who wants to watch a flatscreen? You might as well be stuck reading a book."

Sergei frowned, unsure if the comment was meant to insult him or not.

"We'll put the money from the holovision towards a new one," Val promised. "Just one not so big."

The house echoed. They sold the dining room set and kept the kitchen table. The piano would stay; it wasn't worth the shipping charge because of its size. Clothing and personal belongings were the next to go.

Valeria made each of them pack a carry bag. "Two changes of clothes," she directed, "and anything you can't live without, in case we lose the other luggage." They stacked the finished bags in the empty dining room, but baby Marina, now eleven months old and waddling with increasing speed, soon discovered how to unpack the cases, and they were stacked in the twins' room instead.

Sarah sat on the floor of her room, perplexed. Maybe she wasn't thinking well, but no matter how she packed, she couldn't get two changes of clothes into her carry bag. A stack of school text chips, her personal textreader, her homework pad interface, four plastic-bound printed novels with double-page holographic photo spreads, a deck of cards, the solid ruby-crystal ring Father had given her once – still too big to wear, a Navaran phrase dictionary, her favorite blue socks, a Tsar Nicholas matryoshka doll and several other mementos from Russia, some family photos she'd swiped from Mother's room, and if she carried the study guide, she could close the bag. That left her with no clothes or shoes. At last she found a sheet of plastic, laid out the clothes, laid a pair of soft sandals on them, and rolled the whole thing up snug. Using wide adhesive strips, she bound the roll firmly to the side of her bag. That was the best she could do, like it or not.

The stress of upheaval ate at her.

"No more hospitals," Dmitri still swore.

"How? What are you doing?" Sarah begged. "I want in on it!"

He tousled her hair. "You have to trust me. Just keep your fingers crossed."

She worried daily.

The boys were right; a meter-wide flat vidscreen couldn't compare to a two-meter-cubed 3-D image. Dmitri broke up the boredom one night by starting a soccer game in the house, with the hall and kitchen doorways as goals.

"What are you doing? You can't play ball in the house!" Val objected.

"Shut up, Val," Galina said, pulling on a sport shoe. "Who cares? Are you in, or not?"

Valeria's mouth hung open before she remembered to shut it. "I'm in."

Only the piano, the sofas, and the computer desk were left. They padded the computer and the commlink with suitcases, penned the baby in the kitchen, and played until they were sweaty and exhausted; Dmitri, Gal, Sarah and Vlad against David, Val, Sergei, and Katya. Nikky played both sides until he caught the ball with his face, and retreated to the kitchen with the baby. Then the real bloodsport began.

Sarah wasn't ready to run aggressively, but she made a reasonable goalie, hopping in place when things got exciting, such as Dmitri slamming David against the piano to get the ball, or Galina putting her hands over Sergei's eyes when the ball came near him, or Katya tackling Dmitri and his pants sliding to his knees. Vlad fell over Valeria and was trampled, and Dmitri's nose bled when David tripped him and he went face-first into the wall. No one could remember the score. In the end, lying in a pile on the cool stone floor, they were hot, sore, winded, and tired, but they hadn't felt that great in a long, long time.

A week to go, and Sarah backslid from the stress. She spent the days on the couch, knees pulled up, holding the study guide that she no longer read. Val worried, took her on the hundred last-minute errands to get her out of the house, but the haunted look was back, and Sarah was resolutely silent once more.

Dmitri pulled her aside. "When we go back to court, tell the judge you want to go with me," he instructed. "Nobody but me. I promise, cross my heart, no more hospitals."

Sarah thought back to the lists. Her name had been with Dimi's on every grouping. If Viktor couldn't be there to protect her, Dmitri seemed to be proving a worthy replacement.

She promised.

Three days to the countdown. Work and school ended for the Kirushenko clan. Today would be the final custody hearing; a matter of formality than anything else. The forms had been filed weeks ago; today the judge would interview each of them and give her final approval.

Once again Val had Sarah wear her tan-on-tan dress, but this time Sarah wanted her hair braided up. It was too hot for cutesy stuff. Unfortunately, her sandals were in the clothing roll, and she had to unstrap it to get them back.

Nikky saw the judge first, too young to understand. Val had given him so much attention in the past year he could hardly remember his actual mother.

Sergei went next, then Vlad, then David. Katya and Dmitri had given their interviews earlier in the week, saving time. Sarah, jumpy with the interminable wait, went last.

She entered the office, relieved to find it looked nothing like any doctor's office she'd ever seen. It smelled of cool walls and dusty floors, not disinfectant and ointments. Judge Rush sat behind her desk, a pleasant, dark-skinned woman, her short hair tipped with gray. She smiled and waved Sarah to a chair next to her.

"And you're Sarah! Nice to meet you! Come, sit. I've been wanting to meet you for quite a while. I saw you during your father's trial. You're a very brave little girl."

"Thank you," Sarah said, ignoring the remark about being little.

"Yours is such a special case. I'm interested as to why your brother Dmitri is applying for guardianship as well as your sister. I see he was liberated two weeks ago, but he strongly feels he should have custody over you instead of your sister. I have already spoken to him, but, can you tell me why he might do that?"

Sarah's breath caught, and she relied on her Navaran training to hide her surprise. So *this* was what he'd been plotting! Wait 'til Val got a hold of him! So *he* would have charge over her! And Val wouldn't be able to tell her no unless he thought so, too. If *that* wasn't the best idea! *How to answer?* She'd promised to back him up, and he would keep her out of the hospitals.

Judge Rush broke through her shock. "Do you understand my question?"

"Yes ma'am," Sarah said quickly. "I was thinking. They want me to go with Galina, right?"

"That's what I have in my papers."

"I don't really know Galina that well," Sarah said, feeling terribly guilty over stretching the truth. She liked Galina just fine; she was more patient and fun than Valeria, but Sarah'd made her promise to Dimi. "I was little when she left home. Now she works nights and sleeps days. Valeria takes care of us most of the time. I know Val a lot better, but I understand that she wants the baby. Val's taken care of her since she was born. She's really like Val's own baby."

"Would you rather Valeria make decisions for you?"

"No ma'am! Valeria and I don't agree on anything! We don't get along at all. She tries, but she's too bossy, and we wind up fighting every time.

"That's why Dmitri's seeking custody," Sarah continued, trying to keep a logical line of reasoning. "Dmitri's the one who knows me best; he's been there all my life. He visited me in the hospital; he went through training to learn my programs and treatments and medications. Galina hasn't had any of that."

"And why is that?"

"Because of Valeria. Val has to be the boss. If Val decided she had to see the hospital programs, then Galina automatically has to stay behind to keep things running. Galina just follows Val around. She never goes out and investigates things for herself. Being with Galina is like staying with an aunt who knows you only through correspondence." It was a lie, a horrible outright lie, but Sarah was running out of convincing argument. She had no idea what an aunt was like, she'd never known one except through literature. She hoped Galina would never find out.

"So, you feel your brother knows you best, and can make the best decisions for your care?"

"Yes, ma'am."

"I have some serious reservations about such an arrangement. Your brother Dmitri is almost eighteen. I haven't gone over his school records, but I'll assume he'll go on to a university program next year. What would you do then?"

"I'd go with him!" Sarah said brightly. "I'm in an accelerated program. I'd be graduating in five months if I hadn't been in the hospital." *But Dmitri was almost seventeen, not eighteen?* She counted backwards up the line to make sure. Vlad was a year ahead of her, two to Sergei, then two and two. Yes, he was only sixteen. She was certain, but maybe the judge would think she was a troublemaker if she pointed out the error.

"I'm still concerned over how Dmitri can support you, both now and after he graduates. The stipend allowed to a court-appointed guardian for care of a minor isn't very much. What if Dmitri had a practicum and you couldn't go with him?"

"Then I'd be with the twins," Sarah replied easily. "We all live together anyway. It's not like we'd be on our own."

"What if they didn't have room, or couldn't take care of you? What if Dmitri wants to live elsewhere?"

"I think you have too many if's in your hypothesis to make a conclusive statement." Sarah couldn't stop herself. The ideas were getting a little ridiculous. Of course Dmitri could take care of her. He was already responsible for her two nights a week. And they each had all that money Val wouldn't let them spend. She could cover her own expenses. That kind of money would last forever.

"I see." Judge Rush made a note and changed direction. "Sarah, are you being pressured as to what you're supposed to say to me? Who you are supposed to support?"

Sarah was confused by the implication. "No. This is what I want."

"Have you ever felt threatened by your brother? Been afraid because he hurt you, or thought he might hurt you? Dislike how he treats you or touches you? Not like what he says to you?"

Always, *those* questions… Sure, Dmitri'd plotted with David to get her, threatened dozens of times to punch her, teased her with name-calling, sat on her while tickling her until she nearly cried from rage, but none of that was serious stuff. That was just the two of them being brother and sister. He'd never hit her out of meanness, like Alexei, like Father. Surely he wouldn't have gone to all this trouble if he *didn't* care about her.

"No. Dmitri's taken care of me since I was a baby. Yes, he yells when he's mad, and if Val's not around he swears sometimes, but he's never mean. Since Viktor left, he's been the man of the house."

"And you don't think it might be difficult, being raised by a brother? You wouldn't miss your sisters, miss talking to them, being with other girls?"

"My sisters are all a lot older or younger than me," Sarah said truthfully. "I've been with my brothers all my life. I'm used to them. Even when I leave for university, I can call them on the comm whenever I want."

"One more question, Sarah," the judge said. "If you could live with any of your brothers or sisters, who would it be?"

"I want to live with all of them," Sarah replied, suspicious. No one would keep her away from Vlad, law or no law.

"If you had to pick just one?"

"Well, Vlad and I are like twins, but I take care of him and he's my age, so he can't take care of me," Sarah reasoned. "If I had the choice, I might go with Viktor, but we haven't seen him in six months, and he's half a galaxy away. My second choice is Dmitri, then Katya, I guess, or both. They've always taken the best care of me, before the twins ever came back."

"I see. Thank you, Sarah. That's all I need to know."

The judge called them all into the office. "I've gone over the paperwork, and everything is in order. Your interviews were fine. I have no reservations about granting Katerina liberated adult status; if this were Earth, she could have declared herself ten months ago. I am awarding custody of David, Marina, and Nikolai to Valeria, and custody of Sergei and Vladimir to Galina. Sarah's case is rather complicated, and I've spent many hours talking to various professionals for their opinions. Based on her records, I think that keeping her stress to the lowest possible level is in her best interest, and that stress can be reduced by supporting her decision as to what makes her most comfortable. I have some reservations, but I am going to grant the request for custody of Sarah to Dmitri, but only on a temporary basis. I would like to review the case in six months to see where things stand, before granting permanent custody.

"That's it," the judge said. "Sign the forms, and you're all set."

Valeria nearly dropped the baby. *"What!"*

Galina looked from Dmitri to the judge. "I don't understand..."

David stared at Dmitri, and his jaw fell open.

*"How?"* Val cried in disbelief. "Dmitri's not – Galina's supposed to – What about *Dmitri's* custody?!"

"According to my paperwork, Judge Ellmore emancipated Dmitri to liberated status a week and a half ago," Judge Rush said. "Is there a problem? If you wish to dispute the claim, I can file an appeal."

For the first time in her life, Valeria was struck speechless. She sat, eyes roaming from Dmitri, who avoided her gaze and quickly signed the custody form, to Sarah, who never looked at anyone anymore, to Galina, who looked just as dumbfounded.

Val regained her composure. "I see. No, no appeals. I – hadn't heard that had been finalized. Give me the forms." She and Galina signed and dated their forms, and took the new official identification cards.

The judge shook their hands. "Congratulations, and best of luck to you all."

"We'll need it," Valeria said primly, and walked out of the room.

"That's my girl!" Dmitri lifted Sarah and kissed her on the forehead, then thanked the judge. They left the office hand in hand.

Galina seethed as they passed in the hall. "You better pray she lets you in the flyer."

"No more hospitals?" Sarah double-checked, her hand fast in Vlad's.

"Never again," Dmitri swore.

The tension on the ride home made it difficult to breathe. Obviously, Dmitri hadn't informed Val of his plan. Sarah could see both sides. She felt a little sorry for Val, having such a surprise thrown on her in front of a judge, where she couldn't say something bad. Except for the baby, and Nikky singing a song he made up as he went along, not a sound could be heard inside the cabin but the low whine of the antigrav generators. Valeria parked the flyer at the door and stalked into the house. They tiptoed in after her.

Val stood at the divider, arms crossed, back to them, chin on her chest. Galina put Marina down to run, but no one knew what to do. They stood huddled, all eyes on Dmitri.

Dmitri cleared his throat. "Val, let me explain," he tried, but the bomb went off before he had a fighting chance.

Val exploded. *"Explain?!* I should call City Security and have you *arrested! Liar!* Forget about making a fool out of me in front of the judge! *Ten days!* You liberated yourself *ten days ago* and never said a *word*! Living in this house like nothing was wrong while you plotted against me? Lie after lie after lie? *Traitor!* How did you do it, Dimi? How did you possibly convince the court that a sixteen-year-old brat with no schooling and no employment can better care for an emotionally unstable child? That's kidnapping! You *kidnapped* her away from Galina!"

"It's not like that. I only meant …"

Sarah broke from the pack and slipped her hand into her brother's. He'd need the support in the face of Valeria's storm, but the action only increased her fury.

"And you, you little witch!" She turned on Sarah, slapping her about the head and shoulders. "You had a hand in this too, didn't you! You told him how to do it, didn't you!"

Sarah ducked, arms raised, stepping back, but she caught the hem of her dress with her heel and fell. Before she could scramble up, she was lifted to her feet. She looked up to see David helping her, pulling her close and wrapping protective arms around her. He dragged her back to the group. Sarah'd only seen him look that scared once, the night Father was taken away.

Dmitri grabbed Val's arm. "Now wait a minute! Don't you go hitting on her like that! She didn't know a thing! I didn't tell *anyone* about it."

Val dropped her voice, icy cold. "Get your hand off me! If we hadn't cut Father's whip to pieces, I'd tear your ass this very minute! You can't even keep your skin clear! What makes you think you know right from wrong where Sarah's concerned?"

"If you weren't so goddamned self-righteous all the time you might be able to – "

Valeria lashed out and slapped him. "Don't you swear at me!"

Dmitri raised a fist, and for one dreadful moment looked like he would punch Valeria. With a howl of rage he spun instead, unleashing the fist into the empty air behind him.

*"Fuck you, Valeria! Fuck you!* For once in your life, something hasn't gone the way you wanted! I'm *glad* I did what I did, and I *meant* what I told the court! I *will* take care of her! Now you can't nag her and threaten her until you make her sick! The only reason I did it was to keep you from shipping her off to some goddamned lunatic prison because you admit you don't know what you're doing and you refuse to listen to reason!"

Val pointed to the door. *"Get out!* You no-good, traitorous backstabbing *prick!* You think you're such a *goddamned* adult, take your *goddamned* lunatic and *get out!*"

"She doesn't mean that, Sarah," Sergei said softly.

"Yes, she does," Sarah answered with certainty. The once-fearsome Four clustered together. Even Nikky stood silent. Mother and Father never fought, not even behind doors. Outside of Sarah and Elizabyeta's permanent state of preschool war, they had never had a really serious fight among them. Not like this. Pissed off and not speaking was one thing; Valeria and Dmitri looked ready to draw blood.

Galina eased between the warring parties. "Stop! Before somebody does something they'll really regret, everybody back off, okay? Let's sit down and talk this out."

Valeria burst into tears. "Why? Nobody talks to me! I'm the last one to know anything! Everyone hates me, remember?" She thought further.

"Where did you get the money for the court fees, Dimi? It's a hundred credits for the guardianship, another seventy-five for liberation papers. *Where did you get 175 credits?"*

"I have money," he sneered, not mentioning the twenty-five for false documents. "We *all* have money…"

Valeria's shoulders drooped. "You stole it, didn't you. You went into my things and stole that insurance certificate."

"I can't steal what's rightfully mine."

"How! How could you do this to me! A liar, a kidnapper, *and* a thief!"

Galina held her hand out. "Let me see your guardianship papers. You can have them right back. I just want to see what they say."

Dmitri handed over his hard copies, standing close. It was easy to imagine Valeria grabbing them and tearing them up.

"They look the same as ours. Wait a minute. The date's wrong. This says you're seventeen."

"So?"

Galina handed the paper back. "So it's not correct. It's not your birthdate. That might invalidate it."

"Prove it."

"Anyone can look at your records and see you lied about your age…"

"Looks the same to me." He handed her his revamped ID.

Galina's forehead wrinkled in disbelief. "It is! I don't know how, but it is! Tell me I'm not crazy."

*"Dear Sweet Lord of the Universe!"* Valeria wailed to the high ceiling. "I forgot forgery! Is there anything else I should know about,

Dimi? Is there a body count you failed to mention? That's the kind of shit I expect out of David and his hoodlum friends, not you! I always thought you had more integrity than that!"

If only the ground would swallow Sarah whole. *All this violence on account of her!* If it would rewind time two hours, she'd call and have herself hauled back to Rangler herself. She twisted to see David, arms circling her, chin set tight. Less than an hour ago Val swore to take the best care of him; here she was, already cutting him down, just like Father. It wasn't fair. She reached up and entwined her arms around David's. They'd all have to stick together extra-tight through this.

"Didn't you think someone would question how you were only two *weeks* older than Katya?" Galina wondered.

"You hear about it often enough," Dmitri reasoned. "One twin being taken earlier than the other for some crisis or another. It happens. The Mubana twins in tenth form are three weeks apart."

Galina still looked doubtful. "So why wouldn't they question why I applied for guardianship of you, if Katya was being liberated outright?"

"I told them it was done as a backup, so the paperwork would already be in place if things didn't go through," Dmitri shrugged. "Because you already had custody, they only looked at the records here on Navara. They bought into it better than I ever expected. Honestly, Gal, I'm as surprised as you they approved it."

"You lying, sneaking *bastard!*" Valeria raged from the far end of the dining room. "You even had *backup* plans! I wish Father were here to see this."

Galina held her hands up. "Look, I think you guys need to separate for a while. When you both calm down, we'll find a way to fix it. Dmitri, go to your room. Val, go in the kitchen and we'll talk."

*"I want him out of this house!"*

Dmitri didn't need a second prompt. He stormed off to his room with an anger so great it could be felt rolling off him in waves.

Sarah dragged David down the hall. Dmitri would need David. Where Sarah went, Vlad followed, and soon everyone squeezed into the tiny room.

Dimi kicked the daylights out of a packing box, but the resilient plastic refused to buckle. He knocked the container violently into the corner, then leaned on his desk, breathing hard.

Sarah couldn't ever remember seeing Dmitri this angry. She gathered her courage and hugged him. *What was the worst he could do? Hit her?*

"I'm sorry," she whispered.

Dmitri patted the hands around his middle. "It's not your fault. I didn't think she'd take it this bad. You okay?" He tipped her face up. "I can't believe she hit you like that."

"She hit you, too."

"That's different."

"Dimi, I want to shake your hand!" David said excitedly, flipping his hair back. He held his hand out and grabbed for his brother's. "That is the most wildest thing I ever heard! *That's* what you needed that ID for! I didn't know you had those kind of guts. My robe's off to you, man! All that to save her neck? You are *too* stellar! You couldn't have adopted me?"

Dmitri parked himself on the desk. "I don't know what Sarah said, but she must have done a hell of a convincing job, 'cause I was dead sure they wouldn't do it. Save the laurels. You might need to take my money to bail me out of holding and get me a lawyer. Not that one at the trial – a better one than that. I'd doubt Val will let Sarah testify for me. Anybody know what the penalty is for falsifying documents and lying in court?"

"I think Terry got three months for the ID's," David said. "I don't know about perjury. The kidnapping might stick, too. Depends on how they word the charge."

Vlad and Sergei had climbed to the top bunk, out of the way. "She wouldn't really call Security, would she, Dimi?" Vlad asked anxiously.

Katya leaned against the wall in the space by the door. "I wouldn't put it past her. She's really ripped about this. I can't believe you'd do something so *stupid!*"

"What was so stupid about it?" Dmitri glared. "You would never have done it. You won't even tell Val you don't like the way she makes rice for dinner."

"No, I wouldn't," Katya agreed. "I know I couldn't take good enough care of Sarah, and I take care of her most of the time as it is. I don't understand."

"Neither does Valeria – "

The door opened, but there wasn't much physical space left for Galina to enter. "Out, everybody. I want to talk to Dmitri. *Alone.*" She pushed David toward the door as she squeezed her way in.

Sarah looked small and scared, wedged between the wall and the bed and Dmitri's knee hanging over the side of the desk. "You might as well stay, Sar. You're wrapped up in this, too. Not this time, Vlad. Go." Galina propelled him out and shut the door.

"Now explain to me, Dimi, just what in the name of the Universe made you think you could get away with this?"

"Is Val calling for public security?"

"She wants to," Galina sighed, sitting on his bed. "She has a pretty good case, but for now I convinced her not to."

"I didn't think she'd take it this hard."

Galina resisted the urge to knock on his head with her knuckles. "What did you expect?! You not only embarrassed her, you ripped her heart out and threw it to a wolf! She's spent the last two months planning every last detail, tracking down relatives, coordinating transportation, storage facilities, travel documents, lining up apartments and schools and doctors, to make this move as smooth as possible, *besides* juggling the daily routine and Sarah's ups and downs. Then you go and stab her in the back, telling her she doesn't know what she's doing? Has she really done so bad a job? Where do you get the nerve to tell her she has? Just who the Hell do you think you are?!"

Dmitri sighed. "I guess she hasn't. I just – I only did it to keep her from sending Sarah back to the hospital, but between the time I started and now, the problem passed, and by then it was too late to back out. It didn't seem like such a big deal. Nothing would change, except Val would have to give someone else a real say in Sarah's medical treatment."

"What did you *think*, Dimi? That you could just say, 'Here Val, raise Sarah, but don't forget I make the medical decisions because I don't think your judgment's good enough'? That you're some highly trained specialist who can sit back and dictate orders without getting their hands dirty?"

"I didn't think of it that way… "

"You didn't think at *all*! Guardianship means *total* responsibility! Her clothing, her education, her nutrition, making sure she washes her hair – you can't pick and choose your responsibilities, they're *all* yours! How are you going to support her financially when you're still in school yourself? Are you prepared to find her an educational program fit for her abilities, when she's further ahead in school than you are? How tall is she? Do you know what size shoe she wears? You haven't finished puberty yourself – how are you going to explain it to her? *Can* you explain it to her? If she decides she's not going to take her medication anymore, are you just going to say, 'Hey man, that's orbital with me!'?"

Dmitri wallowed in self-pity. "I screwed up, I admit it. It seemed like a good idea when I thought of it."

"If anyone should be angry, it's me," Galina went on. "I was supposed to have custody of both of you, remember? You're figging me off at the same time. I understand why you did it, even if I think it's the most... childish, most immature thing I ever heard of. My concern right now is Sarah. That contract isn't legal. It's a lie – and technically, that leaves Sarah as her own legal guardian, which she can't be."

Dmitri could see all too clearly in his mind the City Safety and Security enforcement cruisers surrounding the house, and his hands in binders. **FELON** wasn't a word he wanted stamped on his forehead. He'd never get a date after that. "So what do I do?"

Galina paused to think. "To correct it now would delay the move by at least a week. They'll investigate, maybe reopen the custody files, even revoke them. I'll see if Val will hold it together until we get back to Earth. Then you can just say you made a mistake, you can't do it, sign her over to me, and we'll go on as always. It's probably not legal either, but it's better than it is now. You can keep your adult status."

"I don't care. I screwed up. I'm sorry. I just thought I was doing something good for Sarah."

"Well, you didn't. I just hope I can fix it."

# * Twenty-five *

Valeria wouldn't be swayed that easily. When Dmitri, trailed by Sarah, left his room, a melancholy lunch was in progress. Two seats were empty, and neither had been set.

"We don't rate lunch?"

"You're an adult," Val reminded him acidly. "Get your own. And feed your kid while you're at it."

Dmitri mumbled an inaudible reply. He stabbed code into the replicator and removed two plates.

Sarah liked vegetable dumplings, but realized she couldn't eat it. The silence in the kitchen stung like an open wound. She could feel Val's eyes on her and Dimi, and the rest of the table watching Val. She gave Vlad a sad shake of her head, and let go of his hand.

"I'm not hungry right now." She pushed the plate forward and left the table.

Dmitri attacked his lunch with fury, shoveling food into his churning stomach. He cleared and disposed of the plates and stalked out.

Sarah sat outside, wrapped in Sergei's protective robe that she'd grabbed off the hooks by the door. The stone step baked her *zhopa,* even through the thick cloth. The sun had just passed its zenith, clearing the ridge behind the house. The air writhed in the agony of noon; she pulled the robe's hood forward to cool the air as much as possible before she breathed it.

The boring, burning sand. She couldn't sit on the step forever; she'd roast. To stay outside she had to find shade. To walk around to the shadowed side of the ridge would take half an hour, and she'd need to take water with her. She couldn't face that cold kitchen yet. Sarah walked around the north side of the house to the meager stripe of shade by the ridge. Between house and stone ran narrow steps to the flat roof.

The air still wavered up here, but shelter lay under the line of solar collectors humming drowsily as they absorbed the energy in the long bank of storage cells. The big collectors powered the entire house. Picking her way around the various communication arrays, the skylights to her windowless bedroom, and the now-useless holovision receptor dish, Sarah found a shady spot tolerably hot to the touch, between the battery bank and a collector.

She squeezed herself into the gritty space under the collectors, staring off into the blurry distance. Guilt weighed on her stomach like so many kilos of sand. Galina was trying so hard to be sensible about everything, and Sarah had gone and told all those vicious lies about her. Father would have whipped her fierce for telling a lie; she almost wished he could. At least she'd feel justified for feeling this miserable. She just wanted to sit alone for a while, to sort out what had happened and how to help Dmitri, but the lazy hum of the arrays, the overpowering heat, and the endless desert breeze soon lulled her to sleep.

* * *

Afraid of reprisal, Vladimir waited over an hour before saying anything.

"Dimi, you seen Sarah?" He didn't know if he was supposed to be talking to Dimi or not. He didn't know anything anymore. Val could scream all she wanted, but he wasn't going to stop talking to Sarah. Val couldn't yell at him, anyway; only Galina could.

Dmitri was repacking his bags; Val had dumped them on the floor. "Not since lunch. She's not in her room?"

"*Nyet*. Or under her bed, or in her closet."

Dmitri tried to close a bag, readjusted the pile inside, and finally got it to shut. "Well, she's got to be here. Did you try the bathrooms?"

"*Da*. And the linen closet and my room, too."

"Well, she's got to be here," Dmitri repeated. "I'll help you." Sarah could hide in some pretty small places when she wanted. For all he knew, Valeria hid her just to make a point.

Soon everyone – except Valeria – helped search.

"Where could she be?" Dmitri was stumped. The house had no attic, no basement, and they'd checked the locked utility room twice.

"If she was really upset, you don't think – ?" Katya stopped, afraid to finish the sentence. Six people jammed the front door before breaking through.

The heat seared down and reflected up from the salmon sand, instantly drying eyes and skin and the insides of noses. Heat waves rose, thick as water, blurring the landscape with their waver. Katya squinted into the blinding brightness.

"Sarah!" she yelled. "Sarah!" The sound didn't seem to carry beyond the parked flyer, eaten up by the heat and emptiness.

"If you ran out in the desert, where would you hide?" Dmitri wondered.

"I'd dig down where it was cool and bury myself in the sand," Sergei replied, "maybe even my head, breathe through a straw."

The four boys looked down at the sand and almost together took a step backward.

Galina punched the lock code on the flyer door. "I'll search the ridge."

"Where else could she go?" David frowned. "If she walked off ..."

"The roof!" Vlad shouted. "What about the roof? Sometimes we go up there at night."

Dmitri broke into a run, taking the steps two at a time. "Watch the power cables!" he ordered as the boys spread out. If nothing else, he could use the height as a lookout.

"Dimi! Over here!" David yelled, clear across the house. "She's here!"

Dmitri hurdled clear over the hyperspace dish in his rush. "Is she all right?" he panted, moving far too fast for the heat. Sweat poured off him, off all of them, not one having had the sense to grab a robe. *Val would kill him with her bare hands.* In charge of someone for four hours, and he'd screwed up already. Some adult!

David shook her. "She's breathing, but she won't wake up."

"She's too hot," Dmitri realized, lifting the inert form with David's help. Sarah was dead weight. *Half-dead.* "Run! Tell Katya to get some water." Sergei and Vlad raced ahead.

"What was she *doing* up there!" Katya cried as they entered the house. They unwrapped Sarah from the robe and laid her on the cool floor. Katya sponged the baked face with water.

Valeria came over and felt Sarah's skin. "She's not that super hot. It's probably just heat exhaustion. Get her in a cool bath, and when she comes around, get a liter of Hi-Drate in her."

Galina came in, breathless. "You got her?"

"She was on the roof," Vlad explained, holding Sarah's hand while Dmitri wiped her arm.

"Go!" Val ordered again. "She's your problem, Dmitri. Get her in a cool bath."

"Me? I can't do that! I can't give her a bath."

"*You're* her guardian, it's *your* problem," Val insisted. "You're supposed to know where she is and what she's doing at all times. She's overheated and dehydrated. *What are you going to do, Dimi?*"

"*I know that!* She's a girl! I can't... "

Kat glared at Valeria. "I'll help you. Get her up."

"Ekaterina!" Val warned.

Katya stood strong against the icy gaze. "I'm not undermining your authority, Val. As an independent party in this war, I know what you're trying to do, but I'm not going to stand by and see Sarah suffer for Dmitri's mistake. Go!" she ordered her brother.

Dmitri held the unconscious child, while Katya stripped off the shoes and dress. "Look," she told him above the noise of the running water, "I don't know how far Val's going to carry this, but if you come to the room later, I'll give you some pointers on Sarah. Little things to watch for, girlish things she likes. And like now – you can either put her in the water in her underwear, since we're just here to cool her off, or wrap a towel around her. So what if it gets wet. That's what a towel's for. Throw it in the reclaimer when you're done."

"I didn't think of that." Dmitri lifted the half-dressed girl over the side of the cooling tub.

Kat drizzled water over Sarah's head. "Did she do this deliberately, do you think?"

"Who knows?" Dmitri stirred the water with his fingers so the waves splashed higher onto Sarah's legs. "I think Val scared her. Honest, Kat, I didn't do this to piss Val off. I just didn't think she was trying hard enough. I didn't want to have to listen to Vlad crying for another three months."

"We all make mistakes. You meant well. You did it because you cared, and that's what counts."

"Sure. Explain that to Val."

"I've been trying to, but... "

Sarah took a deep breath, stirred, felt and heard the water splash. She sat up, fast as light.

"Hey, hey, easy!" Katya soothed, wiping water from the frightened face. "It's all right. The heat got you, silly! You've got less sense than a sand spider."

Dmitri held out a glass of rehydration juice. "You might as well start drinking, kid. You've got a lot to go."

Sarah downed the liquid without argument.

Katya dripped more water on her head. "Whatever made you go up on the roof in the daytime? Even Nikky knows better than that."

Sarah held the glass out for a refill. "I wanted to be alone to think. The roof was the shadiest place I could find. I got sleepy."

"It's a good thing you were covered, and in the shade. Dimi, run and get her something cool to wear. She should be okay now."

* * *

Dmitri sat alone on the front step after dinner, watching the stars, when Sarah came out in her pajamas and sat next to him, gripping her study guide.

"What're you doing out here?" he asked. "Kat catches you outside again, she'll skin you alive." His robe hung over his shoulders; he lifted a corner, and she moved in close under it.

"I came to say goodnight. Looking for Earth?" she asked, watching the blinking lights from a high-altitude craft pass silently in the distance.

"How'd you know?"

"Vlad and I do it all the time. We sneak out the bedroom window and go up on the roof. We guess what the weather's like, or what time of day it is, or what we'd be doing if we were home. Things like that."

"You're lucky Father never caught you."

Sarah played with a corner of the study guide. "I'm sorry about this afternoon. I didn't mean to fall asleep. If I wanted to hurt myself, I would have just walked into the desert."

"No you wouldn't. You're afraid of being lost out there. Afraid of being lost, afraid of water, afraid of doctors, afraid of hospitals... Is there anything you're not afraid of?"

She grinned impishly. "You!"

"Aw, get out of here. Leave it to a girl to take a simple question and turn it into something mushy. You can tell Valeria I've officially told you to go to bed."

"I know." Sarah scampered inside.

The glittering starlight had a calming, hypnotic effect. Dmitri breathed the cool night air, hearing the soft static of the envirofans buzzing on the roof, and the chirpy insects that came alive after dark. He closed his eyes, listening to the empty silences of the desert and the distant voices going about their business inside the house. The peace was welcome after the horrible day. Outside, the night was almost perfect.

*A smoker.*

That's what would make the night perfect. A dark red Bloodweed smoker, made from the sweet, dried-blood-colored desert grass that grew sparsely wherever the hell it wanted to, defying cultivation. They were legal if you were eighteen and carried a controlled-substance permit, and he had a paper saying he was as old as that. Legal, but expensive. His friend John had an older brother who supplied their crowd at cost, but Dmitri was out. Val would lecture him if she caught him, all the crap about how he was destroying lung tissue and how you needed every cell in the lousy Navaran air, but he couldn't get in much more trouble than he was now. One cough stick every week or so wouldn't kill anybody. A source crossed his mind.

He tracked down David inside the boys' room, fresh from his shower.

"You got any Bloodweeds? I'll buy one off you."

David yanked a half-shirt over his wet hair. "What makes you think I touch that stuff?"

"Because I know you, and I know the people you hang with. I know Hodin Seil supplies you guys with beer behind the school on Friday nights at a twenty-five percent markup, and I know you were probably hanging with Galaxy Remillard the night he got nailed for putting graffiti on the walls of the Kilon'at Street pedestrian tunnel; I know how you spell. If you're into speedbiking and drinking, at least one of you is thinking you're solar because you're carrying a box of Bloods."

David grinned and shook his head. "Damn it all! Never could fool you or Viktor. Vik could see right through me. I only got one left. I was saving it for when we get back home – I doubt they import them, and I don't know what's good there yet. Keep your money. I'm still in awe about this morning. I'll share. Be out in five."

They sat in the sand, relaxing against the far side of the parked flyer, hidden from the house. Faint light from the front windows eased the impenetrable blackness of Navaran night just enough to make each other out. The thin atmosphere caused things to burn a little slower, but they were in no rush. Sand bugs were biting, but after a day like this, they weren't worth whacking at. The stress of the day faded with the thin, dark-blue smoke.

A voice rang out by the nose of the flyer. "What'cha doing?"

David almost swallowed the cigarette. He fumbled it, dropped it in his lap, then finally hid it in the sand behind his back.

Dmitri clutched his chest. "*Na koi herr*, Ekaterina! You took ten years off my life, sneaking up like that!"

"Ten more than the ten Val will take if she catches you with that cigarette?" Katya laughed and dropped down cross-legged next to them. She pulled the elastic tie out of her hair, slipped it over her wrist, and shook her hair loose. "Well, don't waste it. Pass it over."

"Girls don't smoke," Dmitri said. David found the smouldering cigarette, handed it to her, and the boys watched their sister in amazement. She didn't even cough!

"Of course we do," she said, handing back the bloodweed. "You don't buy into that 'My body is a temple and I must keep it holy' crap do you? You think I'm the only girl with brothers? Girls think and do the same things guys do, I hate to tell you.

"I'll make you a bet that even with everything that's happened today, *I* can top everyone for causing the biggest problem this family ever thought of, all of you so-called Bad Boys included."

"You're on!" David said.

"Deal," Dmitri agreed. Katya wasn't prissy, but she couldn't be called wild, either. Kat was just a naturally good person. There was no way she could top his mess.

"Pay up," she said, patting the sand. "Three credits."

"I don't have cash!" David wailed.

Dmitri dug into his pocket. "I'll cover you."

Katya leaned in closer. "Now, I've never told a soul about this, except for the person who helped me through it. If you want to confirm it, you'll have to ask her, but so help me, I better not *ever* hear it repeated otherwise. Seriously! Top secret. I'm trusting you guys on this, above and beyond the stars. Swear!"

"Sarah's the one with the big mouth, not us," Dmitri promised, crossing his heart. "We swear."

"About three years ago," Kat began, "I was kind of seeing this older guy ..."

Dmitri thought back. "Is that the guy who wouldn't leave you alone? Kept following you?"

"That's the one. Anyway, I said I'd be at Terra Century's, but we left and went to a party somewhere else, thinking we were so incredibly cosmic for sneaking off. Must have been a month or two before semester break. I'd seen this gorgeous guy in the halls, talked to him a few times, and here he was at this party. He was a senior I think, seventeen or eighteen. So we're talking, and drinking, and then we start making out, and *drinking*," she emphasized. "That's what you did at a party, wasn't it? Father drank, and Mother drank wine, so why not, you know? Only kids didn't drink.

"So we kissed some, drank some, and so on. I was in way over my head, but I was too drunk to get out of it. I'd never had to deal with that kind of thing before – drunk or sober. I got myself ... forced into a bad situation."

David's face screwed up in a look of disbelief. "You mean he and you – ?"

Katya shrugged. "I was fourteen. I'd never been drunk before. I didn't want to, I really didn't, but I didn't think you could say no at that point, and he was very – *insistent*. What did I know back then? I didn't want to yell or something and have a roomful of people see me and laugh. I let him do it."

Dmitri looked away, anger evaporated by the compelling, subliminal scent of bloodweed. "If we'd known that, Alexei and me and Vik would've killed him for you."

"It gets better!" Kat held up a hand while she took her turn with the cigarette. "Remember during break that year I begged and begged Mother to let me spend the two weeks with Valeria at school?"

"Yeah. Guess who got stuck watching everybody instead," Dmitri grumbled. "Vlad got a stomach bug and puked like a fountain for two days. Sergei got it, then 'Byeta, then *me*."

"It wasn't just to get away from here," Katya confided. She peeked over the nose of the flyer to make absolutely sure they were alone. "*I terminated a pregnancy!*"

David's mouth fell open. "No fucking way!"

"No, that's just how it started. Val was really good about it, though. She took care of me. Told me how stupid I was – and how lucky. She didn't tell." Katya stirred circles in the sand with her finger. "Can you imagine what Father would have done if he found out? Pregnant at fourteen?"

"No wonder you freaked when Father... *You* know...," Dmitri reflected.

Katya snorted. "Talk about a bad flashback! Thank the Gods for Viktor, or Sarah and I could have been roommates at the Funny Farm."

"Last round," said David, passing the stub to his brother. "She's as good as dead."

Dmitri leaned against the flyer, elbows on his knees. He rubbed a pinch of sand between his fingers and watched the shadow sprinkle darkly to the ground, mesmerized. "That's about the only way I can see today being worse. Can you imagine if I walked in there right now and said, 'Oh Val, by the way, I'm going to be a father.' "

David giggled and made a rude comment, but Katya looked sad. "But you *did* do that to her, Dimi. You left the house this morning a boy, and came back responsible for a child. Think about it."

"I don't want to think about it. That's why I came out here."

Katya buried the last of their evidence in the sand. "Anyway... Now you know why I tend to support Val's judgment. Val can be a real life saver if you give her a chance. If you stay out of her way, let her recover, she'll pull you out of this, too. Just give her time."

"Yeah. You win, Kat. That would have been the biggest problem ever."

"But it never caused trouble because no one knew, so it doesn't count," David reasoned.

"Let her have it," Dmitri said, even more depressed by Katya's confession. "It caused her more trouble than anything we ever did." All the times he'd wished he'd gotten that far with a girl... He'd never thought about it from the girl's point of view, never given a thought about the fatherhood risk. That just wasn't supposed to happen.

Brightness blinded them from the direction of the house. Someone had activated the perimeter floodlights.

"Val's coming," Katya warned, peering over the flyer. "Remember, you guys promised!" She snatched her prize.

Val came around the back of the craft. "So this is where everyone went. What are they up to, Kat?"

"Nothing!" Kat assured her. "We were just shooting the breeze. It's nice out tonight."

Val gazed at the cloudless starry sky. "That it is. David, didn't you shower already? You'll be covered with sand again. It's time you went in, anyway."

"I'm going," he grunted, rising.

"I should hit the shower myself." Katya stretched and stood up, brushing sand from her legs.

Dmitri steeled himself for the inevitable criticism. He wasn't disappointed.

"Is Sarah in bed?" Valeria asked curtly.

"Yeah, I sent her a while ago."

"Do you know for a fact? In hers, or Vlad's?"

"One of them."

"Don't you think you should check?"

"I'm going," he muttered, and climbed to his feet.

He lay in bed, lifeless, immobilized by the crushing day and the self-pity in which he coated himself. *Just a screw-up, that's what he was.* The way Dmitri'd had it figured, it should have been easy. Sure, maybe he *had* meant to irritate Val at some level, but not like this. Nothing like this. *Man, oh man.* At least he was in his own bed, not some City Security holding cell. The thought didn't bring as much comfort as he'd hoped. And as if he didn't feel lousy enough, Katya had to go and tell that story.

*Was she joking?*

He didn't think so – why would you make up a story like that? – but he wished she was. Come to think of it, he'd never seen her drink at *any* party he'd been to with her. Poor Kat. Major trouble and unable to tell anyone, and then keep it a secret for three years. He thought back to himself at fourteen.

Fourteen.

*Shit.*

Even good ol' Viktor couldn't have fixed that. Dimi'd certainly think twice next time he considered doing more than just making out with a girl. There were enough kids at home without him making more. He'd cleaned enough babies for one lifetime.

He tried to imagine Sarah coming to him and saying she was pregnant. *How ridiculous was that!* That she'd created life in a bio dish, yes, but pregnant? No – unless she did it herself as a lab experiment, and then panicked because it worked. But Sarah kissing a boy? She was more likely to beat him up. Any suitors would have to stand in line behind Vlad. Besides, if Sarah was fourteen, he'd be... twenty-one! Too out of orbit to think about.

He fought it, hated himself more for it, but finally buried his face in his pillow and wept. Not just messed up his life, but Sarah's, too, the one he swore to protect. *How long could she keep up her brave face?* Anyone could see she was forcing it for his sake. *Who was taking care of whom?* Galina was so right!

A soft tapping at his door interrupted his misery. He wiped his nose on the corner of his pillow and looked at his chronometer. One-twelve. "Yeah?"

"It's me, Dim," came David's low voice. "You still up? I wanted to talk."

Dmitri would have liked to talk, but he didn't want to be seen like this. Not by David. Outside of funerals, it was the first time he could remember crying without Father's assistance. "Not tonight, Dave. I'm kinda crashed."

"Okay. I'll catch you in the morning, I guess."

Dmitri put his head down. His mind ran in rotten circles, reciting the list of crimes he'd committed in the name of decency, and the punishments Val would be sure to inflict. *If only Viktor were home!*

He wiped his face with his hands, and fetched a cup of water from the bathroom. Locking his door, he rummaged in the packed carry bag. He found the confiscated bottle of sleeping pills, took two, and lay down to await their effects.

# * Twenty-six *

Dmitri awoke to an urgent pounding on his door. He squinted at the time. He'd overslept by two hours. His head dropped heavily onto the pillow.

"Come on, Dimi!" Sarah pleaded, banging. "Valeria's leaving in *five minutes,* and she won't let me go unless you're with me!"

Dmitri dragged himself to the door and opened it, rubbing his eyes into focus. *"Shto?"*

Sarah's face fell. "You're not dressed yet? Val's leaving for town and she won't wait. Hurry!"

"Gimme three minutes." *Pants*, he coached himself as he shut the door. *I need pants.*

The flyer's emergency beacon sounded its harsh squawk as Dmitri emerged from the house, shoes in hand, shirt around his neck, hair uncombed, robe on his arm.

Val wrestled to pull Sarah off the switch. "In the back, Sarah. Get in a seat."

Dmitri found space in the third row.

"You look hung over," Katya informed him.

"Just tired," he sighed, crawling into his shirt. "I didn't sleep much."

"I don't think anyone did."

"Split up?" Galina asked Val after they'd left the flyer in the parking bay for an underground shopping plaza. "I can take the boys with me, get haircuts, and get the food you wanted for the trip."

"That's probably best," Valeria agreed, stopping at a market stand. "Meet back in two hours? Don't be late, Dmitri. I won't wait this time." She flipped through a stack of woven wallhangings. "I should find something Navaran to give Grandmother as a gift. Keep an eye out, Kat."

"Val! Val, look!" Sarah ran up, dragging a large, khaki-colored knapsack half as tall as herself. "This is just what I need! My things won't fit in my carry bag. This one's parsecs bigger! Please, can I get it? It holds up to thirty-five kilos. I could even carry Vlad in it."

"Sarah, you can't lift thirty-five kilos."

"Yes I can! And that's just what it's rated for, not how much I'll put in it. Please?"

Val looked the bag over. The sturdy fabric was double-stitched and reinforced on all the corners and stress points. "I'd love to, Sarah," she answered extra-sweetly, "but you'll have to ask your brother. That's his business now."

"Mine?" Dmitri said from the back of the group. "I don't care what you buy her."

"*You* are financially responsible for her, Dmitri. Not me, not Gal. It's *your* problem."

"Crying out loud! Let me see it," he grumbled.

Sarah handed it to him with reservation. "It's got lots of room. You could put some of your stuff in there, too, if you want. I'll carry it for you."

"I don't care. What else are you going to want?"

"That's all," she said, hugging him. "Thank you!"

"Come with me," he told her when he finished the transaction. "I need breakfast."

"We can't stay with Vlad?"

"We'll catch up later. Come on, I'm starving."

Sarah waggled her fingers sadly at Vlad, waiting in the middle of the walkway. He waved back, crestfallen, and ran to catch up with Galina. Divided, after all. Maybe this *wasn't* going to be the best idea.

The short flight home, and all through lunch, Sarah and Vlad had a relentless case of the giggles every time they looked at David. Even Sergei couldn't help a grin, since he alone knew David had planned to do it. To Valeria's utter horror, David had his thick hair chopped short on the sides and spiky across the entire top, except for three long strands that hung down into his eyes. Galina kept apologizing to her twin.

"Shut up!" David yelled at the younger two, stabbing his lunch with his fork. "Shows how much you know about style!"

Sarah burst out giggling. "You – you look like an angry hedgehog! Can I pet it?"

Vladimir slid off his chair with a bump, laughing so hard he couldn't breathe.

"Knock it off, both of you!" Val ordered harshly. "Dmitri, quiet her down."

"Now, Sarah," Dmitri said, imitating Valeria and waving his finger, "You stop this instant. David's hair isn't funny. It's – It's the pet we never had!" He dissolved into laughter.

The entire table laughed except David, who kicked his brother under the table, and Valeria, whose jaw clenched in anger. Galina's shoulders shook, though she hid her smile behind her hand.

"*This* is exactly the kind of maturity I was talking about," Valeria glared.

"Honestly, Dave, I like it," Dmitri told him later, lounging across a couch. "It shows off your ear a lot more."

Two years ago, Father had let David pierce his ear, and he wore two small gold hoops in it, one at the top and one at the bottom. Father himself had two earrings in each ear, two hoops in the left and a hoop and his initials always in the right.

Dmitri pulled on his ear. "What do you think? Should I get one?"

"I think you better quit while you're ahead, or Val will stab you in your sleep," David replied, half-serious.

They could hear the twins in the kitchen, going over their pages of lists and last-minute details. Except for attitude, they sounded identical, too.

"And the extra baby things?"

"Blue bag. B for blue, B for Baby."

"In Standard, maybe, but not in Russian. How did you label everything?"

"Both. The main scanner tags are in Standard, then I added a second label underneath in Russian."

"That makes sense. Did you pack an emergency bag? I expect Vlad to be spacesick as soon as we hit orbit."

"The basics are in a black zippered bag in my carry on. These are the boarding passes?"

"Yeah. Count them again. There should be eight."

"...*Shest, syem, vosyem*. All here. You're really going through with this? I still think it's rather extreme. Where are you going to keep them?"

"Pffft! At this rate, in my shirt." Valeria laughed briefly. "I'm too afraid I'll lose them."

Dmitri walked to the doorway. "What do you mean, eight tickets? Last I counted, there were ten of us."

Val batted her eyes. "Are you going with us, Dmitri? You never told me. I would have picked up your passes for you while I was at the ticket office."

Dmitri's ears weren't hearing right. "You didn't get flight tickets for me and Sarah when you bought those?"

"No. I had no idea what your plans were. You're an adult. I figured you'd bought your passes. I guess we must have had a

320

miscommunication."

*"VAL!"*

The sound carried half a kilometer into the desert. A herd of feet came running to see why.

Dmitri stormed over and gripped the back of a chair. "Goddamn you, Val! This is going too far! I've had it with your snotty digs and insults! I *get* the point! I am *NOT* ready for this responsibility! You *WIN*! I *ADMIT* it! But you are *NOT STRANDING* us here!" He banged the chair on the *not's*.

Val remained brutally calm. "No one has stranded you anywhere, Dmitri. Flights leave Shir P'an every day. You're free to leave any time you want."

Dmitri's hold on his temper stretched impossibly thin, then vaporized. In a rush of fury, he hauled his sister off her chair and slammed her against the cabinets in a manner done to him so many times before.

Galina screamed. *"'Mitya!"*

*"You can't leave us here!"* he shouted, banging Valeria against the cabinets. "It's bullshit and you know it! You knew damned well we were going with you!"

*"Let go of me!"* Valeria hissed. "Or so help me, I'll have you arrested, and this time Galina won't save you!" When he didn't move, she seized him by the throat. Dmitri was strong and agile, but Valeria had thirteen centimeters and eighteen kilos on him. She shoved his jaw upward while hooking his leg with her foot, knocking him backwards, but he pulled her over with him. They rose to their feet, screaming.

"Shouldn't we help Galina?" Sergei asked David at the kitchen doorway. "This is out of control. Who's in charge of Val?"

"I'm not sure," David said.

Vlad pulled on Sarah. "Come on. I'm sick of listening to them fight. Let's go."

Sarah watched from the safe distance of the living room. *If Dmitri could get that mad at Val, what might he do to her? What if Vlad or Katya wasn't around?* She let Vlad haul her away.

Vlad and Sarah hid in the boys' closet, where, through the doors, only the loudest noises came through. The closet seemed spacious now that all the clothes and containers and shoes were gone. Soon Sergei and Nikky joined them.

"There's a lot of words out there Nikky probably shouldn't hear," Sergei justified himself. He shut the closet and sat down.

"Who's winning?" Vlad whispered.

"I don't know. It's pretty bad. David broke into the utility room and disabled the commlink. He's afraid Val will turn Dimi in."

"I'll bet she's being this mean because she doesn't want me back," Sarah concluded wretchedly.

Fifteen minutes passed before they heard Dmitri's door slam, followed by a swarm of unintelligible cursing and the sound of something being smashed.

David's voice came louder from the hallway, fist banging the door. "Come on, 'Mitya! Let me in!"

" – *alone!*" seeped through the thick wall.

"Just talk with me! We'll figure something out. It's not over yet."

They couldn't make out Dmitri's reply. The foursome froze as the bedroom door opened, then slammed hard. Vlad clamped his hand over Nikky's mouth.

"Are you little trolls in here?"

Sergei opened a closet door.

"You can come out now," David sneered. "*You* sure as shit weren't any help. You should have at least had your ass out there, Sergei."

"It's not like I could have stopped them," Sergei said weakly.

"Yeah, well, you better start thinking fast with that big brain of yours. Since Val couldn't use the comm, she took off in the flyer. She'll probably bring the law back with her. She studied those kinds of things, remember?"

Sarah's eyes grew wide. "She can't! What do we do?"

"That's what I said, you idiot!" David shouted. "*Think!*"

"Who started it?" Sergei asked.

"I don't know. Supposedly Val didn't buy enough flight passes for the trip. She's exactly two short."

Nikky's lip shivered. "We can't go on the spaceship? Why? David, why? I packed my toys. I wanna fly in the stars to see the snowy place."

Sarah understood. "I don't believe it," she declared with confidence. "Not even Val is that mean. She said it to get Dimi mad, and he was stupid enough to fall for it. Val told me, she *promised* me, that she wouldn't split anybody up. We're all staying together. Remember? How many times has she said that?"

"She promised she'd never split us up," Vlad echoed. "Those very words."

"Yeah, well, just in case, maybe you better get used to the idea of staying with Dimi in lock-up. He grabbed her more than once, and she wasn't too happy about it," David said to Sarah. "Or she'll put him in lock-up and steal you back."

Galina opened the door, harried-looking and short on patience. "David, whatever you did to the comm, fix it. I need it *now!*"

David handed her a two-pronged piece of colored plastic. "Primary fuse. You probably know where it goes."

"Thank you," she sighed, shutting the door as she ran out.

*"You!"* Dmitri slammed the door open so hard it hit the wall and bounced shut again.

"You!" He pounced on Sarah and grabbed her shoulders so fast she didn't have time to retreat. "Did she tell you anything about this? Not to worry, it was just to punish me, it was just a joke? She has two more tickets she won't tell me about?"

"Stop it!" Vlad yelled, pulling on him. "You're scaring her!"

Sarah *was* scared. Dimi looked so wild, breathless and red-eyed and shouting. She hadn't seen a look that desperate since Father misplaced a grant proposal the day of the deadline. They'd scattered like birds, that day. She didn't fully understand the problem, had too little information to make a conclusion, but she could guess at the hypothesis. Everything in life came down to quantum mechanics: push versus pull, how fast, what direction, number of particles participating, factor in time and relative – *relatives* – dimensions in space, one catalyst to set it off, and the result could be a great big Bang. Like now. This was her fault, for hating Rangler so much, for hating to be away from home. It all came down to her.

"No! No! She's making it up! She wouldn't *do* that to us. She promised!"

Dmitri released her. He ran a shaking hand through his hair. "Fuck, fuck, fuck, fuck, *FUCK!*" he shouted, punching at the air.

"Don't say that in front of Nikky." Sarah rolled across Sergei's bed behind her and knelt out of his reach.

Dmitri paced in a frenzy. "What am I gonna to do? What am I gonna do? All I meant was to help her!"

David acted unusually strong and calm. "We'll figure something out. Pack Sarah on the ship with my ticket, and I'll stay behind with you. Or better yet, what is it, thirteen kilometers to town? We can walk that in two, three hours tops. Leave before dawn, we can be in town and on a shuttle to the spaceport before Val even realizes we're gone. We'll beat her back home. We know we're going to Minsk. How many Ivanovs can there be in Minsk? We'll catch up."

"You gonna carry luggage thirteen kilometers?"

"You can have the pack you bought me," Sarah offered. "It holds thirty-five kilos."

"Take what we can carry. Have Sergei make sure the rest gets boarded with everyone else's stuff. Val won't notice. You got a better idea?"

Dmitri fell back onto David's bed hopelessly. "That's assuming I'm still *here* tonight! Who knows who Val will bring back with her. I am so cooked! I can't believe she'd actually leave us."

"Maybe she changed her mind and went to get your boarding passes," Vladimir said.

David didn't have patience for Vlad on a good day. "Hey Vlad, why don't you go put your head in the sanitary and look for your brain?"

"It's not like I can even hide anywhere," Dmitri whined.

"Well, they can't run us all in," David said. "We'll think of something if we have to. We know how to stick together."

"If it would help," Sarah said quietly, "I can go back to Rangler."

"That's not exactly a place you knock on the door and see if they have a vacancy," David goaded. "How stupid is that?"

"I can do it," she insisted. "All I need is something sharp. It's just mind over matter – "

Dmitri was off the bed in a second. He dove headfirst across Sergei's bed and caught her by the wrist, twisting her arm up until he breathed in her face.

"Don't *EVER* say that! Don't ever *DO* that! You pull crap like that on me and so help me, I'll pound you to a bloody mess, Sarah! I'm in this shit because I was keeping you *OUT* of the damned hospital, remember? *Remember*?!"

Sarah shook. "I'm sorry! I just thought it would solve your problem." He released her, and she scrambled onto Nikky's bed to curl into a protective ball.

Dmitri buried his face in Sergei's bedcover. "I'm sorry, Sar. It's not that I don't appreciate the offer. You'll be on that ship, with or without me, don't worry. Just don't pull anything stupid, okay?"

Nikky flew into the room several hours later. "Val's home!"

Dmitri clambered from the floor where they played cards half-heartedly. "Is she alone?"

"*Da.* Just Val."

"Well, go back! Tell me if anybody else comes." He pushed Nikky out.

Dimi listened at the door while everyone sat motionless, straining to hear anything. The silence grew more unbearable with each passing second.

"I'll go out and see," Sergei said at last.

He returned, as confused as the rest of them. "Nobody's out there. I think they're all in the bedroom."

Dmitri dared to poke his head out the door, then stepped into the hall.

"What's that?" David asked, pointing to Dmitri's door. A sheet of colored paper, covered with print, stuck to it at eye level. It carried an official seal.

Dmitri took it down and began to read.

"What's it say?"

"It's an order of restraint," Dmitri frowned. "... No contact or harassment, verbal, physical, or electronic.... Keep a distance of not less than ten meters at all times... for a period of twenty-six hours, or action may be taken, including but not limited to incarceration for not more than fourteen days.

"There *is* a higher power in the Universe!"

Since Dmitri wasn't allowed near Valeria, they dined picnic-style on the floor of the living room. Where Sarah went, Vlad invariably followed, and Galina let Sergei go as well. Katya, independent now, joined them. David's eyes burned hatefully into Valeria.

"Go," she said with defeat. Nikky followed soon after.

They were determined to show Val she hadn't upset them, and they put on a good show, describing Earth for Nikky, remembering what interstellar flight was like, laughing at the latest stories Dmitri had heard.

Now Katya came in as Sarah pulled on her pajamas for the very last time on Navara. "I have something for you." She sat on the bed, one hand behind her back.

"Kat, what's Val really doing?" Sarah said, tugging her shirt down. "She was kidding about being two tickets short, wasn't she? We're all going tomorrow, right? *Right?*"

Katya's face wasn't as reassuring as she'd hoped. "If I knew, I'd tell you, Sar, but I honestly don't. Am I worried? Yes, but Val's not saying a word. Forget that for now. I bought you a present today." She handed Sarah a light-blue case, lumpy and heavy for its size. "Open it."

Sarah slid the fastener back. Crammed inside were an assortment of bottles, jars, and little packaged items. She looked at Katya quizzically.

"It's girl stuff, silly!" Katya laughed, taking things out. "Look! I got you your own pen of that nailpolish you liked. Here's another – *Neptune Frost*," she said, holding up a glowing blue tube. "And smell this!" She unscrewed the cap to a bottle. "Isn't this pretty? It's soap. And here's skin stuff. Make sure you coat your face with it every day. The cold will peel your skin just as bad as the sun. I know Dmitri will never think of these things. Some day you may decide boys are even more fun if you act like a girl."

Sarah rolled her eyes. "I am a girl. How can I not act like one?"

"You know perfectly well what I mean, *Tom* Irina!" Katya tapped the tomboy's head with the tube of skin cream.

"You're talking like you won't be around if I decide to use these," Sarah said, wary.

"Well, I do hope to be in university in the fall..." Katya tried, but she could see Sarah didn't buy it. "Okay. I'm afraid of what Val might do. But I swear, I'll do everything I can. Don't worry about it, not one bit, you hear?"

"I'm not, really. Dmitri's doing it enough for both of us. Val promised me over and over she won't break us up," Sarah insisted, faith weakened but intact.

Katya held her close. "I'm sure you're right."

Sarah was nearly asleep when Val came in and turned the lights on to half-power.

"Sarah, I want to talk to you. I want you to know that I know you're not responsible for any of this. I'm sorry you have to be caught in the middle. I know you don't trust me right now, but please, trust me on this, okay? Dmitri's got to learn this lesson by himself. No one can tell him what to do, because he's not about to listen. I do have faith in him, I do. I know he can figure it out, he just has to grow up and let himself do it. I know he can take pretty good care of you. I'm not worried about that. Trust me, this will work out right.

"But you're going to have to be strong, Sar, hear me? Don't collapse on me. Once he figures it out, go with him. You may jump to conclusions, but you're smart enough to tell right from wrong. That's why I want to give you these." She opened a magnetic envelope she held.

"Whatever you do, Sarah, *don't lose* any of these! Lose your luggage, but not these. Keep them safe with you at all times." She held up a black plastic computer card. "This here is your ID. Blue is medical records, and school records are all on this striped one. This one here is your interstellar passport. This yellow one is your bank card. Yes, *yours*. I cashed in your insurance form. There are six thousand credits available. I put a string on the card – wear it around your neck, save it for dire emergencies only. *Don't* give it to your brother, whatever you do;

don't even tell him you have it. *Desperate emergency only.* Got that? When we get to Earth, give it back to me, and I'll hold onto it for you. I don't want you to be caught without cash of your own if you need it.

"These here," Val said, laying two white cards on Sarah's lap, "are scripts for your medications, just in case you lose your pharmacy card. I refilled them for you again today, so you should have plenty, but if something happens to them you can get these filled. This one here," she laid a printout on the pile, "is where we're going. Here's grandmother Ivanov's address in Minsk, Uncle Tomas' office in New York, and the direct comm lines for both, all right here."

Sarah tried her best not to jump to conclusions – yet. *"Val!* You promised me – you *promised*! – that everyone was staying together and we weren't splitting up. Val! Why give me all this if we're staying together?"

Val came back just as serious, folding her long legs to kneel by the bed. "Bear with me, Sar. I asked you to be strong. The fact is, we may have to split up – don't *panic*, Sarah! Okay? It's just for the trip – two days at the most. Can you do that? Can you live with Dmitri for just two days? We will all be back together as a group when we land on Earth. I swear with all my heart."

Sarah felt ill, but she had to stay on Val's good side if the rift with Dmitri was ever to heal. "I guess so."

Val patted her knee through the blanket, giving a tired smile. "I know you can. If you get lost, or separated, or if you're just plain scared, call me at one of those numbers. I'll come and get you. Understand?"

"I think so," Sarah lied, eyeing the pile in her lap as if it might poison her.

"Call me – talk to Vlad – three times a day, if you want. I'll get the messages as soon as we arrive. Let me know how you're doing. I do care about you, Sarah, no matter what you think. Promise?"

"Yeah."

"Good. We'll get everything straightened out after we get back to Earth. You'll see. Now put these back in the envelope and put it somewhere safe. Get some sleep. Tomorrow's a busy day."

But sleep was a rare commodity for everyone that night.

# \* Twenty-seven \*

Tomas Ivanov gathered his determination and entered his mother's private suite.

Andrea Ivanov swallowed her bite of dinner in surprise. "Tomas! No one told me you were coming home. I would have held dinner for you. Tatiana!" she called to the wait staff. "Call down to Marya; tell her Master Tomas is home and will need dinner."

"No! Don't bother, Tatiana, please. Tea would be fine, though, thank you."

"Of course, Mr. Ivanov, sir. I shall bring it immediately."

Tomas kissed his mother on each cheek. "I didn't tell anyone, Mamá."

He dropped into a chair, hiding his exhaustion. Mamá was a strong woman despite her tiny stature; strong in will, strong in ideas, strong in opinion. He wasn't sure he could be stronger, and he needed to be stronger.

"What brings you home so unexpectedly, Tomas?"

"What if I had information that would blow you off your chair? Information you may or may not want to hear?"

"You're going to marry that Romanian woman," Mamá sniffed. "That Empress or whatever she is."

"Ilona's a Countess, Mamá. Countess. No. Something much bigger than that." Tatiana brought him a steaming cup of tea, and several light biscuits.

"Don't play games with me, Tomas. I have neither time nor patience. Just spit it out. What are you up to?"

Tomas took a deep breath.

"I'vebeenintouchwithMaryana'sfamilyandI'minvitingtenofherchildrentocomeandstaywithusindefinitely." He crammed an entire biscuit into his mouth.

Andrea Ivanov's silver fork clinked onto her plate. She pressed a hand to her small bosom. "What?"

Tomas pointed apologetically to his overstuffed mouth, and tried to chew.

"Did you say M… *Maryana*?" she whispered, as if her husband would hear her from beyond the grave.

Tomas nodded, and tried to sip his tea.

"Where is she? Is she coming with them? Did you... Did you say *ten* children?"

Tomas shook his head at the second sentence, nodded at the third.

"Tomas Severyan Fedorovitch! *Otvechai!*"

Tomas swallowed at last. "No, Mamá. I'm sorry to tell you, Maryana died shortly after Papa. Her children are currently parentless, and have nowhere to go. I told them they may come here."

"Tomas! My Maryana...? How could you do that without asking me! For *how* long? No! No, Tomas! I cannot have children about underfoot when I am hosting conferences! Have you lost your mind? I'm much too busy for that nonsense. *How* many children did you say?"

"Ten of thirteen."

Andrea sagged over her plate. "Dear God! Oh, Maryana!"

"They are your *grandchildren*, Mamá," Tomas reminded her mercilessly. "Your own offspring. How can you not wish to meet them?"

"What about their... *other parent.*" Madame Ivanova couldn't bring herself to say the 'F' word. "Is he dead, too?"

Tomas shook his head with a sigh. "No, and it could create a nightmare of a public-relations fiasco if we're not careful. That, uh, murder that spun Navara off its axis? It appears he was the, uh, onewhodidit." He grabbed another biscuit.

"PUT that in your mouth, Tomas, and it will be the last thing you ever eat in this house!" his mother commanded, and he placed it sheepishly next to his cup.

Mamá didn't move from her chair, but her attitude cast a shadow that seemed to build until it towered across the ceiling, sucking the light from the room.

"There will be no such visitors in this household, Tomas," Andrea Ivanov ordered with finality. "You will bring no such children here. You will not acknowledge them, you will not see them, you will not contact them. I will not have that incident destroying everything Fyodor and I worked to build. Any daughter of mine would know not to breed like a peasant. I have no daughter, I have no grandchildren, and that is final."

"I'm sorry, Mamá, but they're already en route," he lied. "Anyway, I will take full responsibility for them. I promise to keep them out of your way and under control until they get settled back on Earth."

"No, Tomas."

"I'll keep them in my apartment."

Mamá's thin nostrils widened as if she smelled a foul stench. "This is a house of distinction, not a kennel for homeless pets. I give quite generously to the Children's Welfare League; it's time they paid us back for our charity."

"I'll put them up in the guest house."

"Unsupervised? Presidents and Emissaries have stayed in that house! It contains a small fortune in artistic and historic treasures. They'll have the furniture destroyed in a week, and the walls within two. *No*, Tomas, and that is my final word."

"It's too late, Mamá," Tomas insisted with a helpless smile. "I've already sealed the deal."

He took a large bite of biscuit.

# * Twenty-eight *

" **U**p, Katya!" Sarah sang out in the morning, tying her desert boot. "Val wants the sheets." She took her giant backpack, half-filled with all her possessions *and* two changes of clothes, slung one of the straps over her shoulder, and struggled to grip the three large cases that held her other clothes and belongings. Sarah was big, Sarah was strong, but she couldn't lift them. Her pack alone weighed nine kilos. Leaning to the side, she lifted one case, dragged the second across the floor by its handle, and pushed the third with her foot. She made slow but steady progress, reaching the living room several minutes later.

Val snatched up any remaining loose items. They would eat breakfast in Shir P'an, to be on the orbital shuttle by mid-morning. Galina directed the younger boys in packing the flyer. Dmitri was distinctly absent.

*Fat chance he would oversleep today!* Sarah ran and banged on his door. "Are you up yet?" she shouted. "Hurry!"

"Getting dressed," came a lucid reply.

Katya rushed out to the main room tying her hair back, her overstuffed bag slung over her shoulder.

"Katya, bring me all your bed things," Valeria ordered, stuffing pillows into a shipping crate. "Sarah, go help her."

Dmitri came out and dropped his things at the end of the baggage pile. David and Sergei returned for more, but David stopped.

"Don't put those there," Val warned Dmitri. "They're not part of our luggage." She picked his bags up two at a time and moved them away, then placed Sarah's next to his. "Back up; you're too close."

Dmitri's eyes narrowed, but he took two steps back. "You're really going through with this? You're going to abandon us here?"

"Adults don't get abandoned, Dmitri. Sarah has a guardian – such as it is."

"I said I was sorry. What more do I have to do?"

Sarah carried in an armload of sheets. Val crammed them into the crate. Sarah glanced from Dimi to Val, read the worry in David's face, and decided to wait, too.

David tried the polite and proper way first. "Val? Take Sarah and let me stay. It's not fair to –"

"Absolutely not. I can't trust you unsupervised, David. The two of you alone? You'd spacejack the ship! Keep loading, or we'll be late."

Sarah noticed her luggage moved, and hauled it back to the shrinking pile.

"You won't even give us a ride in?" Dimi asked.

"We're overloaded as it is. There isn't room."

"Sarah, there's more...." Katya walked in with her arms piled high with blankets, and stopped. She surveyed the tense scene before her. "I'll get them." She dropped the blankets in the crate.

Valeria moved Sarah's bags back against the wall.

Dmitri crossed his arms. "So what am I supposed to do?"

"That's up to you." Val put Katya's linens into the crate, closed and sealed it. "You're an adult. You figure it out."

Vlad came in for the last case, save Sarah and Dmitri's. He made hopeful eyecontact with Sarah, but his shoulders drooped at her wordless reply, and he walked slower.

Her bags had moved again. Sarah lined them up, and with a determined heave, pushed them, all together, across the floor. She held the straps to her carry bag and sat down on the cases between Val and Dmitri.

"We're going," she announced. "We stick together and we take care of our own, just like always."

"Is that everything, Kat?" Val asked. "Sarah, I already talked to you about this."

"Bedrooms are clear," Katya replied. "Beds, drawers, and closets all empty."

"Grab the baby and put her in the flyer, then." Nikky and Marina raced room to room screeching and clapping, laughing at the echoes they created.

Katya laid a hand on Dmitri's shoulder as she walked by.

"Good luck," she managed to say. She stood on tiptoe to give him a peck on the cheek. "I'll be waiting for you."

Dmitri closed his eyes briefly and swallowed, nodding.

Kat dropped down behind Sarah and squeezed her tight. "Be good, Sarah. I'll see you in a couple of days, okay? Go easy on Dimi. He feels just as bad as you do."

Sarah stiffened against the contact. *None of this was real. It was only real if she let it be real.* "It doesn't matter. We're all going together. We stay *together*."

"Be good," Katya repeated. She kissed Sarah on the cheek and went to find Marina.

David brought the boys in as Galina fought the cargo hatch to close.

"That's everything but this stuff, Val," Sergei said.

"That's *everything.*" Val stuck the shipping label on the crate before her. Movers would come later for the two crates and the furniture.

Vladimir sat on the suitcases with Sarah, silent and trembling. He moved to hold her hand, but Sarah dug into her shoulder pack instead.

"Here," she said to Sergei, holding out one of the books she'd packed. "You can read this one on the flight. It's full of elves and mysticism and stuff. The third holoart is really beautiful."

"Thanks," Sergei said, taking the thick volume. "I'll start it as soon as we hit orbit. We can talk about it when you get in."

Valeria rushed, taking the baby from Katya and following her to the flyer. "Let's go, boys. Time is short."

"'Bye, 'Mitri," Sergei said, downcast. They slapped hands high, then crossed arms and gripped hands.

"See ya, Serg."

Dmitri felt strangely rooted where he stood. Time seemed to have stopped. Nothing seemed real. He could see out the open door to Val trying to make Nikky sit down in the flyer. Katya was arguing with her; Dmitri couldn't hear what she said, but judging by the hand gestures, it wasn't something Val wanted to hear.

With Val outside, David came up to him. "It's not too late, Dim. I'll push to stay – lock myself in the bathroom, or run off or something. She can't wait too long or she'll miss the flight."

"Don't go getting yourself into trouble right off the launch. She'd just blame me anyway. We'll be okay. Take care of things for me 'til we get there."

"You're following us, aren't you?"

"Of course!" Dmitri promised. "What else am I gonna do with her? We can't stay here."

"David! Vlad! Let's go!" Val called.

"You better go."

David glanced outside. "When I'm damned good and ready."

Dmitri clapped a hand on his brother's shoulder. "Go on. And be nice to Vlad, huh? Just 'til we get back. You know he can't be away from Sarah that long. Don't make it worse on him. You got to take the lead. At least you know what not to do, thanks to yours truly."

"Dimi – ," David started, but couldn't finish. He looked at the floor, shifting his feet.

"I know." Dmitri studied his own feet. He raised a hand; David twisted his arm around his brother's, and they clasped hands in a bone-bending crunch.

"What the hell." Dmitri pulled his brother in close with his free hand. They pounded each other on the back, then quickly stepped apart, studying every mark and crack on the stone floor. "Get going, or Val will have your ass."

"Yeah. She's got it anyway. You're following, right?"

"Soon as we get to the city," Dmitri swore.

Sarah and Vlad whispered back and forth. David squatted before her. "Hey, Scout. Take care of him, okay? Keep him out of trouble – you know how he gets with that goddamned fucking mouth of his." David grinned, punching her lightly on the arm but glancing at his brother for approval nonetheless. "We'll miss you on the flight – can't raise hell right without the entire Fearsome Four. 'Member the flight here? Can't play cards without you unless Kat will fill in, but she isn't as good as you. We'll see you at the 'port." He chucked her under the chin.

"We're going with you," Sarah repeated with less conviction, but she threw her arms around his neck.

"Don't worry," he whispered, squeezing back. "He'll take good care of you."

Sarah's voice broke. *"I know!"*

"David Fyodor!" came an impatient call.

"I'll be there in a *fucking* minute, Val!" he yelled, a fiendish look lighting his face. "That'll give her something to fuss about. Come on, Vlad."

"I'm not going," Vlad replied. "Not without Sarah. Val said she wasn't splitting us up."

David shrugged. "Okay." As he left, he shouted, "Va-al! Vlad said to fuck yourself, he's not going." He winked to Dmitri as he walked away.

Val spouted brimstone as David climbed into the flyer. A moment later she climbed out, patience thin in the roasting sunshine.

"Let's go, Vlad," she snapped. She grabbed for his hand, but he wrapped his arms around Sarah, who did likewise to him.

"No! You're not being fair! You promised!"

Valeria pulled on his arm. "I'm sorry, Vlad. Things changed. Let go. You're being worse than Nikky."

"I'M NOT GOING!"

Time ticked. If the ground-flight lanes to the city were crowded... "Dmitri, get your half, please."

Dmitri found the first bright spot in the rotten day. "Gee, Val. You know I'd like to, but, I've still got eight more hours until I can come that close to you. Anyway, as I see it, your kid grabbed mine first."

If it hadn't been thirty-seven degrees outside, Valeria might actually have given off steam. She stalked back to the flyer.

Galina jogged in. "Come with me, please, Vlad? You're holding everyone up."

"Either Sarah comes or I stay!" he said with rare determination. "Val's breaking her promise."

"I'm sorry, Vlad. I'd change it if I could, but I can't right now. It's only for a couple days. You'll see. Come on," Galina said, pulling at him.

"*NYET!*"

Galina looked up beseechingly. "Please, Dmitri? I know you have every reason not to help me, but I'm asking anyway, for *my* sake. I don't agree with what Val is doing, not in the least, but I can't stop her now. Please, help me here."

"Only because you've been fair to me," Dmitri relented.

He gripped Sarah under her arms. "Come on, Sar, let him go. You'll see him soon."

"No!" Sarah growled.

"No!" Vlad repeated a half-second later, just as desperate. "Val promised!"

Galina held Vlad but didn't pull. She leaned close. "Listen, Dimi. All Val's looking for out of this is for you to show her you have some sense of responsibility. She sees it as a way to come out of this without losing her authority over the rest of the boys. You know as well as I do, David listens to you a lot more than he does to her. She depends on that. I checked the schedules; there's a flight leaving for Earth two hours after ours. Get a taxi, follow us out, you'll be only two hours behind us the whole way. You may land before we clear the baggage claim.

"When you get there, I'll take Sarah off your hands. Keep your Adult papers, or fold them up and I'll adopt you, too, for the year. I won't hold anything against you. Val gave Sarah the addresses; we'll be expecting you."

Dmitri gave her a nod. How she could be genetically identical to Val, and still be so nice, had him beat. "Thanks. I don't know if we'll make the same flight, but we'll be on one of them."

"Ready? Count of three. One, two, three – pull!"

Dmitri pulled hard on one, Galina pulled hard on the other, and the grip stretched.

*"You can't! You can't! We're a team!"* Vlad shouted. He'd never thrown a tantrum in his life, but Father was gone, and he was about to start.

Sarah started with a frantic shriek of "NO!", but she struggled harder to keep her grasp. She let go of Vlad and twisted her fingers in his clothes instead, pulling until the fabric looked ready to tear.

He hated to force her to do it, it wasn't fair, but Dimi slid his hands onto Sarah's and squeezed a nerve between the bones in her wrists. They'd taught him the trick at the hospital, as a way to disarm her should she be using a weapon on herself or someone else. He'd practiced on David, and he'd used it when Sarah had the corkscrew. The pressure on the nerves won out. Her grip eased against her will.

An unearthly scream split the thin air as Galina backed up and Dmitri seized Sarah around the waist. Vladimir had been physically torn from her, the one she'd shared a crib with the first two years of her life, the one she'd bathed with for three years, started school with – even if it was just for a day, the one who was even the exact same age for ten and a half weeks every year. The one who only hospital visits had managed to part.

He was gone.

They could see Galina drag him out to the flyer, screaming and fighting with a violence he'd never shown. Katya helped pull him in, crying along with him. Galina closed the bird's-wing door. The flyer shuddered as Val started the engines, locking them in. The levitators kicked in, and the overloaded craft wobbled and rose a half meter. The accelerator revved up, whining, and the flyer pulled away into the desert.

They were alone.

Sarah had been screaming the entire time, desperate to break Dmitri's hold. His arms were too high on her ribs for her to climb over them, and too far around her for her to break free.

"Shhh." They watched the flyer disappear until nothing remained but the wavering heat. Sarah sagged; the unending scream dropped to a series of high-pitched squawks. He released her once the flyer was out of sight. Sarah sank to her knees, catching her face in her hands just before it hit the floor, weeping. Dmitri attempted to console her, but she wailed until she coughed. He gave up.

He kicked the door shut against the growing inferno, anything to keep his own angry tears from falling. *"God damn you, Valeria!"* The shout reverberated through the hollow rooms. He grabbed the piano bench and threw it, watching it bounce off the sofa and roll onto the floor, unharmed. Unsatisfied, he marched to the kitchen and kicked the cabinets as hard as he could. The first kick opened the spring latch, and each subsequent kick slammed the door shut and back open with a loud bang.

After a minute of hard kicking, Dmitri was out of breath but his anger only slightly assuaged. He leaned against the doorway until he calmed, then dropped sideways in Father's chair, shoes over the side, eyes closed. It wasn't as if there were anyone to complain about it now. Sarah hadn't moved a millimeter, though her sobs were softer.

He sat and brooded.

A cargo carrier crawled by the window and stopped in the front yard, cutting short his stewing. There was a pause before a knock sounded at the door, and two men entered.

"Hello?"

Dmitri got up.

Hearing a strange voice, Sarah lifted her head. She scrambled across the floor to the wall, pulled up her knees, and watched from under the elbow of her crossed arms.

"I'm sorry," the man apologized. "We were told the place would be empty. We're here for the furniture. All chairs, couches, tables, no piano, no overhead lighting, no beds or drawers, two shipping crates," he read off his compad.

"Go ahead," Dmitri said in defeat. "Take my chair. We're supposed to be leaving anyway." He ran his hand over the back of it, then sat out of the way next to his sister as the men brought in anti-grav handles and attached them to the over-sized chair.

He poked Sarah with his elbow. "You should watch this. There goes a piece of our lives. How many nights did he sit in that chair, drinking himself to sleep? How fast could he jump out of it to come after you? I hated that chair, you know."

One purple eye scrutinized him from the bend of her arm, so he continued. "I hated that chair, just because he liked it. I hated the size of it, the way he sat in it, the way he drank in it, and I hated it for being a part of the bastard he was. Like the chair had anything to do with it." He gave a single chuckle.

The two sofas went next, the deadly triangular end tables balanced on top.

"Looks like we'll have breakfast at the piano," Dmitri said, watching the table go by. Sarah followed it with the one eye.

He put his arm out to pull her closer, but Sarah unfolded on him, scratching and pounding as hard as she could.

*"Don't you touch me!"* she screamed hoarsely. "You let them take him away! He wasn't going, but you helped take him away! *I hate you!"*

Dmitri pushed her away, but she didn't stop. Finally he grabbed her fist. "Knock it off!" He shoved her hand back and released it. "Like I wanted this to happen!" Sarah curled up and pounded her head several times with her fists.

He softened again, patting the floor close to him. "Come here." Sarah turned away.

"You're not the only one who lost a best friend today. Last I looked, I was left alone here, too. As far as I see it, we can either go through this ignoring each other and being completely miserable, or we can be friends, to prove to Val she can't beat us. Which would you prefer?"

Sarah ignored him for the longest pause. Without turning, she stretched out her hand. Dmitri accepted it.

*Truce.*

The mover held out the compad. "That's the last crate. Will you sign for it?"

Dmitri started to take the 'pad, then handed it back. "No. We're supposed to have left already. Let the owner worry about it."

"No problem," the man said as he left. "Have a pleasant day."

*Too late for that,* Dmitri thought to himself. "Hungry? I haven't had breakfast yet; how about you?" He pulled Sarah up. "Come on."

Her bottles of medicine sat on the empty counter. "Did you take these yet?"

Sarah shook her head.

"Don't you think you should?" He opened the bottle of liquid Antivox and sniffed it. Finding the scent agreeable, he put a finger over the opening, tipped it, then tasted his finger. He sucked on it, nodding.

"Not bad! A little carbonated water, some vodka, and..." He frowned, tasting the finger again. "...Lime juice!"

Sarah snatched the bottle away. "You are not *drinking* my medication." Pouring the liquid into the dispensing cap, she threw a yellow pill from the second bottle into the liquid and knocked it back. It went down with only one gag and a cough. She replaced the caps and glared at him again.

Dmitri punched the buttons on the replicator to call up breakfast. A minute went by, but the replicator door didn't open.

"Dammit! What now?" He tried again, stomach growling, with the same results. He ran a system check, and a red light glowed on the front of the panel.

A few more choice words, and Dmitri unfastened the large panel below the machine and slid it toward him. Attached to the back were

338

several large bins that recessed into the wall. All were empty.

"There's no matrix!" Dmitri exclaimed. "You bastard, Valeria! You couldn't even leave us something to eat? I'm *starving*! Now what do we do?"

He hiked himself up and sat on the counter. "Guess we'll have to eat in town, huh?"

Sarah nodded. "Don't we have to get going?"

The commlink beeped, interrupting her. Dmitri answered it.

"Sharinna!" he said with delight, his heart-breaking half-smile curling across his face.

The girl on the monitor blushed and smiled. Light-brown hair framed a pretty face. "Hi, Dimi! I wasn't sure if you'd left yet. I just wanted to say goodbye again."

"Not yet. In fact, I've got the house to myself right now. Can you come over?"

"I'm at school. I could come over tonight..."

"We'll be gone tonight," Sarah reminded him from the kitchen doorway. There was no privacy without the earset; the speakers echoed. "We're already late. Shouldn't you be calling for a taxi or something?"

Dmitri made a deadly face at her before turning back to the 'link, cheerful as could be. "Tonight? Tonight's fine! I mean, I have to babysit and all, but... We could make a party of it! Invite a couple people, have some fun. Give you something to remember me by."

"Dimi!" came a protest from the kitchen.

"I'd like that," Sharinna glowed. "Uh oh; there's the buzzer. I have to run. Is 1900 okay?"

"Perfect! See you then."

"See you."

Dmitri broke the connection with a shriek of delight. "Too radical! Me, Sharinna, and not a curfew or a chaperone for thirteen kilometers!"

"What are you *doing*?" Sarah said, stunned. "We won't be here tonight! We have a flight to catch! You can't just go inviting people over. We could get in trouble."

"Lighten up, will ya? Flights for Earth depart a dozen times a day. What difference will it make, as long as we're on one of them? Nobody's here – how the hell are we going to get in trouble? No neighbors, nobody bossing us... So we catch a redeye at two a.m.. I have always, *always* wanted to have a party – the real kind, you know? Where everybody and their friends just hang out?"

Sarah shook her head. The only party she could remember was Vlad's birthday a month ago. "Aren't we supposed to be following

Galina? She said they'd be waiting for us."

"What difference does it make? Let Val hold'er ass a day! We'll need a lot of food – I'll have to restock the replicator. I think I know how. I can get some of the drinks, but everyone will have to bring their own hard stuff."

"And chairs," Sarah added.

Dmitri paced the empty room, thinking. "You don't need chairs for a party. We'll lay everything out on the piano. Lemme make some calls. You don't mind waiting just one day, do you?"

# * Twenty-nine *

Sarah slouched against the piano leg, hypnotized by Dmitri's deep snores, lost in her thoughts. The sudden buzz of the commlink in the dead silence jolted her like an electric shock. She crawled across the littered floor and hit the toggle.

*Val! Val was calling to tell her they were waiting for her and Dimi! Val was coming to get her! Thank goodness! She needed to talk to Vlad!*

John Carver's cheerful face appeared onscreen. "Sarah Irina! I didn't expect you to answer. I promised Valeria I would call to check on you before you left. You look like you just woke up."

Sarah hugged herself. "I didn't sleep last night. Hang on." She disappeared for several seconds as she pulled the piano bench over to sit on.

Carver grew concerned. "Dreams?"

Sarah shook her head, glanced over her shoulder, and massaged her temples with the heels of her hands before hugging herself again.

"No. Dimi had a big party last night. Someone brought a music system, and the noise was so loud it made my insides dance. I tried to hide in my room, but Val took the pillows. Once, I had to… use the sanitary, but there were two people in there kissing pretty hard, and they didn't look like they wanted to leave, so I tried the other lavatory, but there were people in the bedroom and the girl didn't have a shirt on, so I tried to find Dimi, but there were so many *people!*" She hugged herself and rocked on the bench.

"They were laughing and shouting and passing things around and I was so scared. I couldn't find Dimi anywhere, so I ran back and locked myself in my room. I crawled under the bed and hid behind my bag, and I stayed there until it got quiet. When I crawled out, I didn't see anybody, so I came out and I've been sitting here for maybe a half hour. I don't know what to do."

Carver perched on the edge of his seat. "Deep breath, Sarah. Stay with me. Where's Val? Or Katya. Put someone on."

Sarah broke eyecontact with the image and went back to rocking. "Val's gone. They all left yesterday. *And she took Vlad with her!*" Sarah's chin quivered, her voice cracked, but she didn't cry – yet.

"What do you mean, 'Val left'? Sarah, *who's with you?*"

Sarah glanced over her shoulder again. "Just Dimi. He's my guardian now. He and Val had a big fight, and she wouldn't take us with her."

"*Dmitri?!* Sarah, what the hell's happening out there? Put Dmitri on, then!"

"He's sleeping on the piano. Should I wake him?"

"*Yes, I want you to wake him!* Right now! Don't lose me, Sarah – I'm going on another line for a second or two. Don't cut me off."

"Okay." Of course she wouldn't cut him off. There wasn't another soul for thirteen kilometers. He was the only person left in the universe she could talk to.

When Carver returned to the screen, his viewer was blank, but he could hear Russian pleading in the background.

Another minute passed before Dmitri's face appeared, looking as if he'd been in an accident. Dark rings circled his eyes; he had an active tic in one and fought a losing battle to focus the other. Sleep lines and spit covered one side of his colorless face, and he drifted to the left before catching himself.

"G'morn' Dr. Carver," he mumbled without moving his lips.

Carver's voice boomed off the empty walls. "Dmitri, what the hell's going on there?"

"*Aaaaaiiiiii!* Turn that damned thing down!" Dmitri grabbed his forehead to keep the pieces of his skull from flying away.

"I had a going away party last night," he said, rubbing the eye with the tic. "I must have had too much to drink."

"What does Sarah mean, you're her guardian? What happened to Valeria and Galina?"

Dmitri rubbed both eyes this time, gripping the edge of the computer desk with one hand. "Valeria and I aren't speaking. She freakin' abandoned us here."

"Listen to me, Dmitri, Sarah! I don't know what's going on, but I'm coming out there. I've got a flight leaving here in just over an hour. I'll be in Shir P'an in seven hours. Seven! *You hear me, Sarah?* I'll Moley into the spaceport; it's faster than waiting for a shuttle. Can you meet me there in seven hours?"

"Moley Beam! Can we watch you come in?" Sarah squealed with elation at the prospect. The terrors of the previous night fell away with the anticipation of something new and incredibly wonderful. The military used molecular transport beaming all the time, and some VIP's, but moley beaming was an expensive and dangerous luxury for the normal populace. To disassemble someone's atomic structure into energy, move it, and reassemble it took enormous amounts of power generation and computer memory, and there were gruesome accidents. The controversies stirred by the development only added fuel to the debate. Material items, fine, but was the reassembled person really the same as the original? And who was responsible if you materialized at your destination without, say, your pancreas? Or your memory? Sarah had read all about it, understood the theories and complaints from all sides, but she'd never actually seen anything transport.

"Only if you get there before me," Carver said. "I'll see you at the spaceport in seven hours. Carver out."

Sarah burned with excitement. "Did you hear that, Dimi? He's coming by moley beam!" But Dmitri had already run, lurching, for the sanitary.

They checked their bags at the spaceport with an hour and a half to spare. Dmitri promised her, cross his heart, girlfriends notwithstanding, they'd leave before the evening was over. He stopped at a travel office, and after much heated discussion, bought two one-way passages for an evening flight.

Three hours' sleep and a long shower stopped the world from spinning out of control, but did little for Dimi's bone-crushing headache. The common painkillers he'd bought at the spaceport hadn't made a dent. Every breath roared through his head like a hurricane, every heartbeat echoed painfully inside his skull, his bones cracked and crumbled with every step. A sneeze made him cry out in agony, as if a hand had reached through his nose and yanked his nervous system. While Sarah stood at the transport observation window, squealing each time someone arrived or departed, Dmitri slouched motionless against the wall, the hood to his robe far over his face, wishing there was a faster way to die.

*"There he is! There he is!* Just like that!" Sarah shrieked, jumping on her toes. She shook Dmitri's shoulder and bounded over to the exit.

*"Don't do that,"* Dimi groaned, and climbed shakily to his feet.

Sarah could hardly contain her excitement until Carver claimed an overnight bag from incoming cargo and walked through the exit.

"There you are," Carver said with relief.

Sarah's face glowed with awe. She touched him on the arm, increasing the pressure until convinced he was whole. "That's just the wildest thing ever! Wait til I tell Vlad!"

"I'm happy to see you, too." Sarah wrapped her arms around him. Carver bent sideways to peer under the drooping hood. "I take it that's Dmitri in there?"

"Yeah." Dmitri adjusted the hood so his face showed. "How are you, Dr. Carver."

Carver shook the limp hand with amusement. "Better than you, I'm sure."

"Mmmm. I hope you're not here to lecture me."

"Sarah scared the hell out of me this morning. I came to find out what's going on. I promised I'd help if I could, so I'm here. Is there someplace we can sit?"

They settled on a spaceport eatery; Carver wasn't dressed for Navara, and Dmitri couldn't walk far. John ate an early dinner, Sarah sucked down a thick slice of cake and a fizzy fruit shake, but Dmitri clung to a glass of ice water as if his life depended on it.

Carver glared hard at Dmitri. "So you took that responsibility on yourself? At sixteen?"

"Almost seventeen," Dmitri corrected. "Six more weeks."

Carver asked Sarah, "You're happy to see me now, but you couldn't come back and visit?"

She hung her head in shame, scraping chocolate filling off her lip with her thumb. "I didn't want you to be disappointed in me."

"I'm not disappointed, Sarah. I'm very worried."

"You weren't there; it wasn't that simple," Dmitri explained, holding his head up with his hands. "She couldn't even get out of bed. Val started pushing the hospital idea, and Sarah flipped out and tore herself up. *Val* couldn't handle it, plain and simple. *I* went back and read all that stuff you gave us, and most of it worked. *I* got her up and around, then she begged and begged me not to let Val send her back, and I promised her she didn't have to go. What was I supposed to do? Let her hurt herself because Val was too pigheaded? I didn't sit through those boring meetings for fun. It all spiraled up out of that."

"So tell me what happened last night," Carver pressed. "Why the hell did Sarah have to hide under her bed all night? How is that demonstrating responsibility?"

"I don't want to talk about it. It was just... out of hand. A nice little party, ten people tops ... Must have been close to a hundred that showed up. People I didn't know. They brought all kinds of shit – you know, contraband and all? What could I do against a crowd like that? Call Security and tell them I was hosting an illegal party, and could they clear out the uninvited guests?

"I was gonna check on her, honest. But sometime around midnight, Blaike Garibaldi comes up to me, and she's wearing this sleeveless thing that looked like chainmail, you know? Cut down to here, with nothing on under it? And she gives me this *kiss*… " Dmitri took a deep breath and let it out slowly. "Like I've never had in my life. And she makes this really… *adult* suggestion in my ear – You know the kind I mean? – and she offered me some of her drink. I tasted it, and *bam!* That's the last thing I remember until Sarah woke me up this morning. I keep trying, but it all stops there."

"What was she drinking?" Carver wondered.

*"I don't know,"* Dmitri moaned, breathing as if his lungs hurt, "but I think it was laced with Crystal Faze."

*"Crystal?"* Carver leaned across the table. "Tip your head back." He pried the boy's eyelids apart and looked the watering eyes over carefully. "Follow my finger," he demanded, moving it in every direction.

Carver sat. "I think you'll be okay. Ocular hemorrhage is usually the first sign of trouble, and I don't see anything. Dmitri, you've got to stay away from that stuff! I've seen eight DOA's and three cerebral hemorrhages in the last two years from people using Faze. Don't touch it!"

"It wasn't my idea. I *swear*, my friends and I are clean. We don't do anything like that. I've never even been drunk enough to have a hangover. We were just supposed to cool off and have a good time, hopefully – you know – score with my girl. It just got way out of control."

"I brought my field kit with me. I can give you something to help."

"That would be very greatly appreciated," the boy winced. "I feel like I was hit by an energy beam."

"In effect, you were. Except that, instead of a few seconds, your body thinks it was hit with a four or five hour blast. It can blind you, destroy your speech centers, fry your brain right in your skull. By the time anyone realizes you've OD'd, it's too late."

"I believe it. I'm sorry if you were scared last night, Sarah," Dmitri apologized, head hanging. "But I think I'm more scared than you. I've got a… nine hour hole in my memory. I don't know what happened last night. I don't know what happened to Sharinna, or Blaike, or what I might have done, or in front of who. I was supposed to be in charge, and I have *no flying clue* what happened. I can't believe I let myself get taken like that." He folded his arms on the table and let his head fall – softly – on top of them.

"There's a lot you don't know how to handle, Dmitri," Carver said. "That's why you need to get home. Give it two, three years, learn a little more about life. Gain a little wisdom. Then go off with Sarah if you think that's what you need to do."

Dmitri forced himself up. "No! I'm not going back! I've made up my mind on that. What's there to go back to? Val fighting with me every time I breathe, threatening to call for security if I don't do what she wants? Go back and watch Katya be forced to kiss her ass? Watch Val hover over Sarah until she snaps? No, thank you. I'm free now. The more I think about it, the less I want to go back."

"There's Vlad," Sarah reminded him, wearing her brave face. "And David, and Sergei..."

"Then come back with me to Starbase Four," Carver urged. "The starbase itself. I'll pull some strings to get you quarters there. If you need help, I'm a whole lot closer than half a parsec. You've both got schooling to finish."

"That would work, Dimi," Sarah said. "We'd be on our own, but not totally alone, just in case. Like, what if my lungs give out again? There's a hospital right there..."

"No," Dmitri persisted. "We're on that evening flight. We're going somewhere Val won't be able to pull shit."

Sarah reopened the argument from earlier that afternoon. "Couldn't we do it in Australia? Or Venezuela or something? Father always wanted us to go to Seattle... If not Russia, I'd settle for anywhere on Earth." *Anywhere closer to Vlad.*

"You're being irresponsible, Dmitri. Money doesn't last forever. What are you going to do then? How will you support Sarah?" John argued.

"I'll figure that out if and when it happens," Dmitri said. "If we're careful, we can last quite a while."

"That's a stupid, dangerous plan. You're not just fooling with your life, you're fooling with *hers*. Dmitri, I'm serious!" Carver laid a firm hand on his arm, trying to stare some sense into him. "I don't think you should do this."

Dmitri sat back, wary. "You gonna report me?"

"No. No, I won't do that. Would you consider leaving Sarah with me? You don't have to give up custody – call it a visit, a vacation, whatever you want. Go off by yourself and think about things for a few weeks. Cool off. Sow your wild oats. She'll be there when you get back. I promise, no strings."

Sarah watched the two like a ping-pong match. She would be willing to stay a while with John – not on the wards, of course. Surely someone on the starbase must be licensed to give the Basic Education Exam. She'd been over the manual enough to feel confident now. On the other hand, she owed so much to Dmitri… He'd fought so hard for her, and lost everything but her. How could they split up when each was all the other had left?"

"No," Dmitri insisted. "I swore I would take care of her, and I meant it. We stick together. We'll go home, just not right now. Val will be expecting us. By the time she finds out we're not coming, she won't be able to do a damned thing about it. See how she likes it when the tables are turned."

"Let me do one thing, then." Carver opened his bag and took out a medical field kit. "Let me replace Sarah's subdermal pack. I know she's still got time left on the last one, but you'll have six full weeks before you have to worry about it. It's your call."

It was the first time anybody had treated Dmitri like an adult. For the first time, it was his decision, his alone, and he had no idea what to answer. "I guess so. Makes sense to me." Sarah nodded.

He glanced around the cafeteria. "Where? You can't just pull out a knife and start doing surgery in the middle of a lunchroom. People get upset."

"Good point. We'd look kind of funny standing in the restroom together. There's got to be somewhere…"

Sarah perked up. "The library!"

"He wants to *do* surgery, not *read* about it, you bookhead."

"Not the stacks, stupid! The study rooms. They're private."

"She's right," Dmitri agreed. "If anyone knows a library, it's Sarah or Sergei. How the hell do we get there?"

"Cross-city underground." Sarah knew Shir P'an better than Kar Ku'umi.

Carver picked up his bag. "Lead on."

John traced the faint line across her shoulder from the edge of the incision scar. "What's this?"

"That?" Sarah looked at her arm. "That's what happens when you accidentally move when an incision is being made, which ticks off Dr. Carmichael, and he swears at you and puts you in restraints and you vow you'd rather die than ever go back."

"So *that's* what happened. That's why Valeria called me."

"You?!"

"Sure. Who do you think refilled your Antivox?"

"*I* figured that one out," Dmitri said proudly. "I read the signs in those papers. I figured out she was hearing things and got her to admit it to Val."

"Good catch," Carver praised, spreading his kit on the study table. "Remember those symptoms. Okay. I brought three different doses, since I won't know which you've got until I see it. Val told me they upped it. You're going to hold still, now, aren't you? I didn't bring any restraints with me...."

"And Vlad's not here to faint dead on the floor and make me turn at the last minute – ." Sarah's face fell as she realized it now might be some time before she saw Vlad again. "Vlad!" she mourned.

"Don't move," Carver warned. "Good." With ultra-fine forceps, he removed the remaining capsules and examined one. "Twenty-five milligram. I have those. You're still taking one extra, aren't you? I'll use thirties then. Hold still.

"Now listen, both of you," Carver said as he finished. "Save the pills. If you can't get the pack replaced in six weeks, take six of those pills a day. At least five. I know, it's a lot; I know, you don't like them, but do it anyway. Dmitri, *make sure* she does it. That's too heavy a dose to mess around with. You remember not to stop the Antivox fast?"

Sarah nodded. "Absolutely! I won't do that again."

"When you're down to your last half bottle, if you can't get more, take a little less each week. By the end, you should be okay."

"If someone doesn't drink it on me," Sarah muttered.

*"Huh?"*

"Dimi wanted to mix it with vodka and drink it," she snitched, not believing his innocence for a nanosecond. Not after last night. Not after the second change in plans. Not after breaking his promise to reunite her with Vlad in only two days.

"I would *never* have done that!" Dmitri said. "I was just messing with her. I was playing."

Carver's cold gaze bored into the boy. "Take my advice. *Don't* mix it with alcohol. And that goes for you, too," he warned Sarah.

"*I* don't touch that stuff," she assured him, unrolling her sleeve.

"Now, Dmitri. Come here." Carver adjusted the aeroderm and pressed it to his arm. "Better?"

Dmitri's eyes opened fully for the first time that day. "Yes, sir!" he brightened. "Much better! My brain still feels deep-fried, but the pain is gone. Thank you."

"Next time, don't drink anything you didn't pour yourself. Stay away from Crystal Faze. And that new one going around – what's it – Reflex, Reflux, Redux? It's just as deadly."

"I'll remember," Dmitri promised. "I don't think I'll be drinking anytime soon."

"Don't. You need a clear head, for her sake."

* * *

Carver hung around the spaceport to see them off, talking with Sarah and feeling her out. As far as he could tell, she was stable; nervous, sad, but with the hefty dose of medication to hold her up, she was coping. Dmitri was young, stupid, and extremely foolish, but he did seem to know how to handle her, and she wanted to be with him. They might do all right, for a little while. Carver wished he could feel more confident.

"Ten minutes to boarding," Dmitri said, returning from the flight schedule wall.

"You still won't tell me where you're going?"

Dimi shook his head. "I'm sorry. I don't want anybody following us, or calling Val. I'll call her in a day or two to tell her we won't be there. I promise."

"You know all I have to do is look at the schedule to figure it out?"

"You're gonna rat us after we leave?"

*Communication. Rapport. Trust. The tools of his trade.* There was a pause before John said, "No, I won't."

Sarah opened her pack and located a marker. She took Carver's hand and wrote a series of numbers on the back of it.

"What's this?"

"That's where Val and everybody's going," Sarah said, having memorized it the night before, just in case. "Call in a month or so. See if we made it home."

"Absolutely."

Sarah stood stiffly, downcast, fingers picking her nails. It was a look of indecision Carver knew all too well. He held out his hand, but instead found himself tackled in a forceful hug; Sarah didn't let go.

Dmitri held his hand out, like an adult. "Thank you, Doctor Carver. For everything. You've been a real friend to us."

Carver shook the hand. "Keep that in the present tense. Call me. Any time, for any thing. I'll be here. Keep your head clear, Dmitri. Think first. Don't go putting my girl here in danger. I invested too many hours in her for you to go screwing her back up. Mess her up, and I'll come after you."

"I will do my very best, sir."

John clapped him on the shoulder. "I know you will. And you, Miss..." He tried to peel Sarah off, but she wouldn't budge. He settled for rubbing her back. "Don't give your brother any of that nonsense you

349

get into now and then. Behave yourself. And *talk* to him. He's not a mind reader. He's there to help you, remember that. You know where to find me if you need me, no questions asked. If Dmitri won't call, call yourself. Even if all you say is 'Hi'."

Sarah drew a shaky breath and nodded extra fast.

Dmitri tapped her on the shoulder. "Come on. They're boarding us now."

Sarah nodded, but didn't let go until Dmitri prompted again. She stepped back, looking small and scared and on the edge of tears. She reached an arm up to Carver's neck and lightly kissed his cheek.

"Thank you," she whispered. Taking her bag, she slid her arms into the straps, hefted the weight onto her shoulders, and took Dmitri's hand.

"Take care," Carver called as the pair walked away. "And call me!"

Halfway down the boarding corridor, Sarah turned around and gave a sad little wave. When she turned back, Dmitri let go of her hand and put his arm around her shoulders, holding her tight.

John Carver watched them go, an uneasy feeling squeezing his stomach. They were both crazy, he decided. He could have stopped them, *should* have stopped them. Maybe he was as crazy as they were, letting them go like this. He could have pushed to hold them for seventy-two hours. The boy had ingested an illegal, highly dangerous chemical compound; he required observation. The girl had a strong recent history of mental instability, she was still more or less under his care, she was under severe stress, and the risk of crisis was very real. Seventy-two hours would buy enough time for their family to land on Earth, not only for him to contact Valeria but have her return and claim them, settle everything down. He didn't have admitting rights at Ku'umi Trauma, but he could probably work a deal with Carmichael.

*But would it help anything? Should he sacrifice trust simply because he had the power to stop someone from making a mistake?* Sometimes, the hardest part of his job was allowing people to learn from their mistakes.

Carver sighed, letting his indecision decide for him. They should be okay, for a week or so. Something would inevitably happen, one good scare, and they'd be running home within a month. That's the way kids were.

*End, book 1*

*"Get out!" Valeria pointed to the door. "You think you're such a goddamn adult, take your goddamn lunatic and get out!"*

It wasn't supposed to *be* like this! First Valeria promised they'd never separate, then it was only supposed to be for *two days*. Sarah never imagined anything like this when she agreed to let Dmitri take charge of her, and now two days is stretching into a lifetime. How can she tell him how unhappy she is, when he had to sacrifice everything he had for her? She's trying to be patient, but she'd give just about anything to go home again. Disaster follows disaster, and still Dmitri won't stop being so damn stubborn! Time is passing, and things are changing at home. They're changing for Sarah, too - she's growing up, and she can't make it stop. Can she hold herself together in the process? Will Dmitri ever realize that *responsibility* and *maturity* are two very different words?

Sarah's desperation is growing, and the depths to which she'll sink to stop Dmitri's plans may just be unforgivable...

# Best Efforts

*What happens when good intentions aren't enough?*

Part 2 of *Best Intentions*
Susan Staneslow Olesen

351

Susan Staneslow Olesen is a graduate of Chase Collegiate School and studied psychology and writing at Wells College. She is a special-needs foster parent with more than 20 years experience in autism. She has worked all aspects of special education from birth to adult, taught creative writing and beginning Russian language for adult education, spent several years fostering kittens for a local shelter, won several awards for art and costuming, and is a perpetual pest at science-fiction conventions in the Baltimore area. When not writing or intervening, she works as a Tech Assistant for her local public library. She lives in Connecticut with her husband, five children, three dogs, three cats, and a Dumbo rat named Fatticus.

On occasion, she has been known to sleep.

For info and trivia, or to contact the author, follow along at Best Intentions book series on Facebook.com

·